Praise for the
MORGANVILLE VAMPIRES NOVELS

Kiss of Death

"Has everything that Morganville Vampires fans have come to expect from the series—fast-paced plotting, high-octane action, and dangerous vampires, interspersed with witty banner and occasional laughs." —LoveVampires

"Rachel Caine once again takes this band of misfits that always seem to find trouble, and designs an enjoyable ride for the reader. The story is well paced and holds your attention to the end." —Fresh Fiction

Fade Out

"Book seven of the Morganville Vampire series won't disappoint readers as Claire and her friends find themselves in the middle of a potential catastrophe wrought by a publicity-seeking filmmaker." —Monsters and Critics

"Full of drama, pathos, and a touch of romance with characters larger than life especially the teens trying to survive in a town run by vampires . . . This is a must read for teens and adults." —The Best Reviews

Carpe Corpus

"Ms. Caine offers readers an intriguing world where vampires rule, only the strongest survive, and romance offers hope in the darkest of hours. Each character is brought to life in superb detail, with unique personality quirks and a full spectrum of emotions. Carpe Corpus is well-described, packed with action, and impossible to set down." —Darque Reviews

"Rachel Caine has carved out a unique niche in the urban fantasy subgenre with her super young adult Morganville Vampires. The latest thriller contains plenty of action, but as always in this saga, Carpe Corpus is character driven by the good, the bad, and the evil." —Midwest Book Reviews

continued . . .

"The pace is brisk and a number of loose ends are tied up as one chapter on the town of Morganville closes and a new one begins."

—Monsters and Critics

Lord of Misrule

"Book five of the Morganville vampires is filled with delicious twists that the audience will appreciatively sink their teeth into. . . . Rachel Caine provides a strong young adult vampire thriller." —The Best Reviews

"A sinister book. . . . Although marketed to teens, this series is sure to capture plenty of adult fans with the fast moving story line, hints of romance, and well-developed characters." —Monsters and Critics

Feast of Fools

"Fast-paced and filled with action. . . . Fans of the series will appreciate *Feast of Fools*." —Genre Go Round Reviews

"Thrilling. . . . In sharing her well-imagined world, Ms. Caine gives readers the danger-filled supernatural moments they crave while adding friendship, romance, and teen issues to give the story a realistic feel. A fast-moving series where there's always a surprise just around every dark corner."

—Darque Reviews

"Very entertaining. . . . I could not put *Feast of Fools* down. . . . There is a level of tension in the Morganville books that keeps you on the edge of your seat. Even in the background scenes you're waiting for the other shoe to drop. And it always does." —Flames Rising

"I thoroughly enjoyed reading *Feast of Fools*. . . . It was fantastic. . . . The excitement and suspense . . . [are] thrilling and I was fascinated reading about the town of Morganville. I greatly look forward to reading the next book in this series and catching up with the other books. I highly recommend *Feast of Fools* to paranormal readers for a delightful and fun read that you won't want to put down." —Fresh Fiction

Midnight Alley

"A fast-paced, page-turning read packed with wonderful characters and surprising plot twists. Rachel Caine is an engaging writer; readers will be completely absorbed in this chilling story, unable to put it down until the last page. . . . For fans of vampire books, this is one that shouldn't be missed!"

—Flamingnet

"Weaves a web of dangerous temptation, dark deceit, and loving friendships. The nonstop vampire action and delightfully sweet relationships will captivate readers and leave them craving more."

—Darque Reviews

The Dead Girls' Dance

"[*Glass Houses*] left me emotionally spent, in a good way. The intensity is cubed in [*The Dead Girls' Dance*]. It was hard to put this down for even the slightest break and, forget what happens to the kid with the scar and glasses, I want to know what happens next in Morganville. If you love to read about characters with whom you can get deeply involved, Rachel Caine is so far a one hundred percent sure bet to satisfy that need. I love her Weather Warden stories, and her vampires are even better."

—The Eternal Night

"Throw in a mix of vamps and ghosts and it can't get any better than *Dead Girls' Dance*."

—Dark Angel Reviews

Glass Houses

"Rachel Caine brings her brilliant ability to blend witty dialogue, engaging characters, and an intriguing plot."

—Romance Reviews Today

"A rousing horror thriller that adds a new dimension to the vampire mythos . . . a heroine the audience will admire and root for as she swallows her trepidations to ensure her friend and roomies are safe. The key to this fine tale is her plausible reactions to living in a town run by vampires that make going to college in the Caine universe quite an experience. *Glass Houses* is an electrifying enthralling coming-of-age supernatural tale."—*Midwest Book Review*

THE MORGANVILLE VAMPIRES NOVELS

Glass Houses

The Dead Girls' Dance

Midnight Alley

Feast of Fools

Lord of Misrule

Carpe Corpus

Fade Out

Kiss of Death

Ghost Town

Bite Club

THE
MORGANVILLE
VAMPIRES

VOLUME 4

Fade Out

and

Kiss of Death

RACHEL CAINE

 NEW AMERICAN LIBRARY

New American Library
Published by New American Library, a division of
Penguin Group (USA) Inc., 375 Hudson Street,
New York, New York 10014, USA
Penguin Group (Canada), 90 Eglinton Avenue East, Suite 700, Toronto,
Ontario M4P 2Y3, Canada (a division of Pearson Penguin Canada Inc.)
Penguin Books Ltd., 80 Strand, London WC2R 0RL, England
Penguin Ireland, 25 St. Stephen's Green, Dublin 2,
Ireland (a division of Penguin Books Ltd.)
Penguin Group (Australia), 250 Camberwell Road, Camberwell, Victoria 3124,
Australia (a division of Pearson Australia Group Pty. Ltd.)
Penguin Books India Pvt. Ltd., 11 Community Centre, Panchsheel Park,
New Delhi - 110 017, India
Penguin Group (NZ), 67 Apollo Drive, Rosedale, Auckland 0632,
New Zealand (a division of Pearson New Zealand Ltd.)
Penguin Books (South Africa) (Pty.) Ltd., 24 Sturdee Avenue,
Rosebank, Johannesburg 2196, South Africa

Penguin Books Ltd., Registered Offices:
80 Strand, London WC2R 0RL, England

Published by New American Library, a division of Penguin Group (USA) Inc. *Fade Out* and *Kiss of Death* were previously published in separate Signet and NAL Jam mass market editions.

First New American Library Printing (Double Edition), June 2011
10 9 8 7 6 5 4 3 2 1

Set in Centaur
Designed by Ginger Legato

Printed in the United States of America

FADE OUT

To Alan Hanna, who got me going.
To Nina Romberg, who got me out there.
To P. N. Elrod and Carole Nelson Douglas, who showed me the ropes.
To my dear friends Jackie and Bill Leaf,
Heidi Berthiaume, Glenn Rogers, Sharon Sams,
Christina Radish, ORAC, and so, so many
more, who keep me climbing.
To my dear husband, Cat, who's always there when I come back.
Special thanks to Aviva and Aziza, who helped me with specific issues.

ACKNOWLEDGMENTS

To my wonderful bosses, Sondra and Josefine, who truly make this whole balancing act work.

To my fantastic agent, Lucienne Diver.

To Excellent Editor Anne and the entire staff of NAL, who make these books a delight to write.

INTRODUCTION

WELCOME TO MORGANVILLE. YOU'LL NEVER WANT TO LEAVE.

So, you're new to Morganville. Welcome, new resident! There are only a few important rules you need to know to feel comfortable in our quiet little town:

- Obey the speed limits.
- Don't litter.
- Whatever you do, don't get on the bad side of the vampires.

Yeah, we said vampires. Deal with it.

As a human newcomer, you'll need to find yourself a vampire Protector—someone willing to sign a contract to keep you and yours safe from harm (especially from the other vampires). In return, you'll pay taxes ... just like in any other town. Of course, in most other towns, those taxes don't get collected at the blood bank.

Oh, and if you decide *not* to get a Protector, you can do that, too ... but you'd better learn how to run fast, stay out of the shadows, and build a network of friends who can help you. Try contacting the residents of the Glass House—Michael, Eve, Shane, and Claire. They know their way around, even if they always end up in the middle of the trouble somehow.

Welcome to Morganville. You'll never want to leave.

And even if you do . . . well, you can't.

Sorry about that.

ONE

Eve Rosser's high-pitched scream rang out through the entire house, bouncing off every wall, and, like a Taser applied to the spine, it brought Claire out of a pleasant, drowsy cuddle with her boyfriend.

"Oh my God, what?" She half jumped, half fell off the couch. Mortal danger was nothing new around their unofficial four-person frat house. In fact, mortal danger didn't even merit a full-fledged scream these days. More of a raised eyebrow. "Eve? *What?*"

The screaming went on, accompanied by thumping that sounded like Eve was kickboxing the floor.

"Damn," Shane Collins said as he scrambled to his feet, as well. "What the hell is wrong with that girl? Was there a sale at Morbid R Us and nobody told her?"

Claire smacked him on the arm, but only out of reflex; she was already heading for the hallway, where the scream echoed loudest. She would have moved faster, but there wasn't panic in that scream after all.

It was more like . . . joy?

In the hallway, their roommate Eve was having a total fit—screaming, bouncing in hoppy little circles like a demented Goth bunny. It was made especially strange by her outfit: flouncy black sheer skirt, black tights with neon pink skulls, a complicated-looking corset with buckles, and her clunky Doc Martens boots. She'd worn her hair in pigtails today, and they whipped wildly around as she jumped and spun and did a wiggling victory dance.

Claire and Shane stood without saying a word, and then exchanged a look. Shane silently raised a finger and made a slow circle at his temple.

Claire, eyes wide, nodded.

The screaming dissolved into excited little yips, and Eve stopped randomly bouncing around. Instead, she bounced directly at them, waving a piece of paper with so much enthusiasm that Claire was lucky to be able to tell it *was* a piece of paper.

"You know," Shane said in an entirely too-calm voice, "I kind of miss the old Morganville, when it was all scary monsters and dodging death. This would *never* have happened in the old Morganville. Too silly."

Claire snorted, reached out, and grabbed Eve's flailing wrists. "Eve! What?"

Eve stopped bouncing and grabbed Claire's hands, crushing the paper in the process. From the jittery pulse of her muscles, she still wanted to jump, but she was making a great effort not to. She tried to say something, but she just couldn't. It came out as a squeal that only a dolphin would have been able to interpret.

Claire sighed and took the paper from Eve's hand, smoothed it out, and read it aloud. "*Dear Eve,*" she began. "*Thank you for auditioning for our production of* A Streetcar Named Desire. *We are very pleased to offer you the role of Blanche DuBois—*"

She was interrupted by more bouncing and screaming. Defeated, Claire read the rest silently and handed it on to Shane.

"Wow," he said. "So, that's the town production, right? The annual?"

"I've been auditioning *forever*," Eve blurted out, dark eyes as wide as an animé character's. "I mean, *forever*. Since I was twelve. Best I ever got was one of the Russian dancers for the Christmas performance of *The Nutcracker*."

"You?" Shane said. "You dance?"

Eve looked offended. "You've been to parties with me. You know I dance, jackass."

"Hey, there's a difference between shaking your ass at a rave and *ballet*."

Eve leveled a black-nailed finger in his direction. "I'll have you know I was good on pointe, and, anyway, that isn't the issue. I got the part of *Blanche*. In *Streetcar*. Do you know how wicked huge that is?"

"Congratulations," Shane said. He actually sounded like he meant it, to Claire's ears at least, and she was pretty sure he really did. He and Eve yanked each other's chains hard enough to leave marks, but they really did care. Of course, Shane was a guy, and he couldn't leave it at that, so he continued. "Maybe I should go out for it. If they picked you, they'll love my Marlon Brando impression."

"Honey, nobody likes your Brando. He sounds like your Adam Sandler. Which is also terrible, by the way." Eve was calming down, but she was smiling like a lunatic, and Claire could tell she was on the trembling verge of another jumping fit—which was okay, really. Eve excited was quite a show. "Oh my God, I've got to find out about rehearsals. . . ."

"Page two," Claire said, and pointed at the paper. On the back was a neatly printed schedule of what looked like an awful lot of dates and times. "Wow, they're really working it, aren't they?"

"Of course they are," Eve said absently. "The whole town turns out for—oh, damn, I'm going to have to call my boss. I'm going to have to switch shifts for some of these. . . ."

She hustled off, frowning at the paper, and Claire sighed and leaned her back against one wall of the hallway while Shane took the other. He raised his eyebrows. She did, too.

"Is it really that big a deal?" she asked him.

Shane shrugged. "Depends," he said. "Everybody does go, even most of the vampires. They like a good play, although they're usually not so hot on the musicals."

"Musicals," she repeated blankly. "Like what? *Phantom of the Opera*?"

"Last one I saw was *Annie Get Your Gun*. Hey, if they'd put on *Rocky Horror Picture Show*, I'd definitely go, but somehow I don't think they'd have the guts."

"You don't like musicals? Unless they involve transvestites and chain saws?"

Shane pointed both thumbs back toward his chest. "Guy? In case you forgot."

That made Claire smile and tingle in deep, secret places. "I remember," she said, as indifferently as she could, which was not very. "*And* I'm changing the subject, because I need to get to work." A glance at the window told her that it was an ice-cold spring afternoon, with the freezing Texas wind whipping old leaves down the street in miniature tornadoes. "And so do you, soon."

Shane pushed off and crossed the distance fast, pinning her in place with his hands flat against the wall on either side of her. Then he bent his elbows and leaned in and kissed her. The warmth spread from his lips to hers, then out in a rushing summer heat that moved over her entire body in a wave, and left her feeling as if she were glowing inside.

It went on a long time, that kiss. She finally put her palms flat against his chest with a wordless (and mostly weak) sound of pleading.

Shane backed off. "Sorry. I just needed something to get me through another eight hours of the exciting world of food service." He was working at Bryan's Barbecue, which wasn't a bad gig as jobs in Morganville went. He got all the barbecue he wanted, which meant a lot of free brisket and ham and sausage for the rest of them when he carted home a goody bag. The job also brought decent money, according to Shane, and as a plus, he got to use a sharp knife most of the day, carving meats. Apparently that was cool. He and some of the other guys practiced throwing them at targets in the back when the boss wasn't looking.

Claire kissed him on the nose. "Bring home some brisket," she said. "And some of that sauce. I've had enough chili dogs this week to last me a lifetime."

"Hey, my chili dogs are the best in town."

"It's a really small town."

"Harsh," he said, but he was smiling. The smile faded as he said very seriously, "You be careful."

"I will," she promised.

Shane played with knives, but she had the dangerous job.

She worked with vampires.

Claire's job was lab assistant to a vampire mad scientist, which never made sense when she thought of it that way, but it was still accurate. She hadn't *meant* to become Igor to Myrnin's Frankenstein, but she supposed at least it was a paying, steady job.

Plus, she learned a lot, which meant more to her than the money.

She'd been on job leave, with permission, for a couple of months while the vampires got themselves back together and fixed the damage that had been done—at least the physical damage—by the tornado that ripped through town. Or by the vampire war that had burned down part of it. Or by the rioting by the human population, which had left some scars. Come to think of it, the construction was going pretty well, all things considered. So she hadn't been to the lab for a while—today was, in Myrnin's words from his note, the "grand reopening." Although how you had a grand reopening of a hidden lair beneath a tumbledown shack, Claire had no idea. Was there cake?

The alley next to the Day House—a virtually identical twin to the Glass House where Claire lived, only with different curtains and nicer porch furniture—looked the same. The Day House was a shining white Victorian structure, and the alley was narrow, dark, and seemed to get narrower as you went along, like a funnel.

Or a throat. Ugh. She wished she hadn't thought of that.

The shack at the end of the alley—a leaning, faded wreck, tired and abandoned—didn't look any different, although there was a shiny new lock on the door. Claire sighed. Myrnin had forgotten to give her a key, of course. That didn't present much of a problem, though; she tested a couple of boards and found one that easily slid aside enough for her to crawl through.

Typical Myrnin planning.

Inside, most of the space was taken up by a set of stairs that went down, like in a subway station. There was a bright glow coming up from it.

"There'd better be cake," she said, mostly to herself, and hitched her backpack higher on her shoulder as she headed down into the lab.

The last time she'd been here, it had been totally destroyed, with hardly a stick of furniture or a piece of glass left intact. Someone— most likely Myrnin himself—had gotten busy with a broom and maybe a dump truck to sweep out the mounds of shattered glass, scrapped lab equipment, broken furniture, and (worst of all, to Claire's mind) ravaged books. The place had always had a mad scientist–meets–Jules Verne flair to it, but now it *really* did—in a totally good way. There were new worktables, many of them wood and marble, and a few shiny metal ones. New electric lights had been installed to replace the odd collection of oil lamps, candles, and bulbs that Thomas Edison might have wired together; now they had indirect lighting behind elegant fan-shaped shields. Modern, but retro-cool.

The floor was still old flagstone, but the hole Myrnin had punched in it the last time she'd been here had also been repaired, or at least covered with a rug. She hoped there was something *under* the rug, but with Myrnin, you really could never tell. She made a mental note to poke it before she stepped on it.

Myrnin himself was shelving things in a new bookcase that must have been ten feet tall, at least. It came with its own little rolling ladder—no, as Claire looked around, she realized that the entire room was surrounded by the same tall bookcases, and the ladder was on a metal rail so it could slide all around. Neat. "Ah," her boss said, and looked down at her through the little square antique glasses perched on the end of his long, straight nose. "You're late." He was five feet up in the air, on the top step of the ladder, but he hopped off as if it were pretty much nothing, landed light as a cat on his feet, and straightened his vest with an absentminded little tug.

Myrnin wasn't especially tall, but he was just . . . strangely cool. Long, curling, lush black hair that fell to his shoulders. His face was vampire-pale, but it suited him, somehow, and he had the kind of sharp features that would have made him a star if he'd wanted to be in the movies. Big, expressive dark eyes and full lips. Definitely cover-model material.

If the lab was neater, so was Myrnin. He was still favoring old-timey clothes, so the coat was black velvet, and flared out and down to his knees.

The ensemble also included a white shirt, bright blue vest, a pocket watch chain gleaming against the tight black satin pants, and . . .

Claire found herself staring at his feet, which were in bunny slippers.

Myrnin looked down. "What?" he asked. "They're quite comfortable." He lifted one to look at it, and the ears wobbled in the air.

"Of course they are," she said. Just when she thought Myrnin was getting his mental act together, he'd do something like that. Or maybe he was just messing with her. He liked to do that, and his dark eyes were fixed on her now, assessing just how weirded out she was.

Which, on the grand scale of zero to Myrnin, wasn't much.

"I like a good bunny slipper. I'm surprised you didn't get the ones with fangs," she said, and scanned the room. "Wow, the place looks fantastic."

Myrnin's eyes brightened. "They have some with fangs? Excellent." He got a faraway look for a moment, then snapped back to the here and now. "Thank you. I've had quite a time ordering all the instruments and alembics I need, but did you know that you can find almost anything on the new computer network, the Interweb? I was quite amazed."

Myrnin hadn't paid much attention to the past hundred years or so. Claire wasn't too surprised he'd discovered the Internet, though. *Wait until he finds the porn.* That would be a very uncomfortable conversation. "Yeah, it's great; we like it a lot," she said. "So, you said you needed me today . . ."

"Yes, yes, of course," he said, and walked over to one of the tidy lab tables, one laden with boxes and wooden chests. "I need you to go through these, please, and see what we can use here."

"What's in them?"

"No idea," he said as he sorted through a stack of ancient-looking envelopes. "They're mine. Well, I think they are. They might have once belonged to someone named Klaus, but that's another story, and one you don't need to worry about just now. Go through them and see if there's anything useful. If not, you can throw it all away."

He didn't seem to care one way or another, which was another odd mood swing from him. Claire almost preferred the old Myrnin, when the illness he (and the other vampires) suffered from had made him genuinely loony, and desperate to regain control of himself. This version of Myrnin was both more in control, and less predictable. Not violent or angry, just—never quite where she expected him to be. For instance, Myrnin had always struck her as a keeper, not a tosser. He was sentimental, mostly—more than a lot of the other vamps—and he seemed to really enjoy having his things around him.

So what was this sudden impulse for spring cleaning?

Claire dumped her battered canvas backpack in a chair and found a knife to slide through the ropes that held the first box closed. She immediately sneezed, because even the *rope* was dusty. It was a good thing she took the time to grab a tissue and blow her nose, because as she was doing that, a fat, black spider crawled out from under the cardboard flap and began to scuttle down the side of the box.

Claire gave out a little scream and jumped back. In the next fast heartbeat, Myrnin was there, bending over the table, examining the spider with his face only inches from it. "It's only a hunting spider," he said. "It won't hurt you."

"*So* not the point!"

"Oh, pish. It's just another living creature," Myrnin said, and put his hand out. The spider waved its front legs uncertainly, then carefully stepped up on his pale fingers. "Nothing to be frightened of, if handled properly." He lightly stroked the furry back of the thing, and Claire nearly passed out. "I think I'll call him Bob. Bob the spider."

"You're insane."

Myrnin glanced up and smiled, dimples forming in his face. It should have looked cute, but his smiles were never that simple. This one carried hints of darkness and arrogance. "But I thought that was part of my charm," he said, and lifted Bob the spider carefully to take him off to another part of the lab. Claire didn't care what he did with the thing, as long as he didn't wear it as an earring or a hat or something.

Not that she'd put that past him.

She was *very* careful as she folded back the old cardboard. No relatives of Bob appeared, at least. The contents of the box were a tangle of confusion, and it took her time to sort out the pieces. There were balls of ancient twine, some coming undone in stiff spirals; a handful of what looked like very old lace, with gold edging; two carved, yellowing elephants, maybe ivory.

The next layer was paper—loose paper made stiff and brittle and dark with age. The writing on the pages was beautiful, precise, and very dense, but it wasn't Myrnin's hand; she knew how he wrote, and it was far messier than this. She began reading the first paper.

My dear friend, I have been in New York for some years now, and missing you greatly. I know that you were angry with me in Prague, and I do not blame you for it. I was hasty and unwise in my dealings with my father, but I honestly do believe that he left me little choice. So, dear Myrnin, I beg you, undertake a journey and come to visit. I know travel no longer agrees with you, but I think if I spend another year alone, I will give up entirely. I would call it a great favor if you would visit.

It was signed, with an ornate flourish, *Amelie*. As in, Amelie, Founder of Morganville, and Claire's ultimate—although she didn't like to think of it this way—boss/owner.

Before Claire could open her mouth to ask, Myrnin's cool white fingers reached over her shoulder and plucked the page neatly from her hand. "I said determine if we can use these things, not read my private mail," he said.

"Hey—was that why you came to America? Because she wrote to you?"

Myrnin looked down at the paper for a moment, then crumpled it into a ball and threw it in a large plastic trash bin against the wall. "No," he said. "I didn't come when she asked me. I came when I had to."

"When was that?" Claire didn't bother to protest how unfair it was that he wanted her to not *read* things to figure out if they needed them. Or that since he'd kept the letter all this time, he should think before throwing it away.

She just reached for the next loose page in the box.

"I arrived about five years after she wrote to me," Myrnin said. "In other words, too late."

"Too late for what?"

"Are you simply going to badger me with personal questions, or are you planning to do what I told you to do?"

"Doing it," Claire pointed out. Myrnin was irritated, but that didn't bother her, not anymore. She didn't take anything he said personally. "And I do have the right to ask questions, don't I?"

"Why? Because you put up with me?" He waved his hand before she could respond. "Yes, yes, all right. Amelie was in a bad way in those days—she had lost everything, you see, and it's hard for us to start over and over and over. Eternal youth doesn't mean you don't get tired of the constant struggles. So . . . by the time she wrote to me again, she had done something quite insane."

"What?"

He made a vague gesture around him. "Look around you."

Claire did. "Um . . . the lab?"

"She bought the land and began construction on the town of Morganville. It was meant to be a refuge for our people, a place we could live openly." He sighed. "Amelie is quite stubborn. By the time I arrived to tell her it was a fool's errand, she was already committed to the experiment. All I could do was mitigate the worst of it, so that she wouldn't get us all slaughtered."

Claire had forgotten all about the box (and even Bob the spider), so focused was she on Myrnin's voice, but when he paused, she remembered, and reached in again to pull out an ornate gold hand mirror. It was definitely girly, and besides, the glass was shattered in the middle, only a few silvery pieces still remaining. "Trash?" she asked, and held it up. Myrnin plucked it out of her hand and set it aside.

"Most definitely not," he said. "It was my mother's."

Claire blinked. "You had a—" Myrnin's wide stare challenged her to just *try* to finish that sentence, and she surrendered. "Wow, okay. What was she like? Your mother?"

"Evil," he said. "I keep this to keep her spirit away."

That made . . . about as much sense as most things Myrnin said, so Claire let it go. As she rummaged through the stuff in the box—mostly more papers, but a few interesting trinkets—she said, "So, are you look-ing for something in particular, or just looking?"

"Just looking," he said, but she knew that tone in his voice, and he was lying. The question was, was he lying for a reason, or just for fun? Because with Myrnin, it could go either way.

Claire's fingers closed on something small—a delicate gold chain. She pulled, and slowly, a necklace came out of the mess of paper, and spun slowly in the light. It was a locket, and inside was a small, precise portrait of a Victorian-style young woman. There was a lock of hair woven into a tiny braid around the edges, under the glass.

Claire rubbed the old glass surface with her thumb, frowning, and then recognized the face staring back at her. "Hey! That's Ada!"

Myrnin grabbed the necklace, stared for a moment at the portrait, and then closed his eyes. "I thought I'd lost this," he said. "Or perhaps I never had it in the first place. But here she is, after all."

And just like that, Ada flickered into being across the room. She wasn't alive, not anymore. Ada was a two-dimensional image, a kind of projec-tion, from the weird steampunk computer located beneath Myrnin's lab; that computer was the *actual* Ada, including parts of the original girl. Ada's image still wore Victorian skirts and a high-necked blouse, and her hair was up in a complicated bun, leaving wisps around her face. She didn't look quite right—more like a really good computer generation of a person than a person. "My picture," she said. Her voice was weirdly electronic because it used whatever speakers were around; Claire's phone became part of the surround sound experience, which was so creepy that she automatically reached down and switched it off.

Ada sent her a dark look as the ghost swept through things in her way—tables, chairs, lights.

"Yes," Myrnin said, as calmly as if he spoke to electronic ghosts every day—which, in fact, he did. "I thought I'd lost it. Would you like to see it?"

Ada stopped, and her image floated in the air in the middle of an open expanse of the floor without casting a shadow. "No," she said. Without Claire's phone adding to the mix, her voice came out of an ancient radio speaker in the back of the lab, faint and scratchy. "No need. I remember the day I gave it to you."

"So do I." Myrnin's voice remained quiet, and Claire couldn't honestly tell if what they were talking about was a good memory, or a bad one.

"Why were you looking for it?"

"I wasn't." That, Claire was almost sure, was another lie. "Ada, I asked you to please stop coming here, except when I call you. What if I'd had other visitors?"

Ada's delicate, not-quite-living face twisted into an expression of contempt. "Who would visit *you*?"

"An excellent point." His tone cooled and hardened and took on edges. "I don't want you coming here unless I call you. Are we understood, or do I have to come and alter your programming? You won't thank me for it."

She glared at him with eyes made of static and ice, and finally turned—a two-dimensional turn, like a cardboard cutout—and flashed at top speed through the solid wall.

Gone.

Myrnin let out a slow breath.

"What the heck was that?" Claire asked. Ada creeped her out, and besides, Ada *really* didn't like her. Claire was, in some sense, a rival for Myrnin's attention, and Ada . . .

Ada was kind of in love with him.

Myrnin looked down at the necklace and the portrait lying flat in his palm. For a moment, he didn't say anything, and Claire honestly thought he wouldn't bother. Then, without looking up, he said, "I did care for her, you know." She thought he was saying it to himself more than to her. "Ada wanted me to turn her, and I did. She was with me for almost a hundred years before . . ."

Before he snapped one day, Claire thought. And Ada died before he could stop himself. Myrnin had told her the first day she'd met him that he was dangerous to be around, and that he'd gone through a lot of assistants.

Ada had been the first one he'd killed.

"It wasn't your fault," Claire heard herself saying. "You were sick."

Myrnin's shoulders moved just a little, up and down—a shrug, a very small one. "It's an explanation, not an excuse," he said, and looked up at her. She was a little startled by what she saw—he almost looked, well, human.

And then it was gone. He straightened, slid the necklace into the pocket of his vest, and nodded toward the box. "Continue," he said. "There may yet be something more useful than sentimental nonsense in there."

Ouch. She didn't even like Ada, and that still stung. She hoped the computer—the computer that held Ada's still-sort-of-living brain—wasn't listening.

Fat chance.

The afternoon passed. Claire learned to scan the sheets of paper instead of read them; mostly, they were just letters, an archive of Myrnin's friendship with people long gone, or vampires still around. A lot were from Amelie, over the years—interesting, but it was all still history, and history equaled *boring*.

It wasn't until she was almost to the bottom of the second box that she found something she didn't recognize. She picked up the odd-shaped thing—sculpture?—and sat it on her palm. It was metal, but it was surprisingly light. Kind of a faintly rusty sheen, but it definitely wasn't iron. It was etched with symbols, some of which she recognized as alchemical. "What's this?"

Before the words were out of her mouth, her palm was empty, Myrnin was across the room, and he was turning the weird little object over and over in his hands, fingers gliding over every angle and trembling on the outlined symbols. "Yes," he whispered, and then louder, "Yes!" He bounced in place, for all the world like Eve with her Blanche DuBois note, and stopped to wave the thing at Claire. "You see?"

"Sure," she said. "What is it?"

His lips parted, and for a second she thought he was going to tell her, but then some crafty little light came into his eyes, and he closed his hand around the sharp outlines of the thing. "Nothing," he purred. "Pray continue. I'll be—over here." He moved to an area of the lab where he had a reading corner with a big leather armchair and a stained-glass lamp. He carefully moved the chair so its back was toward her, and plunked himself down with his bunny-slippered feet up on a hassock to examine his find.

"Freak," she sighed.

"I heard that!"

"Good." Claire sawed through the ropes on the next-to-last box.

It exploded.

TWO

When Claire opened her eyes again, she saw three faces looming over her. One was Myrnin's, and he looked concerned. One was the shining blond head of her housemate Michael Glass—Michael had her hand in his, which was nice, because he was sweet, and he had beautiful hands, too. The last face took her a moment, and then recognition clicked into place. "Oh," Claire murmured. "Hello, Dr. Theo."

"Hello, Claire," said Theo Goldman, and he put a finger to his lips. He was a kind-looking older man, a bit frayed around the edges, and he had an antique black stethoscope in his ears. He was listening to her heart. "Ah. Very good. Your heart is still beating, I'm sure you'll be very pleased to hear."

"Yay," Claire said, and tried to sit up. That was a bad idea, and Michael had to support her when she lost her balance. The headache hit a moment later, massive as a hurricane inside her skull. "Ow?"

"You struck your head when you fell," Theo said. "I don't believe there's any permanent damage, but you should see your physician and have the tests done. I should hate to think I missed anything."

Claire pulled in a deep breath. "Maybe I should see Dr. Mills. Just in case—hey, wait. Why did I fall?"

They all exchanged looks. "You don't remember?" Michael asked.

"Why? Is that bad? Is that brain damage?"

"No," Theo said firmly, "it is quite natural to have some loss of memory around such an event."

"What kind of event?" There it was again, that silence, and Claire raised her personal terror alert from yellow to orange. "Anybody?"

Myrnin said, "It was a bomb."

She blinked, not entirely sure she'd heard him right. "A *bomb.* Are you sure you understand what that is? Because——" She gestured vaguely at herself, then around at the room, which looked pretty much untouched. All glassware intact. "Because generally bombs go boom."

"It was a light bomb," Myrnin said. "Touch your face."

Now that she thought about it, her face *did* feel a bit hot. She put her fingers on her cheeks. *Burning* hot. "What happened to me?" She couldn't keep the fear out of her voice.

Theo and Michael both tried to talk at once, but Michael won. "It's like a sunburn," he said. "Your face is a little pink, that's all."

Michael wasn't a very good liar. "Great. I'm red as a cherry, right?"

"Not at all," Myrnin said cheerfully. "You're definitely not as red as a cherry. Or an apple. Yet. That will take some time."

Claire tried to focus back on what was—hopefully—more important. "A light bomb?"

Myrnin looked suddenly a great deal more serious. "It's an inconvenience for a human," he said. "It would have been extremely damaging to me, or to any vampire, had I been the one to open the box."

"So who sent you a bomb?"

He shrugged. "Eh, it was so long ago. Might have been Klaus. But I might have actually sent it to myself. I'm not always that rational, you know. Mind you, I wouldn't open the last box if I were you."

Claire sent him a long, wordless look, then accepted the hand Michael extended to help her to her feet. She felt dizzy and—yes—sunburned, and a whole lot filthy. "Great. You might have booby-trapped your own boxes. Why would you do a thing like that?"

"Excellent question." Myrnin left her and went to the table, where he lifted from the open box a complicated-looking tangle of metal and wires—the kind of bomb an insane Victorian inventor might have made—and set it very carefully to one side. "I can only think that I meant it to protect what else was in the container."

He stood there staring into the box, not moving, and Claire finally rolled her eyes and said, "Well?"

"What?"

"What's in the box, Myrnin?"

In answer, he tipped it over in her direction. A cloud of dust fogged the air, and when it cleared, Claire saw that there was nothing in the box.

Nothing at all.

"I'm going home," she sighed. "This job *sucks*."

Michael gave her a ride back to the Glass House, which was what she meant when she said *home*, although technically she didn't live there. Technically, her parents had a room for her in their house, and her stuff was there. Mostly. Well, partly. And, according to the agreement she'd reached with them, she slept there most every night—for a few hours, anyway.

It was all part of her parents' grand scheme to keep her and Shane—well, maybe *apart* was too harsh. *Casual*. They didn't want their little girl shacking up with the town bad boy, even though Shane was *not* the town bad boy, and he and Claire were in love.

In love. That still gave her a delicious little tingle every time she thought about it.

"Parents," Claire said aloud. Michael sent her a look.

"And?"

"They bring the crazy," she said. "Is Shane home?"

"Not yet. I dropped Eve off at her first rehearsal." He smiled slowly. "Was she that excited when she got the letter?"

"Define excited. You mean, did she look like a cartoon character on crack? Yes. I never knew she was all into acting and stuff."

"She loves it. She's always acting out scenes from movies and TV shows in her room. When we were in high school, she used to organize these little plays in study hall, give us all parts she'd written out on little pieces of paper, and the teacher never knew what the hell was going on. Insane, but fun." Michael braked his car; Claire couldn't see beyond the tinted windows, but she assumed there was some kind of red light. Good thing Michael had special vampire vision, or they'd be exchanging insurance with some other driver right about now. "So this is a big deal for her."

"Yeah, I got that. Speaking of big deals, I heard that you're playing at the TPU theater tomorrow."

The tips of his ears got a little pink, which (even in a vampire) was adorable. "Yeah, apparently they heard about the last three sets at Common Grounds." Those had been pretty spectacular events, Claire had to admit—people jammed in shoulder to shoulder, including an impressive number of vampires all playing nice, at least for the evening. "Not a big deal."

"I heard the tickets were sold out," Claire said smugly. "So there. It *is* a big deal, dude. Deal with it."

There was a complicated expression on Michael's face—pride, nerves, outright fear. He shook his head and sighed. "You ever feel like your life is kind of out of control?"

"I just went to work for a vampire, was scared by a spider, and got knocked down by a tanning bomb. And that's just my day, not my week."

"Okay, yeah. Point." Michael turned the wheel and hit the brakes again. "You're home, Pinky."

"Don't even *think* about calling me that."

Except, when she got upstairs and in front of a mirror, she realized that Michael wouldn't be the only one calling her that, or worse. Her face was *shiny* pink. As if she'd been dipped in blush and then wrapped in plastic. Ugh. When she pressed her fingers against her skin, she left dramatic white spots that slowly filled in again. "I'm going to *kill* him," she muttered, and slammed the bathroom door, locked it, and flipped on the shower as she glared at her hot pink reflection. "Lock him in a tanning bed. Drive him out in the desert with the top down. Myrnin, you are toast. Burned toast."

It was worse when she had her clothes off; her naturally pale skin was a violent, gut-wrenching contrast to the sunburn on her face. She hadn't realized it before, but she had burns on the tops of her hands and arms, too—anywhere that had been exposed to the blast of light.

Radiation. UV radiation. It didn't really hurt yet, but Claire knew it would, and soon. She showered fast, already uncomfortable with the sting of water on shocked flesh, and then searched her closet in vain for something that wouldn't clash with her new, hot pink color scheme.

Oh, Monica was going to love this like a new puppy.

Finally, she put on her bra and panties and flopped back on the bed, staring at the ceiling. She knew she should dry her hair, but she was in too bad of a mood to care. Shiny, pretty hair wasn't going to help at all. And tangled, ratty hair would at least fit her current mood.

After spending a solid fifteen minutes of glum brooding—which was pretty much her limit—Claire grabbed her headphones and loaded up the latest lecture from Myrnin on string theory. Well, she assumed it was string theory, although Myrnin had a tendency to confuse science with mythology and alchemy and magic and who knew what. Pieces of it still made more sense than anything she'd heard from a tenured professor—and pieces of it were complete gibberish.

The trick was figuring out which were which.

She didn't even know that anyone was in the room until the bed tilted to one side. Claire opened her eyes on near-complete darkness—when had that happened?—and instinctively grabbed for the covers, then remembered she was on top of them, and nearly naked, and panic went nuclear. She yanked off her headphones and slithered off her side of the bed, away from whatever weight had settled on the other side. . . .

The bedside light snapped on, revealing Eve sitting there in all her Gothy glory. Purple was still the color of the day, but she'd gone informal—purple tights, some baggy black shorts, a purple tee with Gothic lettering all over it.

Eve tilted her head to one side, staring at Claire. "Wow," she said. "Respect, girl. That is one *hell* of a sunburn. I haven't seen one that bad since my cousin fell asleep in a deck chair on the Fourth of July at nine a.m. and nobody woke her up until four."

Claire, still trying to control her racing heartbeat, gulped down breaths and grabbed her bathrobe from the chair in the corner of the room. As she yanked it on, it dragged over the backs of her hands and arms, and she almost yelped, again, from the pain. Her face felt as if it were on fire. Literally, with flames. "It's not a sunburn," she said. "It was some kind of UV bomb. It was meant for Myrnin."

"Ouch. Right, so we should get you some of that sunburn cream crap in the gallon size. Note taken."

Claire belted her robe. "Did you just come to see the freak show?"

"Well . . . entertaining as it is, no. I came to tell you that dinner was ready, but you were all grooved out on tunes."

Claire considered telling her that she'd been listening to lectures, but decided that in Eve's world, that was too much information. "Sorry," she said.

"Hey, I wouldn't have dared come in except that Shane's downstairs setting the table." Eve winked. "And if I'd sent him, well . . . Dinner would get cold, right?"

Oh God. *Shane.* Shane was going to see her like this, looking like some exile from Planet Magenta. "I—I don't think I feel well enough to eat," she lied, even as her stomach rumbled at the thought of food. "Maybe you could bring me—"

"It's only going to get worse," Eve broke in with ruthless cheerfulness. "Oh yeah. Big-time worse. First, the red face, then the blisters, then the peeling skin. Trust me, unless you're going to hide for the next week, minimum, you might as well just get on downstairs. We're having tacos."

"Tacos?" Claire repeated wistfully.

"I even made that funky rice stuff you like. Well. I boiled the water and put the funky rice stuff in it, anyway. That's cooking, right?"

"Close enough." Claire sighed. Across the room, a mirror reflected someone standing in her clothes that she refused to believe was really her. "Okay. I'll be right down."

"Better be." Eve kissed her fingers at Claire and scooted out the door, slamming it behind her.

Claire was still trying to decide whether her pink shirt made her look marginally better or marginally worse, when she felt an ice-cold sensation travel through her like a wave. No drafts, nothing like that—this was internal. It was a warning, straight from the semi-self-aware house.

Something was wrong *in the house.*

Claire grabbed her emergency home defense kit on the way out of her room—a bag of everything from pepper spray to silver-plated stakes—and raced down the hall, then down the stairs, and arrived with a jolt to find everybody else, including Michael, calmly sitting down to dinner.

"What?" Eve asked. Michael rose to his feet, evidently reading the look on Claire's face, if nothing else.

Shane blurted out, "What the hell happened to you?" Under normal circumstances this might have made her feel really bad, but she was off that right now.

"Something's wrong," she said. "Didn't anybody else feel that?"

They exchanged looks. "Feel what?" Michael asked.

"The—cold. It was like a wave . . . of cold?" Her words slowed down, because she wasn't getting any reaction from them. "You didn't feel it. How is that possible? Michael?" Because it was Michael's house, and technically, she didn't even live here anymore. Exactly. The house shouldn't have communicated anything to her before it talked to him.

"I don't know," he said. "Does it feel the same now?"

"Yes." Claire still felt cold, cold enough that she had chills running through her body. She was surprised her breath didn't smoke in the air. "Worse," she managed to say, and Shane got over his shock about her burn and came to take her hands. She winced as the tender skin complained, but she was grateful for the warmth, too.

"You're freezing," he said, and grabbed a fleece blanket from the back of the couch, which he wrapped around her. "Damn, Claire. Maybe it's the sunburn—"

"Not a—sunburn," she said through chattering teeth as he led her to the table and sat her down. "It's the house. It's got to be the house!"

"I—don't think it is," Michael said, and slowly sank back into his chair. "I'd know, Claire; there's no way I wouldn't. This is something else."

She shook her head and hugged the blanket closer, miserable both ways—her face burning hot, her body shaking with cold.

"Try to eat something," Eve said, and loaded tacos on her plate. "How about something hot to drink?"

Claire nodded. The chill seemed to be sinking in deeper, drilling toward her bones. She had no idea what would happen when it got there, but it didn't seem good. Not good at all.

She kept the blanket tight with her right hand and reached out for a taco with the left, hoping her shaking hand wouldn't scatter the contents all over the table . . . and Shane grabbed her arm. "Look," he said, before she could protest. "Look at the bracelet."

It was Amelie's bracelet, the one she wore clasped around her left wrist, the one she couldn't remove, that reminded people who it was Claire worked for (and reminded Claire, every second).

It was supposed to be gold, but its center was now pale white, as if it had turned to crystal.

Or ice.

It was smoking in the air, so cold it was giving off its own mist.

"We need to get it off," Shane said, and turned her wrist over, looking for a clasp. Claire tried to tell him there wasn't one, but he wasn't listening. "Michael, it's cold, man. It's really cold. Something's really wrong."

They were all out of their chairs now, gathered around her. Michael touched the bracelet, drew back, and locked gazes with Shane. "It doesn't come off," Michael said.

"I don't give a crap if it's not *supposed* to come off!" Shane snapped. "Help me!"

"It won't do any good. It's a Founder's bracelet." Michael grabbed Shane's arm when Shane tried to yank on the bracelet. "Dude, *listen!* You can't get it off! All we can do is get to Amelie. She can take it off."

"Amelie," Claire repeated, and tried to control her violent shaking so she could get the words out. The whole world seemed to be turning to ice, cold and toxic. "Something—wrong—with—Amelie—"

Shane glared at Michael. "Let go." When Michael did, he kept on glaring. "Shouldn't you know if something was wrong with Amelie, you being her demonic spawn and everything?"

"It's not like that," Michael said, although anger was starting to build in his blue eyes and in the set of his face. "I'm not her *spawn*."

"Not arguing the demonic part? Whatever you call it. She made you a vampire. Can't you tell if she's in trouble?"

"You're confusing vampires with Spider-Man," Michael shot back, but he'd already left the fight and was pulling out his cell phone. A one-button press, and he was talking, but not to Shane. "Oliver. Are you with Amelie? No? Where is she?"

Whatever the answer, he snapped the phone shut without answering, locked eyes with Shane, and said, "Let's go."

"W-w-wait," Claire managed to say, and grabbed for Shane's arm. "Wh-wh-where—"

"My question, too. Where are you going? Because I'm going with," Eve said, and jumped up to grab her patent leather skull purse.

"No, you're not. Someone needs to stay with Claire."

"Then *she's* going with. Womenfolk don't stay behind anymore, Mikey; it's so last century," Eve said, and Claire nodded. She thought she did, anyway; it was hard to tell, with all the shaking. "Right. Up you go, kiddo."

THREE

The ride in Michael's car felt like a nightmare. Eve had brought loads of blankets, and Claire was almost smothering under them, but she was still cold, and getting colder, as if her thermostat had gone drastically wrong. Her skin was turning white, her fingernails and lips blue.

She was starting to look . . . dead.

Even if she'd been trying to look where they were going, it wouldn't have done any good; Michael's car was vampire-standard, with ultratint on the windows. Human eyes couldn't get anything but murky hints of lights through it, so she just kept her attention on taking another breath, and another.

"Hey, Michael?" she heard Eve say. "Like, soon, okay?"

"I'm already breaking the speed limit."

"Go faster."

A surge of acceleration pressed Claire back in her seat. Shane was holding her, but she couldn't feel it. She'd stopped shivering now, which felt better, but she was also very, very tired, barely able to stay awake. At least the shaking had been something she could hold on to, but now there was nothing but cold, and silence. Everything seemed to be moving away from her, leaving her behind.

"Hey!" She felt something, a flash of heat against her skin, and opened her eyes to see Shane's face inches away. He looked scared. His hands were on her cheeks, trying to force heat into her. "Claire! Don't close your eyes. Stay with me. Okay?"

"Okay," she whispered. "Tired."

"I see that. But don't you go away from me, you hear me? Don't you even think about it." He stroked her skin, her hair, with hands that shook almost as much as she had before. "Claire?"

"Here."

"I love you." He said it quietly, almost a whisper, a secret between the two of them, and she felt a burst of what was almost warmth travel through her chest. "You hear me?"

She managed a nod, and thought she smiled.

Michael brought the car to a quick, sliding stop, and was out of the car before Claire could register that they'd arrived at their destination. "Hey!" Eve protested, and scrambled out after him. Shane opened the back and lifted Claire out in his arms—or rather, lifted the bundle of laundry that Claire felt like, wrapped in half a dozen blankets.

Moonlight fell blue-white over grass, trees, and headstones.

They were at Morganville's official cemetery—Restland.

"Crap," Shane breathed. "Not my idea of a great night out, you know? Claire? Still with us?"

"Yes," she said. She actually felt a little better, and didn't know why. Not *good*, of course. But not going away anymore.

Ahead, she could see that Michael and Eve were making their way together through the maze of leaning tombstones, crosses, and marble statues. A big white mausoleum dominated the hill at the top, but they weren't going that way—they veered off to the right.

Claire thought she knew where they were heading. "Sam," she whispered. Shane pulled in a breath, let it out, and headed in that direction, too.

It had been months since Sam Glass, Michael's grandfather, had died . . . given his life to save them all, really, but most especially Amelie. He was, as far as Claire knew, the only vampire buried here in the cemetery; he'd had a real service, real mourners, and he was maybe the only vampire Morganville had ever had who was universally liked and respected by both sides.

But he'd been loved, too—by Amelie. By vampire standards, Amelie and Sam's had been a whirlwind relationship; he'd been born in Morganville, hadn't even been a hundred years old when he'd died, but from what Claire had seen, it had been an old-style, intense love affair, and one they'd tried to deny themselves more than once.

They found Amelie kneeling at his grave.

From a distance, she looked like one of the marble angels—pale, dressed in white, unmoving. But her long pale blond hair was down, falling in waves around her face and down her back, and the icy wind lifted and fluttered it like a flag.

As cold as Claire felt, Amelie looked far colder. There was no grief in her expression. There was nothing—just . . . nothing. She didn't seem to see them as the four stopped near her; she didn't move, or speak, or react in any way.

"Hey," Shane said. "Stop it, whatever you're doing. You're hurting Claire."

"Am I?" Amelie's voice came slowly, and it seemed somehow distant, too, as if she were miles away but speaking through the body in front of them. "Your pardon."

She didn't move. She didn't say anything else. Shane and Michael exchanged looks, and Michael clearly got the message that if he didn't do something, Shane would, and it wouldn't be pretty.

Michael reached out for Amelie, to help her up. And she turned on him, suddenly and completely alive and viciously enraged, eyes flaring bloodred in her stark white face, fangs snapping down in place in sharp, lethal angles. "Do not touch me, boy!"

He stepped off, holding up both hands in surrender. Amelie glared at him—at all of them—for another few seconds, and then returned her stare to the grave in front of her. The red swirled away, leaving her eyes pale gray and once again distant.

Amelie's surge of rage had burned through Claire like summer, driving off the chill for a moment. She squirmed in Shane's arms, and he let her down. Claire shed blankets, except for the last one, and crouched down across from Amelie, facing her over the grave.

Amelie looked right through her, even when Claire lifted her wrist and showed her the bracelet. The gold was frosting over again, already, and Claire felt the insidious chill coming back.

"You're a coward," Claire said.

Amelie's eyes snapped into focus on her. No other reaction, but that alone was enough to make Claire want to shut up and take it all back.

She didn't. Instead, she took a deep breath and forged on. "You think Sam wants you to sit here and wish yourself to death? I mean, I get that you're hurting. But it's just so high school."

Amelie frowned, very faintly—just a tiny wrinkle of her brow. "What happened to your face?"

Oh. The burns. "Forget about me. What's going on with *you*? It feels—so cold."

While she was talking, she realized there was something strange about Amelie's hands. She was wearing gloves . . . dark ones. No, that wasn't it. There were spots of white skin showing through the . . .

The blood. Her hands were covered with *blood*. And there were slashes on her wrists, deep ones. *Those should have healed*, Claire thought as her skin tightened all over her body, and she shivered in panic-shock. She had no idea why Amelie's wounds stayed open, and kept on bleeding; vampires just didn't do that.

But Amelie had found a way. And that meant she was trying to kill herself, for real. This wasn't some melodramatic cry for help. She hadn't expected help, or looked for it.

That was why she'd been angry.

Claire felt a burst of absolute terror. *What do I do? What do I say?* She looked up at Michael, but he was standing behind and away from Amelie—he couldn't see what she saw.

Eve, though, did. And unlike Claire, she didn't hesitate. She flopped down on her knees on the cold grass next to Amelie, grabbed the vampire's left arm, and turned it so her wrist faced upward. There was something sticking out of the cut, and Claire might have gone a little faint when she realized that Amelie had stuck a *silver coin* into the wound to keep it from healing.

Eve pulled it out. Amelie shuddered, and in seconds, the cut sealed itself, and the blood stopped flowing.

"Idiot child!" she snarled, and shoved Eve back as she reached for the other arm. "You don't know what you're doing!"

"Saving your life? No, I pretty much get the concept. Now *behave*. Bite me and I swear I'll stake you."

Amelie's eyes swirled red, then went back to their normal, not-quite-human gray. "You have no stake."

"Wow, you're literal. Maybe I don't have one now, but just *wait*. You bite me, and it is *on*, bitch. . . . I don't mean you're a bitch; it's just an expression. You know?" Eve's chatter was only meant to distract. While she was talking, she took Amelie's right arm and pulled the silver coin out of that cut, too.

The flow of blood from Amelie's hands into the dirt of the grave slowed to a drip, then stopped.

And Claire felt the chill inside her own body fade, too, as Amelie healed. Finally, she could feel her life again—the heat in her body, the beating of her heart. She wondered if that was how Amelie felt all the time—that icy winter silence inside.

If it was, she understood why Amelie was here.

The night rattled through the branches of the trees and swirled Amelie's pale hair around her face, hiding her expression. Claire watched the wounds on the vampire's arms fade from red slashes to pale lines, then to nothing.

"What the hell were you doing?" Michael asked.

Amelie shrugged. "It's an old custom," she said. "Offering blood to the lost. It takes will and ingenuity to do it properly."

"Don't forget stupidity," Eve said. "That kind of thing would kill most people, never mind most vampires."

Amelie slowly nodded. "It might have."

Michael, who'd been more appalled than any of them, from the look on his face, finally found something to say. "Why?" he asked. "Why would you do this? Because of Sam?"

That actually got a smile, or at least a suggestion of one, on her pale lips. "Your grandfather would be very angry with me if he thought he was the cause. He'd think me a helpless romantic."

Eve snorted. "There's romantic, then there's dramatic, and then there's moronic. Guess which this would be."

Amelie's smile faded, and some of the spark came back into her eyes. She lifted her chin, staring down her nose at Eve. "And you do not wake up daily and paint on your clown makeup, knowing it sets you apart from your fellows? What's the phrase your generation uses? *It takes one to know one?*"

"I'm pretty sure that phrase was hot about fourteen generations back, but yeah, I get your point. And I may be into drama, but hey, at least I'm not a cutter."

"A what?"

"A cutter." Eve pointed to Amelie's bloody wrists. "You know, bad poetry, emo music, I have to hurt myself to feel, because the world's so awful?"

"That isn't why—" Amelie fell silent a moment, then slowly nodded. "Perhaps. Perhaps that is how I feel, yes."

"Well, too damn bad," Eve said, and there was some freaky chill in her voice that made Claire blink. "You want to waste away by your lover's grave, go for it. I'm Goth; I get it. But don't you dare drag Claire along with you, or I'll chase you down in hell and stake you *there.*"

Even Shane was staring at Eve now as if he'd never seen her before. Claire opened her mouth to say something, and couldn't for the life of her figure out what it would be. The silence went on, and on, and finally Amelie turned her head toward Claire and said, "The bracelet. It warned you of my—situation."

"*Warned* her? It almost killed her," Shane said. "You were taking her with you. But you knew that, right?"

Amelie shook her head. "I did not." She sighed, and she looked very young, and very human. And, Claire thought, very tired. "I had forgotten that such a thing could happen, though now I think on it, it is very pos-sible. I must apologize to you, Claire. You are feeling better now?"

Claire was still cold, but figured that it had more to do with the icy wind and the cold ground than any magic. She nodded and tried not to show any shivers. "I'm fine. But you lost a lot of blood."

Amelie shrugged, just a tiny roll of her shoulders, as if it didn't mat-ter. "I will recover." She didn't sound overly thrilled about it. "Leave me now. I have amends to make to Samuel."

"You can bleed all over his grave some other time," Eve said. "Come on, lady. Up. Let's get you home."

She reached out, and once again, Amelie let herself be touched. Odd, Claire thought; Michael was the vampire, but Amelie trusted Eve more right now. Michael was feeling that, too; there was a complicated look on his face, mostly worry.

"No biting," Eve said, as she helped Amelie to her feet. The vampire gave her a withering look. "Hey, all my teachers said that repetition was the only way to learn. You got a car or something?"

"No."

"Um . . . what about your people? Lurking in the shadows, preferably with a limo?"

Amelie raised a single white eyebrow. "If I had brought an entourage, surely they might have objected to my purpose here."

"The dramatic death scene? Yeah, guess so. Okay, then, we'll give you a ride. Blood bank first, right?"

"Unless you are offering a donation."

"Ugh. No. And don't even *look* at Claire, either."

"Me neither," Shane put in. "Homie don't play that."

"I wonder, sometimes, if your generation speaks English at all," Ame-lie said. "But yes, if you would drive me to the blood bank, you may leave me there safely enough. My *people*"—she gave it just enough of an ironic edge to let them know she found it as funny to say as they did—"will find me there."

They were walking away from Sam's grave, moving slowly and in a tight group, when a shadow stepped out from behind the big marble mausoleum at the top of the hill. It was a vampire, but not the kind Claire was used to seeing around Morganville; this one looked like he lived rough, and without access to showers or personal-grooming equipment.

He also didn't look quite *sane.*

"Amelie," the man said—at least Claire thought it a man, but it was tough to be sure with the tangle of hair that hadn't been combed since the last century, and the shapeless mass of dirty clothes, topped by a filthy raincoat. "Come to visit your peasants and distribute charity, like olden times?" He had a thick accent, English maybe—but rough, too, not like Oliver's refined voice. "Oh, please, mistress, alms for the poor?" And he laughed. It was a dry, hollow sound, and it grew . . . until it came from all around them, from out of the darkness.

There were more of them out there.

Michael turned, staring into the night; maybe he could see something, but to Claire it was all just shadows and tombstones, and that *laughter.* Shane put his arm around her.

Amelie shook off the support of Eve's arm and stepped out from their little group. "Morley," she said. "I see you crawled out of your sewer."

"And you've come down from your ivory tower, my lady," he said. "And here we are, meeting in the midden where humans discard their trash. And you brought *lunch.* How kind."

Ghostly chuckles came from the dark. Michael turned, tracking something Claire couldn't see; his eyes were turning red, and she could see him shifting away from the Michael she knew into something else, something scarier—the Michael she *didn't* know. Eve sensed it, too, and stepped back, closer to Shane. She looked calm, but her hands were balled into fists at her sides.

"Do something," she said to Amelie. "Get us out of here."

"And how do you imagine I will do that?"

"Think of something!"

"You really are a very trying child," Amelie said, but her eyes stayed fixed on Morley, the scarecrow next to the marble tomb. "I don't know why I bother."

"I don't know why you do, either," Morley said. "Confidentially, your dear old da had the right idea. Kill them all, or pen them up for their blood; this living as equals is nonsense, and you know it. They'll never be our equals, will they?"

"Right back atcha," Eve said, and shot him the finger. Shane quickly grabbed her arm and forced it down. "What, you're Mr. Discretion now? Is it Opposite Day?"

"Just shut up," Shane whispered. "In case you haven't noticed, we're outnumbered."

"And? When are we not?"

Claire shrugged when Shane looked at her. "She does have a point. We usually are."

"You're not helping. Michael?" Shane asked. "Whatcha got, man?"

"Trouble," Michael said. His voice sounded different, too—deeper than Claire was used to hearing it. Darker. "There are at least eight of them, all vampires. Stay with the girls."

"I *know* you didn't mean that how it came out. And you need me. Amelie's weak, and you're way outgunned, bro."

"Am I?" Michael flashed them a disconcerting smile that showed fang. "Just stay with the girls, Shane."

"I'd say you suck, but why state the obvious?" Shane's words were banter, but his tone was dead serious, tense, and worried. "Go careful, man. Real careful."

Amelie said, "We're not fighting."

At the top of the hill, with the big white mausoleum glowing like bone behind him, Morley cocked his head and crossed his arms. "No?"

"No," she said. "You are going to walk away, and take your friends with you."

"And why would I do that, when you have such delicious company with you? My people are hungry, Amelie. The occasional rat and drunken stranger really don't make a well-balanced diet."

"You and your pack of jackals can come to the blood bank like any other vampire," she said, just as if she were in charge of the situation, even though Claire could see she was weak and exhausted. "All that's stopping you is your own stubbornness."

"I won't bend my neck to the likes of you. I have my pride."

"Then enjoy your rats," Amelie said, and cast a commanding look at the rest of them. "We're going."

Morley laughed. "You really think so?"

"Oh yes." Amelie smiled, and it felt like the temperature around them dropped by several degrees. "I really *do*. Because you may like your games and your displays, Morley, but you are hardly so stupid to think that crossing me comes without a price."

This time, it wasn't laughter coming from all around them; it was a low rumble of sound, picked up and carried all around the circle.

Growling.

"You're threatening us," the ragged vampire said, and leaned against the tomb behind him. "You, who reeks of your own blood and weakness. Who stands with a newborn vampire as your only ally, and three juicy snacks to defend. Truly? You've always been bold, my highborn lady, but there is a boundary between bold and foolhardy, and I think that if you look, you'll find it's just behind you."

Amelie said nothing. She just stood there, silent and icy calm, and Morley finally straightened up.

"I'm not your vassal," he said. "Turn over the prey, and I'll let you and the boy walk away."

Claire guessed, with a sick sensation, that *the prey* meant her, Eve, and Shane. Shane didn't like it, either; she felt him tense at her side.

"Why would you think I'd do such a thing?" Amelie asked. She sounded only vaguely interested in the whole problem.

"You're a chess master. You understand the sacrifice of pawns." Morley smiled, revealing brown, crooked fangs that didn't look any less lethal for never having seen a toothbrush. "It's tactics, not strategy."

"When I want to be lectured on strategy, I'll consult someone who actually won battles," Amelie said. "Not one who ran away from them."

"Snap," Eve said.

"You know what they're talking about?" Shane asked.

"Don't need to know to get that one. She smacked him so hard his momma felt it."

Morley felt it, too; he took a step toward them, and this time when he bared his teeth, it wasn't a smile. "Last chance," he said. "Walk away, Amelie."

"I can open a portal," Claire whispered, trying to make it quiet enough that Morley, twenty feet away, couldn't hear. Amelie shot her a look, one of *those* looks.

"If I simply leave in that fashion, even with all of you, he can claim to have driven me away in defeat," she said. "It isn't enough to simply escape."

"Exactly," Morley said, and clapped. The sound was shocking and loud as it echoed off the tombstones. A flock of birds took off from the trees, twittering in alarm. "You must show me the error of my ways. And that, my dear liege lady, will be difficult. You're all hat and no cattle, as they like to say in this part of the world. Unless you count the three with you as cattle, of course. In which case you are short a hat."

"I'm bored with this. Attack, or do nothing as you always do," Amelie said. "We are leaving, regardless." She turned to the rest of them and said, in exactly the same cool, calm voice, "Ignore him. Morley is a posturing coward, a degenerate, a liar. He skulks here because he is afraid that standing with the rest of us will only show him for the sad, lacking beggar that he—"

"Kill them all!" Morley shouted, and blurred into motion, heading for Amelie.

Michael hit him head-on, and the two of them tumbled over headstones. Claire whirled as shadows appeared out of the darkness, moving too fast to see clearly. Her pulse jumped wildly, and she tried to get ready to fight.

And then Amelie said, "Oliver, please demonstrate to Morley why he has been so badly mistaken."

One of the shadows came forward into the moonlight, and it wasn't a stranger at all. Oliver, Amelie's second-in-command in Morganville, was in his kindly shopkeeper disguise—the tie-dyed shirt with the Common Grounds logo on the front, and a pair of blue jeans—and with his graying hair clubbed back in a ponytail, he looked like a typical coffeehouse radical.

Except for his expression, which looked like he was *not* pleased to be here at Amelie's beck and call, and even less pleased to be dealing with Morley. The shapes coming out of the darkness behind him weren't Morley's people after all, but Oliver's . . . neatly groomed, polished vampires with an edge of chill and distance that made Claire shiver. They were polite, but they were killers.

"Michael," Oliver said. "Let that fool go." Michael seemed just as surprised as Morley—or as Claire felt—but he let go of the other vampire and backed off. Morley lunged to his feet, then paused as he took in the sight of Oliver and all his backup. "Your *followers*—if one can dignify a starving pack of dogs by such a name—have been persuaded to leave. You're alone, Morley."

"Checkmate," Amelie said softly. "Strategy, not tactics. I trust you see the point."

Morley did. He hesitated a moment, then darted between the cover of tombstones and shadows, and then he was just . . . gone.

Crisis over.

"Well," Eve said. "That was disappointing. Usually in the movies there's kickboxing."

Oliver turned his head slightly, looking at Amelie in a fast, comprehensive glance that fixed on the blood on her hands. His mouth tightened in what looked like disgust. "Are you finished here?" he asked.

"I believe so," Amelie said.

"Then may I offer you an escort home?"

Her smile turned cynical. "Are you worried for me, my friend? How kind."

"Not at all. I am so gratified that I could be of use to defend your honor."

"Michael defended me," Amelie said. "You showed up."

Claire thought, *Snap, again.* She could see Eve thinking the same thing. Neither of them was quite brave enough to say it, though.

Oliver shrugged. "Strategy, and tactics. I do know the difference. And I *have* won battles, unlike Morley."

"Which is why I rely on you, Oliver, for your counsel. I trust I can continue to count on you for that."

Their gazes locked, and Claire shivered a little. Morley was bluff; Oliver wasn't. He was the kind of guy who'd do what he said, if he thought he could get away with it. He also wanted Morganville. Maybe not quite enough to kill Amelie to get it, but the line was pretty thin.

In fact, Claire could see the line right now, in the faint and fading scars on Amelie's wrists.

"Michael and his friends were kind enough to offer me an escort to the blood bank," Amelie said. "I will go with them. Perhaps you can summon my car to meet me there."

Oliver's smile was sharp as a paper cut. "As ever, I exist to serve."

"I sincerely doubt that."

Michael fell in next to Amelie, and the five of them moved down the rambling path toward where they'd left the car. When Claire looked back, there was no sign of Oliver and his people, or of Morley. There was just the silent cemetery, and the gleaming mausoleum at the top of the hill.

"Anybody else think that was weird?" Shane asked as they got into the car. Eve sent him an exasperated glance; the three of them were, of course, in the backseat. Amelie had the front, with Michael.

"Ya think? In general, or in particular?"

"Weird that we got through the entire thing, and I didn't have to hit anybody."

There was a moment of silence. Michael said, as he started the car, "You're right, Shane. That *is* strange."

When Michael parked at the blood bank, Amelie's security detail was already in place, with the limousine parked at the curb. Claire half expected to see those little devices the Secret Service wore curved around their pale ears, but she supposed the vampires didn't really need technology to hear one another. They did wear snappy black suits and sunglasses, though, and the second Michael's car came to a stop, one of them was opening the passenger-side door and offering Amelie a hand. She took it without a bit of awkwardness, graceful as water, and looked back before the door closed to say, "I thank you. All of you."

That was it. From Amelie, though, that was kind of a lot.

"Shotgun," Eve and Shane said at the same time, and promptly launched into rock-paper-scissors to settle things. Shane won, then got an odd look on his face.

"You take it," he said to Eve, who was still holding her scissors position, which had lost to his rock.

"Seriously?" Her eyes widened. "You're giving up shotgun? I mean, you did win."

"I know," he said. "I'd rather stay back here."

Meaning, with Claire. Eve didn't waste any time; she bailed and slipped into the front passenger seat, wiggling in satisfaction. Michael smiled at her, and she took his hand.

Shane put his arm around Claire, and she rested her head on his chest. Warm, finally. Warm, safe, and loved. "Man, dinner must be cold," he said. "Sorry. I know how much you like tacos."

"Cold tacos are good, too."

"Sick." He meant that in a good way. "So, after the tacos, you want to watch a movie or something?"

Claire made a vague sound of agreement, closed her eyes, and without any conscious decision to do it, fell asleep in his arms. She remembered waking up, vaguely, to Shane saying, "Better take her home," and then another very fuzzy memory of his lips pressed against hers. . . .

Then, nothing.

Morning dawned, and she woke up in her twin bed, at her parents' house. The first few seconds she felt nothing but a vague sense of disappointment that she'd wasted the opportunity to stay with Shane, but then all that was wiped out by the incredible *heat* she felt on her face. It was as if she'd fallen asleep under a sunlamp, except the room was pleasantly dim.

Claire slid out of bed, stumbled over the pile of clothes on the floor—she didn't remember taking them off, but she was wearing a mom-approved cotton nightgown, which meant *Shane* hadn't taken them off—and made her way into the bathroom.

The blinding lights came on, and they were cruel. Claire whimpered as she stared at the red blotch of her face, with white patches that must have been forming blisters underneath the first layers of skin. She pressed on her face, tentatively; it hurt—a lot. "*Really* going to kill you, Myrnin," she said. "And laugh, too."

The shower was horrible; hot water turned nuclear when it hit the burns, and she got through it mainly by gritting her teeth and chanting a variety of gruesome and creative ways she could kill her boss. Afterward she felt a little better, but she thought she looked worse. Not a great exchange, really.

She ran into her mother in the hallway, as Mom climbed the last few steps with a neatly folded stack of sheets and towels in her arms. "Oh, you're up, sweetie," Mom said, and flashed her a distracted smile. "Want me to change your—oh lord, what happened to your face?"

Mom fumbled the laundry, and Claire caught the toppling stack. "It's not that bad," she lied. "I, ah, fell asleep. In the sun."

"Honey, that's dangerous! Skin cancer!"

"Yeah, I know. Sorry. It was an accident. These go in the linen closet?"

"Oh—wait, let me take those. I have a system." The threat to take her mother's neatly folded laundry and mess it up had the desired effect; Mom left the subject of Claire's sunburn and focused on the task at hand. "Breakfast is ready downstairs, honey. Oh, dear, your face—can I get you some lotion?"

"No, I've got it already. Thanks." Claire went back to her room, finished dressing, and opened up her backpack. Truthfully, the backpack itself had seen better days; the nylon was ripped and frayed in places, there were stains that Claire was queasily sure were blood over part of the back, and the straps were starting to work their way loose, too. Probably that was because of the amount she crammed into it. She wiggled the books until she was able to pull out her *Advanced Particle Physics* and the sadly lame *Fundamentals of Matrix Computations*, which was just about the worst text ever on the subject. Behind that was the giant, backbreaking book of English lit, and all her color-coded notebooks. Behind *that* was the other stuff. *Alchemy and the Hermetic Arts*, which wasn't so much a textbook as an analysis of why the whole field was crap. Myrnin hadn't recommended it; Claire had ordered it off the Internet from a Web site run by a guy who was creepily paranoid. Of course, if he knew what she knew, he'd probably run screaming, so maybe paranoia was the right attitude.

At the back, in a special Velcro pocket, were her *special* supplies—the vampire-related ones: a couple of heavy, silver-plated stakes that she hoped never to have to use; a couple of injectable pens that she and Myrnin had rigged up with the serum Dr. Mills had developed, just in case there were still a few vampires around who hadn't gotten the shot and might be—to put it kindly—unstable. And she wasn't sure Morley from the cemetery didn't qualify, but she was glad she hadn't gotten close enough to use the pen, either.

Folded and shoved all the way to the back was the piece of paper Myrnin had given her with a sequence scribbled on it in symbols. As she did daily, Claire memorized it. She'd test herself later, drawing out the symbols and comparing them against the original. Myrnin had said the reset sequence was only to be used in emergencies, but she had the feeling that if it really got to that point, the last thing she'd have time for would be to try to figure out his sloppy drawing.

She repacked her bag, making sure she could easily slide the books in and out this time, and hefted it experimentally. The strap creaked, and she heard another thread snap. *Really need a new one.* She wondered where Eve picked up her cute patent leather ones, embossed either with the pink kitty or cute skulls; probably not in town, Claire guessed. Morganville wasn't exactly Fashion Central.

Breakfast was a family thing in the Danvers house, and Claire actually kind of looked forward to it. She didn't often make it back for lunch or dinner, but every morning she sat with her mom and dad. Mom asked her about classes; Dad asked her about her job. Claire didn't know how other families in Morganville worked, but hers seemed pretty . . . normal. At least in the abstract. The specifics were bound to be freaky.

Breakfast over (and, as always, delicious), Claire headed out for school. Morganville was a small enough town that walking was easy, if you liked that sort of thing, and Claire did—usually. Today, with her gross-looking face throbbing with the heat of the sun, she wished she'd taken up her dad's offer of buying her a car, even if it had come with the attached strings of also seeing a lot less of her boyfriend. She hadn't told Shane that he meant more to her than having a car. That seemed like commitment any guy would find scary.

Claire stopped in at the first open store—Pablo's Market, near the university district—and found a black cloth cap with a brim that shaded her face. That helped, and it made her feel a bit less obviously disfigured . . . until she heard a horn honk behind her, and looked over her shoulder to see a red convertible gliding up next to her on the street.

Claire turned face-forward and kept walking. Faster.

"What is it?" she heard a voice ask from the backseat of the car. Gina or Jennifer; Claire could never tell their voices apart. "It *looks* kind of human."

"I don't know. Zombie? We've had zombies here, right?" Gina's (or Jennifer's) vocal twin said. "Could be a zombie. Hey, how do you kill a zombie?"

"Cut its head off," a third voice said. There was no doubt about whom that voice belonged to, no doubt at all: Monica. It was cool, confident, and commanding. "Let's find the brain-freak and ask her—she'd know. Hey, zombie chick. Have you seen Claire Danvers, Girl Brain?"

Claire flipped her off and kept walking. Monica—black-haired again, no doubt looking shiny and pretty—was just a vague shadow in her peripheral vision, and Claire wanted to keep it that way.

And she knew, fatalistically, that it was never going to happen.

In fact, Monica didn't like being flipped off. She accelerated the sports car, whipped it around the corner, and came to a hard stop to block Claire's progress across the street. Monica and Gina snapped at each other, probably arguing about the specifics of how to kick Claire's ass without breaking a nail or scuffing a shoe.

Claire gave it up and crossed the street.

Monica threw the car into reverse, and blocked her there, too.

They played the game two more times, back and forth, before Claire finally just stopped and stood there, staring at Monica.

Who laughed. "Oh my God, it *is* the brain-freak. You know *freak* is only an expression, right? You didn't actually have to become a circus attraction just for me."

"It's the new thing. High-speed tanning. I'm on the way to an awesome summer glow; you should try it," Claire said. Jennifer actually laughed. She looked immediately guilty. "I'm going to be late for class."

"Good. That'll move the bell curve back toward the middle."

"Only if you actually attended to drag it down."

"Ooooh, zing," Monica said. "I'm crushed, because brains are my only asset. No, wait—that would be you, right?"

Claire sighed. "What do you want?" Because it was kind of obvious they wanted something—and probably something other than just the daily harassment. Monica had worked at cutting her off, after all, and Monica just didn't do work.

"I need a tutor," Monica said. "I don't get this economics bullshit. There are fractions and stuff."

Economics, in Claire's opinion, was voodoo science, but she shrugged. Math was math. "Okay. Tomorrow. Fifty bucks, and before we get into it, I won't take a test for you, steal the answers, or come up with some high-tech way for you to cheat."

Monica raised her perfect eyebrows. "You *do* know me."

"Yes or no."

"Fine."

"Common Grounds, three o'clock. You buy the mocha."

"Greedy little bitch," Monica said. Business deal concluded, she flipped Claire off with a perfectly manicured finger, smiled, and said, "You look like shit. Love the hat—where'd you get it, Cousin Cletus on the short bus?"

Their laughter lingered, along with the exhaust, as the three girls sped off on their usual mission of chaos and destruction.

Claire took a deep breath, pulled the hat down lower over her face, and went across the street to enter the gates of Texas Prairie University.

Claire loved classes. Oh, not the actual lectures, really—professors were, as a rule, not that exciting in person. But the *knowledge.* That was right there for the taking, as much as you could grab and hold on to—more than you ever wanted, in some classes.

Like English Lit, which she still didn't know why she had to take, and which was her last class of the day. It wasn't as if the Brontë sisters were going to make a difference in her daily life, right? Not like math, which was underneath everything from cooking to construction to going to the moon. No, science was definitely cooler.

At least until today, when her attention was temporarily pulled in by the class assignment.

> *Those who read the symbol do so at their peril. It is the spectator, and not life, that art really mirrors. Diversity of opinion about a work of art shows that the work is new, complex, and vital. When critics disagree, the artist is in accord with himself. We can forgive a man for making a useful thing as long as he does not admire it. The only excuse for making a useless thing is that one admires it intensely.*

> *All art is quite useless.*

It was the strangest thing to read those words of Oscar Wilde's at the beginning of *The Picture of Dorian Gray*, and think of Myrnin saying them, because it was eerily like the kind of explanation he'd give. It gave Claire a strange little lurch, wondering if Myrnin had ever met Oscar Wilde, who had been quite a partyer, apparently. She'd never really considered the lives of vampires much, but now reality set in, and it was strange.

For Myrnin—and Oliver, and Amelie, and most of the vampires she'd ever met—history wasn't just stuff written in a book, or sometimes captured in an old, stiff photo. For them, history happened day after day after day. Oscar Wilde had just happened a whole lot of days ago.

She bet Myrnin had met him. Probably borrowed his hat or something.

That thought distracted her so much, she didn't hear her phone ring at first; she'd set it to ultrasonic, so the professor rambled on down on the stage of the stadium-seating room without noticing a thing. Those around her did, though, and she smiled an apology, switched it to silent, and checked the name on the tiny screen. It was

Eve. Claire texted her back—*IC* for in class. It was their standard code. Eve texted *CG ASAP OMG*. Meaning, get to Common Grounds as soon as she could.

911?

No.

Shane?

No.

Tell!

No!

Claire smiled and folded up the phone, and refocused on the professor, who hadn't noticed a thing. The last ten minutes of class seemed to crawl by, but she did try to pay close attention. If she was going to seriously ask Myrnin about Oscar Wilde, it might help to actually know something about the dude. Something other than he was snarky, and more or less gay.

After class, Claire jogged through the campus quad, across the grass, and out to the gates. It was still midafternoon, so there was loads of time left before sunset. That was a good thing, because it was kind of nice to be out in the fresh air before it got, as Eve liked to title it, THTL—too hot to live, which lasted from about June through October. It didn't take long to make the trip to Common Grounds. Claire kept her head down, mostly using the cap shading her face to keep passersby from staring at her in horror.

She got to Common Grounds, and for the first time it occurred to her that the place might very well be totally packed, and she might really get stared at, for real. *Wonderful.* Well, nothing she could do about that.

Claire took a deep breath, pulled the door open, and stepped inside. The interior was dim after the brilliant sunlight, and she blinked away glare and looked around the room. It was crowded, all right—maybe forty people clustered around small café tables, drinking their mochas and lattes and espresso shots. Students, at this hour. The mix of caffeine enthusiasts changed after dark.

Everybody stared as she passed. Claire tried to pretend it was because of how fabulously cute she was, but that was a leap of faith she really couldn't make, and now her sunburn was worse because she was blushing on top of it, and also, *ow*.

Eve was all the way toward the back, jammed into a corner and defending an empty chair across the table with sharp glares and careful deployment of harsh words. She looked relieved as Claire dropped into the seat, leaned her heavy backpack against the table leg, and sighed, "I *really* need coffee."

Eve stared at her face for a few long seconds, then said, "And I can see why. Yo! Mocha!"

She snapped her fingers.

She snapped her fingers at *Oliver*, who was behind the counter pulling espresso shots. He looked up at her with blank contempt. "Yo," he repeated with poisonous sarcasm. "I am not your waitress."

"Really? Because we tip, if that helps. And you'd look really good in a frilly apron."

Oliver slammed back the pass-through hinged section of the bar and came out to stand over their table, giving them the full benefit of his presence. And that, to put it mildly, was intimidating. "What do you want, Eve?"

"Well, I'd like the blue plate special of you thrown out of Morganville, with a side order of dead, but I'll settle for a mocha for my friend." Eve tapped purple metallic fingernails against the china of her coffee cup, and didn't look away from Oliver's glare. "What you going to do, Oliver? Ban me for life from your crappy shop?"

"I'm considering it." Some of the aggression faded out of him, replaced by curiosity. "Why are you challenging me, Eve?"

"Why shouldn't I? We're not exactly besties," Eve said. "And besides, you're a jerk."

He smiled, but it wasn't a nice sort of smile. "And how have I offended you recently?"

"You were totally going to screw us over last night, weren't you?"

Oliver's smile faded. "I came when Amelie called. As I always do."

"Until you don't, right? Sooner or later, she's going to ring the little bell and faithful servant Ollie isn't going to show up to save her ass. That's the plan. Death by slacking, and you don't even get your hands dirty."

"And how is that any business of yours, in any case?" Oliver's eyes were dark, very dark, and full of secrets that Claire wasn't sure she wanted to know.

"It's not. I just don't like you." Eve tapped her talons again. "Mocha?"

He glanced at Claire's blistered face and said, without too much sympathy, "That's quite disfiguring."

"I know."

"A week should see it right." Which was, weirdly, kind of comforting in its dismissal of her problems. "Very well, mocha." But he didn't leave. Eve widened her eyes and looked irritated.

"What?"

"It's customary to pay for things you buy."

"Oh, come *on.* . . ."

"Four fifty."

Claire dug a five-dollar bill from the pocket of her jeans and handed it over. Oliver left.

"Why are you doing that?" she asked Eve, a little anxiously. Because hey, it was cool and everything, to get in Oliver's face, but it was also not exactly safe.

"Because they cast him as Mitch, which means I have to pretend to actually like the dude. Ugh."

"Oh, the play. Right. I, uh, looked it up. Looks interesting." Claire said that kind of halfheartedly, because it didn't, at least to her. It sounded like a lot of middle-aged people having melodrama.

"It *is* interesting," Eve said, and brightened up immediately. "Blanche is sort of really the symbol of the way women oppress themselves; she just can't live without a man. Come to think of it, based on that, I guess Oliver's casting was genius."

"So . . . you're playing a woman who can't live without a man?"

"It's a stretch, but the director wanted to do this postmodern kind of take on it, so he went with Goth girls for Blanche and Stella."

"Goth girls, plural," Claire repeated. "I kind of thought you were the only one in town."

"Not quite."

"Eve? You 911ed me?"

"Oh—uh, yeah, I did. I wanted you to meet—oh, there she is! Kim!"

Claire looked around. A girl had just come in the door of the coffee shop—not quite as Goth as Eve, but quite a bit farther down the curve than anybody else in the room. She had long hair, dyed jet-black, with bubble-gum pink stripes. Her makeup was mostly eyeliner. She wore less-outrageous stuff, but what she did wear seemed kind of grim—black cargo pants, plain black shirt, black leather wristband, which had (of course) a vampire symbol on it.

Kim had signed up with a vampire named Valerie, apparently. Claire didn't know much about her, but she supposed that was a good thing. If nobody was talking about her, Valerie was probably playing by the rules. Mostly.

"Hey, Eve," Kim said, and slid into the third chair at the small table. "Who's the burn victim?"

Claire felt herself stiffen; she just couldn't stop herself. "I'm Claire," she said, and forced a smile. "Hi."

"Hey," Kim said, and dropped Claire like a bad boyfriend to focus on Eve. "Oh my God, did you hear they cast Stanley?"

"No! Who?" Eve leaned forward, wide-eyed. "God, tell me it's not that kid from high school."

"No. Guess again."

"Um . . . no clue."

"Radovic."

"Get out!" Eve jiggled in her chair, grabbed Kim's hands, and then they both let out a wild, high-pitched scream of excitement.

Claire blinked as a mocha was thumped down in front of her. She looked up at Oliver, who was studying her with cool, distant eyes. He raised his eyebrows, didn't speak, and went back to his job.

"Who's Radovic?" Claire asked, since he seemed to be the most exciting thing since indoor plumbing. She couldn't remember which character Stanley was, but she thought he was the wife-beating rapist—not somebody she felt inclined to squeal over.

"He runs the motorcycle shop," Eve said. "Big biker dude, shaved head, muscles TDF."

"TDF?" Claire cocked her head. "Oh. To die for." She lowered her voice. "So, is he . . . you know?" She mimed fangs. Both of the Goth girls laughed.

"Hell no," Kim said. "Rad? He's just cool, that's all. In that dangerous kind of way. I think he's way more scary than any of *them* I ever met." By which she meant vampires.

"I guess we don't meet the same ones," Claire said. "Because mine? Plenty scary." And . . . she knew that all of a sudden, she was trying to one-up Kim, and she didn't like that about herself. She also didn't like Eve and Kim being besties all of a sudden while she was sitting like a poor, pathetic lump on the sidelines with her disfigured face, with Oliver bringing her sympathy mocha.

That was just *sad*.

Kim barely glanced at her. "Yeah?" She sounded totally uninterested. "Hey, E, can I catch a ride to rehearsal tonight? Would you mind?"

"Nope. Hey, can I come in and see what you're working on?" Eve threw Claire a quick smile. "Kim's kind of an avant-garde artist. She's really cool; I love her stuff." There was a real glow in Eve's eyes, an excitement that made Claire feel cold and a little pissed off. *I'm your friend*, she wanted to say. *I'm cool, too, right?* So she wasn't some weird artist type who made art out of used toilet paper rolls and chicken bones—so what? What made that cool, anyway?

Eve didn't hear all the mental arguments. Kim said something about the script, and they both got out their copies and flipped pages, talking about theme and motif and things Claire honestly couldn't care less about, because she was now officially in a miserable mood.

She gulped the mocha as fast as humanly possible, given that Oliver had heated it up to the surface temperature of lava. She felt truly betrayed, not just because Eve had dragged her into the middle of Common Grounds with her face looking like undercooked hamburger, but because Eve was sitting there chattering away with *Kim*, ignoring Claire's presence entirely now.

As Claire got up, though, Eve blinked and looked at her. "You're leaving?"

"Yeah." Claire couldn't bring herself to sound too apologetic. "I need to get home."

"Oh. I'm sorry, I just thought—I thought you'd like to meet Kim, that's all. Because she's cool."

"It's nice to meet you," Kim said. She didn't sound all that sincere about it, but more like she wished Claire would hurry up and hit the bricks so she could get back to her BFF-fest with Eve. "Hey, you guys live in that house with Michael Glass and Shane Collins, right? What a couple of hotties!"

Claire didn't like that Kim had even *noticed* Shane, much less knew his last name. Eve didn't seem to mind at all. She just nodded, eyes wide. "They are, right? Man candy. We know!"

Claire grabbed her backpack. "I really have to go."

"Claire—you okay?"

"I'm fine," she said. Kim was kind of smirking at her behind her drink, and Claire had a wild impulse to dump that coffee all over her.

But she didn't.

"Bye?" Eve said, and made it a kind of pathetic question. Claire didn't answer. She just pushed past Kim's chair, not being too careful about it, and headed for the door.

Behind her, she heard Kim's clear, carrying voice say, "Wow, what crawled up her ass and didn't die?"

Claire threw a venomous look back over her shoulder, and saw Oliver watching her with a very slight frown grooving his forehead. Eve looked stricken, clearly surprised at Claire's departure. Kim . . . Kim wasn't even watching her. She just lifted one shoulder in an I-can't-be-bothered shrug.

Then Claire was outside, taking deep breaths of the dry air and lifting her face to the sudden, swirling push of the wind. Sand hissed over the sidewalk, blown in from the desert.

Claire, miserably aware that she was in a horrible mood, walked home with the feeling that everyone, absolutely everyone, was watching her.

FOUR

Michael was playing guitar in the living room of the house when Claire stomped down the hall, dumped her backpack without much care for the electronic feelings of the laptop inside, and threw herself full length down on the sofa. Michael stopped in mid-chord, and she sensed he was staring at her, but she didn't look. Eventually, he started up again. The music spilled over her, beautiful and complicated, and as Claire lay there and just concentrated on breathing, she felt some of the awful tension inside her start to ease up. Still a horrible day, but she could never feel too angry when Michael was playing.

"So," he said, not looking up from the frets as he tried out a complicated new flood of sound, "I'm thinking of going electric. What do you think?"

"Eve dumped me. I've been best-friend dumped."

Michael's playing stuttered, then smoothed out again. "Huh. I'm guessing that's a no?"

"There's this girl, Kim? You know who she is?" Michael nodded, but didn't say anything. Claire felt her hands curl into fists, and deliberately, carefully straightened them out. "So this Kim, she's like perfect and all. Ooooh, she's an *artist*. And all of a sudden she and Eve have everything in common and I'm just—the stranger who doesn't get the jokes."

"I've met Kim," Michael said. His voice was neutral, and he kept his gaze on his guitar. "She's like a black hole; she just pulls people right out of their orbits. Eve's still your friend. She's just crushing on Kim because Kim never wanted to hang with her before."

"So what's the story of the fantastic Kim, anyway?"

He shrugged, and shot her a quick, unreadable look. "She went to OLOM, so I didn't know her all that well."

"OLOM?" Claire repeated.

"I forget you didn't grow up here. Our Lady of Mystery. Catholic school across town run by the scariest nuns you've ever seen. Anyway, Kim bailed on school when she was fourteen, I think. She's our resident funky-artist type, I guess—more likely to flip you off than shake your hand."

"I'll bet she sucks."

It looked like Michael was trying hard to hide a smile. "Art's always subjective. She may suck to you."

"She doesn't to you?" Claire felt a little sinking sensation. Oh, great, of course Michael would like Kim, too. Shane probably not only liked her, but had dated her, and was secretly still in love with her. Claire Danvers, New Girl, was probably the only person in Morganville who didn't think Kim was all that, supersized.

Michael stilled the strings on his guitar with the flat of his palm and sat back, finally looking right at her. "You should get to know her," he said. "She's—interesting. Just don't get too close."

"She treated me like crap."

"She does that," he agreed. "Did you know she survived a vampire attack when she was homeless and sixteen?"

Claire swallowed whatever she'd been about to say, which would have been snarky and sarcastic. Instead, she said, "Survived how?"

"Killed the vamp trying to drain her. She could have been executed—town rules. Instead, she was acquitted. No jail time. Brandon wasn't happy about it—he was Amelie's second-in-command at the time—but he had to swallow it. So really, there are only two humans in Morganville who've ever killed a vampire and gotten away with it."

"Kim and who else?"

Michael raised his eyebrows. "You didn't know?"

"Know what?"

"Richard Morrell," he said.

"Seriously?" Because Richard Morrell was now the mayor of Morganville, one of the three most important people in town, and it boggled Claire's mind to think that the vamps had allowed him to just . . . walk away from that. "When?"

Michael didn't have time to answer, because his cell phone started playing "Born to Be Wild," and he pulled it to check the screen. "Got to get ready," he said. "Sorry. Story time later. Hey, trust me, Kim's a force of nature, but like a storm, she moves on. Eve will be fascinated for a while, but Kim will find somebody else soon enough. It's how she rolls."

Claire had the really strong impression that he wasn't telling her everything. Or anything, really. But he didn't give her time to go into it, either, just storing his guitar in the case and heading upstairs.

"Get ready," she repeated, still simmering. "Yeah, everybody's got somewhere to be but me. *You should get to know Kim; she's interesting.*" Claire put a load of mockery into her Michael impression. "Yeah, right."

The back door opened and closed, floorboards creaked in the kitchen, and Claire smelled the delicious wood-smoke aroma of barbecue. She couldn't help but smile, because hey—barbecue.

And, of course, the one bringing it.

"Hey," Shane said, and leaned over the couch to stare down at her. His hair was getting longer, and even more slacker-messy, as if he'd gone after the most annoying bits with a pair of scissors. Or garden trimmers. It should have looked horrible, but on him, somehow . . . it looked hot.

Not that she was in any way prejudiced.

"Hey," she replied, and held up her hand for him to smack. Instead, he took it and kissed it lightly.

"Why the mopey face? Did I forget to say something?"

"From you, *hey* is good enough." She sighed. Complaining about Kim hadn't been the great release she'd thought it would be; Michael had been on the fence, at best, and she had no reason to think Shane would be any different. "I'm just in a terrible mood."

"This I've got to see." Shane leaned over and stared into her eyes. "Wow. Yeah, that's terrifying. I can see that you're one second from snapping, Hannibal Lecter."

She sighed. "Nobody's scared of me."

"Nope. Nobody. That's a good thing, Claire."

"Says the guy who scares everybody."

Shane considered that and smiled slowly. She loved the way one side of his smile pulled higher than the other, and the little dimple that formed there. "I don't scare you."

"Well. Only a little, maybe."

"I'll have to work on getting rid of that little bit," he said. "Speaking of scary, how's your freaky boss?"

"Don't know, didn't go, don't care," she said. "My face hurts."

"So you're moping because your face hurts?"

"I'm ugly and nobody loves me."

"Wrong," he said, "and *really* wrong." He kissed her fingers again, and this time, his lips stayed warm on her skin for a long time. "Michael's getting ready?"

Claire let out an annoyed breath. "Yeah. Everybody's got somewhere to go but me, and—what?" Because she was getting an odd look.

"The theater at TPU? He's playing tonight? Packed house? Remember?"

Oh *crap*. No, she'd forgotten all about it, and now she felt—if possible—even worse. "I'm an idiot," she said. "Oh man. I've been whining like a two-year-old about Kim. I forgot he was trying to get himself together for the show."

"Kim?" Shane's attention snapped into bright focus. "Kim. Goth Kim?"

"Yeah, what's her last name, anyway? Weird Kim. That one."

"Where'd you meet Kim?"

"Eve. I guess they're in the play together?"

"Oh, crap," Shane said. His expression changed, went guarded. "So you talked to her."

"I wasn't worth talking to."

Was she wrong, or was that a little flicker of relief? "Probably a good thing. She's kind of a flake."

"Kind of?" Claire's eyes narrowed. "Did you date her?"

His eyes went wide, and there was a fatal second of silence before he said, "Not—exactly. No. I—no."

"Did you hook up?"

He started to answer, then shook his head. "I've got no good options here," he said. "Whatever I say, you're going to believe I did, right? But even if I did, it was a long time ago, and anyway, I'm with you now. All right?"

"All right," she said. She felt as if pieces of herself were breaking off, and somehow, it was all Kim's fault. *I'm an adult*, she told herself. *Adults don't get stressed out about ex-girlfriends or ex-hookups or whatever.* Except she wanted to go find Kim and punch her out, which was not good, because she was pretty sure Kim would punch back, and harder. "Sure. It's all good."

Shane didn't believe that for a second, but she saw him decide to fake it. "Right," he said. "So. Barbecue. You in?"

"I can't believe you eat barbecue after you serve it all day long. Doesn't that get old?"

"It's *barbecue*," he said. "What's your point? Come on, mopey. Come eat."

He half dragged her off the couch, tickled her into giggles, and chased her into the kitchen.

He was right. Barbecue really was kind of a magic cure for the mopeys.

Claire dressed up for Michael's show at TPU, but given the state of her sunburn, she wasn't sure it was worth the effort—at least, until she got downstairs. Shane and Michael were standing together, talking, and *wow*. Claire lingered on the stairs, admiring.

"What?" Shane asked, catching her.

"Nothing. You guys look great."

Michael shrugged, as if it were no big thing. So did Shane, even though he'd taken the time to put on his good black shirt and black leather jacket, and even sort of comb his hair.

Michael, though—rock star. Not in the glam hair-band sense, no, but he just looked . . . important. Claire wondered if Eve had picked his clothes for him; if she had, she really loved him, because they were completely perfect. Speaking of which—"Where's Eve?"

"Running late," Michael said. "She's meeting us there."

Eve passed up barbecue? That was odd. Claire came down the rest of the steps and did a little inspection twirl for Shane. "Okay?"

"Spectacular," he said, and kissed her—carefully, because of the sunburn. "You know I love that skirt."

She blushed under the burn. "Yes. I know." It was a short, pleated skirt. Plaid. The shoes she had on with it were the ones that Eve had bought for her last Halloween—funky, but cool and kind of sexy. Claire still felt a little uncomfortable with her body in general, but there was something about the signals Shane was giving her that made her feel less awkward. More—confident.

"You guys going with me?" Michael asked, juggling his car keys. "If so, the bus is leaving."

They were, of course; with Eve MIA, they had no other car, and walking in the dark was still not the best idea in the world, even in the new, calmer Morganville. It wasn't a long trip, and Michael drummed his fingers on the steering wheel as if he were practicing fingerings for his guitar; nobody said much. Claire leaned against Shane in the back, her head on his shoulder, and his presence went a long way toward making her forget about how bad her day had been.

At least, until she remembered that he'd once sat like this with Kim, back in undefined olden times. "Hey," she said. "About Kim—"

"Oh man, I knew it. You're not letting it go, are you?"

"I just want to know—did you guys date, or—"

"No," Shane said, and looked away. He'd have been staring out the window, except that the dark tinting prevented him from actually seeing anything out there. "Okay, I took her bowling once. She was pretty good at it. Does that count as a date?"

"It does if you hooked up after."

He hesitated, and finally sighed. "Yes," he said. "Guilty. Dated. Hooked up. She moved on to the next guy. Anything else?"

Claire was totally unprepared for how awful that made her feel. "Did you—did you really like her?"

"Do we need to have this talk now, with witnesses?"

Michael held up his hand. "I want it on the record that I'm not paying attention."

"And . . . yet."

"Dude, you got yourself into this; don't blame me." Michael sounded definitely amused, which didn't make Claire feel any better.

"I'm sorry," Claire said miserably. "I guess—we can talk about it later. It doesn't matter, anyway." Except it did. A lot.

Shane turned back to look into her eyes. His pupils were huge in the faint glow of the dashboard. "I was looking for a girl," he said. "Kim wasn't it. You are, so stop worrying about that. But to answer the question, yeah, I liked her. *Really* liked her? Probably not. I wasn't exactly brokenhearted when she moved on. More like relieved."

Claire blinked. "Oh." She didn't know what to do with that. It made her feel better, and also a little confused and childish and ashamed. Being jealous of a girl he'd been happy to let go? It seemed wrong, somehow.

"Hey," he said, and carefully traced the line of her cheek, avoiding the burned spots. "I like that you care. I do."

She pulled in a deep breath. "I just don't want to share you," she said. "Not ever. Even before I met you. I know that doesn't make sense, but—"

"It does," he said, and kissed her. "It really does."

Michael was smiling; she could see it in the rearview mirror. He caught her watching him, and shook his head.

"What?" she challenged.

"It's a good thing I've got to live with the two of you," he said, "or I'd be putting this on YouTube later. And mocking you."

"Ass."

"Don't forget *bloodsucking* ass."

"Also, *undead* bloodsucking ass," Shane said. "That's kind of critical, too."

Michael stopped the car. "We're here." He grabbed his guitar case and got out, looked in on them, and flashed them a knowing grin. "Lock it when you leave. Oh, and remember—vampires can see through the tinting. I'm just saying."

"Ugh," Claire sighed. "And there goes the mood."

Michael disappeared into the artists' entrance, walking as if he owned the stage already; Claire and Shane walked, hand in hand, through the parking garage toward the front. There were a lot of other people parking, talking, walking in groups toward the entrance to the theater. Like most of TPU's buildings, it wasn't exactly pretty—a product of the blocky 1970s, glass and concrete, solid and plain and functional, at least on the outside.

The lobby was warmer, with dark red carpet and side drapes that looked only about ten years out of fashion. Claire saw people staring at her and wished she'd worn her cap, but since she hadn't, she held her chin up and clasped Shane's hand more tightly as he checked their tickets and led her up to the balcony. On the way, Claire spotted a lot of familiar faces—Father Joe, from the church, standing out in his black shirt, white collar, and red hair. People she recognized from classes, who probably had no idea they were coming to hear a vampire play guitar. Oh, and a ton of vamps, blending in except for the glitter in their eyes and the slightly hungry way they scanned the crowd. Some of them even dressed pretty well.

She didn't see Amelie anywhere, or Myrnin, or Oliver, and they were all pretty notable by their absence. She *did* see the unpleasant Mr. Pennywell, though, looking smug and remote and sexless in his plain black jacket and pants. He was sitting at a small table near the stairs, watching everyone pass. She had the strong feeling he was like those people who stood in front of the lobster tank to choose what was going on their plate.

Ugh.

"Everything okay?" Shane asked her, and she realized that he wasn't talking about the vampires or anything else like that. He quickly added, "You know, between us?"

"Oh. Uh—yeah. I guess so." She must not have seemed too confident, because he stopped climbing the stairs, looked around, and headed her toward a small group of chairs off to the side at the landing. Nobody near them. It was a darker corner, kind of intimate in the glow of the light on the wall. People moved past in a stream, but nobody seemed to look.

"I need to be sure," he said. "Because I don't want you to think Kim is competition. She's not. Until today, I hadn't thought about her twice."

But, by implication, he was thinking about her now—comparing her to Claire. And Claire couldn't be totally sure she was winning, either. "It's just that everybody thinks she's so *interesting*. And I'm just—you know."

"A supersmart apprentice to a bipolar vampire, not to mention just about the only person in town Amelie listens to these days? Yeah. You're dead boring." Shane's warm hands cupped her face and tilted her chin up so he could meet her eyes in the dim light. "There. That's better."

"Why?" The word trembled on her lips, a restrained wail of bitterness. "So you can see how ugly I look, compared to Kim?"

"You got some layers of skin burned off," he said. "Big freaking deal. In a week you'll have a killer tan, and everybody will be wondering where you got the spray-on stuff. It doesn't matter. Not even a little. Get me?"

She didn't want to cry, and for a wonder, she didn't. She gulped in one hitching breath, held it, and let it slowly out, and that was it.

Then she smiled. "I get you."

"All right then. Because I love you. Remember?"

Warmth zipped through her nerves and took up a hot glowing spot somewhere just below the pit of her stomach. "I remember," she said. "I love you, too."

He kissed the tip of her nose. "Jealous. I kind of like it."

Hand in hand, they headed for the concert hall.

Mr. Pennywell blocked their path.

There was something really, unpleasantly *wrong* about Pennywell, in ways Claire couldn't put her finger on; the vampire looked awkwardly built, female in one light, male in another, but that wasn't the thing that made him frightening.

It was the complete, soulless absence of feeling in his expression and eyes. Even when he smiled, nothing happened in the top half of his face. It was just muscles, not emotion.

"Move," Shane said, and Claire felt his hold on her hand unconsciously tighten. "Dude, you are *not* crazy enough to go after us in the middle of neutral ground, in front of witnesses. Right?"

"That would entirely depend on what I planned to accomplish," Pennywell said. "But I am not here to threaten you. I am here to summon you."

"To our seats? Thanks. Don't need an usher."

Pennywell stayed right in their path. The crowd was thinning out around them. The last thing Claire wanted was to be alone out here with him, everyone else inside and cheering and clapping and covering up her all-too-likely screams. She traded a look with Shane.

"Oliver would like a word," Pennywell said, and made a graceful gesture to his left. "If you please."

"Now?"

"He is not taking appointments. Yes. Now."

There didn't seem to be many options available, but Claire could see that Shane was tempted to tell Pennywell to beat it. That would be bad. Pennywell wasn't someone who took rejection well.

It didn't come to that, and for the worst possible reason.

"Shane? Shane *Collins*? Are you kidding me?" A girl's voice came from over Pennywell's shoulder, and was followed by the girl sliding around the vampire and throwing herself all over Shane. He dropped Claire's hand in surprise, and to catch the girl before they both toppled over.

It took a second to put the dyed-black-and-pink hair and voice together, but Claire knew even before her brain supplied the name.

Kim. Oh, perfect.

And Kim was *kissing Shane.*

It wasn't like he was kissing her back . . . more like he was trying to push her off his lips. But still. Her lips. Touching Shane's.

Even Pennywell looked thrown.

"Hey!" Claire protested, not sure what she ought to do, but she wanted very badly to grab a handful of that black hair and yank, hard. She didn't need to. Shane picked Kim up, bodily, and set her at arm's length—and held her there.

"Kim," he said. "Uh—hi."

"How's it going, Collins? Wow, it's been a while, huh? Sorry about the family stuff—that sucks, man. Oh, did you hear I've got a loft now? I'm selling on the Internet. Very cool." Kim's wide eyes were fixed on Shane's face, and there was a sickeningly delighted expression on her face. "I just can't believe it's you, Shane. Wow. So great to see you."

"Yeah," he said, and looked at Claire, just a quick (and panicked) glance. "This is Claire. My girlfriend." He stressed the word. It didn't seem to register, or if it did, Kim shrugged it off. She barely glanced at Claire at all.

"Cool," she said. "Hey, you're the one from the coffee shop. Eve's friend. Small world, right?"

"Claustrophobic," Claire said. "What are you doing here?" She knew she sounded angry; she just couldn't help it. Pennywell looked from her to Kim, clearly trying to decide whom he should kill first. From his expression, he was leaning toward Kim, which didn't distress Claire much at all.

"I came to hear Michael Glass," Kim said. "I mean, Eve told me all about it. Michael's always been the coolest guy in town—present company excepted." She *winked* at Shane. *Winked.* Claire wanted to vomit. "I just wanted to show my support."

"I'm not interested in you," Pennywell said to her. "Go away."

Kim blinked and turned to look at the vampire for the first time. Then she reacted as if she hadn't even known he was there. *Seriously? She got a part in the play?* Because that was the worst reaction Claire had ever seen, outside of really old silent movies. "Oh my God! What the hell are *you*? I mean, yes, obviously—" She held up two fingers in what Claire thought was a peace sign before realizing it was probably a *V*—for vampire. "But damn, you're freaky."

Pennywell had no idea what to do, Claire guessed from the frown that grooved that smooth, high forehead. He cocked his head and looked at Kim without saying a word, just studying her.

Then he said, "You are the historian."

Kim smiled. "Bingo, dude. I'm the historian. And you're kinda new, am I right? I have *got* to get you on camera. Make an appointment, okay? Here. Here's my number." She dug in the small black bag strapped to her wrist, came out with some kind of business card, and handed it to him. Pennywell took it—mostly in self-defense—and tucked it in his coat pocket. "Word of advice? Nehru jackets went out with the groovy sixties. Go for Brooks Brothers. You do not want to be preserved for posterity in a bad look, right? Also, maybe some work with the hair, butch you up some. Think about it."

While she was talking, Shane took Claire's elbow and quietly hustled her around Pennywell, whose eyes remained fixed on Kim as she chattered. By the time the vampire realized what was happening and thrust Kim aside, Shane and Claire were slipping through the door into the hall, out of his reach.

Hopefully.

"Did she do that on purpose?" Claire asked.

"Don't know," Shane said. "But I wasn't about to waste the chance. Call Oliver. Find out if he was really wanting to see us."

Claire nodded. The crowd in the hall was still buzzing around, and the noise level was high. Nobody would notice her on the phone; there had to be a hundred or more of them glowing like jewels in the tiers of seats as people caught up with their friends, gossiped, made dates.

Claire speed dialed a vampire and got his voice mail. Oliver didn't bother to identify himself, but just told the caller to leave a message, which she did, and then she put her phone on vibrate.

Shane kept looking at the closed doors they'd come through. Claire suppressed the urge to grit her teeth. "You're worried about her?" she asked, and tried to keep her voice neutral.

"We left her alone with Pennywell," he said. "Dammit. I thought she was following us."

Well, Kim hadn't followed them. Claire tried to be more worried, but the best she could really summon up was a dim sense of annoyance.

And that really wasn't like her; she was always trying to find excuses for the worst people, and somehow, she just couldn't get on Kim's side, no matter what.

But she knew the right thing to do. "We should go look for her."

"No," Shane said. "You stay here. I'm just going to see if she's out there. I just want to be sure she's all right."

Because you don't at all care, Claire thought, but had enough sense to keep it to herself. She just nodded. Shane let go of her hand and moved to the doors, which he eased open and looked out. After a moment of hesitation, he let it close and came back. "Not there," he said.

"Which one?"

"Both." Shane sounded tense, and she couldn't blame him. He tended to take a lot on himself, and if something ended up going badly with Kim, he'd see it as his failure, which was nonsense, but it was how Shane rolled. "I need to—"

"Need to what?"

Kim again, coming up from right behind Claire. Claire squeezed her eyes shut and almost screamed in frustration—not relief—but she managed to control herself, turn, and say, very calmly, "Need to be sure you were okay. Which you are. Obviously."

Kim looked at her for a moment; then a knowing smile slowly spread over her lips. "Obviously," she almost purred. She transferred the look to Shane. And the smile. "You were worried about me? That's sweet, but gender-bender vamp back there wasn't about to hurt me."

"Why not?" Claire asked.

Kim shrugged. "Eh, you know. Damn, I really haven't seen you in forever, Collins. What you been up to?"

"Not much," he said, and reached out for Claire's hand again. "We've got seats down there. Sorry. Thanks for the intervention out there."

"Sure," Kim said. "Catch you later, then."

Their seats were close to the front, and by the time they'd reached them, the lights were going down. Claire looked back, but couldn't see Kim anywhere in the shadows.

"I think I might really hate that girl," she said.

Shane kissed her fingers lightly. "Don't be jealous. I'm not into her. Now or later."

Claire wished she could believe that, but there was still some small, difficult part of herself that was too aware of her own flaws.

Then the spotlights came up, the house lights went down, and Michael walked onto the stage, to a sudden rush of applause, and he wasn't the Michael Claire knew—he wasn't the one who hung out in the living room and played video games and noodled around on his guitar and picked terrible Westerns for movie night.

This was someone else.

Someone almost frightening, the way he grabbed and held the spotlight. He'd looked good earlier, but now Claire saw him the way that Michael Glass had always been meant to be seen . . . center stage. The light turned his hair brilliant gold, made his pale skin glow like moonstone, turned him into something exotic and fabulous and untouchable—and, at the same time, something you wanted to touch. Badly.

Someone pushed into the chair next to Claire. Eve. She'd put on her best, mostly backless black velvet gown, fixed her hair into a chic, gleaming black cap, and when she crossed her legs, the slit in her dress revealed an acre of leg and stiletto heels.

She was out of breath.

"Oh God, I thought I'd never make it," she whispered to Claire, and snapped open a black silk fan, which she fluttered to cool herself off. "That's my boyfriend, you know."

"I know," Claire said. She'd been prepared to not talk to Eve, but in two sentences, she found herself smiling. There was something so *happy* in sharing her joy. "He's okay, I guess."

Eve smacked her with the folded-up fan. "Bite your tongue. My boyfriend is a rock *god*, baby."

And this, with the first few notes of his song, Michael Glass proved vividly to the entire hall.

The concert was great. The after-party was overwhelming, mostly because Claire hadn't really known there would be one, and she wasn't up for being stared at by a few hundred strangers who were all pressing around, trying to get to Michael and wondering why she was so special that she got to be behind the autograph table, instead of in front of it. Michael had barely had time to say hi since he'd come out the stage door into the lobby; he'd been mobbed, and not even Eve, standing there looking gorgeous and movie-star sleek, could get private time with him while the fans circled. There was no sign of Kim. The vampires didn't bother to mix with the crowd, but as each of them left the building, they stopped to look at Michael, and nod. Claire supposed that was their version of a standing ovation.

As the number of autograph seekers finally died down, there were only a few people left. One was Pennywell, leaning against a marble pillar a hundred feet away, looking bored but eternal, as if he could wait another ten thousand years if necessary without a change of underwear. One was Kim, who was locked in animated conversation with a couple of TPU guys who looked, to Claire's eyes, like liberal arts students. She kept casting glances at their little group, and Claire figured that any minute she'd kick her holding-pattern boys to the curb and make straight for Shane.

The last person, though, was a human—an older guy dressed in a black tailored leather jacket and jeans—kind of like business tough, if there was such a thing. He had great hair, and one of those nice, even, white smiles people had on TV shows—and a tan.

"Michael, great show," the man said, and leaned over to shake Michael's hand. "Seriously, that was out of the park. My name is Harry Sloan. My daughter, Hillary, goes to school here. She wanted me to come and check you out, and I have to say, I was very impressed."

"Thanks," Michael said. He looked a little tired, no longer the mighty god of guitar that he'd been onstage, and Claire thought he just wanted to get this done and get home. "I appreciate that, Mr. Sloan."

Mr. Sloan produced a business card, which he slid across the table toward Michael's hand. "Yeah, here's the thing. I think you've got real potential, Michael. I work for a major recording company, and I want to take a demo CD back with me."

There was a moment where they all stared at him, and then Michael said, blankly, "Demo CD?"

"You don't have one?"

"No. I've been—" Michael didn't know how to finish that sentence. "Busy." Busy getting killed, then being made into a ghost, then turning into a vampire. Fighting wars. Et cetera.

"You really have to get in the studio, man, right now. I'll set it up— there's a good place in Dallas. I'll book the time for you if you tell me dates. But I want to take your stuff into our next discovery meeting. I think we can really do some business. Think about it, will you? First thing is to get that demo CD done. Call me."

He held out his hand again, and Michael shook it. He looked pale, and a little vacant, Claire thought. Mr. Sloan flashed them all that Hollywood smile again, slid on a very expensive pair of sunglasses, and left.

"He can't be," Eve said. "It's a joke, right? Monica's idea of a joke or something."

Michael held up the business card. Eve examined it, blinked, and passed it to Shane, who passed it on to Claire.

"Vice president," Claire read. "Oh. Wow."

"It's not a joke," Michael said. "There was an article about this guy in *Rolling Stone* about six weeks ago." Michael slowly got to his feet, and it really hit home. "He wants to sign me. As a musician."

Shane held up his hand, palm out, and Michael slapped it, then grabbed Eve and spun her around in a rush of velvet and squeals. He went still, buried his face in the soft shine of her hair, and just held her. "All my life," he said. "I've been waiting for this all my life."

"I know," Eve said, and kissed him. "I'm so proud of you."

Across the gap of a hundred feet of outdated carpet, Mr. Pennywell started clapping. It had the crisp, startling sound of gunshots. The two boys Kim was chatting with discovered they had places to be, and hit the doors to flee into the night; Kim, just as Claire had feared, walked back over toward them. Pennywell finished clapping and said, "You do realize, of course, that they'll never allow you to leave?"

Michael raised his head, and it felt to Claire like the rest of them faded out of the world. It was just Michael and Pennywell.

"They?" Michael said. "You mean Oliver and Amelie."

"They want all vampires here, under their control. Under their *care*." Pennywell's sneer was like a slap across the face. "Two frightened little pups trying to control a pack of wolves. Are you a pack animal, Michael? I myself am not."

"What do you want?" Michael asked.

"Of you? Nothing. You are only a dog running to heel." His empty gaze moved away from Michael and fixed with a snap onto Claire. "I want *her*." Shane, Michael, and Eve closed ranks in front of her before Claire could draw a breath. Pennywell clicked his tongue. "No, no, no, children. This is a waste of blood. I will kill you all—yes, even you, fledgling—and take what I want in any case. You, girl—do you want to see your friends dead on this rather unpleasant carpet?"

"Fat chance," Shane said. "We already fought your punk ass once, remember? Go ask Bishop how that went for him if you're scared to think about it."

Pennywell sent him a scorching look of contempt. "You were not alone, boy. You had allies. Here, you have—" He turned a slow circle, and focused on Kim. "Her. Perhaps not your most persuasive argument." He went eerily quiet, and very serious as he moved his gaze back toward Claire. "I have been alive seven hundred years, and I have been a killer since I was old enough to hold a sword. I have hunted witches and heretics down across Europe. I have destroyed stronger than you, in harder times. Do not mistake me when I tell you that I will not give you another chance."

Claire swallowed and stepped out from behind Shane. He tried to grab her arm, but she twisted away, never taking her eyes off Pennywell. "Don't hurt them," she said. "What do you want?"

"I want you to come with me," he said, "and I am entirely out of patience. *Now*."

Claire held out her hands, palm out, to her friends—Michael, in his rock-star clothes, looking pale and focused and dangerous; Eve, dressed in a fall of black velvet, looking like a silent film star, right down to the look of fear on her face.

Shane was practically begging her not to go. His need to protect her pulled at her like gravity.

She said, "He won't hurt me. I'll call as soon as I can. You guys go home. Please."

"Claire—"

"Shane, *go.*"

To her utter dismay, she saw Kim move over to her friends and stand next to Shane. Kim put a hand on his arm, and he looked down at her. "Let her go," she told him. "She'll be fine."

Claire knew that this was *not* the right time to be wanting to scream, *Take your hands off my boyfriend, bitch,* but it was all she could do to hold the words inside. Pennywell's hand closed around her wrist, cold and strong as a handcuff, and as he began to pull her away, Claire met Shane's eyes one last time.

"I'll be back," she said. "Don't do anything crazy."

He probably thought she meant fighting vampires.

What she really meant, deep down, was *Don't fall in love with Kim.*

FIVE

Pennywell marched her out of the concert hall, into the chilly night. There was a smell of rain in the air, and thunder rumbling far off in the distance. Lightning shattered across the sky, briefly turning Pennywell almost luminous, and as Claire blinked away the glare, she saw that he was pulling her in the direction of an idling limousine parked at the curb.

"In," he barked, and shoved her at the open back door. She stumbled, caught herself, and crawled in. It was dark, of course. And it smelled like cigar smoke. Pennywell clambered in behind her, agile as a spider, and slammed the door behind him. The big car accelerated away from the curb.

"Where are we going?" Claire asked.

"Nowhere," said a voice out of the dark—Oliver's voice. The lights in the back slowly came up, revealing him sitting on the bench seat opposite her. Next to him was the source of the smoke, who smirked at her as he took a long pull on his cigar. Myrnin had put on a wine red jacket for the evening, something with elaborate embroidery on it. He looked almost normal, actually. He was even wearing the right shoes.

There was nothing normal about his smile, though.

"Cohiba?" he asked, and took an unlit cigar out of his pocket to offer it to her. She shook her head, violently. "Pity. You know, daring women used to smoke."

"Cancer isn't sexy."

He raised his shoulders in a lazy shrug. "You all die of something," he said. "And we all pay for our pleasures, one way or another."

"Myrnin, what the *hell* is going on? You send this freak to abduct me—"

"Actually," Oliver said, "I sent Pennywell. It seemed to me he would be the one of us you and your friends would be least likely to argue with."

Pennywell laughed. "There you are wrong."

"I never said it would be easy." Oliver slammed the door on that conversation, and focused back on Claire. He leaned forward, elbows on his knees, and she tried not to be intimidated. "Myrnin and I wish to ask you about Amelie."

"Amelie." Claire stared back at him blankly, and then she felt the first tinglings of alarm. "What about her?"

"That display of foolishness last night. How did you know what she was doing? I didn't."

"I think it's the bracelet. I don't know. Maybe—" *Maybe it's Ada*, she thought, but didn't say. Myrnin stared at her thoughtfully through half-lidded eyes and blew smoke in a cloud at the roof. "Maybe she wanted me to know. Deep down. Maybe she wanted someone to stop her."

"Was she surprised to see you?" Myrnin asked. Claire slowly nodded. "Then she didn't summon you, consciously or unconsciously. Interesting."

"Theories?" Oliver asked.

"Not at present." Myrnin shrugged; then he spoiled his cool by catching sight of something outside of the limousine windows and brightening like a three-year-old with a new toy. "Oh, an all-night drive-through! I could murder a cheeseburger. Don't you just love this century?"

"Focus, you fool," Oliver growled. "What is Amelie up to? Is she fit to remain in control?"

"What makes you think she is in control?" Myrnin asked absently, then shot Claire a frown. "What happened to your face?"

"You," she snapped. "Remember?"

"I certainly did not order you to stand out in the sun. What possible good would that do?"

"Box? UV bomb? Ringing any bells?"

"Oh." Myrnin considered this carefully, then sighed. "Yes. Quite my fault. So sorry. What were we talking about?"

"Amelie," Oliver said, almost growling. *"Is she fit to lead?"*

Myrnin stubbed out his cigar in the wineglass. "Careful, my old friend," he said. "You come very close to saying something you would regret. I'm not your creature."

"No," Oliver agreed. "You're her creature to the bone. You built her this madhouse of a town. I would assume you could destroy it, if you chose."

Myrnin's attention seemed to be focused on crushing the cigar into submission. "Your point?"

"Amelie said herself that Morganville was built as an experiment, to see if it was possible for vampires and humans to live openly, and in peace. Well, I think that after all this time, we know the answer to that question. The only way to control humans is through fear, intimidation, and appeals to their greed. This exercise hasn't made us stronger; it's made us weaker."

"We were dying already," Myrnin said. "Out in the world."

Pennywell, who hadn't spoken since entering the limo, let out a derisive laugh. "Some of us," he said. "And some of us were killing."

"Any fool can kill. It takes genius to create."

"Hey!" Claire broke in. "Why me? Why grab me?"

"We're still debating that," Myrnin said.

Oliver looked frustrated enough to claw steel. "No, we are *not* debating it. The girl clearly has a connection to Amelie. It's the one way we can guarantee she will come to us."

"Don't be stupid. Amelie may have a connection to her, but Claire is eminently replaceable," Myrnin said. "No offense, my dear, but you're human. Humans are, by definition, replaceable."

"So are vampires," Pennywell said. "Including you, you bedlamite wretch."

"I was never in Bedlam," Myrnin said. "Although I hear you picked off inmates there when the rats ran scarce."

That must have been a serious vampire insult or something, because Pennywell launched himself across the space to latch his hands around Myrnin's throat.

Myrnin didn't even bother to react. He *yawned*. "Oliver," he said, "control your beast before I am forced to."

Pennywell snarled. His fangs snapped down.

Myrnin's eyes sparked red, and he grabbed Pennywell's wrist in his hand and twisted.

Bones snapped. Pennywell howled, clearly shocked at Myrnin's strength. From the look on his face, Oliver hadn't exactly expected it, either. Myrnin shoved Pennywell back to his place, pointed a finger at him, and smiled. "Next time, I will take your fangs," he said. "Then you'll be a toothless tiger. I don't think you'd enjoy it. Play nicely, witchfinder."

"Boys," Oliver said coolly, "the question at hand is an important one: Do we allow Amelie to continue to run Morganville? Or do we use the girl to take it from her control, once and for all?"

Myrnin sighed. "You do understand that Amelie is aware of your intentions? That she's planned for your eventual rebellion? Because it was plain as the moon that you'd betray her, sooner or later."

"I'd hate to disappoint," Oliver said. "And she has become weak. The weak can't lead."

"I've known Amelie a very long time, and I would never describe her as *weak*." Myrnin lit up another cigar, with much puffing and use of a lighter with a hot blue flame. Claire almost choked on the smoke. Her eyes burned and teared, and she had to wipe them clear. "Wounded, perhaps. Less certain of herself than before. But not weak, which you will discover if you think to push her."

Oliver frowned at him. "I thought you were with me in this."

"Did I say that? Well, I'm not very reliable, as you know." Myrnin closed his eyes in delight as he drew in the smoke from the cigar. "You very nearly succeeded in bribing me with these excellent Cubans. I haven't had the like since Victoria was still Queen of England. But in the end, I must remain loyal to my lady. And I really can't allow you to torment my apprentice. After all, that's my job."

"I thought that might be the case," Oliver said.

He pulled a stake from inside his coat and slammed it into Myrnin's chest.

Claire screamed and lunged for Oliver, or at least she started to—the limousine violently swerved, sending them all flying, and Claire ended up on the carpeted floor with Myrnin's deadweight on top of her. Something hit them, hard, and Claire felt the car lift, twist in the air, and slam down on its top, sending her and Myrnin in a tangle to the roof of the limo.

Oliver and Pennywell had somehow stayed in their seats—holding themselves in by main force, apparently. Claire fought free of Myrnin's body, panting and disoriented. She wasn't hurt, or at least she didn't feel hurt, but everything seemed a little odd. Too bright. Too sharp. Pennywell's eyes were bright red, and his fangs were out.

Oliver was looking at her like lunch, too.

The side window had broken out when the car rolled. Claire grabbed Myrnin's shoulders, crawled backward through the wrecked window, and dragged him along with her. As soon as she had his chest clear of the limo, she wrapped both hands around the stake and yanked it free with a wrench.

"Ahhhhhh!" Myrnin screamed, and came bolt upright, both hands slapping at his chest. "My *God*, I hate that!"

Pennywell dropped down onto his legs like some pale jumping spider. Myrnin slammed a boot into his face and crawled free of the wreckage, grabbing Claire as he rose to his feet. There was blood staining his shirt, and some on his face where he'd been cut by flying glass, but he looked fine, really.

Angry as hell, though.

Pennywell crawled out of the limo. His expression was no longer empty; it was full of hate. "Heretic," he hissed. "*Witch*. I'll see you burn, you and your familiar." He cast a venomous look at Claire, too, and she swallowed hard.

"What's a familiar?" she asked Myrnin.

"A demonic spirit who aids a witch," he said. "Usually in the form of a black cat, but I suppose you'd do. Although in my experience you are not nearly demonic enough."

"Thanks."

"Don't mention it." Myrnin raised his eyebrows and thrust his chin at Pennywell. "Well? Are you waiting for your lynch mob to bring your spine?"

Claire had a very nasty flash of intuition. "Where's Oliver?"

And then a cold hand closed around her neck, choking off her breath and igniting blind panic inside. She was pulled away, completely off balance and out of control, and saw Myrnin spinning toward her but not quickly enough; she was moving away from him, off into the dark. . . .

It all freeze-framed for her: Myrnin, bloody and wide-eyed, reaching out for her. Pennywell smirking from where he stood near the wreckage of the limo. The smoking sedan that had sent the limo rolling—hood crumpled like used tinfoil.

That was a vampire car.

And the driver's-side door was open.

Claire choked, gasped for breath, and tore at the hand holding her throat closed. No good. Her fingernails didn't concern him any more than her heels when she kicked backward.

"Hush," Oliver chided her, and squeezed harder. "I'd like to say this will hurt me more than you, but that wouldn't be strictly true—"

He broke off with a stunned gasp, and his hand slid away from Claire's throat. She stumbled forward two steps, both hands holding her aching neck, and then looked back.

Oliver was staring down at his chest, where the point of a stake had emerged from his rib cage.

"Damn," he said, and pitched down to his knees, fighting it all the way.

Michael was behind him.

Michael had just *staked Oliver*.

He dashed around the older vampire and grabbed Claire. "You okay?"

She couldn't get words out through her bruised throat, but she nodded, eyes wide. In seconds Myrnin was there, too, picking her up and dumping her unceremoniously into Michael's arms. "Take her," he said. "Oliver is not going to be pleased, boy. Better go."

"I had to," Michael said. "I had to stake him. He was going to kill her."

"In point of fact, he wasn't; he was going to hurt her so badly that Amelie would feel it, that's all. But that's not what I meant. You crashed a car into the limousine. Oliver *loves* his limousine."

Michael opened his mouth, then closed it without thinking of anything to say to that.

Myrnin, watching Pennywell, said, "Michael, take the girl and go. I have things to do here. Do leave the stake where it is—I can't have Oliver interfering just yet. The witchfinder and I have old debts to settle." When Michael hesitated, Myrnin's dark eyes flashed toward him in command. *"Take her."*

Michael nodded, and Claire lost all sense of where she was, except that she was held firmly in his arms, and moving fast. Lights flashed by, moving too quickly for her to focus on. The burning in her throat died down from a bonfire to a slow broil, and she tried clearing it. It felt like gargling with glass, but she got a weak sound out.

Michael slowed to a normal human-speed run, then a walk, and Claire saw that they were back at the TPU theater. Eve, Shane, and Kim were standing in front of Eve's car. Two of them looked shocked; Kim just looked like none of it was much concern of hers.

"Claire!" Shane got there first, taking her out of Michael's arms and easing her to her feet. When she faltered, he held on to her, anxiously looking her over. "What the hell happened, Michael?"

"Crash," Claire whispered. "Car crash. Hi."

"Hi," Shane said. "What do you mean, car crash? Jesus, Michael, you crashed your car?"

"Into the limo," Claire said. It seemed important to get it right, for some reason. "Saved me."

Sort of, anyway. She really wasn't sure what would have happened to

her if Oliver had managed to take Myrnin out and had time to do whatever unpleasant thing he'd had planned, or if Pennywell had gotten hold
of her. There were so many nasty possibilities.

"We need to get out of here," Michael said. "Right now. Eve?"

She pulled her car keys out of her tiny black purse, hiked up her velvet
skirt, and climbed behind the wheel of her big boxy sedan. Kim smoothly
claimed the front passenger seat, leaving Claire in the back, sandwiched
between Shane and Michael—which was not at all a bad place to be. She
was shaking, she realized. She supposed that was shock or something.
Shane held her left hand, and Michael her right, and she closed her eyes
as Eve peeled rubber out of the parking lot, heading home.

SIX

"Mom?" Claire looked at the clock, bit her lip, and prepared for the worst. "Hey. Sorry to be calling so late. We just got out of the concert—you know Michael was playing tonight, right? So I'm at the Glass House. I'm going to stay over tonight; I'll see you in the morning, okay? Bye. Love you."

She hung up and gave a long sigh, leaning back against Shane's chest. "Thank God for voice mail," she said. "I don't think I could have done that if she'd picked up."

He kissed her neck gently. "I don't care what your parents say; I'm not letting you out of my sight. Not tonight."

They were home, safe in the warmth of the Glass House. Michael had gone upstairs to change, but Eve was still there, slinking around in her glam-rags. Also, ugh, *Kim* was still with them.

But somehow it felt like the two of them were all alone.

Shane wrapped his arms around her, and she relaxed, all her fear bleeding away. Her small hand wrapped around his forearm, she felt so safe as she sensed his muscles moving underneath his velvety skin.

Even if she wasn't really safe, ever.

"I need to thank Michael," she said, and stopped to clear her throat. It didn't make it feel much better. "He didn't have to come after me."

"I'd have killed his ass if he didn't," Shane said, and there was a grimness behind it that made her wince. "He wouldn't let me come with him."

"You could have gotten hurt in the crash."

"He wasn't worried about *you*."

"He was. I was about to be dinner."

Shane sighed and dropped his forehead onto her shoulder. "And he'd have a point."

"He saved my life."

"I get that. Could we stop talking about Michael for a second?" He sounded actually pained.

"You are *not* jealous."

Shane held up two fingers pinched almost together. "That much, maybe. And only because he's got that rock-star thing going on. You girls get into that."

"Shut up!"

"Seriously, you throw panties and stuff. I've heard."

She turned in the circle of his arms to face him, staring up into his face. No words. He was drawn down to her like gravity, lips warm against hers, lazy at first, then getting hotter, breath coming faster. Her brain exploded in a thousand thoughts and memories . . . the soft skin at the back of his neck, the way he said her name in that sweet, hushed whisper, the sheer heat of him against her.

"Hey." Eve's voice, mostly amused, made Claire jump. "I know, mad love, et cetera, but could you please not make out in the living room? I really want to be able to tell your parents I've never seen anything going on when they bring the Inquisition over for lunch."

Shane kissed her one more time, lightly and softly, and fluffed her hair back from her face. "To be continued," he said.

"I hate cliff-hangers."

"Blame Eve."

Claire stepped back from him, and the world came back to life around her—funny how it all seemed to disappear when she was with him. Eve was sitting on the couch, flipping channels on the TV. Kim was cross-legged on the floor reading the backs of game cases. "Hey," Kim said. "Who plays the zombie game?"

"Ugh," Eve said. "No."

"I have, a little," Claire admitted.

"So that's a no, a maybe—come on, somebody must be game master around here."

Shane finally held up his hand. Kim smiled.

"Rock on, Collins," she said. "Let's see what you've got."

Claire's lips still tingled from the kisses, and her whole body from anticipation, but the gleam in Kim's eyes made her tense up. She could tell Shane was reluctant, but also, Shane wasn't really in the habit of passing up a challenge, either.

Except that this time, he did. "Can't," he said. "Got to check on Michael."

"I already did," Eve said, "which you'd have known if you weren't on Planet Wonderful, the two of you. And he's fine. He's on the phone with Amelie. I wouldn't go there."

"Oh." Shane's excuse had just vanished, and Claire could tell he wasn't quite up to outright telling Kim no. He went to the couch; Eve scooted over and handed him a game controller. Kim snagged the other one from the side table. "Lock and load, I guess."

Claire left him to go upstairs. The bathroom was free, and she used the facilities, cleaned up, mourned the state of her face and the fast-emerging bruises around her neck, then went to her bedroom and found a pair of comfortable jeans and a top. A cute top. And she made sure it showcased the cross Shane had bought her. She also put on a little lip gloss. Just a little.

She could hear the shouts and smack talk from downstairs when she opened her bedroom door; Kim and Shane were all about the competition, which did not make her feel less left out. "Come on, suck it up," she told herself in a harsh, hoarse whisper, plastered a smile on, and started down the hall.

The hidden door opposite Eve's bedroom opened with a soft click, and in the dim reflected light, Claire saw the flicker of a black-and-white image of a woman in full Victorian-style skirts. It looked like a specter, which anywhere but in Morganville would have made Claire scream and make a run for the local ghostbusters.

But this *was* Morganville, and Claire knew Ada all too well. "What?" she demanded. Ada—or Ada's image projection, anyway—made a hushing motion of a finger to her lips. She turned, the way a two-dimensional cardboard cutout turns, disappearing in the middle and then expanding again to a back view, and glided up the stairs beyond the hidden door without touching the wood.

"Seriously?" Claire sighed. "Wonderful. Just great."

She followed Ada up. Behind her, the door shut with the same hushed click. Upstairs the lights blazed on, a kaleidoscope of color through Tiffany glass lamps, and Claire saw Ada's image—face forward again— standing against the wall near the old red velvet sofa. "Okay, I'm here," she said. "What do you want?"

Ada made the shushing motion again, which was deeply annoying. Ada was a computer—a smart one, and arguably kind of human, but still . . . She was acting all secretive and clever, and Claire really didn't like the rather cruel smile on those smooth dark gray lips.

Ada touched the wall, and it shimmered, taking on the darkness of one of the portals that Ada controlled through town . . . a kind of magic tunnel, although Claire hated to call it magic. It was physics, that was all. Scary advanced physics. That meant it was the ultimate fast lane, but dangerous. . . . Claire frowned at the opening, trying to feel where the destination might be on the other end. Nothing. And it looked way too dark to be safe.

"No," she said. "I don't think so. Sorry."

Why she was apologizing to a crazy computer lady, she didn't know. Ada wasn't her friend. Ada didn't even like her very much, although—by Myrnin's orders—Ada kind of had to obey her.

Ada lost her smile. She shrugged, turned, and glided through the portal.

She vanished into the dark. After a few seconds, a slender gray hand came out of the shadows and made a *Come on* impatient gesture.

"No," Claire said again, and this time sat down on the couch. "No way. I've had way too much today. You have your little weird crisis on your own, Ada."

Her cell phone rang, and the sound of the song echoing through the hidden room made Claire jump and dig the phone out of her pocket. The screen read *Shane Calling*. She flipped it open.

"Shane?"

Static, and then came Ada's weird machine-flat voice. "Myrnin needs you. Now. Come!" She sounded angry, and cold, but she usually did unless she was simpering at Myrnin. Claire slapped the phone shut, blew hair off her forehead, and stared at the darkness. It *could* be Myrnin's lab. She just couldn't tell. Myrnin had a vampire's habit of forgetting to turn on lights, which sucked.

"I really need to start carrying flashlights," she muttered, and then had an inspiration. There was a Tiffany-style pole lamp in the corner by the sofa; Claire lifted off the heavy glass shade, set it aside, and rolled the base to the limit of its electrical cord, then lowered it across the threshold of the portal, into the darkness on the other side.

She saw Ada standing there, hands clasped in front of her, cold and expressionless, surrounded by at least *ten* albino-pale vampires, who cried out and flinched back at the touch of the light. They had oversized fangs and sharp talons, and they weren't like the regular vamps. . . . These were tunnel rats, the ones who stalked the dark places, keeping out of the light and existing just to kill. Failures, Myrnin had called them.

Ada had meant for her to walk right into the middle of them.

Claire yelled in shock, and slammed the portal closed in her mind, then put her hand on the blank wall of the room as it took on weight and reality again. There was a way to lock it—maybe—and she searched for the right frequency to trigger the security. It was like a dead bolt, and it would hold against Ada or anyone else who wanted to come through.

She hoped.

Closing the portal had chopped the pole lamp in half, and she dropped the base part as it sputtered and sparked, then kicked the plug out of the wall. Claire stood there staring at the wall, and the mutilated lamp, for a long moment with her hands curled into fists, then took out her phone and dialed Myrnin's lab.

"How kind of you to check up on me," he said. "I'm fine, as it happens."

"We've got a problem."

"Really? The stake in my chest didn't indicate that at all. I must send Oliver a bill for a new shirt."

"Ada just tried to kill me."

Myrnin was silent for a moment. Claire could almost see him, hunched over the old-fashioned wired phone that looked like it had come from a Victorian junk shop. "I see," he said, in an entirely different tone. "Are you certain?"

"She told me you needed to see me, and opened a portal into a nest of hungry vamps. So, yes. I'm pretty sure."

"Oh my. I will have a talk with her. I'm sure it was a misunderstanding."

"Myrnin—" Claire squeezed her eyes closed, counted to five, and started over. "She's not listening to you anymore. Don't you get that? She's doing her own thing, and her own thing means getting rid of the competition."

"Competition for what?"

"For you," Claire said. "Not that I am. But she thinks I am. Because you haven't killed me."

She was babbling, because saying this was making her feel a little sick and giddy. She wasn't in love with Myrnin, but she did love him, a little. He was crazy; he was dangerous; he was a vampire—and yet, he was somehow not any of those things, in his better moments.

"Claire." He sounded wounded. "I do *not* find you attractive, except for your mind. I hope you know that. I would never take such advantage of you." He paused, and thought about it for a second. "Except if I was hungry, of course. But probably not. Most likely."

"Yeah, that's comforting. The point is, Ada thinks you care for me, and she wants me out of the way so you'll care more for her. Right?"

"Right. I'll go have a talk with her."

"You need to pull her plug, Myrnin."

"Over that? Pshaw. It's merely a flaw in her programming. I'll take good care of it." He paused, then said, "Of course, in the meantime, I wouldn't follow her anywhere if I were you."

"No kidding. Thanks."

"Oh, don't mention it, my dear. Enjoy your evening. Oh, and tell Michael that I enjoyed his concert."

"You were there?"

She heard the smile in Myrnin's voice. "We were all there, Claire. All the vampires. We do so enjoy our entertainments."

That was ever so slightly creepy, and Claire hung up without saying good-bye.

Downstairs, the video game raged on; Kim was as good a player as Shane, apparently, which didn't surprise Claire but depressed her kind of a lot. Shane didn't even notice her reappearance; he was wiggling around on the couch, putting body language into his shooting as his game character ducked zombie attacks and kicked, punched, and shot his way out of trouble.

Kim's character was a slinky-looking girl with black hair in a ponytail, and half a costume. She fought in high heels.

Great.

Claire sat down on the stairs, watching through the railing, and hugged her knees to her chest. Eve was gone, probably to change clothes, so it was just Shane and Kim.

They looked oblivious to everything but the drama on the screen.

She was developing some kind of sixth sense where Michael was concerned; he didn't make any noise coming down the steps, but she knew he was coming, and turned her head to see that he'd switched out his rock-star gear for a faded, old gray T-shirt and, like her, jeans. He took a look at what was happening in the living room, then crouched down next to her. "Hey," he said. "You all right?"

"I wouldn't have been if you hadn't crashed into us," Claire said. "Thank you."

He looked ashamed. "Yeah, well, that wasn't quite the plan. I was just trying to make him stop. I didn't think he'd actually *hit* me."

She almost laughed, because he sounded so sad about it. She took his cool hand and squeezed. He squeezed back. "It was still a good plan."

"Except for the part where I nearly killed you, destroyed Oliver's limo, and my own car? Yeah. It rocked the house."

"Are they going to get you a new one? A car, I mean?"

"Amelie said they would."

"I shut all the portals to the house," Claire said. "Ada's acting weird."

"I thought that was normal."

"Weirder."

"Ah. Okay." Michael looked past the railings, at Kim and Shane. "Are you freaking out about Kim?" Claire made the same little-bit mime with her finger and thumb that Shane had earlier. "Yeah, well, don't. Kim's not his type."

"I'm not sure *I'm* his type." Okay, that sounded really, really whiny. Claire bit her lip. "She's just so—much."

"Yep. She is that." He rose to his feet and padded down the last few steps silently, came up behind Kim, and leaned over her to say, "I vant to drink your blood" in a heavy, fake Dracula accent. She shrieked, flailed, and a zombie ate her brains on-screen.

"You *bastard!*" Kim yelled, dropped the controller, and smacked him hard on the chest. "I can't believe you just totally sabotaged me!"

"Can't let him lose," Michael said, as Shane hit the high score and the victory music sounded. "Gotta live with the dude."

They high-fived.

"You're seriously going to take that as a win," Kim said. "When he totally cheated for you."

"Yes," Shane said. "I seriously am." He canceled the game, put the controller down, and rose to stretch and yawn. "Damn. It's late. Don't you have someplace to go or something?"

Kim looked actually hurt for a second, and Claire felt a twinge of—something. Maybe pity. She hoped not.

"Sure," she said. "Johnny Depp's waiting for me back home. Guess I'd better blaze. Hey, where's Eve?"

"What, you're going?" Eve called from the top of the stairs, and jumped down past Claire in her eagerness to get to the bottom. "You can't! Kim, we need to run lines and stuff!"

"No, Shane's right. It's really late. How about tomorrow? I can meet you at Common Grounds—how about three? You're working until about then, right?"

"Yeah," Eve said. She still sounded disappointed. "Sure, that's okay. Hey—you want to go out tomorrow night? Maybe catch a movie? Um— Claire, you want to go, too?"

Great. She was officially an also-invited. "No thanks," she said. "I've got plans."

"Seriously? What?"

Claire looked at Shane, and he took one for the team. "Dinner with me," he said. "It's kind of an anniversary."

"Awwww, really? That's so sweet!" Eve leveled a finger at him. "Do *not* take her to the chili dog place."

"A real restaurant. With tablecloths. Hey, I'm not a complete idiot."

Kim stared at Shane, and in that moment, Claire realized this wasn't just an act. . . . Kim really *did* like Shane—a lot.

She recognized pain when she saw it.

"So," Eve said, and turned to Kim. "Movies, right? Something scary?"

Kim got herself together before Eve could see the same thing Claire had noticed. "Sure," she said. "Whatev. You pick. No girly movies."

Eve looked deeply offended. "Me? Girly movies? Bite your tongue off. No, seriously. Right now."

Kim laughed, and Eve walked her to the door. Claire said to Shane, "Anniversary?"

He raised his eyebrows. "Depends on how you count things," he said. "Yeah. It's got to be *some* kind of anniversary. Probably of one of us not getting killed."

Michael said, "Speak for yourself, man." He picked up the controller and restarted the game. "I can't believe you almost let her win."

"Man, I almost let *you* win sometimes," Shane said, and dropped into his spot on the other end of the couch. "Game on."

SEVEN

The next day, Claire sat through classes without any real sense of accomplishment, took a quiz—which she aced—and dropped in on Myrnin's lab around noon. It looked neat and clean again, which was two miracles in a row as far as she was concerned. She went to the bookshelves and started looking over journals, trying to find the most recent ones, although those would be the most difficult to figure out, given that most of his notes would have been taken when he was sick, and mostly crazy.

But she was curious.

She was struggling through last summer's book when Myrnin popped in through the portal, wearing a big floppy black hat and a kind of crazy/stylish pimp coat that covered him from neck to ankles, black leather gloves, and a black and silver walking stick with a dragon's head on it.

And on his lapel was a button that said, IF YOU CAN READ THIS, THANK A TEACHER.

It was typical Myrnin, really. She was surprised the bunny slippers were absent.

"I didn't know you were coming today," he said, and draped his hat, coat, and cane on a nearby coatrack. "And I assume it isn't just a random occurrence, like gravity."

"Gravity isn't random."

"So *you* say." He came to the opposite side of the table and looked at the book, then turned his head weirdly sideways to read the title. "Ah. Some of my best work. If only I could figure out what it actually meant."

"I was trying to figure out if you ever met a girl named Kim. Kim—" What the hell was her last name? Had anybody even told her? "Kim, something. Kind of Goth?"

"Oh, her," Myrnin said. He didn't sound too impressed, which made Claire just a little happy. "Yes, Kimberlie's known to us. She asked permission to film some of us, for the archives—a sort of permanent record of our histories. As you know, we do value that sort of thing. Many have agreed. She's been named our video historian, I believe."

"You haven't done it, though?"

"I write my own history. I see no reason to entrust it to a human with a video camera. Paper and ink, girl. Paper and ink will always survive, when electronic storage becomes random impulses lost to the ages."

"But the vampires do know her."

"Yes. She's a bit of a pet for the older ones. Besides me, of course. I don't like pets. They bite—ah! I almost forgot! Time to feed Bob." And Myrnin bustled off to another part of the lab, where presumably he'd stashed Bob the spider.

Or possibly Bob the auto mechanic—Claire wouldn't put anything past him. He seemed slightly manic today, from the glitter in his eyes. It made her nervous.

She was about to close the book, when she saw, in his spiky black handwriting, something about her:

New girl. Claire something. Small and fragile. No doubt they believe that will make me protective of her. It only makes me think how easy it is to destroy her. . . .

She shuddered, and decided she didn't really want to read the rest.

She left Myrnin making little weird kissy faces to Bob the spider as he shook a container of flies into Bob's plastic case, and went to the archives.

Since the first time she'd seen the Vampire Archives—which had been on the run, in a time of war, and it had been a place they'd hit up for weapons—she'd been fascinated by the idea. The vampires were pack rats, no doubt about it; they loved *things*—historical things. Also—apparently—junk, because there were entire vaults of stuff that nobody had gotten around to categorizing yet, and probably never would. But the upper floors were amazing. The library was meticulous, and there was an entire section that contained every known book, magazine, and pamphlet with anything about vampires in it, cross-referenced by accuracy. *Dracula* scored only about a six, apparently.

Apart from that, the vampires had donated, bought, or stolen six floors of historical texts, in a wide variety of languages. There were even ancient scrolls that looked too delicate to properly handle, and a few wax tablets that Amelie had told her dated from Roman times.

The audiovisual area was new, but it contained everything from samples of the flickers made for penny arcades in the early 1900s to silent film, sound film, color film, all the way up to DVDs. Again, most of it was concerned somehow with vampires, but not everything. There seemed to be an awful lot of costume drama. And, for some reason, musicals.

Claire found the digital video interviews on the computer kiosk, listed by the vampire's name and date of—birth? Making? What did they call it? Anyway, the date they got fanged.

The newest one was Michael Glass.

Claire brought up the player and blinked as Michael fidgeted in front of the camera. He wasn't comfortable. This wasn't being onstage for him, obviously. He messed with the clip-on microphone until Kim's offscreen voice told him to cut it out, and then he sat, looking like he wished he'd never agreed to any of this, until the questions started. The first ones were obvious—name, current age, age at death, original birthplace.

Then Kim asked, "How did you become a vampire?"

Michael thought about his answer for a few seconds before he said, "Total stupidity."

"Yeah? Tell me."

"I grew up in Morganville. I knew the rules. I knew how dangerous things were, but when you grow up with Protection, I think you get careless. I'd just turned eighteen. My parents had already left town; my mom was sick and needed cancer treatments, so I was on my own. I wanted to sell the house and get on with my life."

"How's that going for you?"

Michael didn't smile. "Not like I'd hoped. I got careless. I met a guy who wanted to buy the house, somebody new in town. It never occurred to me he was a vampire. He—didn't come across that way. But the second he crossed the threshold, I knew. I just knew."

He shook his head. Kim cleared her throat. "Can I ask who . . . ?"

"Oliver," Michael said. "He killed me his first day in town."

"Wow. That sucks completely. But you didn't become a vampire then, right?"

"No. I died. Sort of. I remember dying, and then . . . then it was the next night, and I couldn't remember anything in between. I was fine. No holes in the neck, nothing. I figured maybe I'd dreamed it, but then—then I tried to leave the house."

"What happened?"

"I started to drift away. Like smoke. I got back inside before it was too late, but I realized after a few more tries that I couldn't leave. Didn't matter which door, or how I did it. I just—stopped being me." Michael's eyes looked haunted now, and Claire saw a shiver run through him. "That was bad enough, but then morning came."

"And what happened?"

"I died," Michael said. "All over again. And it hurt."

Claire turned it off. There was something wrong about hearing this, seeing him let down his guard so completely. Michael had always tried to make it all okay, somehow. She hadn't known how much it had freaked him out. And, she found, she didn't really want to know how it had felt when he'd been made a real vampire by Amelie, in order to be able to live outside of the house.

She knew too much already.

There were about twenty other video interviews in the folder, but there was one that made Claire hesitate, then double-click the icon.

The camera zoomed in, steadied focus, and then the lights came up. "Please give us your name, the date you became a vampire, your birthplace, and your death age." It was Kim's voice, but this time she sounded nervous, not at all the smart-ass Claire knew. "Please."

Oliver leaned back in his chair, looking like he'd smelled something nasty, and said, "Oliver. I will keep my family name to myself, if you please. I was made vampire in 1658. I was born in Huntingdon, Cambridgeshire, East Anglia, England, in 1599. So as you see, I was not a young man when I was turned."

"Was it your choice?"

Oliver stared at Kim, off camera, for so long that even Claire felt nervous. Then he said, "Yes. I was dying. It was my one chance to retain the power I'd attained. The thieving trick of it was that once I'd made my devil's bargain, I couldn't hold the power I sought to keep. So I gained new life, and lost my old one."

"Who made you?"

"Bishop."

"Ah—do you want to say anything about Bishop—"

"No." Oliver suddenly stood up, fire in his eyes, and stripped the microphone off in a hail of static. "I'll do no more of this prying. Past is past. Let it die."

Kim, very quietly, said, "But you killed him. Didn't you? You and Amelie?"

Oliver's eyes turned red. "You know nothing about it, little girl with your foolish toys. And pray to God you never will."

Oliver knocked the camera over, and Kim yelped, and that was it.

Fade to black.

"Enjoying yourself?" Oliver's voice said, and for a second Claire thought it was on the computer screen, then realized that it came from *behind* her. She turned her head, slowly, to find him standing near the door of the small room, leaning against the wall. He was wearing a T-shirt with the Common Grounds logo on it, and cargo pants, and he didn't look like a five-hundred-year-old vampire. He even had a peace sign earring in one ear.

"I—wanted to know about the historical interview project, that's all. Sorry." Claire shut down the kiosk and stood up. "Are you going to try to kill me again?"

"Why? Do you want to be prepared?" He cocked his head at her.

"I'd like to see it coming."

That got her a thin smile. "Not all of us have that luxury. But no. I have been schooled by my mistress. I won't raise a finger to you, little Claire. Not even if you ask me to."

Claire edged slowly toward the door. He smiled wider, and his gaze followed her all the way . . . but he let her go.

When she looked back, he was at the kiosk, clicking the mouse. She heard his interview start, and heard his nonrecorded voice murmur a curse. The recording cut off.

Then the entire kiosk was ripped out and smashed on the floor with enough force to shatter a window three feet ahead of her.

Somebody wasn't happy with how he looked on camera.

Claire broke into a run, dodged around another row of books, turned left at the German books to make for the exit—

And tripped over Kim, who was sitting on the floor of the library, staring down at the screen of her cell phone as if it held the secrets of the universe.

"Hey!" Kim protested, and Claire pitched headlong to the carpet. She caught herself on the way down, kicked free of Kim's legs, and crawled backward. "You okay?"

"Fine," Claire said, and got up to dust herself off. "What the hell are you doing?"

"Research," Kim said.

"In *German?*"

"I didn't say I was looking at the books, dummy. But I *could* read German. It's possible."

"Do you?"

Kim grinned. "Just curse words. And where's the bathroom, in case I get stuck in Berlin. Hey, what was the crash?"

"Oh. Oliver. He just found the interview you did with him."

Kim's grin left the building. "He killed my computer, right? He just went all Hulk Smash on it."

"He wasn't happy."

"No," Oliver said, and rounded the corner of the aisle. There were flickers of red in his eyes, and his bone-pale hands were curled into fists. "No, Oliver isn't happy at all. You told me you'd destroyed the interview."

"I lied," Kim said. "Dude, I don't work for you. I was given a job to do by the council, with a grant and everything. I'm doing it. And now you owe me for a new computer. I'm thinking maybe a laptop."

She looked way too calm. Oliver noticed it, too. "That wasn't the only copy."

"Digital age. It's a sad, sad world, and it's just full of downloadable copies."

"You're going to bring them all to me."

"Duh, no," Kim said, and closed up her phone. "I'm pretty sure I'm not. And I'm pretty sure you're going to have to just get over it, because this is Amelie's pet project. We didn't even get that far, anyway. It's not like you told me you collect Precious Moments figures or something embarrassing. Get over it." She checked the big, clunky watch on her wrist, and rolled to her feet. "Whoops, time to go. I have rehearsal in half an hour. And hey, so do you, Mitch. No hard feelings, okay?"

Oliver said nothing. Kim shrugged and headed for the exit.

"I don't like her," Claire offered.

"At last, we have something in common," Oliver said. "But she is right about one thing: I have to get to rehearsal."

That sounded very—normal. More normal than most things Oliver said. Claire felt some of her tension slip away. "So how's that going? The play thing?"

"I have no idea. I haven't done a play in a hundred years, and the idea of Eve and Kim being our leading ladies doesn't fill me with confidence." That just *dripped* with sarcasm, and Claire winced a little.

"A hundred years. What was the last thing you performed?"

"Hamlet."

Of course.

How rehearsal went Claire didn't know; she headed for Common Grounds, where she was set to meet up with (ugh) Monica. At least it was profitable.

"Money up front," she said, as she slid into the seat across from the mayor's favorite—and only—sister. Monica had done something cute with her hair, and it framed her face in feathered curves. For once, she was alone; no sign of Gina and Jennifer, not even as coffee fetchers.

Monica sent Claire a dirty look, but she reached into her designer backpack, got out her designer wallet, and counted out fifty dollars that she shoved across the table. "Better be worth it," she said. "I really hate this class."

"Then drop it."

"Can't. It's a core class for my major."

"Which is?"

"Business."

It figured. "So where do you want to start? What's giving you the most trouble?"

"The teacher, since he keeps giving these stupid pop quizzes and I keep flunking them." Monica dug in her backpack and tossed over three stapled tests, which were marked up in green—the teacher must have read somewhere that red made students nervous or something, but Claire thought that with this many marks, the color of the pen was the least of Monica's problems.

"Wow," she said, and flipped the pages. "So you really don't get economics at all."

"I didn't pay fifty dollars for the pleasure of hearing you state the obvious," Monica pointed out. "So yeah. Don't get it, don't really want to, but I need it. So give me my fifty bucks' worth of a passing grade already."

"Well—economics is really game theory, only with money."

Monica just stared at her.

"That was going to be the simple version."

"Give me my money back."

Actually, Claire needed it—well, she needed to have had Monica pay it to her, really—so she came up with a few kind of cool explanations, showed Monica the way to memorize the formulas and when to use them . . . and before it was done, there were at least ten other students leaning in to listen and take notes at various points. That was cool, except that Monica kept demanding five bucks from each one of them, which meant that she got a free lesson.

Still, not a bad afternoon's work. Claire finished feeling a little happier; teaching—even teaching Monica—always made her feel better.

She felt *much* better when she saw that Shane had come to walk her home.

"Hey," he said as she fell in beside him. "Good day?"

She considered exactly how to answer that, and finally said, "Not bad." Nobody had gotten killed so far. In Morganville, that was probably a good day. "Monica paid me fifty for a private lesson." Shane held up his hand, and she jumped up to smack it without breaking stride. "And yours?"

"There was meat. I sliced it with a big, sharp knife. Very manly."

"I'm impressed."

"Of course you are. So, it's our anniversary—"

"It's not!"

"Well, I told Kim it was, and then I promised to take you out to a nice restaurant."

"With tablecloths," Claire agreed. "I distinctly remember tablecloths."

"The point is, I'm taking you out. Okay?"

"I don't think so. My face is just starting to heal. I've got bruises all over my throat. The last thing I want to do is go to a nice restaurant and have everybody stare at us and wonder if you're abusing me. I wouldn't enjoy my food at all."

"You think too much."

She took his hand. "Probably."

"Okay then. How about a sandwich offered up on a nice, clean napkin, in my room?"

"You're such a romantic."

"It's in my *room*."

They were about two blocks along from Common Grounds—about halfway home—when the streetlights began to go out, one after another, starting behind them and zooming past as each clicked off. It wasn't quite full dark yet, but it was getting there fast as the last hints of red sunset faded from the horizon.

"Claire?" Shane looked around, and so did she, feeling her instincts start to howl a warning.

"Something's wrong," she said. "Something's here."

A bloody form lurched out of the darkness toward them, and Shane shoved Claire behind him. It was a vampire—red eyes, fangs down, blood splashed on the pale face and hands.

Claire knew him, she realized after a second of pure adrenaline and shock. He was wearing the same ragged, greasy clothes from the last time she'd seen him: Morley, the graveyard vampire who'd tried to ambush Amelie.

He saw Claire and gasped out, "Fair lady, tell your mistress—tell her—"

He lunged for Claire, off balance, and Shane stiff-armed him away. Morley went sprawling on the pavement, and rolled up into a ball.

Afraid.

"It's okay," Claire said, and put a hand on Shane's arm. She carefully crouched down near Morley's bloodstained body. "Mr. Morley? What happened?"

"Ruffians," he whispered. "Tormentors. Hellhounds." Something made him flinch, and he listened for a second, then rolled painfully to his feet. Claire jumped backward, just in case, but Morley didn't even look at her. "They're coming. *Run.*"

Something was coming, all right. Morley stumbled away, moving at a fraction of normal vampire speed, and Claire heard the distant sound of running feet, voices calling to one another, and excited whoops.

In a few more seconds, she saw them—six young men, most no older than Shane. Two wore TPU jackets. They were all drunk, mean, and looking for trouble, and they all were armed—baseball bats, tire irons, stakes. They slowed when they caught sight of Claire and Shane, and changed course to come toward them.

"Hey!" one of them yelled. "You seen an old dude running through here?"

"Why? What did he do, steal your purse?" Shane shot back. Claire dug her fingernails into his arm in warning, but he wasn't paying attention. "Jesus, you idiots, what do you think you're doing?"

"Cleaning up the streets," another one said, and twirled his bat as if he really knew how to use it. "Somebody's gotta. The cops don't do it."

"We heard that one killed a kid," said the first man—the least drunk, as far as Claire could tell, and, also, maybe the meanest. She didn't like the way he was watching Shane, and her. "Drained her dry, right on the playground. We don't let that pass, man. He has to pay."

"You have any proof?"

"Screw your proof. These monsters have been running around killing for a hundred years. We catch them, we teach them a lesson they don't forget." He laughed, dug in his pocket, and pulled out something. He tossed it on the ground in front of Shane's feet. Claire couldn't tell what the scattered pieces were at first, and then she knew.

Teeth: vampire fangs, pulled out at the root.

Shane said, "Knock yourself out, man. He went that way." He nodded in a direction Morley hadn't gone. "Keep up the good work."

"It's Collins, right? Your dad was one hell of a guy. He stood up for us."

Shane's father had been an abusive asshole who didn't care about anyone, as far as Claire had been able to tell; he certainly hadn't cared about Shane. The idea that Frank Collins was becoming the underground hero of Morganville made Claire want to puke.

"Thanks," Shane said. His voice was neutral, and very steady. "I'm taking my girl home."

"Her? She's one of them. One of the Renfields. Works for the vamps."

"No better than the vamps," another put in.

"I heard she worked for Bishop," said a third, who had a tire iron resting on his shoulder. "Carrying around his death warrants. Like one of those Nazi collaborators."

"You heard wrong," Shane said. "She's my girl. Now back off."

"Let's hear from her," said the leader of the pack, and he locked stares with Claire. "So? You working for the vamps?"

Shane sent her a quick, warning glance. Claire took in a deep breath and said, "Absolutely."

"Ah hell," Shane breathed. "Okay, then. *Run.*"

They took off, catching the minimob by surprise; alcohol slowed them down, Claire thought, and an argument broke out behind them over whom they should be chasing, humans or vampires. Shane grabbed Claire's hand and pulled her along, running as if their lives depended on it. The streetlights were all out, and Claire had trouble seeing curbs and cracks in the pavement in the dim starlight.

They made it almost a block before she heard a howl behind them. The pack was following.

"Come on," Shane gasped, and pushed her faster. It was harder for Claire; she was a bookworm, not a runner, and besides, her legs were about six inches shorter than his. "Come on, Claire! Don't slow down!"

Her lungs were already on fire. *Need to exercise more*, she thought crazily. *Note to self: practice wind sprints.*

Something hit her in the back, and Claire lost her balance and hit the pavement hard. Shane yelled, stopped, and turned to cover her. In seconds, the pack of guys was on them, and Claire saw Shane taking a bat away from one guy and using it to smack the tire iron away from another attacker.

A shadow loomed over her, and she looked up to see a guy who looked about ten feet tall raise a baseball bat over his head, aiming straight for hers.

Claire grabbed him around the knees and yanked, hard. He yelled in surprise as his legs folded, and he fell backward. The bat hit the ground with a clatter, and Claire picked it up as she climbed to her feet. Shane was swinging with precision, taking out weapons and maybe breaking an arm here and there if he had to. All she had to do was stand there and look threatening.

It was over in a few seconds. Something turned for the pack, and they'd had enough. Claire stood there shaking, bat still cocked in the ready position, as the last guy scrambled up off the pavement and lurched away.

Shane dropped his bat and put both hands on her shoulders. "Claire? Look at me. Are you all right? Anybody hit you?"

"No." She felt shaky, and she had some skinned knees and palms from her fall, but that was all. "My God. They were going to kill us. *Humans* were going to kill us. Because of me."

"It wouldn't have mattered," Shane told her, and kissed her forehead with burning hot lips. "They were going to go after anybody they came across. The vampire thing is just an excuse. God, Claire. Good job."

"All I did was hold the bat."

"You held it like you meant it." He put his arm around her and picked up both bats, slinging them over his left shoulder. "Let's get home."

When they got home, after getting the third degree from Michael, then Eve, they had to answer to the Founder. Not by choice; Claire was all for making a quick phone call to the police and letting it go through the proper channels, but Michael thought Amelie might want to ask more questions.

He must have been right, because as soon as he hung up the phone, a wave of sensation swept through the house—like a gust of wind, only psychic. Claire actually felt the locks she'd put on the portals snap, and the connection open.

Amelie was coming in person.

Michael realized it, too—he and Claire seemed to be more connected to the house than Shane and Eve, generally. "That was fast," he said. "I guess we'd better go up."

"Up where?" Shane asked, frowning.

"Amelie," Claire sighed. "I was hoping for a hot bath, too."

The four of them, in the spirit of solidarity, trudged upstairs to the hidden room. The Tiffany lamps—minus that one pole lamp casualty—were blazing, filling the walls with color and light, but somehow none of it fell on Amelie, who looked pale as bone and just as hard. She was wearing pure, cold white, and her lips seemed almost blue. Her eyes looked more silver than gray, but maybe that was because of the metallic shine of her shirt under the tailored jacket.

Claire wondered why Amelie bothered with the meticulous dressing, when she rarely seemed to leave her home these days; she supposed that growing up as royalty in the distant past had made looking perfect a habit Amelie couldn't seem to shake.

Amelie received the news of the gang beating up on her vampires without much shock, Claire thought; she sat there looking cool and calm, hands folded, and listened to Shane and Claire's experience without any flicker of expression. There was *something* in her face when Claire described the handful of pulled vampire fangs that she'd seen, but what it was, Claire couldn't guess. Disgust, maybe, or pain. "Is that all?" Amelie asked. She sounded way too distant. "What of Morley? Did you see where he went?"

"We don't know," Claire said. "He looked—hurt. A lot hurt, maybe."

"I was afraid of this," Amelie said, and got up to pace the floor.

"Afraid of what?" Michael asked. He was leaning against the wall with his arms folded, looking very serious. "Losing control?"

Amelie stopped to frown at the broken pole lamp, trailing pale fingers over the neat slice through the metal. "Afraid that humans might lose their fear of reprisals if I offered too much leniency," she said. "The rules of Morganville existed for a reason. They were meant to protect the strong few from the fragile many. Even a giant may be destroyed by the stings of insects, if there are enough of them."

"That's not what your rules did," Shane said. "They just made it easier for vampires to kill us without letting humans hit them back."

Amelie sent him a cool glance, but didn't otherwise react. "I've received reports of other incidents, less serious than this. It seems these gangs of thugs are growing bolder, and they must be stopped."

"They said something about Morley killing a kid," Shane said. "Anything to that?"

"I doubt it." Amelie met his eyes for a few seconds, then continued to pace. "I've had no reports of children being victimized. As you know, that is strictly against all our laws, human or vampire. I can't say it never happens, but it happens in human society, as well. Yes?"

"Maybe, but why did they take it out on Morley?"

She shrugged. "Morley is an easy target, like all the vampires who choose not to declare an allegiance. They are powerful in themselves, but vulnerable. Morley's lived rough and alone for some time. It's not surprising that humans are taking vengeance on those easiest to hunt. In other towns, they target the homeless, as well, do they not?"

"Aren't you going to do anything about it?" Claire asked.

"There are laws. I assume they will be enforced. Until these thugs are caught and punished, I will caution all vampires to be careful." Amelie smiled slowly. "And I will allow them latitude in matters of self-defense, of course. That should put a stop to things quickly."

Claire wasn't so sure of that. First, Morley and his vamps had gotten all pushy with Amelie, and then Oliver had seemed about to bolt from her camp and set up as a pretender to the throne. Now, there were humans roaming around looking for trouble, too. And Amelie just seemed . . . disconnected.

It seemed that, as much as they'd tried to pull Morganville together, it was unraveling all around them.

"I believe I have heard enough," Amelie said. "You may go. All of you."

She kept on pacing, as if she didn't intend to leave. Claire hung back, watching her, as the others descended the stairs, and finally said, "Are you okay?"

Amelie stopped, but didn't look at her. "Of course," she said. "I am—troubled, but otherwise fine. Why do you ask?"

Because you tried to kill yourself two nights ago? Claire didn't think it would be smart to bring that up. "Just—if you need anything . . ."

Amelie did look at her this time, and there was something warm and almost human in her expression. "Thank you." Amelie's personal winter closed in again, leaving her face still and cold. "There's nothing you can do, Claire. Nothing any of you can do. Now go."

That last thing wasn't a request, and Claire took it for dismissal. Shane was waiting at the bottom of the stairs, looking up with a worried not-quite-frown that smoothed away in relief when he saw her coming to join him. "Don't do that," he said.

"Do what?"

"There's something off about her right now. Don't you see that? Don't try to help. Just walk away."

Claire tapped the gold bracelet on her wrist. "Yeah, that'll work."

He pulled her out of the stairwell and shut the hidden door. Michael and Eve were already going downstairs, hand in hand. "It's getting late," he said. "You going or staying?"

"Does it have to be one or the other? Maybe I stay for an hour, then go?"

"Works for me," he said, and took her hand. "I've got a surprise for you."

The surprise was that he'd cleaned his room. Not just randomly picked up a few things, but really *cleaned* it—everything put away, bed made, everything. Unless . . . "What did you trade with Eve?"

He looked wounded and way too innocent. "What do you mean?"

"Oh, come *on.* You totally traded with Eve to clean your room for you."

He sighed. "She needed some cash for something, so yeah. But it's good, right? You're impressed I thought of it?"

Claire suppressed a laugh. "Yes, I'm impressed that a boy thought about spending money on a clean room."

"Worth it, as long as you're impressed." He flopped on the bed, leaving space for her, and she curled up next to him in the crook of his arm. Her head rested on his chest, and she listened to the strong, steady beat of his heart. *I wonder if Eve misses that,* Claire suddenly wondered. *I wonder if she forgets, and then . . .*

"Hey," Shane said, and tickled her. She squirmed. "No thinking. This is the no-thinking zone."

"I can't help it."

"Guess I'll have to distract you, then."

She was going to say, *Yes, please,* but he was already kissing her, and his big hands slid around her waist, and all she could think was *yes* as her blood surged faster, hotter, and stronger.

It was more like two hours before she could even stand to think about going home. The temptation to stay here, curled in Shane's arms forever, was almost overwhelming, but she knew she had to keep her promises.

Shane knew it, too, and as he gently combed the hair back from her face with his fingers, he sighed and kissed her forehead. "You've got to go," he said. "Otherwise, it's parents with pitchforks and torches."

"Sorry."

"Hey, me, too. I'll get the keys." He slid out of bed, and she watched the light gleam off his skin as he picked up his T-shirt and pulled it on. It was all she could do not to reach out and pull it off again. "And you really need to get dressed, because if you keep looking at me like that, we're not going anywhere."

Claire retrieved her pants and shirt and put them on, and caught sight of herself in the mirror—for once, in Shane's room, not obscured by random piles of stuff. She looked . . . different. Adult. Flushed and happy and alive, and not really geeky at all.

He makes me better, she thought, but she didn't say it, because she was afraid he'd think that was weird.

Shane borrowed Eve's car to run her back to her parents' house—her home?—and by midnight she was at her bedroom window watching the big, black sedan pull away from the curb and accelerate away into the night.

Mom knocked on the door. Claire could tell her parents apart by their knocks. "Come in!"

When her mom didn't say anything, Claire turned to look at her. She looked tired, and worried, and Claire wondered if she was getting enough sleep. Probably not.

"I just wanted to tell you that I left you a plate in the fridge if you're hungry," Mom said. "Did you have a good day?"

Claire had no idea how to answer that in a way that wouldn't sound completely insane, and finally settled for, "It was okay." She hoped the scarf she'd wrapped around her throat covered up the bruises, which were turning rich sunset colors.

Mom knew that was a nonanswer, but she just nodded. "As long as you're being safe." Which was less about the vampires than about Shane. Claire rolled her eyes.

"Mom."

"I'm serious."

"I *know.*"

"Then stop looking like I'm being an idiot. I'm worried about you getting hurt. I don't doubt Shane means well, but you're just so—" Mom looked for another word, but settled for the obvious one. "So young."

"Not as young as I was when this conversation started."

"Claire."

"Sorry." She yawned. "Tired."

Mom hugged her, kissed her cheek, and said, "Then get some rest. I'll let you sleep in."

The next day Claire missed her first class, because Mom was true to her word and the alarm clock failed in its duty, or at least Claire turned it off before she really woke up. She finally got up around ten o'clock, feeling happy and humming with energy. It might have been the sleep, but Claire knew it wasn't.

She was running on pure Shane sunlight.

Walking to the campus was a delight—the sun was out, warming up the streets and waking a soft breeze that smelled like newly cut grass. The trees were all full of new green leaves, and in the gardens flowers were blooming.

Claire was in such a good mood that when she saw Kim, armed with a video camera, she didn't actually wince.

Much.

Kim wasn't paying attention to her, which wasn't much of a change; she was focused on a guy in a TPU jacket tossing a football, who laughed at her jokes as she filmed. Kim circled around him, waved, and kept filming as she approached a group of girls camped out on the lawn under a spreading live oak tree. More laughter, and smiles all around.

Am I really the only one who doesn't like her?

Apparently.

Kim noticed her about the same time that Claire's phone rang. She turned her back on Kim—and the camera—and answered without checking the screen, because she was rattled. "Hello?"

"You *bitch*." It was Monica's voice. "Where are you?"

"Excuse me?"

"Are you on campus?"

Claire blinked and stepped out of the way of a crowd of students heading out from the English Building. "Uh, no. And why exactly am I a bitch, again?"

"I got that wrong. You are a *lying* bitch. I can hear the bells!" Monica meant the school's carillon, the tower bells that chimed out a silvery melody at the hour change. For some weird reason, it was playing Christmas music. Maybe somebody had forgotten to change over—or just really liked "O Holy Night." "Where are you—never mind, I see you. Stay right there."

Monica hung up. Claire looked around and saw that Kim was filming her—and Monica was charging down the steps of the English Building, heading her way and trailed by an entourage like a comet's tail. It wasn't just Gina and Jennifer this time; she'd picked up two strange girls wearing designer spring dresses and cute shoes, and a couple of big football-type guys—bland and handsome and not too smart, just the way Monica liked them.

Claire considered running, but not if Kim was planning on gleefully filming the whole thing. She could live with the shame. She just didn't think she could live with the reruns on YouTube.

Monica had gone with a floral pattern minidress, and it looked great on her; she hadn't let her tan go during the winter, and her skin looked healthy and glowy and toned. She strode up to Claire and came to a halt a couple of feet away, surrounded by her fashion army.

It was like being menaced by a gang of Barbie and Ken dolls.

"You," Monica said, and leveled an accusatory, perfectly manicured finger at her. Claire focused on the hot pink nail, then looked past it to Monica's face.

"Yes?"

"Come here."

And before Claire could even think about protesting, Monica had her wrapped up in a hug.

A hug.

With Monica.

Claire got control of herself, at least enough to grab Monica by the arms and push her back to a safe distance. "What the hell?"

"Bitch, you are the *best*. Seriously, I cannot believe it!"

Monica was . . . excited. Happy. Not about to beat her up.

Wow. "Don't take this the wrong way, but what are you on?"

Monica laughed, reached into her messenger bag, and pulled out a stapled two-page paper. It was an economics test.

And it had, written in the corner in red, an A.

"That's what I'm on," she said. "Do you know how long it's been since I got an A? Like, ever? My brother is going to fall over."

Claire handed the paper back. "Congratulations."

"Thanks." Monica's good mood faded, replaced by her more normal bitch face. "I guess I got my money's worth, anyway."

For some reason, Claire thought about Shane paying Eve to clean his room. "There's a lot of that going around, trust me. Okay then. We're good?"

"For now," Monica said. "Stay available. I've got other classes I suck at."

Claire bit her tongue before she could say, *I don't doubt it*, and watched Monica and her swirl of hangers-on sweep away, laughing and talking as if they were in their own private shampoo commercial.

She'd almost forgotten about Kim, and when she caught sight of the cold gleam of the camera lens out of the corner of her eye she turned and said, "Cut it out, will you?"

"Not a chance," Kim said cheerfully, camera still running. "Not until I run out of tape."

"It's digital!"

"That's the point. Hey, so, tell me about you and Monica. Secret love affair? Mortal enemies? Are you each other's evil twins? Come on, you can tell me; I won't tell anybody!"

"Except everybody on Facebook?"

"Well, obviously, yeah. Come on, you're wasting my minutes. Talk!"

"I have two words for you," Claire said, "and the second one is *off.* Fill in the blank."

Kim lowered the camera and switched it off, shaking her dark hair out of her face. "Wow. Who got up on the grumpy side of breakfast?"

"I don't like being on camera."

"Nobody does. That's the whole point. I want to catch people as they really are. That guy, for instance, Mr. Football Dude? He's a douche. I got him to talk long enough that you could actually *see* he was a douche. It's fun. You should try it."

"No thanks." Claire didn't think the powers that be in Morganville would take especially well to guerrilla filmmaking, and she wondered if anybody had told Oliver. He didn't seem to like Kim's little projects much.

Maybe it was time for a mocha.

"Hey," Kim said, as Claire started to walk on. "About Shane."

That pulled her to a full stop. "What about him?"

"I just wanted to know—so, are you guys serious or something?"

"Yeah, we're serious." Claire said it flatly, trying not to imagine what Shane might say to the same question. He didn't like to commit. He *was* committed; he just didn't like to go on the record. "You been filming anywhere else?"

"Sure, all over," Kim said. "Why, you want to see?"

"No. Just curious. What are you planning to do with it?"

"You've seen *Borat?* Yeah, kind of like that—sort of a mockumentary." Kim gave a one-shoulder shrug, focused on whatever was playing on the tiny screen of her camcorder. "Only with vampires."

"You're filming the vampires."

"Well, not officially. It's a hobby."

It was a dangerous hobby, but Claire guessed Kim knew that. "Just don't film me, okay?"

"Seriously? I'll make you a star!"

"I don't want to be a star."

As she walked away, Kim said plaintively, "But *everybody* wants to be a star!"

EIGHT

The rest of the day passed quietly enough. Claire dropped in to see Eve at the coffee shop, but all Eve could talk about was the play, how cool it all was, how she was so going to rock as Blanche DuBois, and how she had this plan to wear a black skull-patterned slip instead of the white one that the costume people wanted . . . and when she wasn't enthusing about the play, she was all about Kim. Kim, Kim, Kim.

"Cool necklace," Claire said, out of desperation, and pointed at the one around Eve's neck. It *was* cool—kind of a tribal dragon thing, full of angles and sinister curves. Eve touched it with her fingertips and smiled.

"Yeah," she said. "Michael got it for me. Not bad, right?"

"Not bad at all. Hey, did you clean Shane's room?"

"Actually? I just vacuumed and dusted. He picked it up himself. Why, did he tell you it was all me? Boys lie."

"About cleaning?"

Eve ate a bite of blueberry muffin and swallowed some coffee. "Why not? They think cleaning makes them look un-manly. Eek, sorry Claire Bear, gotta motor. Boss man, he no like breaks. See you later?"

"Sure." Claire slid out of her seat and picked up her book bag. "See you at home."

"Oh, you should totally swing by rehearsal! Three o'clock at the auditorium. You know where it is?"

Claire knew, although she'd never been there—it was kind of a town civic center, and it was off Founder's Square—aka, Vamptown. Like most humans in Morganville, she'd never been really interested in traveling there at night.

Three in the afternoon, though . . . that sounded reasonable. "I'll try," Claire said. "So—I know you were worried about Oliver. Is that going okay, having him in the play?"

"Oh, actually, yeah. He's not bad! I almost believe he isn't a controlling jerk. Most of the time." Eve looked over her shoulder, made a scared face when the boss beckoned her, and waved good-bye.

Claire decided she couldn't put it off any longer, and pulled out her cell phone. She'd written and uploaded a program that allowed her phone to track and display available portals; according to the theory she'd been reading up on in Myrnin's lab recently, it wasn't such a good thing for humans to force a portal open, the way vampires could without too much effort. Over time, things *happened*—to the human. And Claire decided she liked her normal arrangement of eyes, ears, and nose—she liked Picasso okay, but she didn't want to become one of his paintings.

So she looked for a portal that was open—open meant that it was at a low level of availability, not active. The one open at the university just now was in the Administration Building.

She headed over there, blending in with all the other students, and as usual, the part of the Administration Building where the portal was located was empty. The chain-smoking dragon lady secretary at the front desk nodded her in without argument; apparently there'd been some kind of memo since Claire had begun doing this kind of thing—a convenient development.

Moving through the portal was a little like taking a microsecond-long ice bath; it felt like every cell in her body received a shock, woke up, screamed, and then went immediately back to normal. Not exactly pleasant, but . . . memorable. It didn't usually feel that way, and Claire felt some distinct uneasiness. If the portal system went out of balance . . .

"Myrnin?" She stepped away from the portal door of the lab, shoving aside a box of books he'd left lying around, probably for her to shelve. No sign of him here just now. The lab still looked clean and moderately organized, which wasn't like Myrnin at the best of times; she wondered if he'd gotten some kind of maid service. Who cleaned mad scientist lairs, anyway? The same people who did villain lairs and bat caves?

No Myrnin, but he'd left her a note, written in his spiky antique hand, that asked her to—wait for it—sort the box of books he'd left to trip her up. And to feed Bob the spider. Ugh. Why was she even surprised? Claire began unpacking, sorting, and shelving the books, which was surprisingly fun, in the hopes that the universe would end before she had to actually feed a *spider*.

She was in the middle of doing that when Ada's two-dimensional ghost formed in front of her. Claire's heart rate doubled, and she wondered if she ought to just make a dash for the portal . . . but Ada made no threatening moves. In fact, Ada was being polite—she rang Claire's cell phone. She didn't actually have to do that before using the speaker. It was her version of knocking.

Claire swallowed an acidic mouthful of fear, and peered at the fading spine of the heavy book in her hand. German. She wasn't sure what it said. "Do you know German?"

Ada raised her chin and gave her a haughty look, smoothing down the front of her gray scale gown. "Of course," she said. "It's hardly a vanishing tongue."

I have to feed spiders and *put up with a bitchy, homicidal computer. My job really does suck.* Claire didn't say that out loud, and as far as she knew, Ada couldn't read minds. Yet. "Good. Can you tell me what this means?" She held out the book, spine toward Ada. The ghost leaned forward.

"*Alchemical Experiments of the Great Magister Kleiss,*" she read, and the tinny voice sounded a little sad as it vibrated from Claire's cell phone speaker. "Myrnin already has a copy. I remember buying it for him in a little market outside Frankfurt."

Claire put it aside. Ada seemed to be in an odd mood—fragile, confrontational, and oddly nostalgic. "You tried to kill me," Claire said.

"You lied to me, and tried to get me to step through the portal to get eaten. Why?"

A very odd expression fluttered over Ada's smooth, not-quite-human face. If Claire hadn't known better, she'd think it was ... uncertainty? "I did not," she said. "You are mistaken."

"It's not the kind of thing you get wrong," Claire said. "I've got a pole lamp that got cut in half when I had to slam the portal closed for proof. Remember now?"

Ada just—shut down. Not literally: her ghost still hung there in the air, bobbing ever so slightly as if gravity were just a bothersome suggestion, not the law. A flicker like static ran through her image, then another one.

Then she smiled. "You should see a doctor," she said. "I believe you're ill, human."

"You don't remember." Claire heard the flat disbelief in her voice, but what she really was feeling was ... fear. Pure, cold fear. Ada could lie— she had before—but this didn't *feel* like deception.

It felt like something was very, very wrong. And if something was wrong with Ada, it was wrong with Morganville.

"There's nothing to remember," Ada said coolly. "Do you wish to have more translation done, or may I get on with my duties now?"

"No, I'm good. Where's Myrnin?"

Ada paused in the act of turning her back—stopping edge-on, almost disappearing from Claire's perspective—and slowly rotated in place. Her dark eyes looked like burned holes in her pale face.

"That's none of your business," she said.

"What?"

"Myrnin is mine. And you can't have him. I'll kill you first!"

And then she just—vanished.

Claire gaped at the space where she'd been, half expecting her to show up again, but Ada stayed gone. Claire replaced the book she was holding back on the worktable, and walked around toward the rear of the lab. The thick Persian carpet had been rolled back there, and the trapdoor Myrnin had installed—a clever job of painting the door to match the stone floor—was closed. Claire gritted her teeth and clicked the release, which was a book on frogs in the nearby bookcase. The lock released with a snap, and Claire hauled the trap to the catch position.

Myrnin never kept any lights on down there, in the basement/cave where Ada really lived. Claire grabbed a flashlight, checked the batteries, and then looked down into the darkness. "Myrnin?" she asked. No reply. She heard water dripping in the distance. "Myrnin, where are you?"

Great. This made feeding Bob the spider look like a day at the park.

No way am I going down there alone, she thought, and flipped open her cell phone. Michael answered on the second ring. "Yo," he said. "I'm guessing you don't want to go to a movie, or anything fun like that."

"Why would you say that?"

"Because that would be Shane's job. When you call me, it's usually an emergency."

"Well—okay, fair point. But this isn't. Not an emergency, anyway. I just need—some hand-holding. Can you come to Myrnin's lab?"

Michael's voice turned a lot more serious. "Is this crazy maintenance, or is something really wrong?"

Claire sighed. "I don't know, actually. I just don't want to go down into the dark without a big, strong vampire."

"You mean you can't get down there without my help."

"Well, actually, I can't get *out* without your help, since Ada's not letting me do the portal thing near her. It's still a compliment, right?"

"Except the part where you drag me into potentially deadly trouble? Yes. Stay put. I'll be there in ten minutes."

"Be careful," she said. She had no idea why she did; it wasn't as if Michael had anything much to be scared of, especially in Morganville. But it was something her mother always said, and it made her feel better to express a little concern for her friends.

"No exploring on your own, Dora," he said.

She felt lonely and exposed, even here with all the lights burning brightly, once his voice was gone from the call. She considered calling Shane, but honestly, what good would it do? He'd come running, but he needed his job, and Michael was already on the way.

Ten minutes.

Claire decided to get the Bob thing over with. Bob's terrarium sat on Myrnin's rolltop desk, amid stacks of books and some pens—quills, fountains, and rollerballs. Bob looked bigger than she remembered. And blacker. And hairier. Claire shuddered, looking in at him; all eight of his beady eyes looked back. He stayed very still.

There was a small bottle on the table that contained insects—live ones. Claire made a retching sound and tried not to look too hard; she just opened the top of the terrarium and tipped the contents of the jar into the cage.

Bob leaped on her hand.

Claire shrieked, and the bottle went flying to shatter against the wall. Bob didn't budge when she violently shook her hand, trying to get rid of him; he clung to her like Velcro, and he felt *different*, somehow—heavier. Yes, he was larger. Claire batted at him with her right hand, and his fangs glittered as he lunged for her, skittering up her left arm.

She grabbed a book in her right hand.

Bob leaped from her arm, headed to her face.

She smacked him out of the air with the book, and he landed on his back, all eight legs wriggling in the air. Before she could slam the book down on top of him, Bob flipped himself over and skittered underneath the table.

It was *not* her imagination. Bob was getting bigger. In the space of just a few seconds, he'd gone from the size of a walnut to the size of her palm, and now he was almost as big as the book she'd used to smash him out of the air.

"Ada!" she screamed. "Ada, I need you!"

Her cell phone came on, and gave an unearthly screeching noise . . . and then a soft, ghostly laugh.

Something knocked over a pile of papers at the edge of the table, and Claire saw a long black leg waving in the air. She backed away, fast.

When Bob climbed up on top of the table, he was the size of a small dog. His fangs were clearly visible, and if she'd thought he was ugly at small size, he was terrifying now.

"Hi—Bob—" Claire said. Her voice was shaking, and sounded very small. "Nice Bob. Heel?"

Bob bounced off the table, landed lightly on the floor, and skittered toward her, racing incredibly fast. Claire screamed and ran, knocking over anything she could behind her to slow him down. Not that it did, but when she looked back as she reached the stairs, Bob had stopped chasing her.

He was sitting on a table in the center of the lab, trembling. She could actually see him shaking, as if he were having some kind of a fit . . . and then he rolled over on his back, and his legs curled in, and . . .

And he was dead.

"Bother," Ada said. Claire jumped in reaction, bit back a curse, and saw Ada glide out of a solid wall to her left. Ada's image went right up to Bob's motionless body, leaning over him, and shook her head. "So disappointing. I truly thought he'd be able to sustain the change."

"Change?" Claire swallowed hard. "Ada, what are you doing? What did you do to Bob?"

"Unfortunately, I believe I exploded his organs. So fragile, living things. I forget sometimes."

"You did this. Made him grow."

"It was an experiment." Ada's image slowly revolved toward Claire, and her smile was small and cold and terrifying. "We're both scientists, are we not?"

"You call that *science*?"

"Don't you?" Her hands folded primly at her waist, Ada was the image of one of those schoolteachers from the old days. "All science requires sacrifice. And you didn't even like Bob."

Well, that was true. "Just because I don't like something doesn't mean I want to see it die horribly!"

"Really? I find that . . . not very interesting at all, actually. Sentimentality has no place in science."

Just like that, poof, Ada was pixels and vapor, gone. Claire ventured slowly forward, to where Bob the giant spider was curled up on the table. She half expected him to suddenly flip upright in true horror-movie style, but he stayed still.

Claire wasn't falling for it. No way. She backed up to the steps that led out of the lab, and sat down on the cold stone, wrapping her arms around her for warmth.

Minutes ticked by.

The dead spider didn't move, which meant that either he wasn't faking it, or he was really, really good at it.

"Claire?"

She shrieked and jumped, and Michael, standing about a foot behind her, jumped backward, as well. Being a vampire, he somehow made it look cool. She, not so much. "God, don't *do* that! Warn me!"

"I did!" He sounded wounded. "I said your name."

"Say it from across the room next time."

But Michael wasn't looking at her anymore; he was staring past her, at the dead spider. "What the hell is *that?*"

"Bob," she said. "I'll tell you later. Come on."

"Where?"

"Ada's cave."

Which was why she'd called him, because, of course, there were no stairs. Vampires didn't need them. They could jump twelve feet onto solid stone and not even feel a twinge; Claire figured she was sure to have a broken bone, at the very least. She wasn't a superhero, a magical vampire slayer, or even a particularly coordinated athlete. Michael was her way in—and, hopefully, out.

Of course, having a friend with her going down into the dark, that was a plus, too.

Luckily, Michael didn't seem too bothered at being asked to stand in for a ladder; he looked down into the darkness for a few moments, craning to see every detail of what, to Claire, was pitch-blackness. "Looks clear," he said. "You're sure you want to do this?"

"She won't say where Myrnin is. Well, he's not up here, and the carpet was rolled back. He must have gone down there."

"And there's a reason why we can't just wait for him to come back?"

"Yeah. Ada's tried to kill me twice now, and who knows what she's tried to do to him. There's something wrong with her, Michael."

"Then maybe we should call somebody for help."

Claire laughed a little wildly. "Like who, Amelie? You saw her at the cemetery. You really think we should rely on her right now?"

Whether Claire had a point or not, Michael must have realized that debating wasn't getting anything done. He shrugged and said, "Fine. If you get me killed, I'm haunting you."

"Wouldn't be the first time."

He winked at her, and stepped off the edge, dropping soundlessly into the dark. Claire rushed forward, grabbing up the flashlight along the way, and shone its glow down into the trapdoor. A dozen feet below, Michael's pale face looked up. His blue eyes looked supernaturally bright as his pupils contracted in the glare.

"Right," he said. "Jump."

She'd been through this with Myrnin, but it still never felt exactly *comfortable*. Still, it was Michael, and if any vampire was trustworthy . . .

She shut her eyes, took a deep breath, and plummeted, straight into his cool, strong arms. Michael let her slide down, already looking past her into the dark. "There are things down here," he said.

"Vampires."

"Not—sure I'd call them vampires. *Things* is pretty accurate." Michael sounded a little nervous. "They're just—watching us."

"They're sort of guard dogs. Watch them right back, okay?"

"Doing that, yeah. Which way?"

"This way." It was easy to get turned around in the dark, but Claire had a pretty good memory, and there were enough strange shapes in the rocks of the walls that she'd picked some out as signposts. Her flashlight's beam bounced and glittered on granite edges, and pieces of broken glass scattered on the floor. There were some bones. She didn't think these were human, though that was probably wishful thinking.

"Whoa," Michael said, and held her shoulder as the room opened up. She knew what he was seeing—the big cavern where Ada was housed. He'd been here before, but not through the tunnel; it was kind of a shock, the way it opened up into this vast, echoing space.

"Lights," Claire said. "To the left, on the wall."

"I see them. Stay here."

She did, clutching the metal of the Maglite more tightly, until a sudden hum of power accompanied the dazzling arrival of lights overhead. Claire blinked away glare and saw that Ada—the computer, not the flat, generated image she liked to present—was in full-power mode, gears clanking like giant teeth, steam hissing from pipes, liquid bubbling here and there in huge glass retorts.

Myrnin was slumped against the giant keyboard, facedown.

"Oh no," Claire breathed, and raced to his side. Before she could touch him, Michael flashed to her and caught her hand.

"No," he said, and picked up a stray piece of metal from the floor, which he flicked at Myrnin's back, where it landed, electricity arcing, and sizzling. "I can smell the ozone. She's got him wired. If you touch him, it'll kill you."

NINE

"Is he dead?" Claire's heart was racing, and not just because she'd nearly gotten herself barbecued. . . . Myrnin was just getting better, just becoming himself again. For Ada to do this to him, now . . .

But Michael was shaking his head. "More like he's unconscious. I don't think he's hurt too badly. We just have to break the circuit."

Claire hunkered down, trying to get a look at Myrnin's face; his head was turned to the side, but his black hair had fallen over his eyes, so she couldn't see if they were open or closed. He wasn't moving. "We need something wood or rubber to push him off the metal," she said. "See if you can find something."

And with a snap, the lights went off. Claire's breath went out of her, and she felt her heart accelerate to about two hundred beats a minute when she heard Ada's cell-phone-speaker voice whisper, "I don't think you should do that."

"Michael?"

"Right here. The circuit's still on to the keyboard; I can feel it." His hand touched her shoulder, and even though she flinched, she felt reassured. "Here. Take this."

He handed her something. It took her a second to figure out what it was—a hunk of wood? It felt odd.... "Oh God," Claire blurted, "is that a *bone*?"

"Don't ask," Michael said. "It's sharp on one end. Organic, like wood, so it makes a good weapon against vampires. Just don't stab me, okay?"

She wasn't making any promises, really. "Help me with Myrnin." She carefully reversed the bone in her hands to the blunt end, and used the flashlight to check that Michael had something nonconductive, as well. He did, and it was more bone. It might have been a rib. She tried not to think about that too much. "You push from that side; I'll push from here. Push hard. We need to knock him completely away from the panel."

Claire's cell phone screamed so loudly that it seemed like the speaker was melting from the force of it; the sound dissolved into high-pitched static, and Claire took a deep breath and put the end of the bone against Myrnin's shoulder. He was wearing a black velvet jacket, and the bone looked very white against it, almost blue in the Maglite beam.

She saw Michael as a shadow in the backwash of the light. "Ready," Michael said.

"Go!"

They pushed. Michael, of course, had vampire strength, so it was over in a flash—Myrnin's body flying backward from the console, crashing on its back in the darkness. A glittering, frustrated arc of blue sparks from the keyboard snapped toward Claire and fell short.

Claire almost dropped the bone as she turned it in her hand so the sharp end was ready to use, then got on one knee next to Myrnin's motionless body. She carefully brushed hair away from his marble-pale face. His eyes were open, and fixed. They looked dry, but as she watched, moisture flooded over them, and he blinked, blinked again, gasped, and came bolt upright. His gaze fixed on Claire's face, and he grabbed her arm in a tight, grinding grip.

"Let go," she said. He didn't. "Myrnin!"

"Hush," he whispered. "I'm thinking."

"Yeah, great—can you do it without breaking my arm?"

"No." He didn't even try to explain that, but just got to his feet while still clamped on to her wrist like a person-sized handcuff. "That hurt."

"You need to shut her down; she just tried to kill you!"

Myrnin's eyes flashed a bloody red. *"You will not tell me what to do!"* He shoved her abruptly at Michael, and the glare was even angrier for him. "What are you doing here?"

"Talk later. Go now," Michael said, and grabbed Claire up in his arms before she could protest. "Those things are coming for us."

Myrnin looked around into the darkness that hid whatever it was that scared Michael so much. Claire didn't think she wanted to know; she put her arms around his neck and hung on for dear life as she felt his muscles tense. Things moved past, and she noticed a sense of air pressing against her. *The tunnel,* she thought, because things felt closed in, sounds seemed muffled and strange. "Myrnin?" she called behind them, but got no reply. Then she felt Michael jump, and for a breathless second she was weightless, suspended in midair as the light seemed to rush over her.

Michael landed perfectly just beyond the trapdoor set into the lab's concrete and stone, and quickly spun around, backing away at the same time.

Myrnin seemed to almost levitate up out of the hole in the floor, graceful as a cat. As his coat swirled like black fog, he turned in midair, reached out, and slammed the trapdoor shut.

Then he landed on it, light and perfectly balanced, and leaned over to slam his palm down on a red panel on top. It lit up, and a metallic *clunk* echoed through the lab. Myrnin stepped off the door, stared at it for a second, and then carefully unrolled the carpet and smoothed it back over the entrance to Ada's cave.

Claire let go of Michael and slid to her feet. She was still gripping her sharp-pointed bone weapon, and she didn't really feel inclined to put it down. Not yet. "What just happened?"

"I set the lock," Myrnin said, and tapped a toe on the carpet, in case she'd missed the point. "It's quite clever, you know. Electromagnetic. Keyed to my own handprint."

"Yeah, that's great. Why were you down there in the first place? You know she's not—well."

Myrnin fussily adjusted the lapels of his velvet coat, frowned at his bright blue vest as if he didn't remember wearing it, and shrugged. "Something to do with adjusting her emotional responses. Unfortunately, she was ready for me, it seems. She's quite clever, you know." He seemed almost proud. "Now—was there something you wanted, Claire?"

"A thank-you might be nice."

He blinked. "Whatever for? Oh, that. The electricity was only to keep me immobilized. She'd have had to let me go, eventually."

"Not really. She could have just kept you like that until you starved, right?"

"I can't die. Not like that. I can be made very uncomfortable, and very hungry, and quite a bit mad, but not dead. She'd have to have one of her creatures—cut my head—off...." Myrnin's voice trailed away, and he seemed very distant for a few seconds; then he said, "I see. Yes, you're quite correct. She would have options. But she wouldn't kill me."

"Why not?"

"I think we both know why, Claire."

"You mean, because she loves you? I'm not really seeing it right now."

"Ada needs me as much as I need her," Myrnin snapped, suddenly—and very un-Myrnin-like—offended. "You know nothing about her, or me, and I am ordering you to stay out of my affairs where they concern Ada." He suddenly staggered, and had to put out a hand to steady himself against the nearest lab table. "And fetch me some blood, Claire."

"Get it yourself." She couldn't believe she'd said it, but he'd really stung her. "Also, your precious Ada killed Bob by supersizing him and trying to get him to bite me. So maybe *you* don't know anything about Ada."

"Get me blood, or I'll have to take what's available," Myrnin said softly. He didn't seem dramatic about it, and it wasn't a threat. He raised his head and looked at her, and she saw that shine there—lunatic and focused and very, very scary. "I'm very hungry."

"Claire, go," Michael said, and moved to stand between her and Myrnin. "He's not faking it."

He really wasn't, because Myrnin lunged for her. He was faster than she or Michael could have expected, and Michael was off balance and nowhere near the right place as Myrnin shoved him out of the way and sent him crashing into the nearest stone wall....

Then he grabbed Claire by her shoulder and a fistful of hair. He wrenched her head painfully to the side, exposing her neck, and she felt the cool puff of his breath against her skin, and she knew she had only one move left.

She touched the tip of the bone stake to his chest, right over his heart, and said, "I swear to God I'll stake you and cut your head off if you bite me." Her hands were shaking, and so was her voice, but she meant it. She couldn't live in fear of him; it hurt her to see him lose control like this. There was something shining and good in Myrnin, but there were times it just drowned in the darkness. "If I let you do this, you'll never forgive yourself. Now let go, and get yourself a bag of blood."

She could actually feel his fangs pressing dimples into her skin. And Myrnin himself was trembling now, a very fine vibration that told her just how much he was in trouble—well, that and the fact he was about to kill her.

She pressed harder with the stake, and felt the blue satin tapestry vest give way to the point.

She didn't see Michael move, but in only a few breathless seconds he was at her side, carefully putting in her free hand a squishy bag of blood. It was straight out of the refrigeration; he hadn't taken time to warm it, which was probably lifesaving.

"Let go," Claire said.

And Myrnin did, loosening his hands just enough to let her step back. His eyes were wild and desperate, and his fangs stayed down like glittering exclamation points.

Claire held out the blood bag.

After a second's hesitation, Myrnin grabbed it, brought it to his mouth, and bit down so hard, blood squirted over his face, the way a really juicy tomato would.

Claire shuddered. "I'll get you a towel."

She went to the small bathroom—so well hidden, it had taken her forever to find it—and turned on the rusty tap to moisten a towel marked PROPERTY OF MORGANVILLE; it was probably hospital supply, or from a prison. She splashed some water on her face, too, and looked at herself in the mirror for a few seconds. A stranger looked back at her—someone who didn't look that frightened. Someone who had just faced down a vampire intent on feeding.

Someone who could handle that kind of thing, and still be his friend.

The towel was soaked through. Claire squeezed to wring out the excess warm water, then went back to help her boss get cleaned up.

She knew he'd say how sorry he was, and he did—first thing, as she sponged the splatter off his face. *Tomato juice,* she told herself when what she was doing hit home. *It's just tomato juice. You've cleaned up after exploded catsup bottles; this is nothing.*

"Claire," Myrnin whispered. She glanced into his face, then away as she tried to scrub the worst of the stain off his vest. He seemed tired, and he was sitting in his big leather wing chair. "It came on me so suddenly. I couldn't—you understand? I never meant it."

"Is this what happened to Ada when she was alive?" Claire asked. There was blood on his long white hands, too. She gave him the warm towel, and he wiped his fingers on it, then found a clean spot and scrubbed his face again, although she'd gotten the blood off already. He held the warm towel there, covering up whatever his expression was doing. When he lowered it, he was completely in control of himself. "Ada and I were complicated," he said. "This situation is nothing like that one. For one thing, Ada was then a vampire."

"Well, things have changed," Claire said. Myrnin meticulously folded the towel and handed it back to her. "You know she's going to kill you? You get it now?"

"I'm not yet prepared to make any such claim." He looked down at his vest and sighed. "Oh dear. That's never coming out."

"The stain?"

"The hole." He continued to stare at the hole her bone stake had made, and said, "You really would have killed me, wouldn't you?"

"I—wish I could tell you it was a bluff. But I would have. I can't bluff with you."

"You're correct. If you do, I'll know, and you'll be dead. I'm a predator. Weakness is . . . seductive." He cleared his throat. "Mutually assured destruction was good enough for the United States and the Soviet Union; I believe it will be good enough for us. I'd have preferred it not to come to that, but it's hardly your fault—" He broke off, because as he looked up, his gaze fell on the motionless corpse lying on the table in the middle of the lab. "Oh dear. What is that?"

"That would be Bob. Remember Bob? That's what Ada did to him."

"Impossible," Myrnin said, and rose out of his chair to stalk to the table and lean over alarmingly close, poking at the spider's body with curious fingers. "No, quite impossible."

"Excuse me? I was here! He grew, just like in a monster movie!"

"Oh, I can see that. Clearly, that isn't impossible. No, what I meant was your identification of him as Bob."

"What?"

"This isn't Bob," Myrnin said.

Claire rolled her eyes. "He came out of Bob's cage."

"Ah, that explains it. I found a companion for Bob. I thought it was likely they'd try to eat each other, but they seemed content enough. So this must have been Edgar. Or possibly Charlotte."

"Edgar," Claire repeated. "Or Charlotte. Right."

Myrnin left the dead spider and went to Bob's container. He rooted around in it for a few seconds, then triumphantly held out his palm toward Claire.

Bob—presumably—sat crouched there, looking as confused and frightened as a spider could.

"So it was only Edgar," Myrnin said. "Not the same thing at all."

"Was Edgar always the size of a *dog*?"

"Oh, of course not, he—oh, I see your point. Regardless of which spider it is, there are some mysteries to be solved." Myrnin carefully nudged Bob off his palm, back into the container, and then rubbed his hands together eagerly. "Yes, there's definitely work to be done. Ada must have made tremendous strides recently in her research, for her to be able to create this kind of effect. I must know how, and what went wrong."

"Myrnin. Ada made a spider grow into a monster and tried to *kill me with it.* This isn't about *how* she did it. It's *why.*"

"Why is for other people. I am much more concerned with the method, and I'm surprised, Claire; I thought you would be the same. Well, not surprised, perhaps. Disappointed." He carefully uncurled one of the spider's long legs. Claire shuddered. "I'll need a corkboard. A large one. And some very large pins."

Claire and Michael exchanged a look. He'd been standing there, a fascinated but disgusted observer to all this, and now he just shook his head. "If all he wants is for you to fetch and carry, maybe you should just leave him to it."

"She's my *assistant*; it's her job to fetch and carry," Myrnin snapped, and then looked sorry. "But—perhaps you've done enough for one day."

Claire ticked them off on her fingers. "Survived spider attack. Rescued you. Got you blood. Cleaned up blood leftovers."

"I shall therefore fetch my own corkboard. Claire?"

She turned and looked at him as she and Michael headed for the exit. Myrnin looked back in control again, and except for the bloodstain on his vest, you'd never have known he'd been anything less.

"Thank you," he said softly. "I shall consider what you said. About Ada."

She nodded, and escaped.

Michael, as it turned out, was headed for the rehearsal of the play Eve was in, and Claire belatedly remembered that she'd been invited, too. His car was parked at the end of the alley, on the cul-de-sac, and he had an umbrella with him to block the sun. It looked kind of funny, but at least it was a giant golf umbrella, very manly. It had a duck carved into the handle.

Michael even opened the passenger door for her, like a gentleman, but instead of getting in, she reached for the umbrella. "You're the one who combusts," she said. "You get in first." He gave her a funny look as she walked him to the driver's side, and shaded him as he sat. "What?"

"I was thinking how different you are," he said. "You really stood up to Myrnin in there. I'm not sure a lot of vampires could have done that. Including me."

"I'm not different. I'm the same Claire as ever." She grinned, though. "Okay, fewer bruises than when you first met me."

He smiled and closed the car door; she folded the umbrella and got in on the shotgun side. She was careful to open the door only enough to get in; the angle of the sun was cutting uncomfortably close to reaching Michael's side of the car. Inside, the tinting cut the light almost completely. It was like being in a cave, again, only she hoped this one didn't house giant mutated spiders and—what had Michael called them? *Things.*

"Some people come to Morganville and collapse," Michael said as he put the car in motion. "I've seen it a dozen times. But there are a few who come here and just—bloom. You're one of those."

Claire didn't feel especially bloomy. "So you're saying I thrive on chaos."

"No. I'm saying you thrive on challenge. But do me a favor, okay?"

"Considering you came running and jumped into a cave to help me out? Yes."

He shot her a smile so sweet it melted her heart. "Don't ever let him get that close to you again. I like Myrnin, but he can't be trusted. You know that."

"I know." She took his hand and squeezed it. "Thanks."

"No problem. You die, I have to call your parents and explain why. I really don't want to do that. I've already got the whole vampire thing against me."

That took up the entirety of the short drive to the rehearsal hall, which of course had underground parking, being in the vampire part of town. It also had security, Claire was interested to note—a vampire on duty in a blacked-out security booth whom she thought she remembered as being from Amelie's personal security detail. Hard to tell when they all wore dark suits and looked like the Secret Service, only with fangs. Michael showed ID and got a pass to put in his windshield, and within five minutes, they were heading up a sweeping flight of stairs into the Civic Center's main auditorium.

There they found the director having a total YouTube moment.

"What do you mean, *not here?*" he bellowed, and slammed a clipboard to the stage floor. He had an accent—German, maybe—and he was a neat little man, older, with thinning gray hair and a very sharp face. "How can she not be here? Is she not in this play? Who is responsible for the call sheet?"

One of the other people standing in a group around the director on-stage waved her hand. She had a clipboard, a microphone headset, and a tense, worried expression. Claire didn't recognize her. "Sir, I tried calling her cell phone six times. It went to voice mail."

"You are the assistant director! Find her! I don't want to hear about this voice mail nonsense!" He dismissed her with a flip of his hand and glared at the rest of the group. "Well? We must shift the schedule, then, until she gets here, yes? Script!"

He held out his hand; some quick thinker slapped a bundle of paper into his hand. He flipped pages. "No, no, no—ah! Yes, we will do that. Is our Stanley here?"

A big, tattooed guy shouldered through the crowd. "Here," he said. That, Claire guessed, was Rad, the one Eve and Kim were going gaga over. He looked—big. And tough. She didn't see the appeal; for one thing, he wasn't anything like Shane, who was almost as big, and probably just as tough. Shane wore it like part of his body. This guy made a production out of it.

"Good, we'll do the bar scene. We have Mitch? Yes? And all the others?"

Claire stopped listening and glanced at Michael. "Where's Eve? They're missing a *her.*"

"I don't know." He looked at the crowd of people rushing around the stage, resetting the scenery, going over lines, arguing with one another. "I don't see her anywhere."

"You don't think—"

Michael was already walking down the aisle, heading for the stage.

"I guess you do think." Claire hurried after him.

Michael put himself directly in front of the frazzled-looking assistant director, who had a cell phone to one ear, and a finger jammed in the other. She turned a shoulder toward him, clearly indicating she was busy, but he grabbed it and swung her around to face him. Her eyes widened in shock. Michael took the phone from her hand and checked the number. "It's not Eve's," he told Claire, and she saw the intense relief that flooded over his face. "Sorry, Heather."

"It's okay—it's still voice mail." Heather, the assistant director, looked even more worried. She was biting her lip, gnawing on it actually, and darting her eyes toward the livid director, who was stomping around the stage throwing pages of the script to the floor. "Eve's in the dressing room. Man, I am so *fired*."

Michael zipped off, ruffling their hair with the speed of his passage, leaving Claire standing with Heather. After a hesitation, she stuck out her hand. "Hi," she said. "Claire Danvers."

"Oh, that's you? Funny. I thought you'd be—"

"Taller?"

"Older."

"So who's missing?"

Heather held up a finger to silence her, tapped the device strapped to her belt, and spoke into her headset mike. "What's the problem? Well, tell him that the director wants it that way, so just do it, okay? I don't care if it looks good. And quit complaining." She clicked it to OFF and wiped sweat from her forehead. "I don't know what's worse, having a crew who's a bunch of newbies, or having a crew who's been doing this kind of thing since they still used gas in footlights."

Claire blinked. "You've got vampires on the crew."

"Of course. Also in the cast, and of course Mein Herr there." Heather jerked her chin at the director, who was lecturing some poor sap trying to position a potted plant. "He's kind of a perfectionist. He imported the costumes from vintage shops. You tell me, who worries about authentic fabrics when you've just cast two Goth girls as the leads?"

Heather wasn't so much talking to her as at her, Claire decided, so she just shrugged. "So, who's missing?"

"Oh. Our second female lead. Kimberlie Magness."

Kim. Claire felt a slow roll of irritation. "Does she usually show up on time?" Because that would be a surprise.

Heather raised her eyebrows. "In this production, *everybody* shows up on time. According to Mein Herr, to be early is to be on time, and to be on time is to be late. She's never been late."

Still. *Kim*. Probably nothing at all.

"Where is my Stella?" the director bellowed suddenly, and the sound bounced around the stage and also out of Heather's earpiece. She winced and turned down the volume. "Stella!" He drew it out, Brando-style.

And in the wings of the stage, Eve stepped out from behind the curtains, tightly holding Michael's hand. She was dressed in tight black jeans, a black baby-doll shirt with a pentagram on it, and lots of chains and spikes as accessories.

From the director's sudden silence, and Heather's intake of breath, Claire figured that wasn't what Eve was supposed to be wearing. "Oh no," Heather whispered. "This isn't happening."

"What?"

"He insists on rehearsal in costume. Something about getting inside the characters. She's supposed to be in her slip."

The director stomped to Eve, stopping inches away from her. He looked her up and down, and said coldly, "What do you think you are doing?"

"I have to go," she said. Her knuckles were white where she gripped Michael's hand, but she stared the director right in the eyes. "I'm sorry, but I have to."

"No one leaves my rehearsals except in a body bag," he said. "Is that how you'd prefer it?"

"Is that really how *you* want this to go?" Michael asked quietly. "Because somebody could leave in a body bag, but it won't be her."

The director showed teeth in a grimace—it actually looked painful for him to smile. "Are you threatening me, boy?"

"Yes," Michael said, completely still. "I know I'm new at this. I know I'm not a thousand years old with a pile of bodies behind me. But I'm telling you that she has to go, and you're going to let her."

"Or?"

Michael's eyes took on a shine—not red, but almost white. It was eerie. "Let's not find out. You can spare her for the day."

The director hissed, very softly, and held the stare for so long, Claire thought things were about to go very, very wrong . . . and then a mild-looking man in a retro bowling shirt stepped up and said, "Is there a problem? Because I am responsible for these two in Amelie's absence."

And Claire blinked, and realized it was Oliver. Not really Oliver, because he looked . . . different—not just the clothes, but his whole body language. She'd seen him do that before, but not quite this dramatically. His accent was different, too—more of a flat Midwest kind of sound, nothing exotic about it at all.

The director threw him a look, then blinked and seemed to reconsider his position. "I suppose not," he finally said. "I can't have this kind of disruption, you know. This is serious business."

"I know," Oliver said. "But a day won't matter. Let the girl go."

"We're going to find Kim," Eve said. "So really, we're still on company business, right?"

The director's face tensed again, on the verge of an outburst, but he swallowed his words and finally said, "You may tell Miss Magness that she may have *one* rehearsal as a grace period. If she is late one second to any other time I call, she will be *mine.*" He didn't mean fired. He meant lunch.

Claire swallowed. Heather didn't seem surprised. She made a note on her clipboard, shook her head, and then cocked her head again as a burst of words came out of her headphone. "Dammit," she sighed. "Are you kidding me? Great. No, I don't care how you do it; just make it happen." She clicked off and looked at Claire. "Wish me luck."

"Um, luck?"

Heather mounted the stairs to the stage and approached the director to whisper something to him. He shouted in fury and stomped away, waving his arms.

Michael and Eve took the chance to escape down to where Claire waited.

Oliver followed them.

"Nice shirt," Claire said, straight-faced.

He glanced down at it, dismissed it, and said, "Now tell me what's going on. Immediately."

"Kim's missing," Eve said. "I tried to find her before the rehearsal; we were supposed to get together—anyway, she didn't show. I was really worried. I was almost late, and I couldn't find her. She's not answering her phone, either."

"Kim," Oliver said. "Valerie owns her contract. Her unreliability is very much Valerie's problem." He didn't sound overly bothered about it. Claire guessed Kim hadn't made friends there, either.

"We need you to call the police. Tell them to look for her."

"No."

"No?"

"Kim has a Protector, who is responsible for her," he repeated. "I will not order town resources to be spent chasing down someone who is, in all likelihood, a victim of her own folly in one way or another."

"Wait a minute. According to the Morganville rules, she's got rights," Claire said. "Whether she's got a vampire Protector or not, she's still a resident. You can't just abandon her!"

"In fact, I can," Oliver said. "I am required neither to help nor harm. Kim Magness is no concern of mine, or of any other vampire's except Valerie, whom I will inform in due course. If you wish to call Chief Moses and explain the situation, you are free to do so. She and the mayor have jurisdiction over the humans. But I sincerely doubt that a human well-known to be unstable, who's been missing only a few hours, will be a top priority." He dismissed the whole thing, and walked away, back up the steps. By the time he'd reached the stage, he was back in his meek, mild persona.

That was just *weird*.

"Son of a bitch," Eve hissed through clenched teeth.

"Come on, we don't need him," Michael said. "Where first?"

Eve took a deep breath. "I guess her apartment." She cast an almost apologetic look at Claire. "I'm sorry. I know you guys don't exactly, ah, click, but—"

"I'll help," Claire said. Not because she cared so much about Kim, but because she cared about Eve. Eve gave her a quick hug. "Want me to call Shane?"

"Would you?" Eve was making puppy-dog eyes now, really pitiful. "Any help we can get—I'm really worried, Claire. This isn't like Kim. It really isn't."

Claire nodded, took out her phone, and dialed Shane's number. He didn't seem to need a lot of encouragement to yell to his boss that he had to go, family emergency. Claire told him they'd swing by to pick him up.

By the time the call was over, they were heading down into the darkened parking garage again. "I can't believe I did that," Eve said. "I just totally blew my shot at the play, forever. He's going to replace me. I'll never get a part in anything, ever again. My life is over."

"Blame Kim," Claire said. "You're a good friend."

Eve looked miserable anyway. "Not good enough, or she'd be here, right?"

"So not your fault."

Eve raised her eyebrows. "What if it were me missing? Wouldn't you guys feel guilty, somehow?"

That shut Claire up, because she would, and she knew it. Even if she'd had nothing to do with it, she'd feel she should have done something.

She was still thinking that over when she felt the tingle of a portal opening nearby. Claire felt a spike of alarm drive deep, and grabbed her phone to look at the tracking app she'd loaded on it. *Yes.* An unplanned portal was getting forced open, right here, in the shadows about a dozen feet away.

"Get to the car!" she yelled, and sprinted for it. Eve didn't ask why, thankfully; she just tore off in pursuit, and Michael bounded ahead to jump in the driver's side.

A flood of spiders poured out, skittering across the concrete floor—bouncing, as if they were being poured out of a giant bucket.

Thousands of Bobs, only larger, the size of small Chihuahuas. Eve shrieked and threw herself into the backseat, slamming the door as one launched itself toward them; it hit the glass and bounced off. Claire kicked one away as she jumped in the passenger seat, and Michael locked the doors. "What the *hell*?" Eve yelled. "Oh my God, it's like Attack of the Giant CGI!"

"It's Ada," Claire said. She and Michael exchanged a look. "She's tracking me. She's got to be."

"Why?"

Symbols flashed in front of Claire's eyes, the symbols she reviewed and committed to memory every single morning. "Because I know her secret," she said. "I know how to reset her, kind of like wiping her memory. Myrnin won't do it, but I will. And she can't have that."

"Great," Michael said. "And where do you have to go to reset her?"

"Guess."

"You are just all kinds of fun right now." He fired up the engine and hit the gas. Claire hid her eyes as they drove over spiders, because that was just sick and kind of sad. The spiders chased them for a while, then milled around in the distance and, one by one, turned up their legs and died.

Ada hadn't been able to keep them alive for long, which was great news for the next person in the parking garage.

"Kim first," Claire said. "Eve's right. Something could have happened to her."

"You're sure."

"I'm sure Ada would expect me to come running. I'd rather let her wait. And worry."

TEN

Kim's loft was a crime scene. Maybe not literally, but Claire thought if the police had roped it off, nobody would disagree. . . . Things were tossed everywhere, broken junk was piled in the corners, clothes were tossed on every flat surface. It smelled of old Chinese food, and the at-least-month-old trash was overflowing with cartons and pizza boxes. One pizza carton lay on the floor with a couple of slices of sausage withered inside.

"Nice," Shane said, and looked around. "Well, we know she's not a closet neat freak." There was paint all over the walls, too—not paintings, just paint, thrown on in sprays as if Kim had taken a few gallons and spun around in a circle, splashing it all over. It was probably still art, just not Claire's favorite kind.

"She's busy," Eve said, and cleaned up the pizza box and a few Chinese food cartons, which she jammed into a plastic trash bag. "She's an artist."

"She's a slob," Shane said. "I'm not judging, though. So, what's the plan? We look around? Can I have dibs on the underwear drawer?"

Claire winced. "I can't believe you just said that."

Shane took on an angelic look. "Somebody's got to do it."

"Then that somebody will be me."

Shane lost his smile and got serious. "Hey. I'm sorry. I didn't mean—"

"I know." It still hurt. She avoided his eyes and started rummaging through things. It wasn't as if Kim actually *had* an underwear drawer—she didn't seem bothered by leaving her bras and panties all over the place. Claire grabbed a bag and started stuffing the clothes into it, just because.

"Girls," Michael said. "We're here for clues, right? Not cleanup?"

"Right." Eve took a deep breath. "I'll check the bedroom."

"Bathroom," Shane volunteered.

"You're brave. All right, you keep going in here," Michael told Claire. "I'll take the kitchen."

"Good luck." She meant it. She bet mold had formed its own civilization in the refrigerator.

That left Claire on her own in the big, trashed-out room. She had no idea where to even start looking, but when she let herself ignore the trash, strewn clothes, and general mess, she found herself focusing on the walls. One of them had a mural painted on it, creepy elongated faces and staring eyes.

Staring eyes. They glittered. For a frozen second, Claire thought there was someone behind the wall, watching her, and then she got her head together. It was just glass, reflecting; they weren't real eyes. But why would Kim put glass on the eyes—no, on only *one* eye?

Oh.

"Guys?" Claire opened the closet beside the mural, shoved through piles of crap and boxes, and found the camera that looked out through the eyehole. It was a small high-tech thing, wireless. So there had to be some kind of receiver, somewhere. She ducked out of the closet to yell, "Any computers around here?"

"In here," Eve said. There was a Mac set up on a rickety table in the corner of the bedroom, jammed in next to a sagging, unmade bed. It had a screen saver on it, and when Claire tapped the space bar, it asked for a password. She looked at Eve, who raised her shoulders in a clear no-idea shrug.

Claire typed in Eve's name. Nothing. She tried Morganville, but again, nothing.

On a wildly unpleasant hunch, she typed in *Shane*.

The screen cleared, and Claire was looking at herself. She recoiled in surprise, and the screen image did the same, leaning back from the camera. *Oh.* The built-in camera was on. Claire clicked it off and looked at what was on the desktop, which was where she personally put things she wanted to use quickly . . . and there it was. It was a folder, marked *Reality Project Cam #72*.

There were video files there. Claire clicked one, and instantly, Kim was there, filling the screen, leaning in dramatically toward the computer's lens. "Day twenty-two of the project," she said in a loud whisper. "Still not sure whether or not any of the extra sites have been discovered, but I'll run it as long as I can. Great stuff so far. The official history project is still going, but most of the vamps won't talk. It doesn't matter anyway; this is going to be so much better. The Oscars are going to be kissing my ass." She grabbed a handy bottle of soda and held it in both hands, looking over-the-top happy. "Oh, thank you so much; I just can't believe this honor. I'd like to thank the Academy—"

Claire paused it and looked at Eve, and Shane, who'd come out of the bathroom to watch. Michael joined, too.

"What is this?" Claire asked. Eve was shaking her head, eyes fixed on the screen. "Seriously, you don't know?"

"No. What's she talking about?"

Claire fast-forwarded until Kim finished her acceptance speech, then clicked PLAY again. Kim's image was glowing with glee. Whatever she was talking about, to her, it was major.

"I can't believe it; I finally got to put some in the last Founder House. Connections look good—stream is starting up. God, why do people always fall for the stupidest things? The old bathroom trick? She didn't even worry when I was gone for ten minutes, poking around. Sweet." Kim leaned in, close and confidential. "I may have to keep some of this for myself. Shane, undressed. Oh yeah."

"Excuse me?" Shane blurted. "What the hell?"

Eve's eyes widened, and she licked her black-painted lips and said, "When was this?"

Claire checked the date. "Early last week."

"Oh God," Eve said. "I—I met Kim at the auditions. I mean, I already knew her, but not like close friends or anything, and she just seemed really—interesting. She came over after we got done. You were at school, Michael was out, Shane was just leaving."

"And she asked to use the bathroom?" Claire prodded.

Eve looked miserable. "Yeah. She was gone awhile, but you don't ask, right? You're not supposed to hover. I mean, come on. Besides, she was so *cool.*"

"She is cool," Shane agreed. "She's also a raving bitch manipulator. I dated her, remember? Once. You should have asked me. And what is this crap about seeing me naked? I wasn't even there!"

Eve covered her mouth with both hands. "What did she do? Oh my God—she used me, right? She used me."

"She uses everybody," Shane said. "Twenty-four, seven. I'm sorry, but I was kind of worried when you got so head over heels with her. She's not . . . yeah. She's just not."

Claire wondered if she should feel some kind of vindication, but she didn't. She felt nervous. "What did she do in our house?"

"What do you get Oscars for?"

Shane and Michael both said, at the same time, "Movies."

And the four of them looked at one another in silence for a moment. Claire didn't know how they felt, but her stomach seemed to be in free fall, and with no end in sight.

She slowly turned back to the screen, shut down the video, and looked at the folder.

"What?" Shane asked. She pointed at the screen.

"This is Kim's personal video journal," she said. "It's where she recorded all her personal stuff."

"So?"

"Look at the number."

"Reality project cam . . . number . . ." Eve drew in a sharp breath. "Oh, holy crap."

"There are seventy-one other cameras out there in Morganville," Claire said. "Somewhere."

"And at least one of them's in our house," Shane finished.

There was no sign on the Mac in Kim's apartment as to where the video was streaming *to*. . . . She'd need more computing power than a laptop to run seventy-one other cameras, especially if she was saving terabytes of data. "She'd need a server array," Claire concluded, after doing the math. "Or off-line storage dumps. Maybe she only records during certain hours, then dumps everything to DVD-ROM or something."

"What about the university?" Eve asked. "Plenty of servers there, right?"

Claire considered it, then shook her head. "Yeah, there's available space, but how would she get to it without somebody noticing? She's not even an enrolled student. And the TPU computer security's pretty tight—it would have to be, because the vamps monitor it to prevent anybody from sending compromising information out." That led her to another, badder place in her mind. "Kim thinks of herself as some kind of renegade indie filmmaker, right?"

"Right," Eve said. "She talks about that a lot. About TV, cable shows, all that kind of thing. She's kind of obsessed with it. The acting thing was really so she could see all the backstage stuff, the technical parts."

Shane lowered himself onto Kim's sagging bed, which gave Claire unpleasant associations she wished she hadn't made. "She's bugged the town," Shane said. "She's got it rigged up with surveillance. And she's going to cut it all into, what, some kind of über-documentary about vampires?"

"Worse," Claire said. "Seventy-two cameras, all running at once? She's cutting together episodes. She wants a reality show. A *Morganville* reality show." She spun back toward the keyboard and brought up Kim's e-mail. As far as Claire could tell, the built-in in-box had never been used. "She's got to have e-mail."

"Web mail," Michael said. "If she wanted to cover her tracks, she'd do it that way. You think she's in communication with someone outside?"

Claire brought up the browser's history, but it had been cleared. "There's some kind of maintenance app running. It wipes out her temp files and history every twenty-four hours."

"Somebody's working with her," Shane said, and shrugged when they all looked at him. "Makes sense. Webcams don't fall off trees, right? Buying that many takes funding, and Kim isn't making that off her spare-parts art."

"Somebody outside Morganville knows," Claire said. "Do you think the vampires found out? That they're behind Kim's disappearing?"

"Oliver didn't seem bothered. If we knew, I guarantee you that this wouldn't still be here," Michael said, and nodded at the computer. *We*, not *they*. Claire didn't miss that, and she saw it register on Eve, too. "We'd have taken it."

Shane exchanged a look with both the girls. He hadn't missed the us-versus-them implications, either. "What's with the *we*, man?"

"What?"

"You counting yourself on the vampire team now?"

Michael sighed. "Do we need to have this fight right now? Because I think we've got bigger problems."

"No, we don't," Eve said. "Kim's disappeared. She's doing something really dangerous, and a lot of people—including the vampires—might want her stopped, or just gone. But I need to know where you are, Michael. Are you with the vampires? Or are you with us?"

"*Us* meaning what? Humans? Eve—"

"*Us* meaning me, Shane, and Claire," Eve said flatly. "Are you? Or are you going to tell Amelie and Oliver what Kim's doing and make this an all-out witch hunt?"

He didn't answer for a few seconds. Shane got up off the bed, which groaned as the old springs adjusted. "Michael?"

"Don't do this," Michael said, straight to Eve. "It's not a choice. I don't have a choice."

"You always have one—you know that. You had one when you let Amelie turn you, and you've got one now. Sam didn't run with the crowd. You don't have to, either. You can—do good things."

"Not everything vampires do is bad."

Shane slapped his hand on the wall, a sharp gunshot of impact, and they all jumped and looked at him. "Are you going to help us stop this, or are you going to run off and snitch?" he asked. "It's a simple question, man."

"It's not about you three. This is about Kim trying to destroy all of us, make herself some kind of reality TV diva, and get rich."

"Maybe," Shane said. "And maybe it doesn't have to be. The video's streaming somewhere. She must still be trying to cut it together. We can still find her and put a stop to it. Nobody else has to know."

"Why do you want to protect her?" Michael asked. Shane glanced quickly at Claire, just a flash, but she saw the guilt in it. "Old-girlfriend blues?"

"Oh man, you'd *better* shut up."

"Eve wants to save her because they were friends; I get that. Claire just wants to save everybody—"

"Not *everybody*," she muttered.

"But you, you hold grudges. You'd throw Monica under the bus in a hot second, but you don't want Kim to get hurt."

"Seriously," Shane said. "Shut up. Now."

"See how it feels?" Michael said softly. "I don't like people questioning my motives, either. I'm a vampire. I can't help that. I drink blood. Get the fuck over it and don't make this about me. You want to save Kim? Fine. But if we don't find her in the next twenty-four hours, I've got to tell someone, and then it's on."

"It's all on," Eve agreed. There were tears in her eyes, shining like silver, but she blinked them away. "And it's all over. You bet your life on it, Michael."

She turned on her heel and walked out, shoving crap out of her way as she went. Claire looked after her, then began unhooking the computer. "Shane," she said. "Get the camera from the closet in the next room. Maybe we can trace the IP and see where she's sending the video."

Michael went after Eve, but Shane lingered as she stuffed the computer and power cord into the laptop bag. "Hey," he said. His fingers touched her hair lightly, then her shoulder. "I'm not—look, it's not like I'm in love with her. I'm not. It's just—"

"You slept with her once. Yeah, I heard." She snapped the catches closed on the bag and slung it over her shoulder. "She makes a hell of an impression."

Shane got in her way, and despite everything, all her best intentions, she looked up into his eyes, and the light in them took her breath away. His fingertips touched her face, and then he bent down and kissed her. "No," he murmured into her mouth. "She doesn't. You do."

Before she could think of anything to say, he turned and left to grab the camera from the closet. In the other room, Claire saw Michael talking to Eve—well, Eve's rigid back. He turned when he saw her and Shane coming.

Eve opened the front door and slammed it back, charging down the stairs and leaving them all far, far behind. By the time they caught up, she was already in the passenger seat up front, face turned toward the tinted window. If she was crying, Claire couldn't tell. She'd put on a gigantic pair of mirrored sunglasses that she absolutely did not need inside a vampire's car.

"Right," Michael said, and climbed behind the wheel. "Where to?"

"Take me home," Claire said. "I'll work on the technical stuff."

"Drop me off at Common Grounds," Eve said. "I need to talk to some people."

Michael cleared his throat. "Want company?"

"No." Her voice was flat and cool, and Claire winced and looked at Shane. In the dimness, she could only see the broad strokes of his expression, but it looked like a *yikes*. "You've got things to do, right?"

She must have been right, because Michael didn't exactly deny it.

Shane said, "So—I'll stay home and watch TV. Critical job, too. Not everybody can do that under pressure."

"You should come with me," Eve said. "I could use some help." Even though she'd just flatly turned down Michael's offer. *Ouch.*

Shane must have thought that, too; he flashed a look at Michael, clearly apologizing, and Michael nodded slightly.

"Okay, sure," Shane said. "Outstanding." Shane held out a fist, and Eve tapped it. "Claire? You'll be okay alone?"

"Sure," she said, and hugged the laptop bag closer. "What could go wrong?"

Michael's eyes flashed to meet hers in the rearview mirror.

"Besides everything, I mean," she said.

ELEVEN

At home—meaning, at the Glass House; the last thing she wanted to do was put her parents in the middle of all this—Claire unloaded Kim's laptop, set up the webcam, and started trying to access the data stream. That wasn't especially hard, because she knew the IP address of the camera; Kim had helpfully put the info right on a label. The problem was that the other end was on a randomizer, a special program that shifted the signal and rerouted it across the Internet every few minutes. It was right in Morganville; it had to be, because of the packet times, but Claire had no real idea where to start looking. She wasn't especially computer savvy, although she knew her way around; Kim obviously had taken some precautions.

But Claire wasn't giving up that easily, either. She didn't like Kim, but there was a lot at stake here: the vampires' lives, including Michael's; Kim's life; maybe everything they'd built here, at whatever cost.

Michael was right: they couldn't just let Kim sacrifice it all for her own ambition. The truth might come out, but it shouldn't come out like this, as some kind of horrible exercise in voyeurism.

She finally reran the video of Kim they'd watched at her loft. *I can't believe it; I finally got to put some in the last Founder House. Connections look good; stream is starting up.*

Claire went in search of cameras in the Glass House.

She found the first one in an air vent in Shane's room, and had to sit down, hard, on his bed with her head in her hands. It was focused right on his bed.

Oh my God. Oh no. At first she was sick with the thought of Kim combing through hours of video of Shane, invading his privacy, watching him get undressed . . . and then she remembered.

We were in here. Together. And she saw it.

Claire lifted her head and looked right up at the camera. She had no idea what was on her face, but if it was any match for the rage burning inside her, the feeling of total betrayal and exposure, she couldn't imagine Kim was having any fun seeing it. "I hope there's sound on these," she said. "You *bitch.* I officially hope you rot in hell, and I swear, if you post *any* of this online, I will find you."

Then Claire dragged a chair over, stood on the seat, and yanked the vent screen out of the wall. Behind it, the little webcam blinked its light and stared at her with a glass eye every bit as emotionless as Bob the spider's.

Claire picked it up, carried it into her bedroom, and put it next to the first one they'd found in Kim's apartment. Then she started searching the other rooms. She found two more—one hidden on top of a bookshelf, barely visible, in the living room, providing a bird's-eye view of the whole space, and another in Michael's room, focused on his bed.

"Pervert," Claire muttered, grabbed it out of the fake plant on top of his dresser and carried it back to set it with the others. The IP addresses were consistent. Claire tried entering them into the Web browser, and the signal was there, but it just displayed as gibberish.

Encrypted, which went along with the randomizer program that Kim was using.

She was just starting to backtrace the signals when she felt that familiar tingle along the back of her neck, a feeling that the world had just *shifted.*

Portal.

Claire slid out of her chair and grabbed weapons, then waited. It had felt like the portal had opened upstairs, in the attic, and as she waited she heard faint creaks and pops from the old wood floor overhead. *Not spiders*, she thought. Spiders wouldn't be that heavy.

God, she *hoped* spiders wouldn't be that heavy. That was a terrifying thought. She was already entering B-movie horror territory . . . alone in the house! With a giant spider!

And a vampire, maybe.

Which could be worse.

Long minutes passed, and nothing came to eat her. Claire's hand had gotten sweaty, and her muscles hurt from the strength of her grip on the silver knife in her hand. *Come on*, she thought. *Just get it over with already.* It could have been somebody with a lot of power—Myrnin, or Oliver, or Amelie. In which case she'd put the knife down and apologize.

But she thought it was probably Ada, making another run at her.

The creaks overhead paused, and she heard them retreat.

Then she felt the portal activate again, and slam closed. All her protections snapped back into place, as if they'd never been broken. If she hadn't been here . . . she'd never have even known someone had been inside.

Claire edged out into the hall, staring at the hidden door up to the secret room. It was shut, and she heard nothing at all. She wouldn't, of course, it being soundproofed, but still . . . She felt as if she ought to be able to feel *something* . . . and the house usually conveyed a feeling of danger. When it didn't, it was usually because Amelie . . .

Amelie.

Claire opened the hidden door and went up the stairs, and found the lights on at the top. The soft glow thrown through colored glass painted the walls, and on the couch, Amelie lay full length, one white hand pressed to her forehead.

She was wearing a flowing white dress, like a very fancy nightgown, and there were flecks of blood on it. Not as if she'd been hurt—more as if she'd been standing near someone else who had been. As Claire entered the room, Amelie's eyes opened and focused on her, but the Founder didn't move.

"We have a problem. Ada," Amelie said. "You know, don't you?"

"That she's crazy? Yeah. I figured that." Claire realized she was still holding the knife, and put it down. "Sorry."

"A reasonable precaution in uncertain times," Amelie said softly. Nothing else. Claire waited, but Amelie was as still as one of those marble angels on top of a tomb.

"What happened?" Claire finally asked.

"Nothing you would understand." Amelie closed her eyes. "I'm tired, Claire."

There was a simple kind of resignation to the way she said it that made Claire shiver. "Should I—is there somebody I should call, or—"

"I will rest here for now. Thank you." It was a dismissal, one Claire was a little relieved to get. Amelie just seemed—absent. Empty.

"Okay. But—I guess if you need something—"

Amelie's eyes snapped open, and Claire felt it at the same time: a surge of power—the portal reopening.

Amelie's will slammed it closed.

"Someone's looking for you," Claire said. "Who is it?"

"None of your affair."

"It is if they're coming here! Is someone after you?"

"It's my guards," Amelie said. "They'll find me, sooner or later, but for now, I want to be here. Here, where Sam—" She stopped again, and silvery tears pooled in her eyes and ran down into her unbound pale hair. "Where Sam told me he would never leave me. But he did leave me, Claire. I knew he would, and he did. Everyone leaves. Everyone."

This time, when the portal flared, Amelie didn't try to keep it shut. In seconds, the attic door flew open, and it wasn't the guards after all, in their black Secret Service suits.

It was Oliver, still wearing his bowling shirt, graying hair pulled tight into a ponytail. For a second, as his gaze fell on Amelie, he looked like a different person.

No, that wasn't possible. He couldn't really *feel* something for her. Could he?

"You," he said to Claire. "Leave us. *Now.*"

"Stay," Amelie said. There was an unmistakable thread of command in her voice. "You don't order my servants in my house, Oliver. Not yet."

"You're hiding behind children?"

"I'm not hiding at all. Not even from you." She slowly sat up, and in the multicolored glow of the lamps she looked young, and very tired. "We've played our games, haven't we? The two of us, we've schemed and cheated and used each other all these centuries, for our own purposes. What did it bring us? Peace? There's never peace for us. There can't be."

"I can't talk of peace," he said, and went to one knee, looking up into her face. "And neither can you. Morley tried to kill you out there in the graveyard the other evening, and still you wander alone, looking for your own destruction. You must stop."

"Speaking as my second-in-command."

"Speaking as your friend," he said, and took her hand. "Amelie. We have our differences, you and I. We always will. But I would not see you suffer so. Morganville is too much for you right now—there are too many vampires here with too much ambition. Control must be maintained, and if you won't do it, you must put it in stronger hands. My hands."

"How kind of you, to keep the best interests of others so close to your heart," she said. She didn't try to remove her fingers from his, but her tone had taken on a remote kind of chill. "So what do you propose?"

"Until you can put aside your mourning, give me the town," he said. "You know I can keep order here. I'll act as your regent. When you are ready, I'll give it back to you."

"Liar." She said it without particular emphasis, or blame, and Claire saw Oliver's hand tighten on hers. Amelie smiled, just a little. "Liar, and bully. Do you really think such tactics could work, against the daughter of Bishop? You would have done well to pretend to a little more sympathy, or less. Half measures never work for you, Oliver."

"You're losing the town by inches now," he said. "Morley's only the first of the vampires to make a move against you—more will come. The humans, too; there are gangs of them attacking us in the night. I've already been approached to stop it."

"So now it's a plot. A plot to remove me from control. And you are my faithful servant, coming to warn me." Her teeth flashed as she laughed softly. "Oh, Oliver. The only reason you didn't betray me to my father when you had the chance was because the odds were even. Had he courted you for even a moment, you'd have yielded like a lovesick girl. You'd have planted the knife in my back yourself."

"No," he said, and pulled her off balance, down to her knees on the floor across from him. "I wouldn't. You're not a queen anymore, Amelie. Don't presume to sit on your throne and judge me!"

She wrenched a hand free and slapped him hard across the face, and Claire backed up as the two vampires locked red stares. "I'll judge as I see fit," Amelie said. "And I'll have none of your insolence. Scheme all you want, but it doesn't matter. Morganville is mine, and it will never be yours. Never. I'm on my guard now. You may be assured that whatever plots exist against me will be uncovered and destroyed. Even yours."

She shoved him back, and Oliver fell full length on the floor. In a flash, Amelie reached out for the silver knife that Claire had put on the table, and before Claire could blink, that knife was at Oliver's throat. "Well?" she demanded. "What say you, my servant?"

He spread his hands wide in mute surrender.

Amelie stared down at him, then looked at Claire. "Summon my car," she said. "I believe I will go for a drive in Morganville. It's time my people see me, and know I'm not to be underestimated."

She slammed the knife into the floor next to Oliver's head, close enough that the edge left a bloody streak down his cheek, then rose to her feet and swept out of the room and down the stairs. Claire dug her cell phone out and called the number to Amelie's security, and told them to meet her downstairs.

By the time she was done, Oliver was sitting on the sofa. He dabbed at the cut on his face, looking a lot less upset than Claire expected him to be.

"Wow, you planned that," she said. "Right?"

He shrugged. "She loved Sam. She needs someone to fill the void inside her—either a lover, or an enemy."

"And you're the enemy."

Oliver dusted himself off. "Through all the long, long years, it's what we've always had between us. Anger, and respect." He smiled a little. "And sometimes a glimmer of something else, not that we would ever admit it to each other. No, enemies are easier. She likes being my enemy. And I rather enjoy being hers."

Claire really, really didn't get it, but she didn't think that either one of them would care.

"Hey," she said. "You came through the portal. Did anything weird happen?"

"Weird?" He frowned. "I don't understand."

"I mean—never mind. I'm just kind of worried about the portals. I want to recalibrate the system."

"I was planning to walk in any case. It's just as important for the residents of Morganville to see me afoot as for them to see Amelie in her queen's black coach." Oliver straightened his shirt and stood up. "It gives us . . . balance."

"Oliver?"

He stopped at the head of the stairs.

"What would happen if someone got word out about the town?"

"Out?"

"Out in the world. You know."

"Oh, it's happened before. But no one believes. No one ever believes."

"What if—what if they had proof?"

"The only possible proof would be a genuine vampire, and that will never happen. Short of that, any proof can be denied easily enough."

"What about—video?"

"Claire. You go to the cinema, don't you? Do you imagine, in this age of digital trickery, that anyone would believe video of vampires?" He shook his head. "They would believe it now less than ever. The very popularity of vampires in your stories protects us." He sent her a sharp glance. "Why?"

"Just wondering," she said.

"Stop wondering. It's not healthy."

Then he was gone. Claire sat down on the couch and smoothed her palms over her jeans.

Oliver was right; people probably wouldn't believe it. Most people didn't believe all the ghost reality shows, either. The problem was that these days, reality didn't have to be real to be a hit—and Morganville couldn't stand up to real scrutiny.

They had to stop Kim, before it all fell apart.

Plus, as a bonus, they had to really kick her ass about the cameras, because that was just *wrong*.

Eve and Shane got home first, while Claire was devouring a peanut butter sandwich. She didn't tell them about the visit from Amelie and Oliver, and besides, they looked pretty grim. She was sure they wouldn't really care.

"What?" she asked. Shane snagged half her sandwich from her plate as he passed. "Hey!"

"Worked up an appetite, watching Miss Bad Attitude's back," he said around a mouthful of bread. "She goes to the most interesting places. I mean *interesting* in terms of scary as hell."

"Do *not* tell Claire about that club," Eve said, and took off her metallic sunglasses. Behind them, her mascara was smeared, and her eyes were red—not vampire red, but more like an overdose of tears. "Besides, it's not like I just randomly decided to go there. It's where Kim liked to hang out."

"What kind of club?" Claire whispered to Shane.

"Leather," he whispered back. "She's right; you really don't want to know."

"Kim hasn't been there in a couple of days," Eve said. "But we found a few vampires who did interviews with her recently, for her history project."

From the expression on Shane's face, there was more to the story. Claire said, doubtfully, "And they just told you? Just like that?"

"I had to make some deals to get the details." Eve avoided making eye contact on that. She shed her black leather jacket, the one with all the buckles, and snagged a corner of Claire's leftover half sandwich. "Hmm, this is good; did you put honey on it?"

"You did *what?*" Making any kind of deal with any kind of vampire in Morganville was crazy. Making deals with the kind of vampires hanging out in a leather bar was . . . suicidal. Claire rounded on Shane. "You let her do that?"

"Seriously, you can't even think about blaming me when she gets like this. I'm the bodyguard. Unless you wanted me to tie her up and gag her . . ."

"They'd probably have gotten into it there," Eve said. "Look, I can get out of the deals. Amelie's our get-out-of-deals-free card. But I needed to find Kim, and to do that, we needed information. Unless you waved your magic techno-wand and . . . ?"

Claire had to shake her head.

"Okay then, quit looking at me like I broke house training or something." Eve, Claire realized, was really uncomfortable about this. She'd probably had to force herself to talk to these vamps, and the last thing she needed was the postgame analysis on what she'd done wrong.

Claire cleared her throat. "What did you get?"

"I found four vamps that Kim either talked to on camera, or set up interviews with in the next week or so, which means she wasn't planning on leaving town just yet. And a couple of human guys who, ah, visited Kim at her place."

"Hookups," Shane confirmed. "Which is Kim's style. Although I can't say much for her taste. It's kind of gone downhill."

"So, wait—what does that tell us that we didn't already know? And what did you promise these vamps, anyway?"

"Things," Eve said, without adding any details. Shane looked away. "Not important right now. The point is, two of the vamps she interviewed she filmed at Common Grounds, but the other vamps said she took them to a kind of studio."

"A studio," Claire repeated. "That sounds promising."

"Thought so. It wasn't knee-deep in crap, so it couldn't have been her apartment, right?"

"Did they tell you where?"

"No," Shane said, leaning over Eve's shoulder. "They wanted more for that little gem. And I told them to stuff it sideways."

Claire blinked. Vampires. Leather bar. "And they just thought that was okay?"

"Honestly? Not so much. They mostly decided we'd make good chew toys."

"Shane!" Claire looked at him with pleading eyes. "You didn't—"

"Fight? Didn't have to," he said. Before he could explain, the front door opened and closed, and Claire heard the locks clicking shut again. Eve stiffened and looked down, burying her black-painted fingernails in her palms as she made fists.

Michael looked—like he'd been through a rough night in a bad bar, Claire guessed. Mussed, clothes torn at the seams. Something dark on his shirt that could have been blood.

"Are you okay?" Claire came to her feet, staring at him. He wasn't bruised or anything, but he looked tired. There was a little flush of red in his eyes, and his hands were shaking.

"I'm fine," he said. "I just need—something to drink. Be right back."

He disappeared into the kitchen. The silence in the room was sharp and uncomfortable, and Claire looked at Eve, who folded her arms across her chest.

"I didn't ask him to come rescue us," she said, and looked down. "I didn't want him to come at all."

Michael came back carrying a black sports bottle. They all knew what he had in it, but nobody mentioned it as he sipped through the built-in straw.

"I had my reasons for going," Michael said. And he didn't look at Eve. And Eve didn't look at him. "Thanks for getting her out of there when you did, Shane."

Shane nodded. "No problem. What happened?"

That was a question Michael wasn't going to answer, evidently, because he just shrugged. "Fight." One hell of one, from the state of his clothes and his hunger for blood. "It was worth it. One of them told me where Kim took him to interview, and it wasn't any of the places you already had."

Eve slowly raised her head, and her eyes narrowed. "You followed us. You thought we couldn't handle it."

"I knew where you were going. And I was right, wasn't I?"

"No, you were *not* right! Michael—"

He put the bottle down, stepped forward, and caught her hands in his. Eve started to try to pull free, but he held on, willing her to look at him. It seemed really personal, somehow.

"I'm a vampire," he said. "I'm never going to be anything else. You need to decide if you're okay with that, Eve. I am."

"What if I'm not?" Her voice sounded really small and wounded. "What if I just want you to be Michael, not—not Vampire Michael of the Clan, or whatever?"

"I can't," he said. "Because I'm not just Michael anymore. I haven't been since before you moved in. You just didn't know it."

He let go of her hands, uncapped the sports bottle, and drank the blood down in long, thirsty gulps, making sure she was watching. His eyes turned ruby red, and he licked the drops from his lips. He put the empty bottle down, watching her.

She crossed her arms and turned away from him, and Michael closed his eyes in pain. When he opened them again, they were just human, and sad.

Claire wondered if she'd actually just witnessed a breakup. She hoped not.

Shane cleared his throat. "So. You turned up at a place where Kim goes, right? Let's talk about that. Please."

Michael walked over to the chair, where his guitar lay across the seat. He picked it up and cradled it in his arms, still watching Eve. After a few seconds, he began to softly play a series of chords. It was an aching kind of sound, gentle and full of emotion, and Claire saw Eve's shoulders tense and shake as she suppressed tears.

"Kim used to work at KVVV," Michael said. "She was an intern there before it shut down. The vampire said she interviewed him in a booth there at the old studios at the edge of town, by the transmission tower."

Claire couldn't help feeling a little spike of excitement. "That's it. That's got to be it, right? You said it was shut down?"

"Yeah, Amelie shut it down a few years back after—there was an incident," Michael said. "The town council decided we didn't need another radio station. It's been locked up since then."

"We need to go look!" Claire bounced to her feet, but Shane caught her shoulder and guided her back into the chair.

"Cool it. Not at night, we don't. The last thing we need to do is go poking around an abandoned building in the middle of the night in a town full of vampires."

"But what if she decides to close up shop? Cut her losses, take her goodies, and try to leave?" Eve said. "She could get killed. We have to warn her."

"Warn her?" Claire felt short of breath, ready to burst out into wild laughter. "Eve, don't you get it? She rigged our house. She was *watching us.* Watching everything, every private thing—"

"No," Eve said. "No, she wouldn't do that. You're wrong."

"I found cameras in the bedrooms!"

Eve's mouth opened and closed, and Claire didn't think she'd ever seen her look quite so devastated. She slumped down on the couch and covered her rice-powder-pale face with both hands.

Shane was staring at Claire with a frozen expression. "Which bedrooms?"

"Yours," she said softly. "And Michael's."

For a second Shane didn't move, and then he reached out, picked up the nearest thing—a DVD case—and hurled it across the room so hard that it dented the wall. "Son of a *bitch,*" he muttered. "That little—"

Michael's face had gone completely still, and he wasn't playing anymore. He held the guitar as if he'd forgotten he had it. "She was recording us. Her own little *Big Brother* reality show, with vampires."

Eve said nothing. Claire couldn't even imagine what she was thinking, but she looked utterly miserable.

"We have to go," Eve finally said. "We need to find where she keeps the recordings, and wipe them out. Every little bit. This can't happen. She can't do this."

"I just hope she hasn't *already* done it," Claire said. "She's been putting this together for almost a month. She's got to be almost done by now. If we're right about her having some kind of sponsor outside of town . . ."

"Then we *really* have to go. Now. Tonight."

"No," Michael said. "Not at night."

"She's going to *get away with it!*"

"That's a chance we're going to have to take," Michael said. "Shane's right. No charging off into the dark. It has to wait until morning." He started playing again. His head was down, as if he were concentrating on his music, but Claire didn't think he was. There was something a little wrong with the way he said it, the way he wouldn't look at them. "How about more of those sandwiches?"

Eve raised her head and stared at him, tears smearing her mascara into clown makeup. "Unbelievable," she said. "You know what's on those recordings. You *know*, Michael. You'd let her take that and sell it?"

"We need to be smart about this. If we go running off without a plan—"

"Screw your plans!" she shouted, and jumped off the couch, then pounded up the stairs, chains jingling. "Screw you, too!"

Michael looked at Claire, then Shane.

"She's not wrong," Shane said. "Sorry, man."

Michael had lied to them, and Claire caught him at it.

She was on her way to the bathroom with her tank top and pajama bottoms over one arm, thinking about curling up warm in Shane's arms, when she heard Michael talking in his room. The door was open a crack. Shane and Eve were still downstairs, cleaning up the kitchen.

He was on his cell phone. "No," he was saying. "No, I'm sure. I just need to go check it out, tonight. Make sure nobody is using the facility without—"

Claire pushed the door open, and Michael twisted around to look at her. *So busted.* He froze for a second, then said, "I'll call you back," and hung up.

"Let me guess," she said. "Oliver. You're telling him everything, aren't you?"

"Claire—"

"We asked you. We asked you if you were with us, and you said you were. You *promised.*"

"Claire, please."

"No." She stepped back when he stretched out a hand. "Eve was right. You're not Michael anymore. You're Vampire Michael. It's really us and them, and you're with them."

"*Claire.*"

"What?"

"That wasn't Oliver."

"Then who was it?"

"Detective Hess. He was going to meet me at the station and check it out, tonight. Eve was right. We really can't wait, not even for morning." Michael's expression took on a dangerous edge. "Kim crossed the line. She tricked her way in here, and she screwed us over. I can forgive a lot of things, Claire, but I can't forgive her for this."

"So you were going to leave us behind."

His eyes flared hot. "Because I care about you. Yes. Do you know how close Eve came to getting herself killed tonight? And Shane? No more. I'm not risking you guys, not for this. Not for *her.*"

"Hey! You're not our father! You can't just decide we need protecting—we're all in this together!"

"No," he said. "We're not. Some of us get hurt a lot easier than others, and I love you guys. I'm not going to lose you. Not like this."

He stripped off his ripped shirt and pulled on another one, grabbed his keys from the table, and very gently picked Claire up and moved her when she tried to block his path. "Don't," he said. "Claire, I mean it. Don't tell them where I went. Let me handle this."

She didn't say anything.

She didn't want to lie to him.

Michael stared at her for a few long seconds, long enough that she was almost sure he could read her mind, and then he shoved his keys in his pocket and moved off down the stairs.

She sat down on his bed, staring up at the vent where she'd found the camera. Claire didn't actually know what she was going to do until she heard Michael's new replacement car starting up outside, and then she stood, walked down to the kitchen, and interrupted an intense conversation between Shane and Eve at the sink to say, "Michael's gone to get Kim, and we need to go, right now."

They both stopped and looked over their shoulders at her. Eve had her arms elbow-deep in soapy water. Shane held a dish towel and a plate.

"Right now," Claire repeated. "Please."

Eve yanked the plug on the sink, grabbed the towel from Shane's hands, and wiped her hands and arms. She three-pointed the towel onto the counter. "I'll drive," she said, and ran to grab her keys. Shane stayed where he was, still holding the plate in one hand, watching Claire. He opened his mouth.

"Don't you dare tell me I can't go," she said. "Don't even, Shane. I'm on those videos, too. You *know* I am."

He put the plate down. "Michael went alone?"

"Mr. Vampire Superhero doesn't need backup." Well, that wasn't quite fair. "He's meeting Detective Hess there. But still."

The kitchen door swung open, and Eve blazed back in, vivid in black and white, a mime on a mission. She tossed her keys in a nervous jingle of metal and said, "Weapons."

Nobody argued that it would only be Kim they were going up against. Shane grabbed a black nylon bag from under the counter—in other towns, people might keep emergency supplies of food and water, maybe a medical kit, but in Morganville, their emergency readiness kit consisted of stakes and silver-coated knives. "Got it," he said, and tossed it over one shoulder. "Claire—"

"Don't *even!*"

He grinned and tossed her a second bag. "Silver nitrate and water in a Super Soaker," he told her. "My own invention. Ought to be good at twenty feet, kind of like wasp spray."

Oh. "You get me the nicest things."

"Anybody can get jewelry. Posers."

Eve rolled her eyes. "Let's go, comedian."

As she tossed the keys again, Shane grabbed them in midair. "I may be a comedian, but you look like a mime. Anybody ever tell you that?"

He dashed for the door. Eve followed. Claire shouldered the nylon bag and prepared to shut the door of the house; as she did, she felt a wave of emotion sweep through her. The house, Michael's house, was worried. It was *almost* alive, some of the time. Like now.

"It'll be okay," she told it, and patted the countertop. "He'll be okay. *We'll* be okay."

The lights dimmed a little as she shut the door.

Eve's car wouldn't start.

"Um ... this isn't good," Eve said as Shane cranked the engine again. There was a click, and nothing. "You've got to be kidding me. This is *not* the time, stupid evil hunk of junk!" She slapped the dashboard, which had zero effect. "Come on, *work!*"

It was very dark outside—no streetlights on, and the moon and stars were veiled by thick, fast-moving clouds. In the glow of the dashboard, Shane and Eve looked worried. Shane pulled the old-fashioned lever under the dash, and the hood of the car popped up with a thick *clunk* of metal. "Stay inside," he said. "I'm going to take a look."

"Because you've got guy parts, you're automatically a better mechanic than me? I don't *think* so," Eve said, and bailed out of the passenger side. Shane banged the back of his head against the seat.

"Seriously," he said. "Why is it always so hard with her?"

"She's worried," Claire said.

"We're all worried. *You* stay in the car."

"*I* don't know anything about cars. I will."

"Finally, a girl with some sense." He leaned over the seat to kiss her, then got out to join Eve as she hauled the giant, heavy hood of the car upward. From that point on, Claire had a limited view of what was going on—the hood, the dark night outside, some lights glowing in nearby houses. . . .

A car turned the corner, and its headlights swept color over darkness, lighting up the Glass House in all its decaying Victorian glory, then the sun-faded picket fence, the spring crop of weeds along the curb. . . .

And then came a group of vampires out of the darkness, heading for Shane and Eve. One of them was Morley, the skanky homeless dude from the cemetery. She supposed the others were his friends; they didn't look as polished and well-groomed as most of the other vamps seemed to be. These looked hungry, mean, and dirty.

Claire lunged across the big bench seat from the back and slammed her hand down on the horn. It was as loud as a foghorn, and she heard a sharp bang as either Eve or Shane hit their head on the hood of the car as they straightened up.

"Guys!" she yelled. "Trouble!"

Shane, one hand held to the top of his head, opened the back door and pulled her out. "Door," he said. "Get back inside. The car thing isn't happening."

Claire didn't argue. She dug her front door key out of her jeans pocket as she ran, banged open the front gate, and skidded to a halt in front of the door. The porch light flickered on.

"Thanks," she told the house absently, jammed the key into the lock, and opened the door.

Shane was at the foot of the steps, but he'd stopped, looking back.

Eve was trapped between the car and the house, and she was surrounded by vampires. Claire gasped, and saw that neither Shane nor Eve had had time to grab the weapons bag out of the car.

She still had hers.

Morley lunged forward, slamming Eve against the rounded fender of her car, and Eve's scream of panic split the night. Shane rushed toward her, pulling a stake from his jacket, but it wasn't going to help. There were six of them, all with vampire strength.

He'd get himself killed.

Claire zipped open the bag and pulled out the big plastic Super Soaker. It was a totally absurd color of neon, and it was heavy with a full load of water.

God, please work. Please work.

Claire moved forward at a run, and pressed the trigger. A shockingly thick spray shot out, hit the sidewalk, and splashed; she quickly angled it up, over the fence, and sprayed it in an arc across Shane's back, the vampires turning to meet him, Morley, Eve.

Where it hit exposed vampire skin, the solution of silver powder and water lit them up like Christmas trees. The bony woman with long dark hair heading for Shane broke off with a yelp, slapped at her burning face, and then gaped at the burns on her hands as the solution began to eat away at her flesh.

Claire pumped the toy gun again, building up pressure, and put it to her shoulder as she came to a flat-footed stop. "Back off!" she yelled. "Everybody just *stop!* You, let her go!" That last was directed at Morley, who had Eve by the shoulder and was holding her in front of him. He was wearing a filthy old raincoat, and it had protected him from the spray; she could see a livid burn spreading across his cheek, but nothing that would really hurt him.

Shane backed up next to Claire, breathing hard. She aimed the Super Soaker directly at Morley and Eve. "Let her go," she repeated. "We didn't do anything to you."

"Nothing personal," Morley said. "We're starving, love. And you're so juicy."

"Ewww," Eve said faintly. "Has anybody ever told you that you smell like tombstones?"

He glanced at her and smiled. "You're the first," he assured her. "Which is a bit charming. I'm Morley. And you are . . . ? Ah yes. Amelie's friend. I remember you from the cemetery. Sam Glass's grave."

"Nice to meet you. Don't eat me, 'kay?"

He laughed and combed her hair back from her pale face. "You're cute. I might have to turn you and keep you as a pet."

"Hey!" Claire said sharply, and took a step forward. "Didn't you hear me? *Let her go!* She's under Amelie's protection!"

"I see no bracelet." Morley grabbed Eve's arm and lifted it to the dim light, turning it this way and that. "No, definitely nothing there." He kissed the back of her hand, then extended his fangs and prepared to munch out on the pale veins at her wrist.

Eve twisted and punched him in the mouth.

Morley stumbled backward against the car, and Claire triggered the sprayer, coating him in silver spray. This time, he screamed and flapped his arms and lunged away from Eve, toward the darkness. Claire sprayed the rest of his crew again as they followed, waking howls of pain and anger.

Shane dashed forward, vaulted the gate, and helped Eve stand up from where Morley had shoved her. "That went well," he said. His voice was shaking. "No fang marks, right?"

"Lucky me," Eve said, and laughed wildly. "Get the weapons bag. I can't *believe* you left it in the car; what was that? What town did *you* grow up in?"

"I was trying to help you fix the car!"

"Bozo." She hugged him, hard, and smacked him on the back of the head; then she took a deep breath as Shane left her to retrieve the black nylon bag out of the car. "And you."

Claire lowered the Super Soaker. "What? What did I do?"

"Saved my life? Redefined awesome in our time?"

"Oh. Okay." She felt a smile bloom from deep inside, and for a moment, it was all good.

Really good.

"Ladies," Shane said, and slammed the car door. "Let's have the champagne inside, okay? And talk about who pulled the wires in the engine, and how we're planning to back Michael up with no wheels?"

He had a point. Claire covered their retreat with the Super Soaker, feeling kind of like a neon-gunned Rambo, and Eve slammed and locked the door, then put her back to the wood and breathed a deep sigh of relief.

The second Claire put the water gun down, Shane wrapped her in his arms and kissed her, really tender and sweet and a little bit desperate. Hot.

"Hey," Eve said. "Michael, remember? What are we doing for transpo, cabbing it?"

There was exactly one taxicab in Morganville, and he didn't work at night, so that wasn't much of an option. They didn't even bother to discuss it. "Well," Claire said, very reluctantly, "there's another way. But you won't like it."

"I'll like it less than getting molested by a vampire in a flasher raincoat who smells like graveyards? Try me."

"I could open a portal," Claire said. "But I've never been to the radio station, so I can't risk doing it blind. I have to go someplace close that I know. What's around it?"

"Hang on a second," Shane said, and dropped the weapons bag to the wood floor with a thump. "What about Ada? You said she was out for blood, right?"

"I said you wouldn't like the idea."

"So just to recap—Ada wants to kill you, and you're going to walk through a portal she controls?"

"Well—"

"No, Claire. Next."

"But—"

"Not happening."

She sighed. "What if I get Myrnin to open it for us? He's better at it. I don't think she dares mess with him directly."

"And tell Myrnin what's happening? Bad idea. The dude is half crazy all the time."

"So what's *your* bright idea?" Claire asked. Shane spread his hands out. "That's what I thought."

She pulled her cell phone out and checked the screen. Her battery was getting low; she hadn't had a chance to charge it up recently, although that was Morganville Survival 101. She picked up the old-fashioned landline phone on the hall table and dialed Myrnin's lab.

It rang, and rang, and rang, and finally, Myrnin picked up. "What?" he snapped. "I was in the middle of dinner."

Claire was afraid to ask who that was. "I need help," she said.

"Claire, you are my assistant. Not the other way around. Perhaps it would be helpful if I prepared an organizational chart you could keep on your person. Possibly tattooed on your arm."

He *was* in a mood. Claire bit her lip. "Please," she said. "It's a little favor."

"Oh, all right. What?"

"You know the old radio station outside of town? KV—" Her mind blanked. She looked at Eve, who mouthed the answer. "KVVV. Could you open me a portal?"

"Hmmm," he said. She heard the sound of liquid being poured in the background, and him swallowing it, and him smacking his lips. "Well, I suppose I could get you close, if not inside the building. Would that do?"

"Sure. Anything."

"And why can you not do this yourself?"

"Ada . . . ?"

Myrnin was silent for a long few seconds. "She's better," he said. "I don't know what got into the old girl. But I've had a talk with her, and really, she's much better now. Much better."

"That's good." It would be, if it were true, but Claire didn't trust Myrnin's judgment when it came to Ada. "Um, about that portal—"

"Yes, fine, coming right up. I will be there in a moment."

"No, Myrnin—"

He hung up before she could explain that she didn't actually need him to come along. Not that he was going to listen to her, anyway. Claire replaced the phone on its cradle.

"Crazy boss is coming," Shane interpreted, just from the expression on her face. "Lovely. This ought to be fun."

About five seconds later, Claire felt a psychic wave sweep through the house, so strong she was surprised neither Shane nor Eve seemed to feel it, and then a dark opening formed in the far wall of the living room, and Myrnin stepped over the threshold.

"I *so* want his wardrobe," Eve sighed. "Is that shallow, or just strange?"

"Don't sell yourself short. It's both," Shane said, and cocked his head to take in Myrnin's latest effort at blending in. It was ... interesting. Claire couldn't decide if it was some deliberate, unholy mix of Victorian lord and hippie, or just what had been on the floor of his closet.

He had on his bunny slippers.

These had fangs.

They all stared at them in silence for about a heartbeat, and then Shane said, "*That* is impressively wicked. Crazy, but wicked."

Myrnin frowned at him, then looked down at his shoes. He seemed genuinely surprised. "Oh. Those. I thought—well, they're appropriate, I suppose."

"Wouldn't want to be inappropriate," Claire said. "You really didn't have to come. I'm sorry."

"I did, in fact. I tried to open the portal to the radio station, and I couldn't do so." Myrnin's dark eyes were wide and gleaming, clearly fascinated. "Claire, do you know what this means?" He paced, the bunny slippers flopping their ears in a very distracting way. "Someone locked down the area. And it wasn't me."

"Who else could?"

"No one."

"But—"

"Exactly!" He smacked his hands together in glee. "A mystery! Thank you for calling and imposing on me for a favor; this is very exciting stuff, you know. Chaos, mayhem, someone stealing a march on me—ah, I've missed it these past few months, haven't you?"

"No," they all said, exactly together. Claire took Shane's hand and said, "Myrnin, who else could lock down areas of town and freeze out portals?"

"Amelie," he said, "but it's not her. There's a certain signature to her work, and by the way, she's been here recently. Did you know? She reeks of pain these days. It's most disturbing."

"Dude, *focus*," Eve said. "Who else?" She threw Claire a why-am-I-even-asking look, but Myrnin got hold of himself and nodded as he thought about it.

"There have been a total of six others in the history of Morganville," he said. "But they're all dead. All but you, Claire."

They all looked at her. She blinked. "Well, *I* didn't do it!"

"Oh. Pity. Then I have no idea."

She cleared her throat. "What about Ada?"

"Ada is not the boogeyman behind every shadow, my dear," Myrnin said, and flopped himself down in Michael's chair, taking hold of the acoustic guitar and picking out a surprisingly competent series of chords. "Ada does as she's told. Unlike you, I might add, which is not an attractive quality in a lab assistant."

"Could she do it?"

He stilled the strings with one hand, and looked up. His dark hair fell back from his pale face, and for a moment, he looked entirely serious. "Ada can do anything," he said. "I don't think even she understands that. But I find it highly unlikely—"

"You're a vampire wearing bunny slippers with fangs. Highly unlikely kind of goes with the territory," Eve said. "How close can you get us? To the radio station?"

"Why do you want to go there? It's hardly safe for untagged blood donors to roam around out there after dark. Even Claire would be at risk, and she's wearing the strongest protection available. I don't advise it." He put the guitar aside and steepled his fingers together. "But you're not quite foolish enough to be doing it for the thrill, I think, so you do have a reason. Tell me."

Claire exchanged a quick look with her friends, and then said, "Michael went alone out there. We need to help him."

"Michael is a vampire. Vampires go out at night." Myrnin shrugged and dusted a bit of fluff from his black velvet jacket, which was pretty elegant, if you were heading off to a costume party. "Why concern your-self, unless you think there will be trouble? Stop lying by omission, Claire. Tell me everything. Now."

Eve shook her head, a tiny spasm that was probably involuntary. Even Shane looked like he thought it was a terminally bad idea. Claire said, "We can trust him. We have to trust him."

"Oh, this sounds interesting," Myrnin said, and leaned forward in Michael's chair. "Please continue."

She did. She even brought down one of the wireless cameras, showed it to him, and explained how it worked, which was a complete delight to his obsessively scientific side. "But this is amazing," he said, turning the little device over in his nimble fingers. "This girl, she's quite the enterpris-ing little thing. How many of these, you say?"

"We think seventy-two."

He lost his smile, focusing on the object in his hand. "She can't be doing it alone, then. There must be a larger purpose. A larger plan. Still, this Kim, she may be using it for her own purposes; have you thought about that?"

"We know she's getting her own thing out of it," Claire said. "But you're saying . . . she didn't come up with it in the first place?"

"Exactly."

So, maybe Kim had been recruited to put cameras out, and then hi-jacked it for her own reality-show dream project . . . but that meant some-one else was in charge.

Someone smart enough to not get caught. Or even suspected.

"You really should tell Oliver," Myrnin said. "I know he's not the most pleasant of allies, but he is effective in the right circumstances. Rather like one of those nuclear bombs."

"If we tell Oliver, Kim's dead," Eve said. "She may be an epic bitch, but I don't want her executed, either."

"Valid," Myrnin agreed. "However, if this goes wrong, she's dead in any case. I will come along. You need an adult chaperone."

"Once again, bunny slippers," Shane said. "I'm just pointing that out."

"I suppose they would get dirty. I'll be right back." Myrnin jumped out of the chair and dashed for the portal. It snapped shut behind him with a flare of energy.

"Do you think—"

Before Shane could finish the question, the portal opened again, and Myrnin hopped out on one foot, pulling on serious pirate boots, the knee-high kind with the cuff of leather. He finished tugging the left one on and did a runway pose for Claire. "Better?"

"Um . . . yeah, I guess." He now looked like a demented version of that pirate captain from the rum bottles.

"Then let's go."

As he turned to concentrate on the portal, Eve tugged on Claire's shirt.

"What?"

"Ask him where he got the boots."

"*You* ask." Personally, Claire wanted the vampire bunny slippers.

TWELVE

The closest Myrnin could get them was a few blocks away. Claire was glad, actually, that he hadn't warned her where they were going; she wasn't sure she'd have been able to step through if he had.

German's Tire Plant had closed at least thirty years ago, and the gigantic, multistory facility was basically one big gold mine of creepy. Claire had been in it exactly twice before, and neither visit held pleasant memories—and those had been daytime excursions. At night, the terror level went way, way up.

The only reason she knew they were at German's Tire Plant was that the weapons bag Shane had brought contained flashlights, and one of the first things Claire's lit up was the spooky clown face graffitied around a big open maw of a doorway. She'd never forget that stupid clown face. Ever.

"Oh man," Shane breathed. He wasn't fond of this place, either.

"Buck up," Eve said. "At least you didn't get locked in a freezer here like next month's entrée. I did."

Myrnin, blue-white in the flashlight beams, looked offended. "Young lady, I put you there for safekeeping. If I had meant to eat you, I would have."

"That's comforting," Eve said. And then, under her breath, "Not."

"This way." Myrnin put out his hand to shield his eyes from their flashlights, and picked his way around a pile of tottering, empty beer cans left by adventurous high schoolers, a stained, torn mattress, and some empty crates. "Someone's been here."

"No kidding?"

"I mean, recently," he said. "Not humans. Vampires. Many of them." He sounded a little puzzled. "Not my creatures, either. They all died, you know. The ones I turned."

Back in his crazy (crazier?) days, Myrnin had experimented on some hapless victims, trying to turn them into vampires but failing as his illness took hold. The results hadn't been pretty—more like zombies than vampires, and not focused on anything but killing. Claire wondered how they'd died, and decided she really didn't want to know. Myrnin was a scientist. He was used to putting down lab animals at the end of a test.

"Are these vampires hanging around now?" Shane asked. He had a stake in his left hand, and a silver-coated knife in the other—a steak knife he'd used a car battery and a fish tank full of chemicals to electroplate. Stinky, but cheap and effective. "Because a heads-up would be nice."

"No, they're gone." Myrnin continued to hesitate, though. "I wonder. . . ."

"Wonder later. Move now," Eve said. She sounded nervous, and she kept shining the light around erratically, reacting to every rustle in the dark. There were a lot of those. Rats, birds, bats—the place was full of wildlife. Claire kept her own light trained on the path ahead of her, making sure she didn't trip or cut herself on rusty juts of metal as Myrnin led the way. Shane's warmth behind her felt good. So did the weight of the Super Soaker in her arms.

Myrnin threw open a metal door with a snap, shattering the lock and scattering links of the big chain that had secured it all over the pitted concrete outside. "There," he said, and pointed as they gathered around him. The clouds thinned a little, allowing some diffuse moonlight to paint the ground with cool blue and silver, and a mile or so away sat a concrete block of a building, and a tall, skeletal metal tower. Big white letters on the tower said KV V; one of the Vs was long gone, and the other was tilting drunkenly to one side, not far from dropping off entirely to join its missing mate. The place looked deserted. Wind rattled over the flat landscape, whipping up dust and scattering trash, and made an eerie whistling sound through the metal of the tower.

"I don't see Michael's car."

"One way to be sure," Myrnin said. "Let's go."

The closer they came, the creepier the place was. Claire wasn't a fan of blighted industrial buildings, and Morganville was full of them—the half-destroyed hospital, German's Tire Plant, even the old City Hall had its decaying side.

This one looked so . . . grim. It was just a cinder block building, not very large, and the one window in front had been long ago broken out and boarded over. Someone had spray-painted KEEP OUT on the bricks, and part of it was heavily decorated in multicolored swirls of graffiti. Beer cans, cigarette butts, empty plastic bags—the usual stuff.

"I don't see a way in," Eve whispered.

"Why are you whispering?" Myrnin whispered back. "Vampires can hear us, anyway."

"Is there a vampire in there?" Claire asked.

"I'm not psychic. I have no idea."

"You could tell in the tire plant!"

He tapped his nose. "Five senses. Not six. It's not so easy to sniff them out standing outside the building." He gently moved the business end of her Super Soaker away from himself. "Please. I bathed already, and I'd rather not do it in the vampire equivalent of pepper spray."

"Sorry."

They made their way around the side of the building, closer to the tower, and there they found Michael's dark sedan sitting in the shadows.

Empty.

"Michael?" Eve called. "Michael!"

"Hush," Myrnin said sharply, and flashed supernaturally fast across the open space to grab the knob of a door Claire could barely see. It sagged open, and he disappeared inside.

"Wait!" Claire blurted, and darted after him. She switched on the flashlight as soon as she reached the door, but all it showed her was an empty hallway, with peeling paint and a floor covered in mud from some old flood. "Myrnin, where are you?"

No answer. She yelped when Shane's hand closed over her shoulder; then she pulled in a breath and nodded. Eve crowded in behind them.

Down the hallway was a dead end, with more hallways stretching left and right. The fading paint had some kind of mural on it, something West Texas-y with cows and cowboys, and the letters KVVV in big block capitals.

The whole place smelled like mold and dead animals.

"This way," Myrnin's voice said quietly, and with a hum, electricity turned on in the hall. Some of the bulbs burned out with harsh, sizzling snaps, leaving parts of the space in darkness.

Claire followed the hall to the end, where it took a right turn into a small studio with some kind of engineering board. The equipment looked ancient, but clean; somebody had been here—presumably Kim—and had taken care to put everything in working order. Microphones, a chair, a backdrop, lighting . . . everything in the studio needed for filming, including a small digital video camera on a tripod.

On the other side of the room was a complicated editing console, which had a bank of monitors set up. They obviously weren't original to the setup—decades more modern than the soundboard—and Claire identified different components that had been Frankensteined into the system.

These included an array of fat black terabyte drives, all portable.

Michael was sitting at the console. "Michael!" Eve blurted, and threw herself on him; he stood up to catch her in his arms, and hugged her close. "You incredible *jerk!*"

He kissed her hair. "Yeah, I know."

She smacked his arm. "Really. You are a jerk!"

"I get that." He pushed her off a little, to look at her. "You're okay?"

"No thanks to you. You had to go running off in the middle of the night and not even say boo . . ."

"I should have known you guys wouldn't stay put."

"Where's Detective Hess?" Claire asked. "I thought you were meeting him here."

"Yeah, I did."

"Where did he go?"

"I'll tell you that in a minute." Michael seemed preoccupied, as if he were trying to figure out how to tell them something they weren't going to like at all. "This is Kim's data vault. At least, most of it. Claire, that's a router, right? I think this is her receiving station for the signals."

"She's using the tower to amplify the signals," Claire said. "Did you find—?" She didn't want to get more specific than that. Michael shook his head, and her heart fell. "What about the other ones?"

"She's been a busy girl," Michael said. "There are video files there from City Hall, Common Grounds, spots all over town. It will take hours, maybe weeks, to look at everything, but she's done a rough cut." He hit some controls, then pointed at the central monitor. "This is the raw file."

After some old-fashioned leader signals, there was a shot of the Morganville town limits sign, creaking in the wind . . . and then, in special effects, the word *Vampires* appeared in bloody streaks right below the sign.

"Subtle." Eve snorted. "She's got a future in Hollywood."

Kim's voice came on, breathlessly narrating. "Welcome to Morganville, the town with bite. If you've ever driven across the barren landscape of West Texas, you may wonder why people live out here in the middle of nowhere. Well, wonder no more. It's because they can't live anywhere else without people knowing what they are."

The visuals cut to a montage of Morganville daily life—normal, boring stuff.

And then a night-vision shot of a vampire—Morley, Claire realized with a shock—sucking the blood out of someone's neck. It was an extreme close-up. His eyes were like silver coins, and the blood looked black.

Cut to Eve, working the counter at the coffee shop in all her Goth glory. Eve sucked in a quick breath, but said nothing. More shots of Morganville, some handheld. Claire saw footage of students, and remembered Kim running around the campus with her digital camera, asking people stupid questions.

It was in there, and so was Claire, saying, "I have two words for you, and the second one is *off.* Fill in the blank."

Claire covered her mouth with both hands. God, she looked so *angry.* And kind of bitchy.

It got worse, with the voice-over. "Even the normal people of Morganville aren't so normal. Take my friends who live in this house."

A shot of the Glass House, full daylight. Then some kind of hidden-camera thing of Kim knocking on the door, Eve answering.

A shot of Shane. One of Michael.

"Living in a town full of terror doesn't mean you can't find true love—or at least, real sex."

The video morphed into Claire and Shane in his bedroom. *Oh God no . . .* Claire felt sick and hot and breathless, full of horror at seeing herself there on that screen. She stumbled away and almost threw herself into Shane's arms. He, lips parted, was staring at the picture, looking just as horrified as she felt. But he couldn't look away, while she simply couldn't watch.

"Goodness," Myrnin said quietly. "I don't think I should be watching this. I don't think I'm old enough."

"Turn it off," Shane said. "Michael."

Instead of turning it off, Michael hit FAST FORWARD. He slowed it down as the scene changed. More Kim voyeur porn, this time Michael and Eve. No voice-over. Claire couldn't imagine what she was intending to say, but it couldn't have been good.

"I'll kill her," Eve said. It sounded calm, but it really wasn't. "Why are you showing me this?"

Michael looked at her, and Claire's stomach did a little flip at the grimness in his expression. "Sit down," he said, and wheeled the chair closer to Eve. She looked at it, then at him, frowning. "Trust me."

She did, still frowning, as the scene changed on-screen.

It was some dark-paneled room, with a big wooden round table, an ornate flower arrangement in the middle. Of the several people around the table, Claire recognized three immediately, with a shock. "Amelie," she blurted. Amelie clearly had no idea she was being filmed; the camera was high up, at an angle, but it caught their faces clearly. Next to her at the table was Richard Morrell, the mayor, neat and handsome in a dark suit. At his right sat Oliver, looking—as usual—angry. Several other people around the table were talking at once; arguing, and finally Oliver slammed his hand down on the wood with so much force it silenced them all.

Then came Kim's voice-over. "Morganville is ruled by a town council, but one not like any other. Nobody elects these people. That's Amelie, Founder of Morganville. She's more than a thousand years old, and she's a ruthless killer. Oliver's not much younger, and he's even meaner. The mayor, Richard Morrell, he's new, but his family has ruled the humans of Morganville for a hundred years. Richard's the only human on the council. And he gets outvoted . . . constantly."

She cut back to the sound as Richard was saying, ". . . want to revisit the decision we made earlier, about Jason Rosser."

"What about him?" Oliver asked irritably. "We've heard your arguments. Let's move on."

"You can't execute him. He gave himself up. He tried to save the girl."

"He did *not* try to save Claire," Amelie said. "He left her to die. Granted, he did turn himself in to the police and told us about his accomplice in these murders, but we must be clear: he is far from innocent, and his history tells us he can't be trusted."

"He's still a kid," Richard said, "and you can't just arbitrarily decide to execute him. Not without a trial."

"With a majority vote, we can," Oliver said. "Two for, one against. I believe that is a majority. It won't be a public event. He'll just quietly—disappear."

Eve's mouth dropped open. She leaned forward, frantically searching the screen for a clue. "When was this? Michael? When did she record this?"

"I don't know," he said. "I thought you should know. Your brother's been sentenced to death."

"Oliver—he didn't even—he didn't say *anything.*"

"Well," Myrnin said, "I don't suppose he felt it was necessary. I expect they were planning to arrange something quiet, perhaps an accident. Or suicide."

Eve fell into the chair, and blindly reached out for Michael, who took her hand. "They can't just kill him. Not like some—rat in a cage. Oh God, Michael . . ."

"I told you Detective Hess was here. He left right after we found that. He's going straight to the jail to be sure Jason's okay. He'll put him in protective custody, okay? Don't worry."

She gave out a breathless, broken laugh. "Don't worry? How do I not worry after you show me things like this?"

"Good point," Shane said. "Michael, Kim bugged the council meeting. How could she possibly do that?"

"She couldn't," Myrnin said. "The human parts of town, yes, of course, but not the vampire parts. She has no excuse to be there, and she'd be caught if she'd gone anywhere near the official chambers. Or Amelie's house." He held up another black hard drive, which was clearly labeled in silver ink. "Or Oliver's, for that matter."

Claire caught her breath. "Your lab?"

"No. Oddly enough, nothing. But the evidence she has here is damning enough, I would say."

"But nobody would believe it," Eve said. "I mean, sure, she might get some off-brand cable station to air it, but everybody would think it was some kind of hoax."

"Doesn't matter," Claire said. "Even if nobody does, tourists will come flocking to town, and how long do you think things will hold together once that happens?"

"I'd give it a week," Myrnin said. He sounded quiet, and not at all amused. "This is our refuge, Claire. Our last safe place in this world. Don't be fooled; we might be willing to compromise, but we are territorial. Kim has violated the deepest covenant of Morganville. She can't survive this."

"She didn't do it alone; you said so yourself. It took a vampire to bug the council, let alone Amelie's house."

"And we will find them," Myrnin said. "And we will destroy them. There are rules to Morganville, and Kim and this vampire have shattered them beyond all repair. Amelie must never know of this. I'm afraid what she would do."

That seemed a strange left turn. "Why? We're going to catch them, right? We've got the video."

"Do we?" Myrnin looked at the array of hard drives. "You spoke of more than seventy cameras, but I see only sixty or so hard drives. What's missing, Claire? You know Amelie. You know that her first concern is for her people. If she believes that we've been compromised here, she will cut our losses."

"Losses being humans," Shane said.

"She'd rather move us and destroy all evidence we were ever here. It's always been her final option. You have no idea how many times she's come close recently."

Claire swallowed. "We can't let her do that."

"We cannot stop her," Myrnin said. "Not even I can do that. But what we can do is remove the evidence."

He crushed the hard drive he was holding into junk and dropped it to the floor, then moved on to the next, and the next.

Michael helped Eve out of the chair, picked it up, and smashed it into the editing station. He ripped out the hard drive from the video editing system and smashed it against the wall.

Claire and Eve backed up against the wall, holding hands, as the two vampires systematically destroyed every bit of data storage in the place. It took a while, but they were thorough, and when the last piece of equipment was broken into random parts, Shane said, "I thought that would feel better, somehow."

"We're not finished," Myrnin said. "We need to find every camera and destroy those, as well. And we *must* find Kim and force her to tell us who helped her. This is not negotiable. A vampire traitor is far too dangerous to live."

Kim had kept records—a hard copy printout stuffed in a cabinet drawer next to the wrecked editing machine. It listed a total of seventy-*four* cameras, all over Morganville. "She must have added a couple at the last minute. This is going to take hours," Eve said. "We'll have to split up, each take ten or so. Myrnin and Michael, you've got the Vamptown cameras. Claire, Shane, here you go. Knock yourselves out."

"What about Kim?" Claire asked, taking the page of locations. "We still need to find her."

"I will ask Ada to locate her," Myrnin said.

"She can do that?" Claire asked, and then blinked. "Of course she can. *Will* she do that?"

"Possibly. If she's in a good mood, which is never certain, as you know. But I assure you, Ada is no longer angry at you, so don't be worried about that." Myrnin checked a gleaming gold pocket watch he kept in his vest pocket, some complicated dragon-shaped thing. "We must meet back before sunrise. Where?"

"Someplace deserted," Claire said. "Much as I hate it, how about German's? I don't want anybody overhearing us."

"Paranoid much?" Eve asked. "Yeah, me too. I'm never taking my clothes off again, I swear."

"German's it is," Myrnin said. "You know the portal frequency. Be there before sunrise, and do try to avoid getting yourself killed, if at all possible."

He led them out of the studio, out into the night. Michael took his car, heading off with his list of camera locations. At German's, Myrnin stepped through the dark clown-mouth doorway and was gone on his own errands, leaving Shane, Eve, and Claire standing there in the dark, in a fragile circle of flashlight.

"So?" Eve prodded. "Fire it up, Teleport Girl. I want this over with."

Claire checked the list. "Right. The first twenty are easy—all in common areas. Eve, I'll send you and Shane to the alley behind Common Grounds. I'll take the university."

"Hey," Shane said. "Wait a minute. I don't want you out there alone."

"University," Claire reminded him. "Protected ground. Besides, I'm the one with the bracelet." She flashed the gold at him, and he didn't look happy, but he did look resigned. "Also, we've got no time to argue. Go."

Shane looked back at her before he stepped through the portal, and

Claire felt a moment's sick fear that she'd never see him again. Morganville was a dangerous place. Every good-bye could be the last.

We'll get through this.

She focused on the portal, shifted frequencies, and started on her camera-destroying mission.

She hoped Myrnin was right about Ada.

Four hours later, it was approaching sunrise. Claire was bone-tired, and she'd bagged all of the cameras on her list, including the one in the football team's shower room, which was an interesting experience. Kim had clearly been combining business with personal pleasure. She took the portal back to the alley behind Common Grounds, intending to pick up Shane and Eve, but they were nowhere in sight. She called Shane's cell, and heard it ringing, but it was distant and muffled.

She found him standing braced against the wall, holding Eve's ankles as she stood on his shoulders to reach a camera set on top of the roof of a shed. "Got it!" Eve called, and nearly overbalanced. Shane staggered around, got his equilibrium again, and helped her down to the pavement. "We should totally join the circus."

"One of us already looks like a clown."

"Hi, guys," Claire said, and they both jumped and turned her way. "Sorry. Didn't mean to scare you."

Shane hugged her. "How'd you do?"

"Twenty cameras. There was one missing. I think somebody found it and swiped it from the University Center. You?"

"That was the last one on the list," he said. "Guess it's time to see how Team Vampire did."

Claire opened the portal to German's Tire Plant, and stepped through, with Shane and Eve right behind her. The portal snapped shut as soon as they were inside, and Claire flipped on her flashlight.

"Um . . ." Eve turned on her light, as well. "Okay. Wrong number, Claire."

"No," Claire said. "That can't happen. I mean, it's the right frequency. I don't know what happened, but we *should* be at German's."

"Well, we're not," Shane said, and shone his light around. They were in an underground tunnel. It was damp and dark and it smelled really foul—much worse than most of the vampire highway tunnels under Morganville. This one didn't look like it had been used for a road, either. "Wrong turn."

Eve said, in an entirely different voice, "*Really* wrong turn." She pointed off down the tunnel, and Claire saw shapes moving in the darkness. Pale skin. Shining red eyes. "Oh man. Dial us out, please."

The only problem was that the portal system refused to pick up. They were locked out.

Claire looked at Shane and Eve and shook her head. Her heart was pounding a mile a minute, and she could see the light trembling from the force of her pulse beats. "We're stuck," she said.

Shane dropped the bag he was carrying, unzipped it, and passed weapons to Eve, then took out a wicked-lethal crossbow with silver-tipped bolts. "Somebody up there doesn't like you, Claire."

Claire primed the Super Soaker. "It's Ada," she said. "This time, I'm not letting Myrnin talk me out of it."

The vampires—well, vampirelike *things*, sort of like Myrnin's experimental attempts to turn humans back in his crazy days—hurled themselves out of the darkness with high-pitched, batlike squeals. Claire resisted the urge to scream, and let loose with the water gun. A blast caught three of them in midleap, and they shrieked even louder, hit the ground, rolled, and kept rolling. She could see the ghostly blue flare of flames around them as the silver ate into their exposed skin—which was most of it, because these things were more like tunnel rats than anything approaching human. Giant undead tunnel rats.

Only in Morganville . . .

Shane aimed and fired, taking one of them out just as it was preparing to leap, and reloaded with an ease that told Claire he'd been practicing. Eve had a handful of what looked like darts—regulation darts, the kind you threw at a target in a bar. She was dead-on accurate with them, too, as soon as any tunnel rat came within ten feet of her.

By the time Claire was starting to worry about her water reservoir, and Shane was running low on crossbow bolts, the attacking forces were running. "Let's go," Eve said, tossing another dart that landed in the ass of a retreating vampire. "Ooooh, trip twenty!"

"You're enjoying this way too much," Shane said. "Darts? When did you come up with that?"

"I was playing with your electroplating thingy. After I did all my jewelry, I started in on pointy things." Eve held out a dart for inspection. It had—of course—a skull on the fletching. "Sweet, right?"

"Cute. Time to run now."

Claire slung the Super Soaker around her back and ran up the hill, chasing Shane, who was, as always, faster—the result of longer legs, not really dedicated practice. Shane only ran when someone chased him; he was more of a weights kind of guy.

The fact that the tunnel tilted uphill was a good sign—it was basically an entrance ramp, which meant they'd come up to ground level soon enough. Then Claire could figure out where they were, how to find a working portal, and how to get back to the business at hand—find Kim, beat Kim like a taiko drum to find out who her vampire coconspirator was, and then hit Ada's RESET button.

Simple.

Except, of course, it wasn't.

Shane slowed, and Claire almost crashed into him. He dashed over to the side of the tunnel, hugging the wall, and Claire and Eve piled in next to him. "What?" Eve asked between breathless pants. She wasn't much for running, either.

"Someone's coming," Shane said. "Shhhh."

Eve choked and strangled on a cough, and muttered, "Got to cut down on the cigarettes."

"You don't smoke," Claire whispered.

"Then I'm completely screwed."

Shane whirled toward them and put hands over both their mouths. His face looked fierce. They nodded.

It was dark where they were, but not dark enough. A shape appeared ahead of them, coming down the tunnel . . . then another. Then more. Six—no, ten. Claire lost all will to snark, and she was pretty sure, from Eve's wide-eyed look, that Eve felt the same. They'd done pretty well against the tunnel rats, but these were *real* vampires.

Hunters.

Morley stopped about twenty feet away, still facing straight ahead, and held up a hand to stop the group of vampires following him. Claire recognized some of them from earlier. Some of them were still healing from the burns left by her water gun.

"Look who's come to visit," he said, and turned his head in their direction at the side of the tunnel. "Claire and her friends. I wonder if they want to stay for dinner."

Shane snapped the crossbow up and took aim on Morley. "Don't even think about it."

Morley stuck his hands in the pockets of his dirty raincoat. "I tremble in fear, boy. Obviously, in all my long life, no one has *ever* threatened me with a weapon before." His tone changed, took on edges. "Put it down if you want to live."

"Don't," Eve whispered.

Morley smiled. "The boy's got two arrows left," he said. "You have a handful of darts. Little Claire's water weapon is almost empty. And by the way, I am aware of your strategic position. I hate to repeat myself, but I will: put down your weapons if you want to live."

"No choice," Shane said, and swallowed hard. He crouched down and put the crossbow on the concrete, then rose with his hands up.

I could get in one good spray, Claire thought, but she knew it was a terrible idea. She lifted the strap of the toy gun over her head and let it fall. It sounded empty.

"Shit," Eve said, and threw down her darts. "All right. What now? You get all *Nosferatu* on our asses? If you make me a vampire, I'll make you eat those fangs."

Morley eyed her with a bit of a frown. "I believe you might," he said. "But I'm not interested in converts. I'm much more interested in allies."

"Allies," Claire repeated. "You've tried to kill us a whole bunch."

"That wasn't about you," he said. "The first time, you were simply with Amelie. The next, well, I was doing a favor for someone else. Another ally, as it happens."

"What do you want?"

"We want freedom," Morley said. "We want to live as God meant us to do. Is that such a terrible thing?"

There were a few vampires in his group that Claire recognized with a nasty jolt of surprise. "Jacob," she said. "Jacob Goldman? Patience?" Two of Theo Goldman's family—and Theo was the last vampire she'd expect to be in the middle of this. His kids, though . . . she really didn't know them very well.

Jacob looked away. Patience, on the other hand, stared right back, and lifted her chin as if daring Claire to say anything else. From her last encounter with the Goldmans, Claire had been aware the younger generation was starting to hate the whole philosophy of their parents; it made sense that they'd found someone here in Morganville more like-minded.

"Amelie and Oliver are trying to make us into something we never were," Patience said. "Tame tigers. Performing bears. Toothless lions. But we can't be those things. Vampires are not caretakers of humanity. I'm sorry, but it will never be true, however much we wish it could be."

"You're not making much headway on this *Let's be friends* argument," Eve said. "I'm just saying."

Morley let out an impatient sigh, and looked back at the other vampires. "Surely you want us out of your town," he said. "As much as we'd like to go. But Amelie won't allow us to leave. We have only two choices: destroy Morganville, or destroy her. Destroying Morganville seems easier, in many ways."

The light dawned. "You were working with Kim. She suggested the cameras, didn't she?"

"It seemed a way to achieve what she wanted, and what we wanted," he agreed. "The end of Morganville. The beginning of her career. Granted, spying is an unseemly way to go about it, but it's probably less objectionable than murder."

"Until the camera's on you," Eve shot back.

"A valid point." Morley bowed slightly in her direction.

"You're the one who put the cameras in Vamptown for her."

"Me?" His thick eyebrows climbed into his tangled hair. "No. I'm hardly welcome there, you know. Nor are any of my people. I know nothing about how she managed that."

"Then let us go find out who did."

"You know, I don't have to bargain with you. I could just distribute you among my followers as a treat if you'd prefer that."

"No," Jacob Goldman said. He and Patience exchanged a look that was more like a silent argument, and then he stepped forward. "Not her. Morley, if you hurt her, we walk away."

"Patience?"

She sighed and shook her head. "The girl helped, before," she said. "Theo wouldn't want us to hurt her."

"The girl left you in a cell to die at Bishop's hands!"

"That was my father's mistake, not hers," Jacob said. "I will do many things to get our freedom. I won't do this."

The tension was ramping up fast. Claire swallowed. "Then let's make a deal," Claire said. "We want Kim, and whatever video she turned over to you."

Morley frowned at her. "In exchange for . . . ?"

"I'll ask Amelie to let you all leave."

"*Asking* is an easy task; there's no commitment required. *Doing* is accomplishment. So you will *get* Amelie to let us leave. Here is my incentive: if you don't manage to secure her permission, your two friends here sign lifetime contracts to me." Morley turned to Jacob and Patience, who nodded. "You see? Even they agree with that."

"Oh *hell* no," Eve said.

"And you are in a position to bargain . . . how?"

Shane held out a hand toward Eve, trying to restrain her a little. "No lifetime contracts," he said. "One pint a month, blood bank only. Ten percent of our income."

"Hmmmmmm." Morley dragged the sound out, still staring through half-lidded eyes. "Tempting. But you see, I can simply insist on a lifetime contract with none of your silly restrictions, or kill you right now."

"You won't," Shane said. That made Morley's eyes open wide.

"Why not? Jacob and Patience were quite specific—they're concerned for Claire. Not for you, boy."

"Because if you kill me and Eve, you'll make her your enemy. This girl won't stop until she sees you all pay."

Claire had no idea whom he was talking about—she didn't feel like that Claire at all, until she imagined Shane and Eve lying dead on the ground.

Then she understood. "I'd hunt you down," she said quietly. "I'd use every resource I have to do it. And you know I'd win."

Morley seemed impressed. "She is small, but I see your point, boy. Besides, she has the ear of Amelie, Oliver, and Myrnin; not a combination I would care to test. Very well. Limited contract, one year, one pint per month at the blood bank, ten percent of your income payable to me, in cash. I will not hunt, bite, or trade your contracts. But I insist on standard punishment clauses."

"Hey," Eve said. "Don't I get a vote?"

"Absolutely," Morley assured her. "Your thoughts?"

"I'd rather die," she said flatly. Shane turned toward her, and from the look on his face, that was not at all what he'd expected her to say. "Don't look at me like that. I told you, I'll never sign a contract. *Never.* If Morlock here wants to kill me, well, I can't stop him. But I don't have to die by inches, either, and that's what this town does to us, Shane; it takes little pieces of us away until there's nothing left and *I won't sign!*" Eve's eyes flooded with tears, but she wasn't scared; she was angry. "So bite me, vampire. Get it over with. But it's a one-time thrill."

Morley shrugged. "And you, boy?"

Shane pulled in a deep breath. "No deals if Eve doesn't buy in."

Claire's mouth tasted like ashes, and she was trying frantically to think of something, *anything* to do. She tried to build a portal behind them, but the system bounced her back, wouldn't let her so much as begin the process.

Ada.

She took Shane's hand in hers. "You'll have to kill me, too," she said. "And you can't. Not without consequences."

Morley looked positively unhappy now. "This is getting far too complicated. Fine, then we do it this way. I give you the video you're looking for, and if you don't manage to secure Amelie's permission within, let's say, a month, your friends' lives are forfeit. Yes?" When she hesitated, he bared his stained teeth. "It's not a question, really. And my patience is wearing thin. In fact, it's positively threadbare."

"Yes," Claire said.

He spit on his palm and held it out. They all just looked at him. "Well?" he demanded.

"I'm not shaking that," Shane said. "You just spit on it."

"It's the way deals are sealed—" Morley made a sound of frustration and wiped his palm against his filthy clothes. "Perhaps not anymore. Better?"

"Not really," Shane said.

Claire stepped forward and shook Morley's hand. She'd done worse.

He turned, dirty raincoat flapping, and the other vampires fell in behind him. Jacob Goldman held back, staring at Claire. He looked unhappy and tormented.

"I wouldn't have let him do it," he said. "Not to any of you. But you understand why I have to do this? For myself, and Patience?"

"I understand," Claire said. She didn't, really, but it seemed to make him feel better.

Claire, Eve, and Shane picked up their weapons and followed them into the dark.

Morley's hideout was a series of what looked like limestone caves, hollowed out into actual rooms, with doors and windows—a city underground. Not fancy, but it was definitely livable, if you were sunlight averse. There were more vamps here, living rough, hiding out. Claire figured a lot of those who'd decided not to take sides during the Amelie and Bishop fight had fled down here, taken up with Morley's crew.

"I guess this means you aren't really homeless," she said. Morley looked back at her as he opened up the ancient, cracked door of one of the rooms. "I'd still look into running water." Because the place stank, bad. So did the vampires.

"We grew up in ages when running water meant streams and rivers," he said. "We've never been overly comfortable with modern luxuries."

"Like baths?"

"Oh, we had baths in the old days. We called them stews, and they caused diseases." He shoved open the door and lit a row of candles set into a kind of shelf along the side of the room, which gave off just enough light to make Claire feel she could turn her own portable lamp off. "What you're looking for is here, in the box."

The box was a rickety-looking crate with rope handles. Inside were more hard drives—the ones that had been missing from the radio station—and some DVDs. One was labeled, in black Sharpie, MICHAEL & EVE. Claire choked a little at the sight of it. She frantically combed through the others, but there was nothing marked SHANE & CLAIRE.

"Don't worry," Shane said. "The lighting was terrible on ours, anyway."

"Not funny."

"I know." He put his arm around her. "I know. Speaking of not funny, where's Kim? I'd like to tell her just how much I appreciate all she did to make us stars."

Morley nodded. "Follow me."

Three doors down was a much smaller cave—more like a cell—and Morley combed through an ancient ring of ancient keys until he found one to fit the huge rusty lock. "I keep her here for her own safety," he said. "You'll see."

He opened the door, and Kim cowered back from the wash of the flashlights—but not Kim. The face was the same, but all the Goth had been scrubbed off except the dyed hair. She was dirty, dressed in filthy clothes, and there was zero bad attitude left.

Claire had been prepared to let loose a flood of anger, but this was just . . . pathetic. "Kim?" No response. "Kim! What did you do to her?"

"Nothing. She doesn't respond to her name," Morley said. "It seems she's lost her mind."

"Bullshit," Eve snapped. "She's an actress."

"I've seen rehearsals," Morley responded. "She's not that good."

Eve shoved past him to crouch down next to Kim, who covered her face and tried to curl into a ball. "Hey!" Eve said, and shook her, hard. "Kim, snap out of it! It's Eve! Look at me!"

Kim screamed, and Claire caught her breath at the sound of it; there was real terror in it, and pain, and horror. Eve let her hand fall away, and she leaned back against the nearest wall, frowning.

"What happened to her?" Shane asked. Morley shrugged.

"Something bad," he said. "Something permanent, as far as I can tell. She crossed someone who didn't take well to her initiative."

"You said you keep her locked up for protection."

He flashed Claire a dark smile. "Consider it locking up the wine cellar. The girl's still a good vintage, if not a brilliant conversationalist."

Ugh. "I need her," Claire said. "I need to take her with me."

Morley's vampire followers didn't seem especially happy about her act of kindness. "She's got no family," Patience said. "No one is going to miss her. No one was even looking for her."

"We were."

"To punish her! We will do that for you."

Even Shane looked a little sick at that. "We'll do our own punishing, thanks," he said. "Humans, I mean. Not me, personally."

Morley's eyes narrowed, but he shrugged as if he didn't really care. "Take her," he said. "Take the black boxes she thought were so important. Take it all, and remember your promise, Claire: you have one month to secure Amelie's permission for us to leave Morganville. If you don't get it, I'll be paying your friends a visit."

Kim was too scared to fight, but Shane took some strips of cloth and wrapped her wrists and ankles tight before slinging her over his shoulder. Eve took the box with the hard drives and DVDs.

Morley and his vampires stood in their way.

"One month," he said. "Remember what I said."

Then they parted ranks, and the three of them, carrying Kim, walked uphill toward the light at the end of the tunnel.

Ada was standing right at the very edge of the darkness, hands clasped before her, eyes like burned paper holes.

"I see you found her," Ada said. "Good. I want her."

"Why? Why did you bring us here?"

"Morley was supposed to kill you. I suppose one must do everything oneself these days."

Claire felt a sick wave of understanding flood over her. "You," she said. "You would have known all about the cameras. You probably found out the first time Kim placed one."

Ada smiled.

"You let her do it."

"Oh no," Ada said. "I *helped* her do it. The girl told me she would use the video she'd collected to rid me of Amelie and Oliver, and I gave her access. I helped her place her cameras. But she was a liar. A cheat. A thief." Ada's image contorted, taking on a monster's shape for a flicker, then smoothed back to her Victorian disguise. "She was going to cheat me out of my revenge and destroy Morganville altogether. I won't have that. Unlike Morley and his rabble, I can't simply leave. I *am* Morganville. I must survive."

"You're not Morganville," Claire said. Kim, draped over Shane's shoulder, had caught sight of Ada, and she was thrashing wildly, screaming. It was all Shane could do to hold on to her. "You're just a science project. One that doesn't work right."

"I am the force that holds this lie of a town together," Ada said, and glided closer, so close Claire could feel the cold chill generated by her image projection. "As far as Morganville is concerned, I am its goddess."

"Word of advice," Eve said. "It's time for a change of religion."

Ada's image became distorted again, and she stretched out a hand. Claire controlled the natural impulse to flinch. *She's not real. She's just a ghost—*

Ada's fingers touched her face. Not quite real, but almost.

Claire jumped back. "Outside!" she yelled. "Get outside!"

Ada smiled. "I'll see you soon."

They made it outside, into the faint hint of sunrise, without anyone jumping them again.

Claire flagged down a passing police cruiser and got them to take

Kim, who shrieked and fought so hard they had to use a Taser on her. Eve winced, and so did Shane.

Claire didn't. She felt bad about it, but she just couldn't bring herself to really feel sorry for Kim. *Karma,* she thought. They'd end up putting her in a padded cell, and eventually maybe Kim would recover enough to function as a normal person. Maybe even a better one. Claire didn't even resent that, so long as she never, ever had to talk to her again.

Ever.

By ten a.m. they were back at the Glass House, and Michael was waiting. "Where were you?" he demanded as soon as they opened the door. Claire said nothing; he was focused on Eve, anyway. "I've been calling; it went straight to voice mail."

"I turned it off," Eve said. "We were kind of being stealthy."

"Since when do you turn off a phone?" Michael put his arms around her, and Eve relaxed against him, and for just a moment, it looked like everything was the same again.

Then Eve pulled free and walked away down the hall, head down.

Michael looked awful. "What do I have to do—?"

Shane slapped his shoulder as he passed. "Give her space," he said. "It's been a hard couple of days. Where's Myrnin?"

"He never showed at the rendezvous," Michael said. "I wasn't really worried about him. More about you."

"Yeah, about that—we kind of had to make a deal with Morley. You know, Graveyard Guy?"

"What kind of deal?"

"The kind where we don't want to pay up," Shane said. "Ask Claire."

She shook her head, walking on. "Ask Shane," she said. "I'm not done yet."

"What?" Shane grabbed her wrist, pulling her to a stop. His face was tense and pale. "You can't be serious. Not done with what? We've got the videos, the cameras, Kim. What else?"

"Myrnin," she said. "He didn't show up at the rendezvous."

"And? Dude's crazy, in case you didn't notice recently. He probably went off to chase butterflies or something"

"He'd have been there. Something happened to him." Claire knew already, knew it all the way down to her bones. "Ada did something. She sent us to Morley, thinking he'd kill us. She'd go after Myrnin, too. I have to find him."

"Not by yourself."

"No," Michael agreed.

"Ditto," Eve said, and picked up a fresh weapons bag from the closet to sling over her shoulder. "Definitely not by yourself."

Claire looked at each of them in turn, saving Shane for last. "You're sure. Because it's going to be dangerous."

"You're going after Ada, right?" Eve put stakes in her pockets, then tossed a crossbow to Shane, who caught it in midair. "You're going to need backup. Especially if she's got Myrnin. Besides, if we just sit here and wait, she can get us anytime she wants."

"We should take the car," Claire said, heading toward the closet to get her own weapons stash. "It's not safe now going through the portals anymore. . . ."

A black hole formed in the wall next to her, and Claire felt the storm of force rip through the house. The portal wavered as the house itself fought back, trying to heal the rift, but whatever was tearing the entrance held firm. *Ada.*

Claire didn't have time to run.

Ada's blue-white hands came out of the darkness, grabbed Claire by the shirt, and dragged her into the portal.

It snapped shut on the shocked, angry faces of her friends.

She heard Shane scream her name.

So, Ada really could touch things. Claire kind of wished she'd taken that idea more seriously.

Claire woke up lying on cold, damp stone, feeling damp little feet skittering over her arm—rats, probably. She hoped it wasn't roaches. She'd just die if it was roaches.

She was in the dark—utter, velvety darkness that pressed in on her like smothering cloth. When she moved, she heard the scrape of her shoes echo off into the distance.

Cave. Probably not Ada's cave, because Claire couldn't hear the distinctive hissing and clanking that came from Ada's gears and pipes. *It doesn't have to be her cave*, Claire reminded herself. Ada could open any portal, anywhere within Morganville—or under it. From the ragged, crude way she'd done it at the Glass House, though, she might not be able to keep up that sort of thing for long.

She was unraveling in control, even while she was getting stronger in raw power.

"Ada," a voice said in the distance—weak and faint. "Ada, you must let me go. I order you to let me go."

"No." Ada's voice came from nowhere, and everywhere; not out of Claire's speakerphone this time. Claire slapped at her pockets, but she had nothing—no weapons, no phone; Ada had taken everything. "You're going nowhere. I've waited all these years, you know. So many years for you to love me."

"Ada, please." Myrnin sounded very weak; Claire could hardly believe it was really him. "I do love you. I always have. Please stop this. You don't know what you're doing. You're not well. Let me help—"

He broke off with a strangled gasp. She'd hurt him, and it took a lot to hurt Myrnin.

Claire slowly climbed to her feet, put her hands on the nearest stone wall, and began to feel her way through the darkness.

"Going somewhere?" Ada's voice asked from right behind her, as if the computer was leaning over her shoulder. Claire yelped and flailed out a hand, but there was nothing there. "I brought you here so that I can get rid of you once and for all, and you can help me make Myrnin better at the same time. Isn't that clever of me?"

Her voice was breaking up into strange harmonics, not really a voice at all—mere noise. "How are you talking?" Claire asked. "You're not using my phone."

"Does it matter?"

"No," Claire said. She sounded a lot less scared than she actually was, which she supposed was a good thing. "I'm just curious."

"You'd be curious at your own autopsy," Ada said, and broke into distorted laughter that reeled wildly out of control. "I'd like to see that."

"Where's Myrnin?"

"Don't you dare try to take him away from me!" Ada shrieked. The echoes filled the cave, bounced, magnified until Claire had to clap her hands over her ears. She could feel the sound waves on her skin, like speakers booming at a rave. "He is mine; he's always been mine; I will never give him up, never!"

"I'm not trying to take him away!" Claire shouted. "I just want to be sure he's all right!"

The sound cut off, just like that. Even the echoes. Claire slowly lowered her hands and touched the wall again; she was afraid to try to move without keeping it under her fingers, because there was no possibility of seeing a thing. Not with human eyes.

"Claire?" Myrnin's voice again, coming from ahead of her and to the right. He sounded weak, and concerned. "You have to get out of here. Please go away."

"Kind of not an option," she said. "Unless Ada wants to open me a portal . . . ?"

Ada laughed softly.

"Guess not." Claire took a couple of more steps forward, but it took her off the angle toward Myrnin's voice. "Myrnin, I can't see. I'm going to try to get to you, but you have to keep talking, okay?"

"Don't," he said. "Don't try to reach me. Claire, I'm asking you, please stay where you are. Get out if you can. *Do not come near me.*"

She was ignoring that, mostly because the idea of staying alone in this darkness, listening to Ada do bad things to him, was worse than anything he could do to her himself. "Keep talking," she said. She heard him take in a deep breath, then let it out. He didn't say a word. She guessed he thought that if he didn't encourage her, maybe she'd give up.

He should have known better.

"Stop!" Myrnin's voice suddenly rang out of the black, urgent and sharp, and Claire paused with her right foot still raised. "Back up. Slowly. Two steps. Do it, Claire!"

She did, putting one foot carefully behind the other, and stopped. "What is it?"

"The floor isn't stable. If you try to cross that way, it'll break through under your weight. You *must* stay where you are!"

"So concerned for the new girl," Ada's voice said, vibrating out of the cave walls. "Never so concerned for me, were you? Even though you always knew how much I loved you. How much I wanted to be with you. I let you drink my blood, Myrnin. I let you take *everything*. And then you did *this* to me."

"Oh, stop whining," Myrnin snapped. "You were grateful enough to become a vampire, and it had nothing to do with your being a lovesick schoolgirl. You wanted a thousand lifetimes to explore the world, to discover, to learn. I gave you that, Ada."

"You were supposed to take care of me."

"According to whom?"

"According to me!" The echoes built again, bouncing wildly, and Claire crouched down in place, hands firmly over her ears again. This time, the echoes died gradually. Once it was quiet, Claire rose to her feet and started moving carefully forward at an angle to her original course, testing the floor before putting her full weight on the stone.

It felt solid.

"Claire, please stop," Myrnin said raggedly. "You can't see. You don't know how dangerous this is."

"Describe it to me. Help me! If you don't, I'll just keep walking."

"That's exactly what she wants. She wants you to try to reach me—" Myrnin broke off with a small cry of pain.

"Myrnin?" Claire forgot all about being careful, and took a step forward. Too fast. She felt the stone snap and crumble and fall away, dark on dark, and she teetered off balance over the edge of a hole that led to the center of the world, apparently. She didn't even hear the falling rocks hit bottom.

Claire slowly shifted her weight to her back foot and stepped back to solid stone again. Her heart was pounding so hard it hurt, and she couldn't seem to slow down her panicked breathing.

"Myrnin, you have to help me," she said. "Tell me which way to go. We can do this."

"Even if you reach me, it's no help to either of us," he said. "She has me. There's no point in your dying, as well."

"Just tell me how to get there."

After a few silent seconds, Myrnin said, "Two steps to your right, then one forward." As she accomplished that, he said, "Claire, she's right. I did take advantage of her. She did love me. I used that to get what I wanted from her."

"You mean, like a guy?" Claire counted steps carefully, then stopped. "Next."

"One step forward, then one diagonally to your left. What I did was considerably worse than you think. I made her a vampire so I could have a reliable assistant, one who loved me and would never betray me. I made her a slave."

"Next. And one thing I can tell you about Ada, she was never a slave, not to you or anybody else. And you really did love her, or you wouldn't have kept her locket all these years."

"Another step straight to your left, then six forward. And don't be daft. I keep gum wrappers. It doesn't mean I love the gum that was once in them."

She counted. He didn't say anything else. Once she got to the end of the directions, she said, "Next. I'm not wrong about Ada. You did love her."

"Straight ahead, one step."

"You're not going to tell me I'm wrong?"

"What's the point? Three steps to your right."

"The point is to keep us talking so I'm not so terrified out of my mind," she said. "What are we going to do about her?"

"Nothing. There's nothing we can do."

"I'm there. Next? Also, there's got to be something. What about—"

She was about to say *the reset code*, and he must have known it, because he let out a sharp hiss for silence. She swallowed the words.

"Focus," Myrnin said. "Forward three small steps. Be careful not to overshoot."

She found out why when she took the steps; her toes overhung what felt like another sinkhole.

Myrnin's voice was close now, very close. "Next," she said.

"This is the difficult part," he said. "You're going to have to jump."

"Jump?" She wasn't sure he was thinking straight. "I can't jump. I can't see!"

"You wanted to get to me, and this is what it takes. If you want to stay where you are—"

"No. Tell me."

"Two steps to your left, and jump straight forward, hard. I'll catch you."

"Myrnin—"

"I'll catch you," he whispered into the dark. "Jump."

She took two running steps and, before she could let herself think about what she was doing, dug in her toes and leaped forward.

She crashed into Myrnin's solid body, his cold arms wrapped around her, and for a few breaths he held her close as she shivered. He smelled like metal. Like cold things.

He didn't let go.

"Myrnin?"

"I'm sorry," he said.

And then he bit her.

THIRTEEN

When Claire came awake again, there were lights in the cave—diffuse and dim, but enough to make things out. Like Myrnin, sitting huddled against the cave wall. She must have made some noise, because his head came up, and he looked straight at her.

She didn't think she'd ever seen anybody look so miserable in her life, and for a moment she couldn't think why he would look that way, and then it all came crashing back.

The throbbing in her neck.

The hollow, disconnected feeling inside her.

The panicked thudding of her heart trying to speed too little blood through the racetrack of her veins. Yeah, she recognized that feeling all too well.

"You bit me," she said. It came out surprised, and a little sad. She started to sit up, but that didn't go so well; she sank back to the cold stone floor, feeling sick and vague, as if she were fading out of the world.

"Don't move," he said softly. "Your pressure is very low. I tried—I tried to stop, Claire. I did try. Please give me the credit."

"You bit me," she said again. It still sounded surprised, although she really wasn't anymore. *You can't trust him.* Shane had said that. And Michael. And Eve. Even Amelie.

You can't trust me.

Myrnin had told her that, too, from the very first. She'd just never really, really believed it. Myrnin was like a thrill ride, one of those dark carnival tracks where scary things swooped in close but never *quite* touched you.

Now she knew better.

"I told you I'd kill you if you did that. I *promised.*"

"I am so sorry," Myrnin said, and lowered his head. "Lie still. It won't be so bad if you keep yourself flat." He sounded tired and defeated. Claire blinked back gray fog, fighting her way back into the world, and almost wished she hadn't when he shifted a little, and she saw—really saw—what had happened to him.

There was a silver bar through his left arm, driven in between the two bones. On either side of it hung silver chains that rattled on the stone and were fixed to a silver-plated bolt. The wound continued to drip red down his arm and hand, to patter into a large puddle around him.

Claire had a flash of Amelie at Sam's grave, silver driven into the wounds to keep them from closing. But Amelie had chosen to do that. This had been done to keep Myrnin here, pinned and helpless.

He shuddered, and the chains rattled. Even as old as he was, the silver must have been horribly painful to him; she could see tendrils of smoke coming from his arm, and he was careful to keep his hand away from the chains. His skin was covered with thick red burns.

"I'm sorry," he said again. "I tried to warn you, but I couldn't—I needed—"

"I know," Claire said. "It's—" What was it? Not okay, okay would be a real stretch. Understandable, maybe. "It's not so bad." It was, though. Still, Myrnin looked a little relieved. "Who did this to you?"

The relief faded from his face, replaced with a blank, black rage. "Who do you think?" he asked.

And from all around them, from the faint shimmer of crystal embedded in the walls, came a soft, smoky laugh.

"She touched me," Claire said, remembering. "She dragged me here. I didn't think she could do that."

"No," Myrnin agreed. "I didn't think she could do a great many things, although she was capable of them on a purely theoretical level. I've been a fool, Claire. You tried to warn me—even Amelie warned me, but I thought—I thought I understood what I'd created. I thought she was my servant."

"And now," Ada said, gliding out of the wall in cold silver and black, "you belong to me. But am I not a generous master? You starved me for so long, barely giving me enough blood to survive. Now I give you a feast." Her cutout image turned toward Claire, and she folded her hands together at her waist, prim and perfect. "Oh, Myrnin. You didn't finish your dinner. Don't let it go bad."

Myrnin stripped his black velvet coat off his right arm, then shrugged it down his left until it was covering the chain. He took hold of it, right-handed, and pulled. Claire tried to get up to help, but her head went weird again, and she had to rest. She rolled on her side and watched Myrnin's right arm tremble as he tried to exert enough pressure to snap the chain, and then he sat back against the wall, panting.

He stared at Ada as if he wanted to rip her into confetti.

"Don't pout," she said. "If you're good, I'll let you off the chain from time to time. In a few years, perhaps"

Claire blinked slowly. "She's sick," she said. "Isn't she?"

"She's insane," Myrnin said. "Ada, my darling, this would be amusing if you weren't trying to kill us. You do realize that if I die, you waste away down here. No more blood. No more treats. No more anything."

In answer, Ada's image reached out and grabbed Claire by the hair, dragging her up to a sitting position. "Oh, I think I can hunt up my own blood," Ada said. "After all, I control the portals. I can reach out and snatch up anyone I wish. But you're right. It would be terribly boring, all alone in the dark. I'll have to keep you all to myself, the way you kept me all to yourself, all these years." She dropped Claire and wiped her hand on her computer-generated gown. "But I can't share you with *her*, my love."

Myrnin's eyes flared red, then smoothed back to black, full of secrets. "No, indeed," he said. "Why, she's in the way. I see that now. Send her out of here, lock her out of the portals. I never want to see her again."

"Easily done," Ada said, and grabbed Claire's hair again. She dragged her backward, and Claire flailed weakly, grabbing at loose stones and breaking nails on sharp edges of rock.

She looked over her shoulder in the direction they were going.

Ada was dragging her to the edge of the sinkhole.

"No!" Myrnin said, and got to his feet. He lunged to the end of his chain, reaching out; his clawing fingers fell short of Claire's foot by about two inches. "No, Ada, don't! I need her!"

"That's too bad," Ada said. "Because I don't."

Claire's hand fell on a sharp, ancient bone—a rib?—and she stabbed blindly behind her head. A second later it occurred to her that she was trying to stab an image, a hologram, an empty space—but Ada let out a yell and the pressure on Claire's hair eased.

Ada's pressed both hands over her midsection, which slowly spread into a black stain.

She was bleeding.

Where the blood hit the stone, it vanished in a curl of smoke.

But the wound didn't heal.

"Yes!" Myrnin cried out. "Yes, by manifesting enough to touch you, she makes herself vulnerable—Claire! Here! Come here!" Myrnin cried, and Claire crawled back in his direction. The second she was within reach, he dragged her toward him, putting her against the wall.

Ada was still standing where she'd been, looking down at her and the spreading dark stain on her dress. Her image guttered, flared, sparked, and then stabilized again.

She flashed toward them, screaming that awful, echoing shriek from all the walls. Myrnin pivoted gracefully and hooked the slack of his chain around her silver, two-dimensional throat. Where it touched her, it burned black holes, and her scream grew louder, until it was cracking stone in the walls. She tried to pull free, but the silver wouldn't let her go. "I've got her!" he said, although Claire could see that his whole body was trembling from the strain, and the burn of silver on his hands must have been horrible. "Go, Claire! Get out of here! You have to go!"

She was too weak, too dizzy. The room was a minefield of sinkholes and false floors, and even if she'd known where to step, chances were she'd simply collapse halfway across and disappear into one of those deep, dark chasms. . . .

And she couldn't just *leave* him.

"Claire!" His voice was desperate. "You have to go. Go *now*."

Now that the lights were on, she could see a clear trail that looked solid, leading all around the room's edge. Claire stumbled out onto it, guiding herself with both hands on the stone wall, and took one torturous step after another. The lights flickered, and the screaming suddenly cut off behind her.

Claire didn't dare look back. She was at the door, a black unknown facing her.

Portal.

She couldn't think. Couldn't get her head together. Couldn't remember all the frequencies to align to take her where she needed to go.

Behind her, she heard Ada laugh.

You have to do this. You can do this!

Claire's eyes snapped open, and without thinking about it, without even meaning to do it, she threw herself forward into the darkness.

And fell out on the other side, into the tunnel beneath Myrnin's lab. Overhead, the trapdoor was open, letting in streams of pale lamplight. Claire staggered into a wall, bounced, and ran away from the light, into the damp chill of the tunnel.

Twelve long steps, and she heard the cavern echoing overhead. She slapped the wall until she found the lights, flipped them on, and ran toward the keyboard at the center of Ada's hissing, steaming, clanking metal form.

A cable slithered across the stone, trying to trip her, but she stumbled on, caught herself against the giant keyboard, and took a second to gasp for breath. Her body was shaking all over, cold as a vampire's, and she just wanted to fall down, fall and sleep in the dark.

Claire closed her eyes, and the symbols began to burn against her eyelids. The symbols she'd memorized every day since Myrnin had given her the sketch on paper of the order. She knew this.

She *had* this.

She opened her eyes . . . and gasped in utter anguish, because the keys were all *blank.*

Somewhere in the darkness, Ada's tinny voice scratched out a contemptuous laugh. "Surprised, little wretch? What's wrong, not as easy as you'd thought?"

You've got this. Claire chanted that to herself, and closed her eyes again. This time, she didn't just imagine the symbols she wanted to push, but with a huge effort, she imagined the keyboard as it had been the last time she'd seen it. She fixed the image in her mind, opened her eyes, and touched the first key.

Yes. Yes, that was right.

The force required to push the key down seemed enormous, like trying to squeeze a boulder. She got the first symbol pressed, then pushed her palm down on the second and leaned her whole weight against it. It slowly, reluctantly clicked and locked.

Ada's laughter died away.

The third symbol was Amelie's Founder's Symbol, the same as on Claire's gold bracelet, and Claire clearly remembered its position right in the center of the keyboard. She put her palm on it and pushed until it locked down. As she reached for the fourth key, she lost her balance and almost fell.

Behind her, Ada's voice came out of the scratchy, ancient speakers. "Stop. You're going to make a mistake."

"I won't," Claire gasped, and pushed the fourth key down. Two more to go.

She couldn't remember the fifth symbol. She knew it was there, but somehow, her mind wouldn't focus. Everything seemed blurry and odd. She closed her eyes again and concentrated, concentrated very hard, until she remembered that it had been hidden down on the bottom-left side.

When she opened her eyes, Ada was *right there*, inches from her face. Claire shrieked and jumped back, slamming her fist forward.

It went right through Ada's form. She wasn't able to stay physical anymore. Myrnin had really hurt her. She hadn't fixed the damage to her image, either—there were black wounds on her throat and hands, and a black stain covering most of her dress.

Her eyes were glowing silver.

"Stop," Ada said.

"No," Claire panted, closed her eyes, and stepped through Ada's image. She found the key she was looking for, and pushed it.

One more.

"All right," Ada said. "Then I'll stop you."

Claire felt cold against her skin, and heard the hiss and clank of the computer grow loud, almost like chatter.

The lights went out, but the noise got louder—and louder.

Ada's cold fingers brushed the back of her neck.

Claire turned toward the darkness behind her. "So that's it?" she yelled. "That's all you've got? Turn off the lights? Scary! I'm totally shaking, you freak! What do you think I am, five and scared of the dark?"

"I think you're defeated," Ada said. "And I think I will kill you, when and how I wish." Ada had made herself physical again, but it wouldn't last. It couldn't. She was still bleeding from where Claire had hurt her, and now her neck and face were scarred and burned from the chain. Her head was at a strange angle, but she was still alive. She glowed a very faint, phosphorous kind of silver.

"You'll never find the key in the dark," Ada almost purred. "You're defeated. And now you die."

"You first," Claire said.

Claire reached behind her from blind instinct and memory, and slammed her palm down on a key. It almost went down, but then it popped up again.

Wrong.

Ada's ice-cold hands—not really hands anymore—closed around her neck. "Stupid girl," she said. "So close."

Ada's fingers squeezed, locking the breath in her throat, and Claire wildly hammered her palm down on the next key to the right.

It locked down with an almost physical snap.

As Claire's fingers slipped off the key, it clicked into place, and the clattering of the machine . . .

. . . stopped.

For a breathless second those cold fingers kept on strangling her, and then they softened, turned to mist . . .

And then they were gone.

A steady, quiet glow came up around her.

Lights.

Claire sank down, back to the keyboard, gasping in breaths through her bruised throat, and watched a silvery light flicker in midair, then take on form.

Ada, but not Ada. The same image, but immaculate, perfectly groomed, and with an entirely blank expression.

"Welcome," Ada said. "May I ask who you are?"

"Claire," she said. "My name is Claire."

"My name is—" Ada cocked her head and frowned. "I'm not quite sure. Addy?"

"Ada."

"Ah yes. Ada." Ada's flat image smiled, but it was a fake kind of smile, with nothing behind it. "I'm not feeling very well."

"You just got reset."

"No, I know all about that. I don't feel at all well, quite beyond that. There's something very wrong with my mind." Her image flickered, and a spasm of emotion flared across her perfect, blank face. "I'm scared, Claire. Can you fix me?"

"I—" Claire coughed. She was so tired, and she really, really hurt. "I don't know." She knew she sounded discouraged. "Maybe I don't want to."

"Oh," Ada said softly. "I see. I really am broken, aren't I?"

"Yes."

"And I can't be fixed."

"No," Claire said softly. "I'm sorry. I think—I think you've got brain damage. I don't think you're ever going to be right."

Ada was silent for a moment, watching her, and then she said, "I loved him, you know. I really did."

"I think he really loved you, too. That's why he tried to hang on to you all these years."

Ada nodded. "Please tell him that I still love him. And because I love him, I can't take the risk that I might hurt him again."

Claire had a very bad feeling. "What are you—"

"Just tell him." Ada smiled, and it was a real smile. A sweet one. "Good-bye, Claire."

And the panel at the wall blew up in arcs of electricity and flames and shredded metal, and Claire ducked and covered her head.

The lights went out.

Ada's image flickered in place for a moment, and then she said, very quietly, "Tell Myrnin I'm sorry I hurt him."

Then she was gone, and the low-level hum of the computer just . . . died.

Claire crouched there, trembling in the dark for a while and listening to the escaping hiss of steam. On one of the round screens on the computer, she saw Ada's image appear. It moved to the next screen—and then to the next. It grew a little fainter every time.

Then Ada's image faded to a single dot of white, and the screen went totally black.

Silence. Real, total silence.

Claire put her head on her upraised knees.

I'll just take a nap, she thought, and then it all just went away for a while.

When she woke up, Amelie was standing in front of the silent, dead computer, one pale hand on the keyboard touching the metal and bone.

"We'll have to get this running again as soon as possible," she said, and then turned toward Claire. "I see you're awake."

"Not really," Claire said. "I don't know what I am right now."

"Your friends are coming." Amelie's tone was cool, and her face was a mask. Claire couldn't tell anything about what she was feeling. "I called them."

"Where's Myrnin?"

Amelie's gray eyes focused on her neck. "He bit you."

"Well—a little." Claire put her hand to the wound, and winced when it throbbed. "Is it bad?"

"You'll live." Amelie turned back to the keyboard. "I'm afraid Ada is beyond help. When the electrical power failed, the nutrients that sustained her organic remnants turned toxic."

"She's dead?"

"She was always dead, Claire. Now she is well beyond our attempts to revive her." Amelie looked at her with cool, calm eyes. "Did you kill her?"

Claire swallowed. "No. I reset her, and she figured out that she couldn't be fixed. She did it herself." That seemed . . . sad, somehow. And a little bit brave. "Where's Myrnin?"

"Here," he said, and crouched down next to her, all long arms and legs, awkward and graceful at the same time. He was still wearing his black velvet coat. Claire fixed her gaze on the bloodstained, ragged hole in his left sleeve. Under it, the skin still looked red and torn. "I'm all right now. Don't worry."

"I'm not," she lied. "Does it hurt?" she asked, because he was holding his arm at an odd angle.

"A little." He was lying, too—a lot. "Claire—"

"No, don't say you're sorry. I know, you had to do it."

"I was going to say thank you for stopping Ada. She always knew you would be the one to destroy her, you know."

"What?" Claire rubbed at the headache forming between her eyes. "What are you talking about?"

"She had taken it into her head that you were going to kill her," Amelie said. "She believed it. So she tried to kill you first, and in doing so, she forced you to this. Unfortunately, it is a great deal of trouble for me; Ada was very valuable. Without her, we cannot maintain many of the less scientific measures of security and travel in the town."

"No more portals," Myrnin said, and sighed. "No more barriers to keep people from leaving. And we won't be able to track those who leave, at least for now."

He turned away, looking at the computer, and for a moment—just a moment—Claire saw the agony clearly visible on his face. His hand was clenched, and as he opened it, she saw the locket she'd found in the box. Ada's portrait. "Oh my dear," he said, very softly. "What we did to each other . . . I am so very sorry."

Amelie watched him and said nothing. Myrnin closed his eyes for a moment, then slipped the locket into his vest pocket and turned toward her, clearly making an effort to make himself seem normal again. As normal as Myrnin ever got. "Right. I'll need a viable candidate to replace Ada. Do you have someone in mind?"

Amelie was still watching Claire. Claire swallowed.

"I do," Amelie said softly. "But I think not quite yet. Let's see where this takes us, Myrnin."

Myrnin said, "I believe it will take us straight into trouble, if experience is any guide at all. Ah, there they are. Claire, your friends—"

She hardly had time to turn before Shane had her and was smothering her in a hug, then devouring her in a kiss, and even though she wasn't exactly in the best possible shape, she felt a hot flush race through her veins to warm her whole body. "Hey," Shane said, then gently combed her hair back from her face. "You look—"

He saw the bite mark, and froze.

Michael and Eve were right behind him, and Claire heard Eve make a funny, strangled noise. Michael's head snapped toward Myrnin.

"I'm okay," Claire said. "A little juice, a steak—I'll be fine. It's just like the blood bank. Right?"

Amelie exchanged a glance with Myrnin, then turned away. He said, "Absolutely," and bounced to his feet to join Amelie at the hissing hulk of the computer. "Take a few days off. With pay."

Shane's face turned red. "You son of a—"

"Don't," Claire said, and put her hand on his cheek. "Shane. I need you. Don't do that."

"I need you, too," he said. "I love you. And it is *not okay*."

Myrnin didn't look at either of them again. After a moment, though, he reached into the pocket of his jacket and came up with a small, portable hard drive.

SHANE & CLAIRE, it read in silver Sharpie.

"I think this is yours," he said.

Claire felt a wave of weakness that had nothing to do with loss of blood. "Where did you get it?"

"Ada," Myrnin said. "She was planning to do something creative with it, I expect—put it on the Internet, or send it to your parents. Her idea of a prank. You can thank me later."

She stopped, staring at his back. "You didn't watch it, did you?"

He didn't turn around. "Of course not."

It even sounded as if he might be telling the truth.

"My car's outside," Michael said. "Come on. Let's get you home."

"In a moment," Amelie said, and turned to face them. In that moment, with her hands clasped at her waist, she looked very much like Ada, which gave Claire a severe attack of the terrors. "I've made a decision. About the three of you."

That didn't sound good. They all exchanged looks.

Claire felt something odd happen inside her, like a flash of heat, followed by one of cold . . . and then the bracelet on her wrist, a constant, heavy presence, clicked, and fell off to roll away on the stone floor.

Claire cried out and rubbed at her wrist. It was dead white where the bracelet had been, and indented with the shape of the band.

"I've decided to record you as Neutrals," Amelie said. "Friends of Morganville. You will be issued special pins, which you must wear at all times. Your names will be recorded in the archives. You are not to be menaced or hunted by any vampire from this point onward. In return, I will require services from you, as I do from other Neutrals, from time to time. You will be listed as employees of the town."

Even Myrnin seemed surprised, Claire thought. "Generous," he said.

"Pragmatic," Amelie said. "Less trouble for me. The four of them are stronger together, and less vulnerable. And I'm well aware that there are those within Morganville who would prefer to split them apart, for their own uses. I can hardly have people with such intimate knowledge of us running around without . . . restrictions."

Claire licked her lips. "About that—I kind of made a deal with Morley. That you'd let him and his people leave Morganville, or else Eve and Shane get hunted."

"Why on earth would you do such a thing?" Amelie shook her head. "I can't protect you from deals made prior to the announcement. If Morley can make a claim, he can register the hunt. It would be legal, according to law. It would be up to you to protect yourselves."

"But you could let Morley and his people leave, right? That's all they want. To be set free, to go where they want."

Amelie was silent for a moment, and then she said, "No." That was all. No *Sorry* or *Hope you don't die.*

She turned back to the dead computer.

"But—"

Shane shook his head. "Let's go home. Come on, we have a month. We'll work it out."

Claire didn't think so, but she shut up and let Michael ferry them, one by one, out of the trapdoor and up to the lab. As they headed for his car, Eve's cell phone rang.

"Hello? Oh, hi, Heather." Eve sighed. "Don't tell me, I'm fired, right?"

Heather? Claire remembered, finally, that Heather was the assistant director for the play. It was the last possible thing Claire could think of, importance-wise, but Eve's face gradually lit up with a smile. "I'm not? Seriously? He didn't—oh wow. Okay. Yes. I'll be there. Yes, of course! . . . Oh, sure, hang on." She handed the phone to Claire. "She says she wants to talk to you."

Claire carefully put the phone to her ear. "Yes?"

"Claire, look, we need a new Stella. Mein Herr says you're perfect. He's already cleared it with your boss."

"He *what?*" And how did Myrnin get to make that kind of call, anyway? "I'm not an actress! I don't know anything—"

"That's what he likes," Heather said. "You're cast. Be at rehearsal tomorrow. Eve will tell you when."

She hung up.

Claire stared at the dead phone, then handed it back.

"I guess I'm in the play," she said.

"Good news," Eve said. "You've already got on-camera experience."

"Yeah, speaking of that, what's going to happen with Kim? Not that I care," Shane said quickly when Claire looked at him. "Just curious."

"I asked," Eve said. "Chief Moses says they'll keep her in the nuthouse for a while, see if she gets better. But even if she does, she'll be in jail a long time."

"You okay with that?"

Eve took in a deep breath. "Yeah," she said. "Yeah, I guess I am."

Claire looked down at the hard drive in her hand, the Sharpie-marked evidence, took it out, and handed it to Shane. "You do the honors," she said.

One smash against the bricks, and it shattered. He kept on smashing it, just to be sure, and then tossed the remains into a handy trash can at the end of the alley.

"The end," Shane said.

It wasn't. Michael and Eve were walking together, but not touching; Claire could see the tension between them. Ada was dead, and that meant the vampires were risking everything, at least for a while. As for Amelie's "gift," Claire knew there had to be a catch, and a big one.

It wasn't the end at all . . . but Claire was content to pretend for now. With Shane warm at her side, and the future stretching out in front of them, she could pretend for today that it was happily ever after.

Of course, tomorrow was another day.

TRACK LIST

In case you want to listen along to the songs I used to help me write this book, here they are! Buy the tracks, please. Don't be a vampire preying on the artists.

"Ghost Town"	Shiny Toy Guns
"Falls Apart"	Hurt
"Under the Gun"	Supreme Beings of Leisure
"Auditorium"	American Princes
"Devil in Me"	22-20's
"John Barleycorn"	Traffic
"Glory Box"	Portishead
"The Hop"	Radio Citizen feat. Bajka
"Roads"	Portishead
"My Old Self"	Wide Mouth Mason
"I Got Mine"	The Black Keys
"C'mon C'mon"	The Von Bondies
"Every Inambition"	The Trews
"Ladylike"	Big Wreck
"Numb"	Holly McNarland
"Beauty of Speed"	Tori Amos
"Best Way to Die"	Jet Set Satellite

"Love Hurts"   Incubus
"Little Toy Gun"   HoneyHoney
"I Don't Care"   Fall Out Boy
"Many Shades of Black"   The Raconteurs
"Headfirst Slide into Cooperstown"   Fall Out Boy
"URA Fever"   The Kills
"Manic Girl"   Radio Iodine
"Take Me to the Speedway"   The Dexateens
"Alsatian"   White Rose Movement
"Poison Whiskey"   Tishamingo
"Welcome Home"   Coheed & Cambria
"Tick Tick Boom"   The Hives
"Jockey Full of Bourbon"   Joe Bonamassa
"Leopard-Skin Pill-Box Hat"   Beck
"The Ballad of John Henry"   Joe Bonamassa
"Funkier Than a Mosquito's Tweeter"   Joe Bonamassa
"Happier Times"   Joe Bonamassa
"Faster"   Rachael Yamagata
"Around the Bend"   The Asteroid Galaxy Tour
"Slow Dance with a Stranger"   Danger Radio
"Ardmore"   Cardinal Trait
"Prayer"   Lizzie West
"Bounce"   The Cab
"Time Bomb"   Jessy Greene

KISS OF DEATH

To the wonderful people in Des Moines, Carroll, Fort Dodge,
Rockwell City, and Clive for making me
welcome in the great state of Iowa!
To my wonderful friends at Legacy Books (Dallas),
the Mystery Bookstore (LA), Murder by the
Book (Houston), and Borders Express (Exton, PA)
for all your support and enthusiasm. See you soon,
I hope!

ACKNOWLEDGMENTS

Far too many awesome people have made it possible for this book to be in your hands today, but I must send extra-special thanks to my Sunday Night pals (Pat, Jackie, Bill, Heidi, J.T., and Joanne), who make even the worst weeks bearable. Also, Joe Bonamassa, Lucienne Diver, Anne Sowards, Jim Suhler, Felicia Day, Jim Conrad, and M. Conrad—all of whom make my days a little brighter. Bless.

INTRODUCTION

WELCOME TO MORGANVILLE. YOU'LL NEVER WANT TO LEAVE.

So, you're new to Morganville. Welcome, new resident! There are only a few important rules you need to know to feel comfortable in our quiet little town:

- Obey the speed limits.
- Don't litter.
- Whatever you do, don't get on the bad side of the vampires.

Yeah, we said vampires. Deal with it.

As a human newcomer, you'll need to find yourself a vampire Protector—someone willing to sign a contract to keep you and yours safe from harm (especially from the other vampires). In return, you'll pay taxes . . . just like in any other town. Of course, in most other towns those taxes don't get collected by the Bloodmobile.

Oh, and if you decide *not* to get a Protector, you can do that, too . . . but you'd better learn how to run fast, stay out of the shadows, and build a network of friends who can help you. Try contacting the residents of the Glass House—Michael, Eve, Shane, and Claire. They know their way around, even if they always end up in the middle of the trouble somehow.

Welcome to Morganville. You'll never want to leave.

And even if you do . . . well, you can't.

Sorry about that.

ONE

The way the Glass House worked, on a practical level, was that there was a schedule for the stuff that had to be done—cooking, cleaning, fixing things, laundry. Technically, they were all on every housemate's list. In practice, though, what happened was this: the boys (Michael and Shane) bribed the girls (Eve and Claire) to do the laundry, and the girls bribed the boys to fix things.

Claire glared at her new iPod—which was actually really nice—and put it on shuffle as she looked at the mess she'd made of her latest laundry effort. And there was the problem: she loved the hot pink iPod, which had been a *heck* of a good bribe, and she really didn't deserve it, because the laundry was . . . also *pink*—which would have been almost fine if it had been a load full of girls' underwear or something.

But not so much with guy clothes; she could not even imagine what kind of screaming that was going to bring.

"Yeah." She sighed, staring at the very definitely pink piles of shirts, socks, and underwear. "Not going to be a good afternoon." It was amazing what one—*one*—stupid red sock could do. She'd already tried running it all through the washer again, hoping the problem would just go away. No such luck.

The basement of the Glass House was big, dark, and creepy, which wasn't really such a surprise. Most basements were, and this was *Morgan-ville*. Morganville went in for dark and creepy the way Las Vegas went in for neon. Apart from the area Claire was in, with a battered washer and dryer, a table that had once been painted some kind of industrial green, and some shelves filled with unidentifiable junk, the rest of the basement was dim and quiet. Hence the iPod, which pumped cheery music through the headphones and made the creepy retreat a little less creepy.

Creepy, she could fight.

Pink underwear . . . apparently not.

She had the music cranked up so high that she failed to hear steps coming down the stairs. In fact, she had no clue she wasn't completely alone until she felt a hand touch her shoulder and hot breath against her neck.

She reacted as any sensible person living in a town full of vampires would. She screamed. The shriek echoed off the brick and concrete, and Claire whirled, clapped her hands over her mouth, and backed away from Eve, who was collapsing in laughter. The Goth look usually didn't go well with hysterical giggles, unless they were *evil* giggles, but somehow Eve managed to pull it off.

Claire ripped the headphones out of her ears and gasped. "You— you—"

"Oh, spit it out already," Eve managed to say. "*Bitch.* I am. I know. That was evil. But, oh my God, funny."

"Bitch," Claire said, late and not at all meaning it. "You scared me."

"Kind of the point," Eve said, and got herself under control. Her mascara was a little smeared, but Claire supposed that was all part of the Goth thing, anyway. "So, what's up, pup?"

"Trouble," Claire replied with a sigh. Her heart was still pounding from the scare, but she was determined not to let it show. She pointed at the laundry on the table.

Eve's eyes went wide, and her black-painted lips parted in horrified fascination. "That's not trouble; that's *fail*. Tell me that isn't all the whites. Like, Michael's and Shane's, too."

"All the whites," Claire said, and held up the guilty red sock. "Yours?"

"Oh, damn." Eve snatched it out of Claire's fingers and shook the sock like a floppy rattle. "Bad sock! Bad! You are *never* going anywhere fun ever again!"

"I'm serious. They're going to kill me."

"They'll never get the chance. *I'm* going to kill you. Do I look to you like someone who rocks pastel?"

Well, that was a definite point. "Sorry," Claire said. "Seriously. I tried washing them again, without the sock, but—"

Eve shook her head, reached down to the lowest level of the shelf, and pulled out a bottle of bleach, which she thumped down on the table next to the laundry. "You bleach; I'll supervise, because I'm not taking the chance of getting a drop on this outfit, 'kay? It's new."

The outfit in question was hot pink—it matched Claire's new iPod, actually—with (of course) black horizontally striped tights, a black pleated miniskirt, and a blazing magenta top with a skull all blinged out in crystal on it. Eve had done up her dyed black hair in a messy pile on top of her head, with stray bits sticking up in all directions.

She looked creepy/adorable.

As Claire reloaded the laundry, with a shot of bleach, Eve climbed up on the dryer and kicked her feet idly. "So, you heard the news, right?"

"What news?" Claire asked. "Do I do hot? Is hot good?"

"Hot is good," Eve confirmed. "Michael got another call from that music producer guy. You know, the one from Dallas? The important one, with the daughter at school here. He wants to set Michael up with some club dates in Dallas and a couple of days at a recording studio. I think he's serious."

Eve was trying to sound excited about it, but Claire could follow the road signs. Sign one (shaped like an EXIT sign): Michael Glass was Eve's serious, longtime crush/boyfriend. Sign two (DANGER, CURVES): Michael Glass was hot, talented, and sweet. Sign three (yellow, CAUTION): Michael Glass was a vampire, which made everything a million times more complicated. Sign four (flashing red): Michael had begun acting more like a vampire than the boy Eve loved, and they'd already had some pretty spectacular fights about it—so bad, in fact, that Claire was not sure Eve wasn't thinking about breaking up with him.

All of which led to sign five (STOP).

"You think he'll go?" Claire asked, and concentrated on setting the right temperature on the washer. The smell of the detergent and bleach was kind of pleasant, like really sharp flowers, the kind that would cut you if you tried to pick them. "To Dallas, I mean?"

"I guess." Eve sounded even less enthusiastic. "I mean, it's good for him, right? He can't just hang around playing at coffee shops in Jugular, Texas. He needs to . . ." Her voice faded out, and she looked down at her lap with a focus Claire thought the skirt really didn't deserve. "He needs to be out there."

"Hey," Claire said, and as the washer began chugging away, washing away the stains, she put her hands on Eve's knees. The kicking stopped, but Eve didn't look up. "Are you guys breaking up?"

Eve still didn't look up. "I cry all the time," she said. "I hate this. I don't *want* to lose him. But it's like he just keeps getting farther and farther away, you know? And I don't know how he feels. What he feels. *If* he feels. It's awful."

Claire swallowed hard. "I think he still loves you."

Now she got Eve to look at her—big, vulnerable dark eyes rimmed by all the black. "Really? Because . . . I just . . ." Eve took a deep breath and shook her head. "I don't want to get dumped. It's going to hurt so bad, and I'm so scared he'll find somebody else. Somebody, you know, better."

"Well, *that's* not going to happen," Claire said. "Not ever."

"Easy for you to say. You haven't seen how the girls throw themselves at him after shows."

"Yeah, you'd *never* do that."

Eve looked up sharply, smiled a little, then looked back down. "Yeah, okay, whatever. But it's different when he's *my* Michael and *they're* the ones who are all, you know . . . Anyway, he's just always so *nice* to them."

Claire jumped up next to her on the dryer and kicked her feet in rhythm with Eve's. "He has to be nice, right? That's his job, kind of. And we were talking about whether you guys were breaking up. Are you?"

"I . . . don't know. It's weird right now. It hurts, and I want the hurt to be over, one way or another, you know?" Eve's shoulders rose and fell in a shrug that somehow managed to be depressed at the same time. "Besides, now he's running off to Dallas. They won't let me go, if he does. I'm just, you know, *human*."

"You've got one of the cool frat pins. Nobody would stop you." The cool frat pins were a gift from Amelie, the town's Founder, one of the most frighteningly quiet vampires Claire had ever met, and Claire's boss, technically. They worked like the bracelets most people in town wore, the ones that identified individuals or families as being Protected by a specific vampire, only these were better. . . . People who wore *these* pins didn't have to give blood or take orders. They weren't *owned*.

As far as Claire knew, there were fewer than ten people in all of Morganville who had this kind of status, and it meant freedom—in theory—from a lot of the scarier elements of town.

This was all because they'd gotten in over their heads, had to fight their way out of it, and done some good for Amelie in the process. It was heroism by accident, in Claire's opinion, but she definitely wasn't turning down the pin or what the pin represented.

"If they decide Michael can go, I'll still have to file an application for temporary leave," Eve said. "So would you, or Shane, if you wanted to tag along. And they could turn us down. They probably would."

"Why?"

"Because they're mostly asshats? Not to mention *bloodsucking vampire* asshats, which doesn't exactly make them fair from the beginning."

Claire could see her point, actually, which was depressing. The air filled with the smells of laundry, which was homey and didn't go too well with depressing. Claire remembered her iPod, which was still blaring away through her headphones, and clicked it off. They sat in silence for a while, and then Eve said, "I wish the dryer were running, because *man*, I could use a good . . . tumble dry."

Claire burst out laughing and, after a second, Eve joined her, and it was all okay.

Even in the dark. Even in the basement.

In the end, the laundry was only a *little* pink.

Dinner was taco night, and it was Claire's turn for that, too, which somehow seemed wrong, but she'd switched with Michael when she'd been staying late at the university library, so she was stuck with Chore Day. Not that she minded making tacos; she liked it, actually.

Shane blew in the door just as she was chopping the last of the onions, which was typical Shane timing; five minutes earlier, and she'd have made him do the chopping. Instead, he arrived just as she was wiping tears away from her stinging eyes. Perfect.

He didn't care that her eyes were red, apparently, because he kicked the kitchen door shut, slammed the dead bolt with a gesture so smooth it looked automatic, set a bag on the counter, and leaned over to kiss her. It was one of those hi-I'm-home kisses, not one of his really good ones, but it still made Claire's heart flutter a little bit in her chest. Shane looked . . . like Shane, she guessed, which was fine with her. Tall, broad, he had sunstreaked slacker hair and a heartbreaker's smile. He was wearing a Killers T-shirt that smelled like barbecue from his job.

"Hey!" she protested—not very sincerely—and waved the knife she'd been using to chop onions. "I'm armed!"

"Yeah, but you're not very dangerous," he said, and kissed her again, lightly. "You taste like tacos."

"You taste like barbecue."

"And that's a win-win!" He grinned at her, reached over, and rattled the paper bag he'd set on the counter. "How about some brisket tacos?"

"That is so wrong, you know. Brisket does not go in tacos."

"Twisted, yet delicious. I say yes."

Claire sighed and dumped the chopped onions into a bowl. "Hand me the brisket." Secretly, she liked brisket tacos; she just liked giving him a hard time more.

"You know," Claire said as she got the barbecue out of the bag, "you really ought to talk to Michael."

"About what?"

"What do you think? About what's going on with him and Eve!"

"Oh *hell* no. Guys don't talk about that crap."

"You're serious."

"Really."

"What do you talk about?"

Shane looked at her as if she were insane. "You know. Stuff. We're not *girls*. We don't talk about our *feelings*. I mean, not to other guys."

Claire rolled her eyes and said, "Fine, be emotionally stunted losers; I don't care."

"Good. Thanks. I'll do that." The door opened, and Michael shuffled in, rocking the worst bed head Claire had ever seen him with. "Whoa. Dude, you look like crap. You getting enough iron in your diet?"

"Screw you, and thanks. I just woke up. What's your excuse?"

"I work for a living, man. Unlike the nightwalking dead."

Michael went straight past them and from the refrigerator took a sports bottle, which he stuck in the microwave for fifteen seconds. Claire was grateful the smell of the onions, brisket, and taco meat covered the smell of what was in the bottle. Well, they all knew what it was, but if she pretended *really hard*, it didn't have to be quite as obvious.

Michael drank from his sports bottle, then wandered over to look at what they were doing. "Cool, tacos. How long?"

"Depends on whether or not she lets me do the chopping," Shane said. "Five minutes, maybe?"

The doorbell rang. "I'll get it!" Eve yelled, and there was something in her voice that really didn't sound quite right. More . . . desperate than eager, as if she wanted to stop them from getting to it first. Claire glanced over at Shane, and he raised his eyebrows.

"Uh-oh," he said. "Either she's finally dumping you, Mikey, and her new boy's coming for dinner, or—"

It was the *or*, of course. After a short delay, Eve opened the swinging door just wide enough to stick her face inside. She tried for a smile. It almost worked. "Uh—so I invited someone to dinner."

"Nice time to tell us," Shane said.

"Shut up. You've got enough food for the Fifth Armored Division *and* all of us. We can fill one more plate." But she was having trouble keeping eye contact, and as Claire watched, Eve bit her lip and looked away completely.

"Crap," Michael said. "I'm not going to like this, am I? Who is it?"

Eve silently opened the door the rest of the way. Behind her, standing with his hands stuffed in the pockets of his jeans jacket, head down, was her brother, Jason Rosser.

Jason looked—different, Claire thought. For one thing, he usually looked strung out and dirty and violent, and now he looked almost sober, and he was definitely on speaking terms with showers. Still skinny, and she couldn't say much for the baggy clothes he was wearing, but he looked . . . better than she'd ever seen him.

And even so, something inside her flinched, hard, at the sight of him. Jason was associated with several of her worst, scariest memories, and even if he hadn't actually *hurt* her, he hadn't helped her, either—or any of the girls who'd been hurt, or killed. Jason was a bad, bad kid. He'd been an accomplice to at least three murders and to an attack on Claire.

And neither Shane nor Michael had forgotten any of that.

"Get him out of here," Shane said in a low, dangerous-sounding tone. "Now."

"It's Michael's house," Eve said, without looking at any of them directly. "Michael?"

"Wait a second—it's *our* house! I live here, too!" Shane shot back. "You don't get to drag his low-life ass in here and act as if nothing happened with him!"

"He's my *brother*! And he's trying, Shane. *God*, you can be such a—"

"It's okay," Claire said. Her hands were shaking, and she felt cold, but she also saw Jason lift his head, and for a second their eyes met. It was like a physical shock, and she wasn't sure what she saw, or what he saw, but neither one of them could hold it for long. "It's just dinner. It's not a big deal."

Shane turned toward her, eyes wide, and put his hands on her shoulders. "Claire, he *hurt you*. Hell, he hurt *me*, too! Jason is not some stray mutt you can take in and feed, okay? He's psycho. And *she* knows it better than anybody." He glared at Eve, who frowned but didn't glare back as she normally would have. "You expect us all to just play nice with him now that he figures out the bad guys aren't winning, so he cranks out a quick apology? Because it's not happening. It's just not."

"Yeah, I figured it would go this way. Sorry I bothered you," Jason said. His voice sounded faint and rusty, and he turned and walked away, toward the front door and out of their line of sight. Eve went after him, and she must have tried to stop him, because Claire heard his soft voice say, "No, he's not wrong. I've got no right to be here. I did bad things, sis. This was a mistake."

Of all of them, only Michael hadn't spoken—hadn't moved, in fact. He was staring at the swinging door as it swayed back and forth, and finally he took a deep breath, set down his sports bottle, and went out into the hallway.

Claire smacked at Shane's arm. "What the hell was that, macho man? You have to come to my rescue all the time, even when nobody's trying to hurt me?"

He seemed honestly surprised. "I was just—"

"I know what you were *just* doing. You don't speak for me!"

"I wasn't trying to—"

"Yes, you were. Look, I know Jason's no saint, but he got himself together, and he stuck with Eve when all of us were—out of commission, when Bishop was in charge. He protected her."

"And he let his crazy buddy Dan grab you and almost kill you, and he didn't do anything!"

"He did," Claire said flatly. "He left me to find help. I know because Richard Morrell told me later. Jason went to the cops and tried to tell them. They didn't believe him or they'd have gotten help to me a lot earlier." Earlier would have meant a lot less terror and pain and despair. It wasn't Jason's fault that they'd figured him for crazy.

Shane was thrown, a little, but he came back swinging. "Yeah, well, what about those other girls? He didn't help *them*, did he? I'm not friending up somebody like that."

"Nobody said you had to," Claire shot back. "Jason's done his time in jail. Sitting at the same table isn't like swearing eternal brotherhood."

He opened his mouth, closed it, and then said, very tightly, "I just wanted to make sure he didn't have a chance to hurt you again."

"Unless he uses a taco as a deadly weapon, he hasn't got much of a shot. Having you, Michael, and Eve here is about the best protection I could want. Anyway, would you rather have him where you can see him, or where you *can't?*"

Some of the fire faded out of his eyes. "Oh. Yeah, okay." He still looked uncomfortable, though. "You do crazy crap, you know. And it's contagious."

"I know." She put her hand on his cheek, and got a very small smile in return. "Thanks for wanting to keep me safe. But don't overdo it, okay?"

Shane made a sound of frustration deep in his throat, but he didn't argue.

The kitchen door swung open again. It was Michael, looking fully awake and very calm, as if bracing for a fight. "I talked to him," he said. "He's sincere enough. But if you don't want him here, Shane—"

"I damn sure don't," Shane said, then glanced at Claire and continued. "But if she's willing to give it a shot, I will."

Michael blinked, then raised his eyebrows. "Huh," he said. "The universe explodes, hell freezes, and Shane does something reasonable."

Shane silently offered him the finger. Michael grinned and backed out of the kitchen again.

Claire handed Shane the biggest knife they had. "Chop brisket," she said. "Take out your frustrations."

The brisket didn't stand a chance.

Jason didn't say much at dinner. In fact, he was almost completely silent, though he ate four tacos as if he'd been starving for a month, and when Eve brought out ice cream for dessert, he ate a double helping of that, too.

Shane was right. The brisket *was* delicious in the tacos.

Eve, compensating for her brother, chattered like a magpie on crack the whole time—about dumb-asses at the coffee shop where she worked, Common Grounds; about Oliver, her vampire boss, who was a full-time jerk, as far as Claire was concerned, although apparently he was a surprisingly fair supervisor; gossip about people in town. Michael contributed some juicy stuff about the vampire side of town. (Claire, for one, had never considered that vampires could fall in and out of love just like regular people—well, vampires other than Michael, and maybe Amelie.) Shane finally loosened up on his glares and brought up some embarrassing stories from Michael's and Eve's pasts. If there were embarrassing stories he knew about Jason, he didn't get into telling them.

It started out deeply uncomfortable, but by the time the ice cream bowls were empty, it felt kind of—normal. Not great—there was still a cautious tension around the table—but there was guarded acceptance.

Jason finally said, "Thanks for the food." They all stopped talking and looked at him, and he kept his own gaze down on the empty dessert bowl. "Shane's right. I got no right to think I can just show up here and expect you not to hate my guts. You should."

"Damn straight," Shane muttered. Claire and Eve both glared at him. "What? Just sayin'."

Jason didn't seem to mind. "I needed to come and tell you that I'm sorry. It's been—things got weird, man. Real weird. And I got real screwed up, in all kinds of ways. Until that thing happened with Claire . . . Look, I never meant—she wasn't part of it. That was all on him." *Him* meant the other guy, the one none of them mentioned, ever. Claire felt her palms sweating and wiped them against her jeans. Her mouth felt dry. "But I'm guilty of other stuff, and I confessed to all of it to the cops, and I did time for it. I never killed anybody, though. I just—wanted to be somebody who got respect."

Michael said, "That's how you think you get respect around here? As a killer?"

Jason looked up, and it was eerie, seeing eyes exactly like Eve's in suc' a different face, simmering with anger. "Yeah," he said. "I did. I still

And I don't need a frigging *vampire* to set me straight about that, either. In Morganville, when you're not one of the sheep, and you're not one of the wolves, you'd better be one mean-ass junkyard dog."

Claire glanced over at Shane and was surprised to see that he wasn't hopping on the angry train. In fact, he was looking at Jason as if he understood what he was saying. Maybe he did. Maybe it was a guy thing.

Nobody spoke, and finally Jason said, "So anyway, I just wanted to say thanks for helping get me out of jail. I'd be dead by now if you hadn't. I won't forget." He scraped his chair back and stood up. "Thanks for the tacos. Dinner was real good. I haven't—I haven't sat at a table with people for a really long time."

Then, without making eye contact with any of them, he walked away, down the hall. Eve jumped up and ran after him, but before she got to him, he was out the front door and slamming it behind him. She opened it and looked out, but didn't follow. "Jason!" she called, but without any real hope he'd come back. Then, finally, hopelessly, she called again, "Be careful!"

She slowly closed the door again, locked it, and came back to flop in her chair at the dinner table, staring at the remains of their taco feast.

"Hey," Shane said. "Eve."

She looked up.

"It took guts for him to come here and try to apologize. I respect that."

She looked surprised, and for a second she smiled. "Thanks. I know Jason's never going to be . . . well, a good guy in any kind of way, but he's—I can't just turn my back on him. He needs somebody to keep him from going off the rails."

Michael took a drink from his sports bottle. "He's the train," he said. "You're on the tracks. Think about what's going to happen, Eve."

Her smile faded. "What are you saying?"

"I'm saying that your brother is a junkie and one sick dude even if he's feeling sentimental right now. That's probably not really his fault, but he's trouble, and now we sat down with him and he apologized and it's all done, okay? He's not coming back. He's not family. Not in this house."

"But—"

When Claire had first met Michael Glass, he'd been cold and kind of harsh to her, and now that Michael came out again.

At Eve.

"Eve, we're not going to argue about it," Michael said flatly, and he looked like an angry, angry angel, the smiting kind. "House rules. You don't bring that kind of trouble in the door."

"Oh, *please*, Michael, don't even think about pulling that crap. If that's the rule, are you throwing Claire out now? Because I'm betting she is the most trouble that ever walked in here on two feet. You and Shane drag your own hassles in all the time. But I don't get to have my own brother over for dinner?" Eve's voice was shaking, she was so angry now, and she was trying not to cry, but Claire could see the tears welling up in her dark eyes. "Come on! You're not my dad!"

"No, I'm your landlord," he said. "Bringing Jason in here puts everybody at risk. He's going to go back to the dark side on us, if he ever left in the first place. I'm just trying to keep things sane around here."

"Then try talking to me instead of just ordering me around!" Eve shoved dishes off onto the floor, spilling the remains of tacos everywhere, and dashed for the stairs.

Michael got there first, easily; he moved in a blur, vampire speed, and blocked her access. Eve came to a skidding halt, pale even underneath her rice-powder makeup. "So you're proving your point by going all vamp on me?" she said. "Even if Jason was still here, you'd be the most dangerous thing in the room and you know it!"

"I *know*," Michael said. "Eve. What do you *want*? I'm trying, okay? I sat down with Jason. I'm just saying once was enough. Why am I the bad guy?"

Shane muttered, loud enough for only Claire to hear, "Good question, bro." She hissed at him to be quiet. This was private, and she was feeling bad for both Eve and Michael, having witnesses to all this. It was bad enough to be fighting and worse to have Shane making snarky comments from the sidelines.

"I don't know, Michael. Why *are* you the bad guy?" Eve shot back. "Maybe because you're acting as if you own the world!"

"You're being a brat."

"A *what?*"

"You're going to dump crap all over the floor and walk away? What else do you call it?"

Eve looked so shocked, it was as if he'd hit her. Claire winced in sympathy. "It's okay; we'll do it," Claire said, and started picking up plates and piling them up. "It's not a big deal." Shane was still staring at their friends as if they were some kind of sideshow exhibit; she kicked him in the shin and shoved plates at him. "Kitchen," she said. "Go."

He raised his eyebrows, but he went. She began cleaning up the mess on the floor. In Shane's absence, it felt as if things changed, as if the balance shifted again. Claire kept herself small, quiet, and invisible as she worked at scraping up the spilled food into a pile with napkins.

"Eve," Michael said. He wasn't angry anymore, Claire realized. His voice had gone soft and quiet. She glanced up and saw that Eve was silently crying now, tears dragging dirty trails of mascara down her cheeks, but she didn't look away from him. "Eve, what is it? This isn't about Jason. What?"

She threw herself into him, wrapping her arms around him. Even with vampire reflexes, Michael was surprised enough to rock backward, but he recovered in just a second, holding her, stroking her back with one hand. Eve put her head down on his shoulder and cried like a lost little girl. "I don't want to lose you," she finally snuffled. "God, I really don't. Please. Please don't go."

"Go?" Michael sounded honestly baffled. "What? Where would I go?"

"Anywhere. With anyone. Don't— I love you, Michael. I really do."

He sighed and held her even more tightly. "I'm not going anywhere with anyone else," he said. "I swear. And I love you, too. Okay?"

"You mean it?"

"Yeah, I mean it." He seemed almost surprised and let out a slow breath as he hugged her tighter. "I mean it, Eve. I always have, even when you didn't believe it."

Eve dabbed at her running mascara, hiccuping little breaths, and then looked past Michael to Claire, who was getting all the mess put onto one plate for disposal. Eve looked stricken. "Oh God," she said. "I'm sorry. I didn't mean— Here, let me. I'll get it."

And she pulled free of Michael and got down on her hands and knees to clean up the rest.

And Michael got down there with her. Claire backed through the kitchen door with a load of stuff, and as it swung closed, she saw Michael lean over and kiss Eve. It looked sweet and hot and absolutely real.

"Well?" Shane asked. "World War Fifteen over out there, or what?"

"I think so," she said, and hip-bumped him out of the way at the sink to dump her armload of plates. "You're washing, right?"

"I'll play you for it."

"What?"

"Best high score wins?"

That was the same basic thing as doing it herself now and saving herself the humiliation, Claire thought. "No bet," she said. "Wash, dish boy."

He flicked suds at her. She shrieked and laughed and flipped more at him. They splashed water. It felt . . . breathlessly good, when Shane finally captured her in his soapy hands, pulled her close to his wet T-shirt, and kissed her.

"And that's World War *Sixteen*," he said. "Officially over."

"I'm still not playing *Dead Rising* with you."

"You're no fun."

She kissed him, long and sweet and slow, and whispered, "You sure?"

"Well, I'm certainly changing my mind," Shane said, straight-faced, at least until he licked his lips. His pupils were large and dark and completely fixed on hers, and she felt as if gravity had reversed, as if she could fall up into his eyes and just keep on going.

"Dishes," he reminded her. "Me dish boy. And I can't believe I just said that, because that was lame."

She kissed him again, lightly this time. "That's for later," she said. "By the way? You look really hot with suds all over you."

The kitchen door opened, and Eve walked in, dumped a plateful of trash in the can, and practically danced her way over to the sink. She still had smeared mascara, and her tears weren't even dry, but she was smiling, and there was a dreamy, distant look in her eyes.

"Hey," Shane said. "How about you? Want to play *Dead Rising?*"

"Sure," Eve said. "Fine. Absolutely."

She wandered out. Shane blinked. "That was not what I expected."

"She's floating," Claire said. "What's wrong with that?"

"Nothing. But she didn't even insult me. That's just *wrong*. It disturbs me."

"I'm taking advantage of all this calm," Claire said. "Study time."

"Bring it downstairs," Shane said. "I need a cheering section, because she is going to *suck* at zombie killing tonight. Just way too happy."

Claire laughed, but she dashed upstairs and grabbed her book bag, which promptly ripped right down the seam, spilling about twenty pounds' worth of texts, supplies, and junk all over the wooden floor. "Great," she said with a sigh. "Just great." She gathered up what she needed in an untidy armload and headed back downstairs.

She was halfway down the stairs when someone knocked at the front door. They all stopped what they were doing—Michael, in the act of picking up his guitar; Shane and Eve, taking seats on the couch with game controllers. "Expecting anybody else?" Shane asked Eve. "Is your distant cousin Jack the Ripper dropping in for coffee?"

"Screw you, Collins."

"Finally, the world is back to normal. Still not up to the usual Rosser Olympic-level insult standards, there, sunshine. Never mind. I'll get it."

Michael didn't say anything, but he put down the guitar and followed Shane to the end of the hall, watching. Claire descended the rest of the steps quickly, trying to keep her pile of stuff from tottering over, and dumped it on the dining table before hurrying over to Michael's side.

Shane checked the peephole, stepped back, and said, "Uh-oh."

"What?"

"Trouble?"

Michael crossed the distance in a flash, looked out, and bared his teeth—*all* his teeth, including the vampiry ones, which didn't exactly bode well. Claire sucked in a deep breath. Damn stupid book bag, picking a bad time to break; usually, she'd have brought all the stuff down, but she'd left her antivamp supplies upstairs in the ruined bag's pocket.

"It's Morley," Michael said. "I'd better go out and talk to him. Shane, stay here with them."

"Word of advice—stop telling me to stay with the girls," Shane said, "or I will seriously bust you in the mouth one of these days. Seriously. I could break one of those shiny fangs."

"Today?"

"Ah . . . probably not."

"Then shut up." Michael opened the door just wide enough to slide out, looked back, and said, "Lock it."

Shane nodded, and as soon as the wood thumped closed, he shot all the bolts and glued his eye to the peephole.

Claire and Eve, by common silent decision, dashed to the living room window, which gave them an angled view of the porch—not perfect, but better than nothing.

"Oh no," Eve whispered.

Michael was standing in a wash of moonlight, facing not just one vampire, but *three*. Morley—a ragged, rough vampire who rocked the homeless look, although Claire knew he actually did have a home—was standing there, with two of his crew. He had quite a number of them, disaffected vampire youth, although *youth* was a relative term when you talked about vampires. It was mostly a matter of status, not just age: the have-nots, or the ones feeling squeezed by those who had power over them.

They also had a human with them.

Jason.

And he wasn't there voluntarily, as far as Claire could tell. One of the vampires had a hand around his arm in what looked like a friendly grip but was probably bone-crushing hard.

"Jase," Eve whispered. "Oh God. I *told* you to be careful!"

Shane left the door, came into the living room, and dragged a black canvas bag out from under a chair. He unzipped it and took out a small crossbow, cranked it back, and loaded it with an arrow. He tossed silver-coated stakes to Claire and Eve, then joined them at the window. "So," he said, "your brother's already said he was a vampire wannabe. Does he need rescuing, or is this his idea of a really great date?"

"Don't be an asshole," Eve said, and gripped the stake so hard her whole hand turned paler than normal. "They wouldn't turn him, anyway. They'll just drain him." It was a lot of work for a vampire to turn a human, and from what Claire had seen, they didn't seem all that eager to go through it themselves. It hurt. And it took something out of them. The only one she'd ever seen take any real pleasure out if had been Mr. Bishop, Amelie's vile, old vampire father. She'd seen him turn Shane's father, and that had been—horrible. *Really* horrible.

This was why Shane, however he felt about Jason Rosser, was loading up a crossbow, and was more than prepared to use it.

"What's Michael doing?"

"Talking sense," Shane said. "It's always his A game. For him, it usually works. Me, I'm usually Plan B, all the time."

"B for brute force?" Eve said. "Yep, that's you."

Shane slotted the arrow in place and raised the window sash. He kicked out the screen on the other side and aimed the crossbow right at Morley.

Morley, who was dressed in clothes that seemed pieced together out of rags, except for one brand-new Hawaiian shirt in disgustingly bright shades of neon, looked straight at the window, smiled, and tipped his head just a little in acknowledgment.

"Just so we're clear, bloodsucker," Shane said.

"Can he hear you?"

"He hears every word. Hey, Morley? I will put this right between your ribs, you got me?"

Once again, Morley nodded, and the smile stayed in place.

"You sure that's a good idea?" Eve whispered. "Threatening him, I mean?"

"Why not? Morley speaks fluent threat."

It went on for a while, all the talking; Shane never took his eyes off

Morley. Claire kept her hand on him, somehow feeling as if that were helping—helping them both—and finally Morley made some polite little bow to Michael, then waved at the other vampire, who was holding Jason.

The vampire let go. Jason stumbled backward, then took off at top speed, running flat out down the street. The vampires watched him. Nobody followed.

Eve breathed a slow sigh of relief and leaned against the wall.

Shane didn't move. He still had the crossbow aimed at Morley's chest.

"Emergency's over," Eve said. "Stand down, soldier."

"Go open the door. I stand down when Michael's back inside." Shane smiled, all teeth. Not quite as menacing as a vampire smile, but it got the point across. Eve nodded and ran to the door. Once it was open, Michael—still looking cool and calm—backed in, said good night, and shut the door. Claire heard him shooting the locks, and still Shane kept his aim steady until Morley, touching a finger to his brow, turned and walked off into the dark with his two followers.

Claire slammed down the window and locked it, and Shane let out his breath in a slow sigh, removing the arrow from the bow. "Nothing like a little after-dinner terrification," he said, and gave Claire a quick kiss. "Mmmm, you still taste like brisket tacos."

She would have called him a jerk, but she was shaking, and she was too short of breath, anyway. He was already down the hall by the time she pulled in enough air, and she used it to follow him. Michael was standing beside Eve, an arm tight around her waist.

"So?" Shane asked. "What's Morley hanging around for? Waiting for us to get ripe?"

"You know what he was here for," Michael said. "We haven't gotten his people passes to leave town yet, which is what you promised him in return for not killing you three when he had the chance. He's getting impatient, and since you three are on the hook as his own personal blood donors, I think we need to get serious about making that happen."

"He wouldn't dare."

"No? Can't say that I agree with you. Morley isn't afraid of much

that I can tell, including Amelie, Oliver, or a wooden arrow in the heart."
Michael nodded at Shane. "Still. Thanks. Nice."

"Brute force. It's what I do."

"Just keep it aimed the right way."

Shane looked as innocent as Shane ever could and put his hand over his heart. "I would never. Unless you flash fang at me again, or ever tell me to stay with the girls. Except for that."

"Cool. Let's go shoot some undead things on the TV, then."

"Loser."

"Not if I win."

"Like *that* ever happens."

TWO

The next day, Claire had classes at Texas Prairie University, which was always a mixture of fascinating and annoying; fascinating, because she'd managed to finagle her way into a lot of advanced classes she really didn't have the prerequisites for, and annoying because those not in the know about Morganville in general—which was most of the students at the school—treated her like a kid. Those who didn't, and knew the score about the vampires and the town of Morganville itself, mostly avoided her. It occurred to her, the second time somebody tried to buy coffee for her but not make eye contact, that some people in town still looked at her as *important*—as in Monica Morrell–level important.

This seriously pissed off Monica, Queen Bee of the Morganville Under-Thirty set. Still, Claire had come a long way from the clueless early-admission freshman she'd been last year. When Monica tried to bully her—which was virtually certain to happen at least a couple of times every week—the outcome wasn't usually in Monica's favor, or always in Claire's, either. But still, a draw was better than a beat-down, in Claire's view. Everybody was left standing.

Claire's first stop was at the campus student store, where she bought a new backpack—sturdy, not too flashy, with lots of pockets inside and out. She ducked into the first bathroom she found to transfer the contents of her taped-together book bag to the new one, and almost threw the old one away . . . but it had a lot of sentimental value, somehow. Ripped, scuffed, stained with all kinds of things she didn't want to remember, but it had come with her to Morganville, and somehow she felt that throwing it away would be throwing away her chance of ever getting out of here.

Crazy, but she couldn't help it.

In the end, she stuffed the rolled-up old backpack into a pocket of the new one, hefted the weight, and jogged across campus to make her first class of the day.

Three uneventful (and mostly boring) hours later, she ran into Monica Morrell, who was sitting on the steps of the Language Arts building, sunglasses on, leaning back on her elbows and watching people go by. One of her lipstick mafia girls was with her—Jennifer—but there was no sign of the other one, Gina. As always, Monica looked expensive and perfect—Daddy's estate must be holding up well no matter what the economy dudes were saying on TV—and Jennifer looked as though she shopped the cheap knockoffs of what Monica bought for full price. But they both looked good, and about every thirty seconds some college boy stopped to talk to them, and almost always got shot down in flames. Some of them took it okay. Some of them looked as if they were one more rejection from ending up on a twenty-four-hour channel as breaking news.

Claire was heading up the steps, ignoring them, when Jennifer called out brightly, "Hey, Claire! Good morning!"

That was creepy enough to stop Claire right in her tracks. She looked over, and Jennifer was *waving*.

So was *Monica*.

This, from the two girls who'd punched and kicked her, thrown her down a flight of stairs, abducted her at least twice, threatened her with knives, tried to set her house on fire . . . yeah. Claire didn't really feel like redefining the relationship on their new buddy-buddy terms.

She just gave the two of them a long look, and kept on up the stairs, trying to focus on what it was she was supposed to remember today about early American literature. Nathaniel Hawthorne? So last week . . .

"Hey!" Monica grabbed her two steps from the top, yanking on the strap of her new book bag to drag her to a halt. "Talking to you, bitch!"

That was more like it. Claire glanced down at Monica's hand and raised her eyebrows. Monica let go.

"I figured it couldn't be me," she said. "Since you were acting so nice and all. Had to be some other Claire."

"I just thought since the two of us are more or less stuck with each other, we might as well try to be friendly, that's all. You didn't have to act as if I stole your boyfriend or something." Monica smiled slowly and pulled her sunglasses down to stare over the top. Her big, lovely blue eyes were full of shallow glee. "Speaking of that, how *is* Shane? Getting bored with the after-school special yet?"

"Wow, that's one of your better insults. You're almost up to junior high level. Keep working on it," Claire said. "Ask Shane yourself if you want to know how he's doing. I'm sure he'd be glad to tell you." Colorfully. "What do you want?"

"Who says I want something?"

"Because you're like a lion. You don't bother to get up unless you're getting something out of it."

Monica smiled even wider. "Hmmm, harsh, but accurate. Why work harder than you have to? Anyway, I hear you and your friends made a deal that's getting you into trouble. Something with that skanky homeless Brit vamp—what's his name? Mordred?"

"Mordred is from the King Arthur stories. It's Morley."

"Whatever. I just wanted to tell you that I can take care of it for you." Her smile revealed teeth, even and white. "For a price."

"Yeah, I didn't see that coming," Claire said with a sigh. "How are *you* going to take care of it, exactly?"

"I can get him the passes out of town he wants. From my brother."

Claire rolled her eyes and adjusted her book bag a little more comfortably on her shoulder. "Meaning what? You're going to forge his signature on a bunch of photocopies that will get everybody thrown in jail except you? No thanks. Not interested." Claire had no doubt that whatever Monica was offering, it wasn't real; she'd already talked to Monica's brother, Mayor Richard Morrell, several times about this and gotten nowhere. But Monica liked to pretend she had "access"—with full air quotes. "If that's all, I've got class."

"Not quite," Monica said, and the smile vanished. "I want the answers to the final exam in Lit 220. Get them."

"You're kidding."

"Do I look like I'm kidding? Get them, or—well, you know what kind of *or* there is, right?" Monica pushed the sunglasses back up. "Get them to me by Friday or you're fried, special needs."

Claire shook her head and took the last two steps, walked to her class, dumped her bag at her lecture hall seat, and sat down to think things over.

By the time class began, she had a plan—a warm, fuzzy plan.

Some days, it was absolutely worth getting out of bed.

When Claire got home, the sun was slipping fast toward the horizon. It was too early for most vampires to be out—not that they burst into flames that easily; most of the older ones were sort of flame-retardant—but she kept a sharp lookout, anyway. Instead of going straight to the Glass House, she turned at the cross street and went a few more blocks. It was like déjà vu because her parents' house looked almost exactly like the Glass House; a little less faded, maybe. The trim had been painted a nice dark green, and there were fewer bushes around the windows, different porch furniture, and a couple of wind chimes; Claire's mom loved wind chimes, especially the big, long ones that rang those deep bell sounds.

As Claire climbed the steps to the porch, a gust blew by her, sounding the bells in a chorus. She glanced up at the sky and saw clouds scudding by fast. The weather was changing. Rain, maybe. It already felt cooler.

She didn't knock, just used her key and went right in, dumping her backpack in the entry hall. "Hey, I'm home!" she yelled, and locked the door behind her. "Mom?"

"Kitchen," came the faint yell back. Claire went down the hall—same as in the Glass House, but Mom had covered this version with photos, framed ones of their family. Claire winced at her junior high and high school photos; they were unspeakably geeky, but she couldn't convince

Mom to take them down. *Someday, you'll be glad I have them*, Mom always said. Claire couldn't imagine that would ever be true.

The living room was, again, disorientingly familiar; instead of the mismatched, comfortable furniture of the Glass House, the stuff from Claire's childhood occupied the same space, from the old sofa to her dad's favorite leather chair. The smells coming from the kitchen were familiar, too: Mom was making stuffed bell peppers. Claire fortified herself, because she couldn't stand stuffed bell peppers, but she almost always ate the filling out of them, just to be nice.

"Why couldn't it be tacos?" She sighed, just to herself, and then pushed open the door to the kitchen. "Hi, Mom, I'm—"

She stopped dead in her tracks, eyes wide, because *Myrnin* was sitting at her mother's kitchen table. Myrnin the vampire. Myrnin her boss. *Crazy* mad scientist Myrnin. He had a mug of something that had *better* not be blood in front of him, and he was almost dressed like a sane person—he had on frayed blue jeans, a blue silk shirt, and some kind of elaborate tapestry vest over it. He wore flip-flops for shoes, of course, because he seemed to really love those. His hair was long around his shoulders, black and glossy and full of waves, and his big, dark eyes followed Claire's mother as she busied herself at the stove.

Mom was dressed the way Mom usually dressed, which was way more formal than people Claire's age would ever think was appropriate for lounging around the house. A nice pair of dress pants, a boring shirt, mid-heeled shoes. She was even wearing jewelry—a bracelet and earrings, at least.

"Good evening, Claire," Myrnin said, and transferred his attention over to her. "Your mother's been very kind to me while I waited for you to get home."

Mom turned, and there was a false brightness to her smile. Myrnin made her nervous, although Myrnin was obviously making a real effort to be normal. "Honey, how was school?" She kissed Claire on the cheek, and Claire tried not to squirm as her mom rubbed at the lipstick mark left on her skin. At least she didn't use spit.

"School was great," Claire said, which completed the obligatory school conversation. She got a Coke from the fridge, popped the top, and settled in across the table from Myrnin, who calmly sipped from his coffee cup. "What are you doing here?"

"Claire!" her mother said, sounding a little scandalized. "He's a guest!"

"No, he's my boss, and bosses don't drop in on my parents without an invitation. What are you doing here?"

"Dropping in on your parents without an invitation," Myrnin said. "I thought it would be good to get to know them better. I've been telling them how satisfied I am with the work you've been doing. Your research is some of the best I've ever seen."

He really *was* on his best behavior. That didn't even sound a little crazy; overdone, maybe, but not crazy.

"I'm off today," Claire pointed out. Myrnin nodded and rested his chin on his hand. He had a nice smile, when he chose to use it, as he did now, mostly directed at Claire's mother, who brought over a coffeepot and refilled his cup.

Oh, good. Not anything red being served, then.

"Absolutely. I know you had a full class schedule today," he said. "This is a purely social call. I wanted to reassure your parents that all was going well for you." He looked down into his coffee. "And that what happened before would never happen again."

What happened before was code for the bite marks on her neck. The wounds were healed, but there was a scar, and as she thought about it, her hand went up and covered the scar, on its own. She forced it back down. Her parents didn't have any idea that Myrnin was responsible for that; they'd been told that it had been some other random vamp, and that Myrnin had helped save her. It was partly true, anyway. Myrnin *had* helped save her. He'd just also been the one to bite her.

Not that it had really been his fault. He'd been hurt, and desperate, and she'd just been there. At least he'd stopped himself in time.

She certainly hadn't been able to stop him.

"Thanks," she said. She couldn't really be mad at him, not for any of it. It would have been easier if she could have. "Are you staying for dinner?"

"Me? Delicious as it smells, I fear I'm not one for bell peppers," he said, and stood up with one of those graceful moves vampires seemed so good at pulling off. They moved like humans, but *better.* "I'd better take my leave, Mrs. Danvers. Thank you so much for your hospitality, and the delicious coffee. Please tell your husband I thank him as well."

"That's it?" Claire asked, mystified. "You came to talk to my parents, and now you're leaving?"

"Yes," he said, perfectly at ease, and perfectly weird. "And to drop this off for you, from Amelie." He patted his vest pockets, and came up with a cream-colored envelope, which he handed over to her. It was heavy, expensive paper, and it was stamped on the back with the Founder's Seal. It was unopened. "I'll see you tomorrow, Claire. Don't forget the donuts."

"I won't," she said, all her attention on the envelope in her hands. Myrnin said something else to her mother, and then the kitchen door opened and closed, and he was gone.

"He has such beautiful manners," her mother said, locking the back door. "I'm glad you work for someone so—civilized."

The scar on Claire's neck throbbed a little. She thought of all the times she'd seen Myrnin go off the rails—the times he'd curled up weeping in a corner; the times he'd threatened her; the times he'd raved like a lunatic for hours on end; the times he'd begged her to put him out of his misery.

The time he'd actually given her samples of his own brain—in a Tupperware container.

"Civilized," she repeated softly. "Yeah. He's great." He was; that was the awful thing. He was great until he was horrible.

Kind of like the world in general.

Claire slit open the envelope with a kitchen knife, slipped out the heavy folded paper inside, and read the beautiful, looped handwriting— Amelie's, without a doubt.

*In accordance with recent requests, I hereby am providing you with passes
to exit and return to Morganville. You must present these to the checkpoints at*

the edge of town. Please provide them to your party and give them the same instructions. There are no exceptions to this rule.

Coordinate with Oliver to arrange your exit time.

Claire's breath left her in a rush. Morley's passes! Perfect timing, too; she didn't know how much longer any of them could keep Morley and his people from losing patience, and coming to take it out in blood. They wanted out of Morganville.

She could give it to them.

She realized immediately, however, as she took the passes out of the envelope, that there weren't *nearly* enough. Morley's people would need about thirty passes in total. Instead, there were only four in the envelope.

The names read *Michael Glass, Eve Rosser, Shane Collins,* and *Claire Danvers.*

What the hell was going on?

Claire pulled out her cell phone and hit SPEED DIAL. It rang, and rang, but there was no answer. She hung up and tried another number.

"Oliver," said the voice on the other end.

"Um, hi, it's Claire? Is—is Amelie there with you?"

"No."

"Wait, wait, don't hang up! You're on the town council—I just got a letter that has some passes in it, but it's not enough for—"

"We turned down Morley's request for emigration out of Morganville," Oliver said. He had a low, even tone to his voice, but Claire felt herself go cold anyway. "He has a philosophy that is too dangerous to those of us who wish to remain . . . What's the phrase? Under the radar."

"But—we made a deal. Me, Shane, Eve, and Michael. We said we'd get them passes."

"I'm aware of your deal. What is your question?"

"It's just—Morley said he'd kill us. If we didn't get the passes for him. We told you that."

Oliver was silent for a long second, then said, "What part of *I'm aware* did you not comprehend, Claire? You and your friends have passes out of

Morganville. As it happens, Michael requested leave to travel to Dallas for his recording and concert session. We've decided to allow that, under the condition that all of you travel together. With an escort."

"Escort?" Claire asked. "You mean, like police?" She was thinking of Sheriff Hannah Moses, who would be good company in addition to a bad-ass bodyguard; she'd liked Hannah from the moment she'd met her, and she thought Hannah liked her, too, as much as a tough ex-soldier could like a skinny, geeky girl half her age.

"No," Oliver said, "I don't mean police." And he hung up. Claire stared at the screen for a moment, then folded the phone closed and slipped it back in her pocket. She looked down at the passes, the envelope, the letter.

Amelie had decided to really piss off Morley, but at least she'd also decided to get Claire and her friends out of town.

With an escort.

Somehow, Claire knew it wouldn't be as simple as just picking a responsible adult to go with them.

"Go get your father," her mom said, and began setting dishes on the table. "He's upstairs on the computer. Tell him dinner's ready."

Claire gathered up everything and put it in her backpack before heading upstairs. Another wave of same-but-not-quite washed over her; her mother and father had reserved the same room for her here that she had over in the Glass House, though the two were nothing alike. *Home*—in name, anyway—had her frilly white bed and furniture, stuff she'd gotten when she was ten. Pink curtains. Her room at the Glass House was completely different—dark woods, dark fabrics. Adult.

Dad's computer room would have been Shane's bedroom in the other house, which woke all kinds of thoughts and memories that really weren't appropriate right now and caused her face to heat up as she poked her head in the room and quickly said, "Dad, dinner's ready! Help me eat the stuffed bell peppers before I gag and die?"

Her father looked up from the computer screen with a surprised, guilty jerk, and quickly shut down what he was doing. Claire blinked. *Dad?* Her dad was . . . normal. Boringly normal. Not an activist, not a freak, not somebody who had to hide what he was doing on the computer from his own daughter. "Tell me you weren't looking at porn," she said.

"Claire!"

"Well, sorry, but you did the guilty dance. Most people I know, that means porn."

Her dad pulled in a deep breath, closed his eyes, and said, "I was playing a game."

That made her feel oh-so-much better. Until he said, "It's one of those online multiplayer games."

"Yeah? Which one? One of the fantasy ones?"

He looked mortally embarrassed now. "Not—not really."

"Then what?"

In answer, he brought up the screen. On it was a night scene, a castle, a graveyard—typical horror fare, at least if you were from the 1950s.

A character appeared on the screen—pale, tall, dressed in a Dracula cape and tuxedo.

With fangs.

Her mouth dropped open, and she stared at her father, her normal, boring father. "You're playing a *vampire* game?"

"It's called *Castlemoor*. I'm not just playing it. I get paid to be there, to watch what people are doing online."

"You—get paid—to play a vampire? By *who*?"

Her father sat back in his chair, and he slowly shook his head. "That's my business, Claire."

"Is it Amelie? Oliver?"

"Claire." This time, his voice had the parental ring of authority. "Enough. It's a job, and I get paid well enough to do it. We both know it's the best thing I can find, with all my restrictions. The doctors don't want me exerting myself too much."

Her dad wasn't well, and hadn't been for a while now. He was frail, fragile, and she worried about him more and more. About her mother, too. Mom looked frayed around the edges, with a kind of suppressed panic in her eyes.

"You'll be okay?" Claire said. Somehow she made it a question, although she didn't mean to. "Did they find anything else?"

"No, honey, everything's fine. I just need time to get stronger."

He was lying to her, but she could tell that he didn't want her to pursue it. She wanted to; she wanted to yell and scream and demand to know what was going on.

But instead, she swallowed and said, "Playing a vampire online. That's a pretty wild career move, Dad."

"Beats unemployment. So, stuffed bell peppers, huh? I know how much you love those." Claire made a gagging sound. Her dad reached over and ruffled her dark hair. "Why don't you just tell her you don't like them?"

"I did. I do. It's a Mom thing. She just keeps telling me I *used* to like them."

"Yeah," he agreed. "That's a Mom thing."

Dinner passed the way it normally did, with Claire picking out edible parts of the bell pepper and her mother holding forth about whatever she was doing for the week. Claire contributed when direct questions came her way; otherwise, she just stayed out of it. She always knew what Mom was going to say, anyway. And she knew Dad wouldn't say much, if anything.

What he *did* say was, "Why don't you bring Shane over some night for dinner?"

It was as if time stopped. Her mother froze, fork halfway to her mouth; Claire froze, too, but unfortunately she was in the process of gulping down a mouthful of Coke at the time, which meant coughing and sputtering, watering eyes, the whole embarrassing bit.

"Honey, I'm sure Shane's very busy," her mother said, recovering. "Right, Claire?"

"I'd like to talk to him," her father said, and right now there wasn't any warm-and-fuzzy daddy vibe. It was more PARENT, in big, flashing red letters. "Soon."

"Uh—okay, I'll see if— Okay." Claire frantically cut up a piece of stuffed bell pepper and ate it, bell pepper and all. She nearly choked again, but she managed to get it down. "Hey, I might be taking a trip."

"What kind of a trip?"

"To Dallas. With my friends."

"We'll see," Dad said, which meant *no*, of course. "I'd need to talk to Shane first."

Oh God, now they were bargaining. Or she was being blackmailed. Sometimes it was hard to tell the difference. Claire mumbled that she'd try, or something like that, choked down another bite of food that no longer tasted even a *little* good, and jumped up to clear her plate. "Claire!" her mother called after her as she dashed into the kitchen. "You're not running off tonight, are you? I was hoping we could spend some time with you!"

"You just did," Claire muttered as she rinsed the plate and put it in the dishwasher. She raised her voice and yelled back, "Can't, Mom! I've got to study! All my books are over at the Glass House!"

"Well, you're not walking over there in the dark," Mom said. "Obviously."

"I told you, I've got a pin from Amelie! They're not going to bother me!"

Her dad opened the door of the kitchen. "And what about just garden-variety humans? You think that little pin protects you from everything that could hurt you?"

"Dad—"

"I worry about you, Claire. You take these risks, and I don't know why. I don't know why you think it's okay."

She bit her lip. There was something in his voice, a kind of weary disappointment that cut her to the core and nearly brought tears to her eyes. She loved him, but he could be so *clueless*.

"I didn't say I'd walk, Dad," she said. "I make mistakes, sure, but I'm not *stupid*."

She took out her cell phone, dialed a number, and turned her back on her father. When Eve answered with a bright, chirping, "Hit me!" Claire said, "Can you come get me? At my house?"

"Claire," her father said.

She turned to look at him. "Dad, I really have to study."

"I know," he said. "I'll drive you home." He said it with a funny little smile, sad and resigned. And it wasn't until she smiled that she realized what he'd really said.

Home. The Glass House.

"It's hard for us to let go," he said. "You know that, right?"

She did. She hesitated for a second, then said into the phone, "Never mind, Eve. Sorry. Dad's bringing me."

Then she hugged her father, and he hugged her back, hard, and kissed her gently on the forehead. "I love you, sweetie."

"I know. I love you, too."

"But not enough to eat more stuffed bell peppers and play Jenga with your folks."

"No more bell peppers, but I'd completely play Jenga," she said. "One game?"

He hugged her even harder. "I'll get the game."

Three games of Jenga later, Claire was tired, happy, and a little bit sad. She'd seen her mom laugh, and her dad look happy, and that was good, but there'd been something odd about it, too. She felt like a visitor, as if she didn't fit here anymore, the way she once had. They were her family, but seen from the outside. She had too many experiences now that didn't include them.

"Claire," her dad said as he drove her home through the darkened streets of Morganville. It was quiet out, only a few cars moving about. Two of them were white police cruisers. At least three other cars they passed had heavy tinting, too heavy for humans to see through. "Your mom had a talk with me, and I'm not going to insist you keep on living at home with us. If you want to live with your friends, you can."

"Really?" She sat up straight, looking at him. "You mean it?"

"I don't see how it makes much difference. You're seventeen, and a more independent seventeen than I ever was. You've got a job and responsibilities beyond anything I can really understand. It doesn't make much sense for us to keep trying to treat you like a sheltered little girl." He hesitated, then went on. "And I sound like the worst dad in the world, don't I?"

"No," she said. "No, you don't. You sound like—like you understand."

He sighed. "Your mother thinks if we just put more restrictions on you, things would get back to normal. You'd go back to being the same little girl she knew. But they won't, and you won't. I know that."

He sounded a little sad about it, and she remembered how she'd felt at the house—a little out of place, as if she were a visitor in their lives. Her life was splitting off on its own.

It was such a strange feeling.

"But about Shane—," her father continued.

"Dad!"

"I know you don't want to hear it, but I'm going to say it anyway. I'm not saying Shane is a bad guy—I'm sure he's not, at heart—but you really need to think about your future. What you want to do with your life. Don't get in too deep, too fast. You understand what I'm saying?"

"You married Mom when you were nineteen."

He sighed. "I knew you'd bring that up."

"Well? It's okay for you to make decisions before twenty, but not me?"

"Short answer? Yes. And we both know that if I really wanted to, I could make Shane's life a living hell. Dads can do that."

"You wouldn't!"

"No, I won't, because I do think he really loves you, and he really wants to protect you. But what Shane may not get at that age is that he could be the worst thing in the world for you. He could completely derail you. Just—keep your head, okay? You're a smart girl. Don't let your hormones run your life."

He pulled the car to a stop at the Glass House, behind Eve's big monster of a car. There were lights blazing in the windows—warmth and friendship and another life, *her* life; one her parents could only watch from the outside.

She turned to her father and saw him watching her with that same sad, quiet expression. He moved a strand of hair back from her face. "My little girl," he said, and shook his head. "I expect you for dinner soon."

"Okay," she said, and kissed him quickly. "Bye, Daddy. I love you."

He smiled, and she quickly got out of the car and ran up the cracked walk, jumped up the steps to the porch, and waved at him from the front door as she got out her keys. Even so, he waited, watching until she'd actually opened the door, stepped in, and closed it. Only then did she hear the engine rev as his car pulled out.

Michael was playing in the living room. *Loud.* That wasn't normal at all for him, and as Claire came around the corner, she found Eve and Shane sitting on the floor, watching the show. Michael had set up an amplifier, and he was playing his electric guitar, which he rarely did at home, and *damn.* That was impressive stuff. She sank down next to Shane and leaned against him, and he put his arm around her. The music was like a physical wall pushing over her, and after the first few seconds of fighting it, Claire finally let herself go; she was pulled away on the roaring tide of notes as Michael played. She had no idea what the song was, but it was fast, loud, and amazing.

When it was over, her ears were left ringing, but she didn't care. Along with Shane and Eve, she clapped and whooped and whistled, and Michael gravely took a bow as he shut down the amp and unplugged. Shane got up and high-fived, then low-fived him. "Nothing but net, man. How do you do that?"

"No idea, really," Michael said. "Hey, Claire. How are the folks?"

"Okay," she said. "My dad says I can officially move back in." Not that she'd ever really moved out.

"I knew we'd wear them down," Eve said. "After all, we really are amazingly cool." And now it was Eve's turn for the high five with Shane. "For a bunch of misfit geeks, slackers, and losers."

"Which one are you?" Shane asked. She flipped him off. "Oh, right. Loser. Thanks for reminding me."

Claire dug in her backpack and came out with the passes Myrnin had delivered. "Uh—I got these today. Somebody want to fill me in?"

Michael, at vampire speed, crossed the distance and snatched the paper out of her hand. He spread out the individual passes and stared at them with a blank, shocked expression. "But—I didn't think—"

"Apparently, somebody agreed," Claire said. "Eve?"

Eve frowned. "What? What is it?"

"Passes," Michael said. "To leave town, to go to Dallas. To do the demo."

"For you?"

"For all of us." Michael looked up and slowly smiled. "You know what this means?"

Shane threw back his head and let out a loud wolf howl. "Road trip!" he yelled! "Yes!"

Michael put his arms around Eve, and she melted against him, her pale-painted face against his chest, hands on his waist. Claire saw her dark eyes flutter closed, and a kind of peaceful happiness came over Eve's face—and then her eyes snapped open. "Wait," she said. "I've never—I mean—outside? Of Morganville? To *Dallas*? You can't be serious. Michael?"

He held up a pass with her name on it. "It's signed. Official."

"They're letting us *leave town*? Are they *insane*? Because once I hit the shops in Dallas, I don't think I'm ever coming home." Eve made a face. "And I can't believe I just thought of Morganville as *home*. How much of a saddie am I?"

"Eight out of ten," Shane said. "But we do have to come back, right?"

"Right," Michael said. "Well, *I* have to come back. I've got nowhere else to go. You guys . . ."

"Stop," Eve said, and put a hand over his mouth to enforce the order. "Just stop there. Please."

He looked down at her, and their eyes locked. He took her hand away from his mouth, and then lifted the backs of her fingers to his lips for a long, slow kiss. It was just about the sexiest thing Claire had ever seen, full of sweetness and love and longing. From the expression on Eve's face, it was just about the sexiest thing *she'd* ever seen, too. "We'll talk about it on the road," Michael said. "The passes are good for a week. I'll make some calls and see when they need me in the studio there."

Eve nodded. Claire doubted she could put any words together, right at that moment.

"Hey," Shane said, and tapped Claire on the nose. "Snap out of it."

"What? What!"

"Seriously. You've got this chick flick hit-by-the-romance-hammer look. Stop it."

"Ass."

He shrugged. "I'm not one of those romantic guys," he said. "Hey, date Michael if you want that."

"No, don't," Eve said dreamily. "Mine."

"And there goes my blood sugar level," Shane said. "It's getting late, Claire has school tomorrow, I've got a long day of chopping fine barbecue—"

"I think we'll stay down here," Michael said. He and Eve still hadn't blinked or looked away from each other.

"I am *really* not sticking around for that." Shane took Claire's hand in his. "Upstairs?"

She nodded, hitched her bag on her other shoulder, and followed him up. Shane opened the door of his room, turned, and lifted her hand up to his lips. He didn't *quite* kiss it. His dark eyes were wicked with laughter.

"Ass," she said again, more severely. "You couldn't be romantic if your life depended on it."

"You know what's lucky? Most bad guys don't ask you to be romantic on command, so that probably won't matter."

"Only girlfriends do that."

"Well, they *can* qualify as supervillains. But only if they have a secret underground base. Wait—you've got a mad scientist for a boss, and a lab—"

"Park it," she said, and smacked his arm. "Are you going to kiss me good night, or what?"

"Romantic on command. See?"

"Fine," Claire said, and this time she actually *did* feel a little annoyed. "Then don't. Good night."

She pulled away from him and walked away the few steps to her own room, opened the door, slammed it, and flopped on her bed without bothering to turn on the lights. After a few seconds she remembered that in Morganville that was never a smart choice, and switched on the bedside Tiffany lamp. Rich colored light threw patterns on the wood, the walls, her skin.

No monsters were hiding in the shadows. She was too tired to check under the bed or in the closet.

"Ass," she said again, and put her pillow over her face to scream her frustration into it. "Shane Collins is an ass!"

She stopped at the sound of a soft knock on the door. She put the pillow aside and waited, listening.

The knock came again.

"You're an *ass*," she yelled.

"I know," came Shane's voice through the door. "Let me make it up to you?"

"As if you can."

"Try me."

She sighed, slid off the bed, and went to open up.

Shane was standing there, of course. He came inside, closed the door behind him, and said, "Sit down."

"What are you doing?"

"Just sit down."

She did, perching on the edge of the bed and already frowning. There was something really different in the way he was acting now—the flip side of how he'd been just a few moments ago, teasing and teen-boy.

This seemed much more . . . adult.

"When you were in the hospital, after Dan . . . well, you know." He shrugged. "You were kind of drugged up. I'm not sure what you remember."

She didn't remember all that much, really. A boy had abducted her and hurt her pretty badly. She'd lost a lot of blood, and they'd given her something for the nightmares. She remembered everybody coming to see her—Mom, Dad, Eve, Michael, Shane. Even Myrnin. Even Amelie and Oliver.

Shane . . . he'd stayed with her. He'd said . . .

She couldn't really remember what he'd said.

"Anyway," Shane said, "I told you this was for later. I guess it's kind of later, so, anyway."

He took out a small velvet box from his pocket, and Claire's heart just . . . stopped. She thought she might faint. The top of her head felt very hot, and the rest of her felt very cold, and all she could look at was the box in his hand.

He wasn't. He *couldn't.*

Was he?

Shane was looking at the box, too. He turned it in his fingers restlessly. "It's not what you think," he said. "It's not—look, it's a ring, but I don't want you to think—" He opened the box and showed her what was inside.

It was a beautiful little ring, silver, with a red stone in the shape of a heart, and hands holding it on either side. "It's a claddagh ring," he said. "It belonged to my sister, Alyssa. My mom gave it to her. It was in Alyssa's locker at school when she—when the house burned." When Alyssa died. When Shane's life completely collapsed around him.

Tears burned in Claire's eyes. The ring glittered, silver and red, and she couldn't look at Shane's face. She thought that might destroy her. "It's beautiful," she whispered. "But you're not asking—"

"No, Claire." He suddenly sank to his knees, as if the strength had just gone out of him. "I suck, I know, but I can't do something like that, not yet. I'm . . . Look, family doesn't mean to me what it means to you. Mine fell apart. My sister, my mom—and I can't even think about my dad. But I love you, Claire. That's what this means. That I love you. Okay?"

She looked up at him then, and felt tears break free to run hot down her cheeks. "I love you, too," she said. "I can't take the ring. It means—it means too much to you. It's all you have left of them."

"That's why it's better if you have it," he said, and held out the box, cupped in one hand. "Because you can make it a better memory. I can barely look at this thing without seeing the past. I don't want to see the past anymore. I want to see the future." He didn't blink, and she felt the breath leave her body. "You're the future, Claire."

Her head felt light and empty, her whole body hot and cold, shaking and strong.

She reached out and took the velvet box. She pulled the ring out and looked at it. "It's beautiful," she said. "Are you sure—"

"Yes. I'm sure."

He took the ring from her and tried it on her right hand. It fit perfectly on the third finger.

Then he lifted her hand to his lips and kissed it, and it was *definitely* better than Michael had done it, *definitely* sexier, and Claire dropped to her knees with him; then he was kissing her, his mouth hot and hungry, and they fell back together to the throw rug next to the bed, and stayed there, locked in each other's arms, until the chill finally drove them up to the bed.

THREE

Of all the mornings Claire didn't want to get up, the next one was the worst. She woke up warm and drowsy, cuddled like a spoon against Shane, their hands clasped even in sleep. She felt *great*. Better than any day, ever, in her whole life.

In the still hush of early morning, she tried to freeze the moment, the sound of his soft, steady breathing, the feel of him relaxed and solid next to her.

I want this, she thought. *Every day. For life. Forever.*

And then her alarm clock went off, shrieking.

Claire flailed and slapped at it, then succeeded in knocking it to the floor. She dived for it and finally got it switched off, feeling like a complete fool that she'd ever left it on in the first place. She twisted around and saw Shane had opened his eyes, but hadn't otherwise moved. He looked drowsy and sweet and lazy, hair mussed, and she leaned back down to kiss him, sweet and slow.

His arms went around her, and it felt so natural, so perfect, that she felt that glow again, that feeling of absolute *rightness*.

"Hey," he said. "You're cute when you're panicked."

"Just when I'm panicked?"

"Ouch. Yeah, that didn't come out as absolutely complimentary as I'd planned. And you hang around Eve *way* too much." His fingers drew lazy circles on her back, which felt like trails of sunlight. "What's the plan for today? Because I'm in favor of nothing but this."

She *so* wanted that, too. But there was a reason her alarm had gone off. "I have class," she said with a sigh.

"Skip it." He kissed her bare shoulder.

"I—you've got work! Remember? Sharp pointy knives and beef to chop?"

"Fun as that is, this is better."

Well, his arguments were persuasive. *Really* persuasive. For about another thirty minutes, and then Claire forced herself to get up, grab the shower before Shane could get to it, and try to get her mind off the fact that he was lying in her bed.

And he still was when she came back in to grab her backpack. His hands were behind his head, and he looked ridiculously satisfied with the world—and with himself.

She smacked his bare foot, which was sticking out from under the sheet. "Get up, Lord of the Barbecue."

"Ha. Don't have to yet. You're the one who had the bad idea to sign up for seven a.m. classes. Me, I go to work at a sensible hour."

"Well, you're not lying around in my bed all day, so get up. I don't trust you alone in here."

His smile was wicked and really, really dangerous. "Probably a good idea," he said. "Not that you can exactly trust me in here when you're with me."

Oh, she was *not* going to climb back in bed with him. She was *not*. She had things to do. After gulping in a few deep breaths, she leaned over, gave him a quick kiss, avoided his grabby hands, and dashed to the door. "Out of my bed," she said. "I mean it."

He yawned. She grinned and shut the door on her way out.

Downstairs, the coffee was already brewing, and Michael was sitting at the table, a laptop computer open in front of him. She was a little surprised; Michael wasn't really the computer type. He had one, and she supposed he had e-mail and stuff, but he wasn't always on it or anything. Not like most people their age. (Not like her, honestly.)

He looked up at her, then down at the screen, and then back up, to stare at her as if he'd never seen her before.

"What?" she asked. "Don't tell me some of Kim's skanky home video made YouTube." That was something she really didn't ever want to think about again. Kim and her little sneaky spying habits. Kim and her plans to make herself a star with all her hidden video cameras recording every aspect of life in Morganville.

Yeah, that hadn't gone so well for Kim, in the end.

He shook his head and went back to the computer. "I've been checking about the studio, the recording session, you know? They're serious, Claire. They want me in there on Thursday."

"Really?" She grabbed a cup of coffee and slid into a chair across from him, then doctored up her drink with milk and sugar. "So we have to leave Thursday morning?"

"No, I'm thinking we leave tonight. Just in case. And besides, it gives us some time to get used to Dallas, and I don't want to travel during the day." Right. Vampires. Road trip. Sunlight. Probably not the best idea.

"We can't take your car, can we? I mean, the tinting's not legal outside of Morganville."

"Yeah. Which is another reason for night driving. I figure we can take Eve's car. It's roomy and it's got a big trunk, in case."

In case they got caught in the sun, he meant. Claire tapped her fingers on the coffee cup, thinking. "What about supplies?" she said. "You know."

"I'll stop at the blood bank and pick up a cooler," he said. "To go."

"Seriously? They do that?"

"You'd be surprised. We can even put Cokes in there, too."

That didn't seem too sanitary, somehow. Claire tried not to think about it. "How long are we going to be gone?"

"If we leave tonight and I do the demo on Thursday during the day, we could be back on Friday night. Or Saturday, depending on what kind of stuff you guys want to do. I'm easy."

That made Claire remember something. "Uh—you know we're going to have an escort, right?"

"Escort?" Michael frowned. "What kind of escort?" Claire mimed fangs. Michael rolled his eyes. "Perfect. Who?"

"No idea. All I know is Amelie's letter said we had to clear our departure time with Oliver."

Michael kept on frowning. He reached for his cell phone and dialed as he sipped more coffee. "It's Michael," he said. "I hear we have to clear leaving town with you. We're planning on going tonight, around dusk."

His face went entirely blank as he listened to whatever Oliver said on the other end. Michael didn't say anything at all.

Finally, he put the coffee cup down and said, "Do we have a choice?" Pause. "I didn't think so. We'll meet you there."

He hung up, carefully laid the cell phone down on the table next to his coffee, and sank back in his chair, eyes closed. He looked—indescribable, Claire decided. It was as if there were so many things inside him fighting to come out that he couldn't decide which one to let off the leash first.

"What?" she finally asked, half afraid to even try.

Eyes still shut, Michael said, "We've got an escort, all right."

"Who?"

"Oliver."

Claire set down her own coffee cup with a thump that slopped brown liquid over the rim. *"What?"*

"I know."

"We have to be trapped in a car with *Oliver?*"

"I *know.*"

"So much for the fun. Fun all gone."

He sighed and finally opened his eyes. She knew that look; she remembered it from when she'd first met him. Bitter and guarded. Hurt. Trapped. Then, he'd been a ghost, unable to leave this house, caught between human and vampire.

Now he was just as trapped, only instead of the house, his boundaries were the town limits. He'd felt, for the last few hours, as if he could break free, be someone else.

Oliver had just taken that away from him.

"I'm sorry," Claire said. He shut the computer, unplugged it, and stood up. He didn't meet her eyes again.

"Be ready at six," he said. "Tell Shane. I'll tell Eve."

She nodded. He kept his head down as he walked toward the kitchen door. When he got there, he stopped for a few seconds without turning back to look at her. "Thanks," he said. "Sucks, you know?"

"I know."

Michael laughed bitterly. "Shane would have said, *And so do you.*"

"I'm not Shane."

"Yeah." He still didn't turn around. "I'm glad you're happy with him. He's a good guy, you know."

"Michael—"

He was already gone by the time she said his name, with just the swinging door left behind. There was no sense chasing him. He wanted to brood in private.

She called Shane to tell him what time they were leaving, but *not* about Oliver. Frankly, she didn't want to have that grief just yet. She went on to class. After her early ones, she had a two-hour break, which meant she had things to do, so she could leave town with a clear conscience.

And besides, she'd been looking forward to this since she'd first thought of it.

First step—she walked the few blocks from campus to Common Grounds, Oliver's coffee shop, and ordered up a mocha. He was behind the bar—a tall older man, with hippie hair and a tie-dyed T-shirt under his coffee-stained apron. When he was serving customers, you'd never know he was a vampire, much less one of the meanest she'd ever met.

Mocha in hand, Claire texted Monica's cell. *Meet me at Common Grounds ASAP.*

She got back an immediate *Btr B good.*

Oh, it would be.

Claire sipped and waited, and Monica eventually rolled up in her hot red convertible; no Gina and Jennifer this time. Monica seemed to be getting out more and more without her backup singers, which was interesting. Claire supposed even they were getting tired of providing constant on-demand validation.

Monica blew in the front door of the shop in a dress that was too short for her, but that showed off her long tanned legs; the swirl of wind *almost* made it illegal. She shoved her expensive sunglasses up on top of her glossy black hair and scanned the room. The sneer that twisted her full lips was probably mostly reflex.

After putting in her coffee order, Monica slipped into a chair across from Claire. "Well?" she said, and dropped her tiny purse on the table. "Like I said, this had better be good."

When Oliver brought over Monica's coffee, Claire said, "Would you mind staying for a minute?"

"What?"

"As a moderator." Oliver was a broker of deals in Morganville. Common Grounds was a key place where humans and vampires could meet, mingle in safety, and reach all kinds of agreements that Oliver would witness and enforce.

Pretty rarely between humans, though.

Oliver shrugged and sat down between the two girls. "All right. Make it quick."

Monica already looked thunderously angry, so Claire spoke first. "Monica made a deal with me for test answers. I want you to witness me handing them over."

Oliver's eyebrows twitched up, and the look on his face was bitterly amused. "You're asking me to witness a schoolyard transaction for cheating. How . . . quaint."

Claire didn't wait. She pushed a thumb drive toward Monica. "There's an electronic file on there," she said. "It's password protected. If you can figure out the password, you can have the answers."

Monica's mouth dropped open. "*What?*"

"You said I had to give them to you. I did. That's what I wanted Oliver to see. Now you have them, so we're done. No comebacks. Right?"

"You put them under a *password?*"

"One you can guess," Claire said. "If you did the homework. Or can read fast."

"You little *bitch.*" Monica's hand flashed out—not for the thumb drive, but for Claire's arm. She crushed it to the table, her nails digging in deep enough to draw blood. "I told you, I'll fry your ass."

"With you, I know that's not an empty threat," Claire said. "Alyssa Collins is proof of that."

Monica went very still, and something flickered across her eyes— shock? Maybe even regret and guilt. "I'm not taking this thing. You give me the answers without the password."

Oliver cleared his throat. "Did you specify how she had to give you the answers?"

"No," Claire said. "She just said I had to. I did. Hey, this is the nicest way I could have done it. I could have given it to her in Latin or something."

"Let go of her," Oliver said mildly. When Monica didn't, his tone turned icy. "Let. *Go.*"

She pulled her hand back and folded her arms over her chest, glaring at Claire, her jaw set hard. "This isn't over."

"It is," Oliver said. "Not her fault you made a poor definition of what it was you wanted from her. She satisfied all requirements. She's even given you a reasonable chance of discovering the password. Take it and walk away, Monica."

"This isn't over," Monica repeated, ignoring him. When she reached for the thumb drive, Oliver's pale, strong hand slapped down over it, and over her fingers, holding her in place. Monica yelped. It must have hurt.

"Look at me," he said. Monica blinked and focused on his face, and Claire saw her pupils widen. Her lips parted a little. "Monica Morrell, you are my responsibility. You owe me respect, and you owe me obedience. And you *will* leave Claire Danvers alone. If you have cause to attack her, you will tell me first. *I* will decide whether or not you can take action. And you do *not* have my permission. Not for this." He let go. Monica yanked her hand back and cradled it against her chest. "Now, take your business and your coffee elsewhere. Both of you."

Monica reached out and snatched up the small memory stick. As she did, Claire said, "The thumb drive cost me ten bucks." Monica's glare reached nuclear levels, but since Oliver was still sitting there, she dug in her tiny purse, found a crumpled ten-dollar bill, and flung it over the table to Claire. She smoothed it out, smiled, and put it in her pocket.

"If you're quite finished," Oliver said. "Leave. Monica, go first. I won't have you doing anything messy. I'm not your maid."

Monica sent him a look that was definitely *not* a glare; it was much more scared than angry. She picked up her purse and the coffee, and stalked to the door. She didn't look back as she piled into her convertible and burned rubber pulling out.

"One of these days," Oliver said, still looking toward the street, "you're going to be too clever for your own good, Claire. You do realize that."

She did, actually. But sometimes, it was just impossible to do anything else.

"I guess you're coming with us tonight?"

Oliver turned his head to look at her this time, and there was something so cold and distant in his eyes that she shivered. "Did you hear me when I told you to leave? I don't like being used to settle your problems."

She swallowed, picked up her stuff, and left.

The afternoon was spent with Myrnin at his freaky mad-scientist lab, which was actually much nicer after the renovations he'd done: new equipment; computers; nice bookcases; decent lighting instead of crazy turn-of-last-century things that emitted sparks when you tried to turn them off or on.

Still, no matter how nice the decor, Myrnin was never less than half crazy. He was under pressure from Amelie, Claire knew; with the death— could computers die?—of Ada, the town's master computer, he was struggling to figure out a way to make a replacement, but *without* putting a human brain into it, which Claire strongly discouraged, given how well that had worked out with Ada and the fact that Claire herself was almost certainly the next candidate.

"Computers," Myrnin said, then shoved the laptop she'd put out for him aside and glared at it as if it had personally insulted him. "The technology is entirely idiotic. Who built this? Baboons?"

"It works fine," Claire said, and took command of the computer to bring up the interface she'd designed. "All you have to do is explain to me how Ada was connected into the portal and security systems, and I can build some kind of connector. You can run it right from this screen. See?" She'd even gotten an art student at the school to design the interface in a steampunky kind of way, which she thought would make Myrnin feel more at home. Myrnin continued to frown at it, but in a less aggressive way. "Try it. Just touch the screen."

He reached out with one fingertip and pressed the screen over the icon of the shield. The security screen came up, all rusted iron and ornamental gears. He made a humming sound in the back of his throat and pressed again. "And this would control the programming."

"Yeah, it's GUI—a graphic user interface."

"And this program would be able to detect vampires and humans, and treat them differently?"

"Yeah. We just use heat-sensing technology. Vampires have a lower body temperature. It's easy to tell the difference."

"Can it be cheated?"

Claire shrugged. "Anything can be cheated. But it's pretty good."

"And the memory alteration?"

That was a problem—a big problem. "I don't think you can actually do that with a computer. I mean, isn't that some kind of vampire mind thing?" Because Ada had, in fact, been a vampire. And the machine that Myrnin had built to keep her brain alive had somehow allowed her to broadcast that vampire power on a wide field. Claire didn't really understand it, but she knew it worked—*had* worked.

"That's a rather large failure. What's this?" Myrnin tapped an icon that had a radar screen icon. Nothing happened.

"That's an early-warning system, to monitor approaches to town. In case."

"In case what?"

"In case someone like Mr. Bishop decides to visit again."

Myrnin smiled and leaned back in his chair, folding his hands in his lap. "There is no one like Mr. Bishop," he said. "Thank the most holy. And this is excellent work, Claire, but it doesn't solve our fundamental problem. The difference engine needs programming to allow for removal of dangerous memories. I know of no other way to achieve what we need than to interface it with a biological database."

"A brain."

"Well, if you want to be technical."

Claire sighed. "I am *not* getting you a brain, because I am not that kind of lab assistant, Dr. Frankenstein. Can we go through the map again?"

The map was a giant flowchart that stretched the length of the lab on giant notepads. She had painstakingly mapped out every single *if*, *then*, and *and/or* that Myrnin had been able to describe.

It was huge. Really huge. And she wasn't at all sure it could be done, period—except that he had done it, once, to Ada.

She just wanted to take the icky brain part out of the equation.

"It's so much easier," Myrnin insisted as they walked the row of pages. "The brain is capable of processing a staggering number of calculations per second, *and* is capable of incorporating variables and factors that a mere computer cannot. It's the finest example of a calculating machine ever developed. We're fools not to use it."

"Well, you're not putting my brain into a machine. Ever."

"I wouldn't." Myrnin picked a piece of lint from his shiny vest. "Unless it was the only answer, of course. Or, of course, unless you weren't using it anymore."

"*Never.* Promise."

He shrugged. "I promise." But not in any way that mattered, Claire thought. Myrnin's promises were kind of—flexible. "You're leaving town the rest of the week?"

"Yeah, we're leaving tonight. You'll be okay?"

"Why wouldn't I?" He clasped his hands behind him and paced back and forth, staring at the charts. He was wearing shorts today, and flip-flops, of course—like some homeless surfer from the waist down, some Edwardian lord from the waist up. It was strange, and ridiculously Myrnin. "I'm not an infant, Claire. I don't need you to take care of me. Believe me."

She didn't, really. Yes, he was old. Yes, he was a vampire. Yes, he was crazy/smart—but the crazy part was always as strong as, or stronger than, the smart part. Even now.

"You're not going to do anything stupid, are you?" she asked him. He turned and looked at her, and looked utterly innocent.

"Why in the world would I do that?" he asked. "Have a good time, Claire. The work will still be here when you return."

She shut down the laptop and closed the lid, packing it up to put it away. As she did, he finally nodded at the machine. "That's not bad," he said. "As a start."

"Thanks." She was a little surprised. Myrnin didn't often give out random compliments. "Are you feeling okay?"

"Certainly. Why wouldn't I be?"

There was just something off about his mood. From visiting her parents to the way he was restlessly prowling the lab—he just wasn't his usual, unsettlingly manic self. He was a *different* manic self.

"I wish I were going with you," he finally said. "There. I've said it. You may mock me at your will."

"Really? But—we're just going for Michael, really." That wasn't true. It was a chance to get out of Morganville, experience life out in the real world. And she knew it would be amazing to feel free again, even for a little while. "Couldn't you go if you wanted?"

He sat down in his leather wing chair, put on his spectacles, and opened a book from a pile next to it. "Could I?" he asked. "If Amelie didn't wish me to leave? Not very likely."

She'd never considered that Myrnin, of all people, could be just as trapped in Morganville as everybody else. He seemed so . . . in control, somehow; at the same time he was wildly *out* of control. But she could see that of everyone in town, Amelie would trust Myrnin the least in terms of actually exiting the town limits. He had too much knowledge, too much insanity brewing around in that head of his.

As careful as Amelie was, she'd never take the risk. No, Myrnin, of everybody in Morganville, would be the next to last to leave, right before Amelie herself. He was her—pet? No, that wasn't right. Her *asset.*

It had never really occurred to Claire that he might not altogether like that.

"Sorry," she said softly. He waved at her, a shooing motion that left her feeling a little lost. She genuinely liked Myrnin, even though she was always intensely aware, these days, of the limits of that friendship—and of the dangers. "Call me if you—"

"Why? So you'll come running back to Morganville?" He shook his head. "Not likely. And not necessary. Just go, Claire. I'll be here."

There was a grim sound to that that she didn't like, but it was getting late. Michael had said to be ready at six, and she needed to pack for the trip.

When she looked back, Myrnin had given up the pretense of reading and was just staring off into the distance. There was something horribly sad about his expression, and she almost turned back. . . .

But she didn't.

FOUR

The Glass House was chaos when Claire opened the door. Mostly that was Eve and Shane, fighting stereo wars and yelling at each other upstairs. Eve was favoring Korn; Shane was fighting back by blasting "Macarena" at the limit of the boom box knob. There was no sign of Michael, but his guitars were cased and sitting in the living room, along with a duffel bag and a rolling cooler that looked like it could hold any normal drinks. Claire just wasn't sure what it *did* hold, and she didn't open it to find out.

She dropped her backpack, which she figured she'd take anyway, and jogged upstairs. Eve was standing in a pile of clothes, an open suitcase on the bed, holding two identical-looking shirts and frowning at them. Terminal fashion indecision. Claire dashed in, tapped her right hand, and Eve gave her a grateful grin and tossed the shirt into the suitcase. The music was so loud, conversation was impossible.

As she passed Shane's door, she saw him sprawled on his bed. He had a duffel bag, like Michael's but brown instead of blue. He looked bored, but he brightened up when he saw her.

"Seriously?" she yelled. "'The Macarena'?"

"It's war," he yelled back. "I had to bring out the heavy artillery. Next up, Barry Manilow!"

Claire hit the POWER button on the stereo, leaving Korn thunder-
ing victoriously through the house. After a second or two, Eve turned it
down. "See how easy that was?" Claire said.

"What, giving up? Giving up is *always* easy. It's the peace that follows
that sucks." Shane slithered off the bed and followed her as she headed
for her room. "How was it?"

"What?"

"Everything."

"You know." She shrugged. "Normal." Yeah. She'd manipulated the
second most powerful vampire in town into taking her side against a
psycho bitch-queen sorority girl. She'd talked rationally about putting
people's brains into computers. This was a normal day. No wonder she
was screwed up. "How was yours?"

"Brisket. Chopping block. Cleaver. It's all good. You packed yet?"

"Did you just see me walk in?"

"Oh. Yeah. Guess not, then."

He parked himself on her bed, flopped out again as she opened up her
one battered suitcase and began filling it. That wasn't tough; unlike Eve,
she wasn't a clothes fanatic. She had a couple of decent shirts, a bunch of
not-so-great ones, and some jeans. She put in her one skirt, along with
the shoes that matched it, and the fishnet tights. Shane watched, hands
laced behind his head.

"You're not going to try to tell me what to take?" she asked. "Because
I figured that was why you followed me."

"Do I look crazy? I followed you because your bed is more comfortable." His smile widened. "Wanna see?"

"Not right now."

"Last chance before we hit the road."

"Stop it!"

"Stop what?"

"Looking so . . ." She couldn't think of a word. He looked just as
ridiculously hot to her now as he had this morning, when it had been so
tough to leave. And that was a good thing. "I've got to get stuff out of
the bathroom."

"Good luck. I think Eve took everything already except the aftershave."

Actually, Eve hadn't; it was just that Claire didn't have a whole lot. Shampoo and conditioner, all in one bottle. A little makeup bag. A razor. She didn't really need a blow-dryer, but if she did, Eve would have packed one—or two. From the size of her suitcase, Eve was planning to take everything she'd ever owned.

Back in the bedroom, Claire almost shut her suitcase, then stopped and frowned. "What did you take?" she asked. "For, you know, protection?"

Shane lifted himself up on his elbows. "What, like, uh, *protection*?"

"No!" She felt her face flush, which was pretty ridiculous, considering what they'd done this morning. "I mean, against any vampire things that might happen. You know."

"Stakes in the bottom of the duffel bag," he said. "Brought some extra silver nitrate in bottles, too. We should be okay. It's not as if there's a big vampire problem where we're going."

Maybe not, but living in Morganville had made it a reflex. Claire couldn't honestly imagine *not* planning for it, and she hadn't been raised here, in the hothouse. She was surprised Shane seemed so . . . calm.

But then, Shane had been outside of Morganville, for two years. And they hadn't been a good two years, either, but at least he knew something about what it was going to be like; more than Michael and Eve, anyway.

Claire dug in her underwear drawer, came up with four silver-coated stakes, and dumped them in on top of her clothes. Just in case. Shane gave her a thumbs-up in approval. She slammed the bag shut and locked it, then wrestled it off the bed. It was heavier than she'd expected, and it wasn't one with wheels and a handle. Shane, unasked, slid off the bed and took it from her. He lifted it as if it were the weight of a bag of feathers, went into his room, grabbed his duffel, and headed toward the stairs. As he passed Eve's room he looked in, shook his head, and yelled, "You are totally on your own for that one!"

Claire saw why, as she looked in. Eve had closed the suitcase and somehow gotten it to the floor, but it was the size of a trunk.

At least it had wheels.

Michael was downstairs when Shane and Claire came down; Shane thumped their bags down and said, "You'd better wrangle your girlfriend's bag, man. I would, but I don't want to spend the entire trip in traction."

Michael grinned and zoomed upstairs. He came down carrying the suitcase as if it were nothing. Claire noticed it was new and shiny, and had hand-applied death's-head stickers and biohazard marks. Yeah, that was definitely Eve's. Oh, and it was black. Of course.

"Snacks!" Eve yelped, and dashed into the kitchen. She came back with a bag full of things. "Road food. Trust me. Totally necessary. Oh, and drinks—we need drinks." She caught sight of the cooler. "Okay, not you, Michael. The rest of us."

They were loading the second cooler with non-blood-related drink items when the doorbell rang. Claire opened it to find Oliver standing on the doorstep. The sun was still up, but he was wearing a hat and a long black coat, which didn't in any way make him less sinister. His hair was tied back and must have been tucked up under his hat. She wondered if it was flammable, like the rest of him. Age had made him flame-retardant, but he'd still suffer out in the sun, and eventually burst into flames, if he couldn't get out of it.

He came in without waiting for an invitation. "Yeah, welcome." Claire sighed and shut the door. "We're getting stuff together. Uh, is that all you brought?" It was one bag, smaller even than Michael's or Shane's.

Oliver didn't bother to answer her. He walked past, into the living room, and straight for Michael. Eve and Shane, who were bickering over the placement of the Cokes versus the bottled iced coffees, fell silent, and Claire joined them.

"You're surely not taking all this," Oliver said, looking at the pile of stuff on the floor. It was, Claire had to admit, a lot—mainly because Eve's suitcase was the size of Rhode Island, but they'd all contributed. "Is there room?"

"I have a major trunk," Eve said. "It'll fit."

Oliver shook his head. "I hate traveling with amateurs," he said. "Very well. Get the car loaded. Michael and I will wait inside until the sun is down."

He acted as if he were the boss, which was annoying, but the truth was, he *was* the boss. Amelie had assigned him as escort, and that meant he could boss them around all he wanted. Heaven, for Oliver. Hell, for everybody else.

Claire shrugged silently, then picked up her suitcase and backpack and led the way.

Packing the car was hilariously awful, because trying to get Eve's suitcase wedged in was a drama nobody needed. It finally worked, and everything else fit in, including the guitars and the coolers. It left the three of them sweaty, annoyed, and exhausted, but by the time they'd worked it all out, the sun was safely down.

Nobody tried to call shotgun. Oliver took the front seat, Michael got in the driver's seat, and Eve, Claire, and Shane took the back. It wasn't even all that crowded.

"Passes," Oliver said, and held out his hand. Michael handed them over, and Oliver examined them as if he didn't know they'd already been cleared to leave town. "Very well. Proceed."

"Tunes!" Eve said. "We need—"

"No music," Oliver said. "I will not be subjected to what you consider *tunes.*"

"FYI, I know it's a disguise, but you even suck at being a hippie," Eve muttered. "At least like the Beatles or something."

"No."

"It's going to be a really long trip," Shane said, and put his arm around both Claire and Eve, since he was in the middle. "But at least I've got all the babes. Backseat, for the win."

"Shut up," Michael said.

"Come back here and make me, *Dad.*"

Michael and Shane exchanged rude gestures, and then Michael started up the car and pulled away from the curb. Eve squirmed in her seat and clapped her hands.

Oliver turned and glared at her. He took off his black hat and set it on the dashboard, next to Eve's nodding skeletal figurine. "Enough of that," he said. "It's bad enough I have to be trapped in a car with you children. You'll do your best not to *act* like children."

"Oliver," Michael said, "back off. It's our first time out of town. Let us enjoy it a little."

"The first time for some of you," Oliver said, and looked out the window as the houses of Lot Street began to roll by, one after another. "For some of us, this is not quite as life-changing an event."

That was kind of true, but still, Claire felt Eve's excitement was contagious. Michael was smiling. Shane was enjoying being the dude in the backseat. And she was . . . leaving Morganville behind, at least for a little while.

At the town limits, Claire watched the WELCOME TO MORGANVILLE sign approach. This side said PLEASE DON'T LEAVE US SO SOON!

They rocketed past it doing at least seventy, maybe eighty miles an hour. Beyond the sign sat a police cruiser—one of Hannah Moses's crew. Claire felt her breath rush out, but the cop behind the wheel just waved them on, and Michael didn't even slow down.

Morganville, in the rearview mirror.

Just like that.

It shouldn't have been so easy, Claire thought. After all that, all the fighting and the terror and the threats.

They just . . . drove away.

Michael switched on the radio and found a scratchy rock 'n' roll station, and although Oliver kept glaring, he turned it up, and before long they were all singing "Born to Be Wild," out of tune and at the top of their lungs. Oliver didn't, but he didn't pitch an übervamp fit, either. Claire was almost certain that once or twice, she saw his lips moving with the lyrics.

The sunset was glorious, spilling colors all over the sky in shades of orange and red and gold, fading into indigo blue. Claire rolled down the window and smelled the cool, crisp air, flavored with dust and sage. Outside of Morganville there was scrub desert, and a lot of it. Nothing to see for miles except flat, empty land, and the two-lane blacktop road stretching into the distance, straight as an arrow.

"We have to do some jogging around on farm roads," Michael said, once the song was over and the music shifted to something not as karaoke worthy. "Should be on the interstate in about two hours or so."

"You're sure you know where you're going?" Shane asked. "Because I don't want to wake up in the Gulf of Mexico or something."

Michael ignored that, and Claire slowly settled into her seat, feeling relaxed and light. They'd *left*. They'd actually *left Morganville*. She could feel the same suppressed thrill and relief in Shane, and, on his other side, from Eve, whose dark eyes just glowed with excitement. She'd been dreaming of this her whole life, Claire realized. Maybe not being trapped in a car with Oliver, or that Michael would be a vampire, but leaving town with Michael had always been one of Eve's top-ten fantasies.

And here they were, more or less, anyway, which just went to show you that your top-ten fantasies might turn out to be completely different experiences than you'd ever thought.

"We're out," Eve said, almost to herself. "We're out, we're out, we're *out*."

"You'll go back," Oliver said, and turned his head to stare out the side window. "You all go back, eventually."

"Even for a vampire, you're a ray of sunshine," Shane said. "So, we should probably talk about what we're going to do in Dallas."

"Everything!" Eve said, instantly. "Everything, everything, everything. And then everything else."

"Whoa, hit the brakes, girl. We've got, what, a hundred bucks between the two of us? I'm pretty sure the all-inclusive everything party package costs more."

"Oh." Eve looked surprised, as if she hadn't even thought about money at all. Knowing Eve, she likely hadn't. "Well, we have to at least go to some of the good clubs, right? And shopping? Oh, and they have some really good movie theaters."

"Movies?" Michael repeated, looking in the rearview mirror. "Seriously? Eve."

"What? *Stadium seating*, Michael. *Digital*. With three-D and everything."

"You're going to waste your first trip outside of Morganville inside a movie theater?"

"No, well, I—*stadium seating!* Okay, okay, fine. Museums. Concerts. Culture. Better?"

Shane just shook his head. "Not really. Where's the fun, Eve?"

"That *is* fun!"

Oliver sighed and let his head fall against the window glass with a soft thump. "One of you is going to be left to walk to Dallas if you don't *shut up.*"

"Wow. Who got up on the wrong side of the coffin this evening?" Eve shot back. "Well? You're the expert. Where would you go?"

Oliver straightened up and looked back at her. "Excuse me?"

"I'm asking your opinion. You probably know where the best places are to go."

"I——" Oliver seemed at a loss for words, which was pretty funny; Claire couldn't imagine the last time that had happened to him. Probably not in the last couple of centuries, she guessed. "You're asking for my recommendations. Of things to do in Dallas."

"Yep."

He stared at Eve for a long, silent, chilly moment, then turned back, face forward. "I doubt our tastes have anything in common. You're too young for the bars, and too old for the playgrounds. I know nothing of what you'd like." Then, after a second's pause, he continued. "Perhaps the malls."

"Malls!" Eve almost shrieked it, then clapped both hands over her mouth. "Oh my God, I forgot about the malls. With actual stores. Can we go to the mall?"

"Which one?"

"There's more than one! Okay, uh—one with a Hot Topic store."

Oliver was—from Claire's point of view—almost *smiling.* "I believe that could be arranged."

"Great." Shane sighed, and let his head drop back against the seat. "The mall. Just what I always wanted."

Claire reached up and threaded her fingers through his. "We can do other stuff." When he glanced over at her, and she realized that everybody *else* was looking at her, too, she colored and added, "Cultural stuff. You know. Bookstores. Museums. There's a cool science museum I'd like to see."

"Is there not a video game store in this entire town?"

"Let's just get there first," Michael said.

That was good advice, Claire thought as the last colors faded from the sky and night took over. That was *really* good advice.

She dozed a little bit, but she woke up when the car jerked violently, veered, and she heard the tires squeal. She was still trying to understand what had happened when Oliver snapped, "Pull over."

"What?" Michael, in the glow of the dashboard, looked like a ghost, his eyes wide and his face tense.

"You've never driven outside of Morganville. I have. Pull over. Vampire reflexes will put you into an accident, not save you from one. Humans can't react in the same way you can. It takes practice to drive safely around them on the open road."

So Michael must have tried to dodge a car. Wow. Somehow, Claire had never considered that vampire reflexes could have a downside. Michael must have felt spooked enough to agree with Oliver, because he pulled the car off to the shoulder, gravel crunching under the tires, and got out. He and Oliver changed places. Oliver checked the car's mirrors with the ease of long practice, steered the car back on the road, and the whole thing settled into a steady, rolling rhythm. Claire looked over at the other two in the backseat. Eve had her headphones on and her eyes closed. Shane was sound asleep. It was . . . peaceful, she supposed. She looked out at the night. There was a quarter moon, so it wasn't all that bright out, but the silver light gilded sand and spiky plants. Everything in the wash of the car's headlights was vivid; everything else was just shadows and smoke.

It was like space travel, she decided. Every once in a while you could see an isolated house, far out in the middle of nowhere, with its lights blazing against the night. But mostly, they were out here alone.

Oliver took a turn off the two-lane highway, heading for the interstate, she supposed. She didn't ask—not until they passed a road sign that had an arrow pointing to Dallas.

The arrow pointed left. They headed straight on.

"Hey," she said. "Hey, Oliver? I think you missed your turn."

"I don't need advice," Oliver said.

"But the sign—"

"We have a stop to make," he said. "It won't take long."

"Wait, what? What stop?" It was news to Michael, apparently. That didn't ease the sudden anxiety in Claire's chest. "What's this about, Oliver?"

"Be still, all of you. It's none of your affair."

"Our car," Michael pointed out. "And we're in it. So it looks like it *is* our affair. Now, where are you taking us, and why?"

Shane woke up, probably sensing the tension in Michael's voice. He blinked twice, swiped at his face, and leaned forward. "Something wrong?"

"Yeah," Michael said. "We're getting hijacked."

Shane sat up slowly, and Claire could feel the tension coiling in him.

"Easy, all of you," Oliver said. "This is a directive from Amelie. There's a small issue I need to address. It won't take long."

Eve, who'd removed one earphone, gave a jaw-cracking yawn. "I could stretch my legs," she said. "Also, a bathroom would be good."

"What kind of small issue?" Shane asked. He was still tense, watchful, and not buying Oliver's no-big-deal attitude. Oliver's cold eyes fixed on him in the rearview mirror.

"Nothing of consequence to you," he said. "And this isn't a debate. Shut up, all of you."

"Mikey?"

Michael gazed at Oliver for a long few seconds before he finally said, "No, it's okay. A short stop would do us all good, probably."

"Depending on where," Shane said, but shrugged and sat back. "I'm cool if you are."

Michael nodded. "We cool, Oliver?"

"I told you, it's not a debate."

"Four of us, one of you. Maybe it could be."

"Only if you want to answer to Amelie in the end."

Michael said nothing. They drove on through the inky night, surrounded by a bubble of backwashed headlights, and finally a faded sign glowed green in the distance. Claire blinked and squinted at it.

"'Durram, Texas,'" she read. "Is that where we're going?"

"More importantly, does it have an all-night truck stop?" Eve groaned. "Because I was serious about that bathroom thing. Really."

"Your bladder must be the size of a peanut," Shane said. "I think I see a sign up there."

He did, and it was a truck stop—not big, not very clean, but open. It was crowded, too—six big rigs in the lot, and quite a few pickup trucks. Oliver took the exit and pulled off into the truck stop, edging the car to a halt at a gas pump. "Top off the tank," he told Michael. "Then park it and wait for me inside. I'll be back."

"Wait, when?"

"When I'm done. I'm sure you can find something to occupy yourselves." And then the driver's-side door opened, and Oliver walked away. As soon as he was outside of the wash of the harsh overhead lights, he vanished.

"We could just leave," Shane pointed out. "Fill up and drive off."

"And you think that's a good plan?"

"Actually? Not really. But it's a *funny* plan."

"Funny as in getting us killed. Some more than others, I might add."

"Fine, rub the resurrection in our faces. But seriously. Why are we doing this? We ditch Oliver; we never have to go back to Morganville. Think about it."

Claire licked her lips and said, softly, "Not all of us can walk away, Shane. My parents are there. Eve's mom and brother. We can't just pick up and leave, not unless we want something bad to happen to them."

He looked actually ashamed of himself, as if he'd really forgotten that. "I didn't mean—" He gave a heavy sigh. "Yeah, okay. I see your point."

"Added to that, I'm Amelie's blood now," Michael said. "She can find me if she wants me. If you want to include me in the great escape, I'm like a giant GPS tracking chip of woe."

"Whoa."

"Exactly."

Eve said, plaintively, "Bathroom?"

And that closed the discussion of running away.

At least, for the moment.

The Texas Star Truck Stop was worse on the inside than the outside.

As Claire pushed open the door—with Shane trying to open it for her—a tinny bell rang, and when she looked up, Claire found herself being stared at—a lot.

"Wow," Shane murmured, close behind her as he entered the store. "Meth central."

She knew what he meant. This was a scary bunch of people. The youngest person in the place, apart from them, was a pinched, too-tanned skinny woman of about thirty wearing a skimpy top and cut-off shorts. She had tattoos—a lot of them. Everybody else was older, bigger, meaner, and uncomfortably fixed on the newcomers.

And then Eve stepped in, in all her Goth glory, bouncing from one Doc Martens–booted foot to the other. "Bathroom?" she asked the big, bearded man behind the counter. He frowned at her, then reached down and came up with a key attached to a big metal bar. "Thank you!" Eve seized the key and dashed off down the dark hall marked RESTROOMS; Claire wasn't sure she'd have the guts, no matter how much she had to pee. That did *not* look safe, never mind clean.

Michael stepped in last, and took it all in with one quick, comprehensive look. He raised his eyebrows at Shane, who shrugged. "Yeah," he said. "I know. Fun, huh?"

"Let's get a table," Michael said. "Order something." Under the theory, Claire guessed, that if they spent money, the locals would like them better.

Somehow, she didn't think that was going to work. Her gaze fell on signs posted around the store: YOU DRAW YOUR GUN, WE DRAW FASTER. GUN CONTROL MEANS HITTING WHAT YOU AIM AT. NO TRESPASSING— VIOLATORS WILL BE SHOT; SURVIVORS WILL BE SHOT AGAIN.

"I don't think I'm going to be hungry," she said, but Michael was right. This really was their only option, other than sitting outside in the car. "Maybe something to drink. They have Coke, right?"

"Claire, people in Botswana have Coke. I'm pretty sure Up the Road a Piece, Texas, has Coke."

By the time they'd gotten seated at one of the grungy plastic booths, still being stared at by the locals, Eve finally joined them. She looked more relaxed, bouncy, and more—well, Eve. "Better," she announced, as she slipped into place next to Michael. "Mmm, *much* better now."

He put his arm around her and smiled. It was cute. Claire found herself smiling, too, and snuggled up against Shane. "How was the bathroom?"

Eve shuddered. "We shall never speak of it again."

"I was afraid of that."

"You want a menu?"

"Absolutely. They might have ice cream."

The last thing bouncy, happy Eve needed was a sugar rush, but ice cream did sound good. . . . Claire looked around for a waitress and found one leaning against the cracked counter, whispering to the man on the other side. They were both staring straight at Claire and her friends, and their expressions weren't exactly friendly.

"Uh, guys? Maybe ixnay on the ice eam-cray. How about we wait in the car?" she asked.

"And miss *ice cream*? Hella don't think so," Eve said. She waved at the waitress and smiled. Claire winced. "Oh, relax, CB. I'm a people person."

"In Morganville!"

"Same thing," Eve said. She kept on smiling, but it started getting a little strained as the waitress continued to stare but didn't acknowledge the wave. Eve raised her voice. "Hi? I'd like to order something? Hellooooooo?"

The waitress and the guy behind the counter seemed frozen in place, glaring, but then they were blocked out by someone stepping into Claire's line of sight—more than one someone, in fact. There were three men, all big and puffy, and with really unpleasant expressions.

Shane, who'd been slumped lazily next to her, straightened up.

"Don't y'all got no manners where you come from?" the first one asked. "You wait your turn. Sherry don't like being yelled at."

Eve blinked, then said, "I wasn't—"

"Where you from?" he interrupted her. The men formed a redneck wall between the table and the rest of the room, pinning the four of them in place. Shane and Michael exchanged a look, and Michael took his arm away from Eve's shoulders.

"We're on our way to Dallas," Eve said, just as cheerfully as if the situation hadn't gone from inhospitable to ominous. "Michael's a musician. He's going to record a CD."

The three men laughed. It wasn't a nice sound, and it was one Claire recognized all too well—it was deeper in register, but it was the same laugh Monica Morrell and her friends liked to give when stalking their prey. It wasn't amusement. It was a weird sort of aggression—laughing *at* you, not *with* you; sharing a secret.

"Musician, huh? You in one of those *boy* bands?" The second man— shorter, squattier, wearing a dirty orange ball cap and a stained University of Texas sweatshirt with the arms cut off. "We just love our *boy* bands out here."

"I ever meet those damn Jonas Brothers in person, I'll give 'em what for," the third man said. He seemed angrier than the others, eyes like black little holes in a stiff, tight face. "My kid can't shut up about 'em."

"I know what you mean," Eve said with a kind of fake sweetness that made Claire wince, again. "Nobody's really been worth listening to since New Kids on the Block, am I right?"

"What?" He fixed those dead, dark eyes on her.

"Wow, not a New Kids on the Block fan, either. I'm shocked. Okay, I'm thinking not Marilyn Manson, then. . . . Jessica Simpson? Or . . ." Eve's voice faded out, because Michael's hand had closed over her arm. She looked over at him, and he shook his head. "Right. Shutting up now. Sorry."

"What do you want?" Michael asked the men.

"Your little freak vampire girlfriend needs to learn how to keep her mouth shut."

"Who you calling *little?*" Eve demanded.

Shane sighed. "Wrong on so many levels. Eve. *Shut up.*"

She glared at him but made a little key-and-lock motion at her lips, folded her arms, and sat back.

Michael had locked gazes with the third man, the angry one, and they were staring it out. It went on for a while, and then Michael said, "Why don't you just let me and my friends have our ice cream, and then we'll get back in our car and leave? We don't want a problem."

"Oh, you don't, you whiny little bitch?" The angry man shoved the other two aside and slapped his palms flat against the table to loom over Claire and her friends. "Why'd you come in here, then?"

Eve said, in a very small voice, "Ice cream?"

"Told you to shut the hell up." And he tried to hit her with a back-handed smack.

Tried because Michael leaned forward in a flare of motion, and had hold of the man's wrist in a flicker of time so fast Claire didn't even see it. Neither did the angry man, who looked just kind of confused by being unable to move his hand, then put it all together and looked at Michael.

"Don't," Michael said. It was soft, and it was a warning, through and through. "You try to hurt her again and I'll pull your arm off."

He wasn't kidding, but the problem was, *none* of them was kidding. While he was holding the angry one, the guy in the orange cap reached in his pocket, flicked open a big, shiny knife, and grabbed Eve by the hair. She squeaked, raised her chin, and tried to kick him. He was good at avoiding her. It looked as if he'd had practice. "Let Berle go," Orange Cap said. "Or I'll do a hell of a lot worse than slap this one. I can get me real creative."

Shane was cursing softly under his breath, and Claire knew why; he was stuck in the corner, she was in front of him, and there was no way he could be effective in helping Michael out from that angle. He had to just sit there—something he wasn't very good at doing. Claire stayed very still, too, but she looked Orange Cap in the eyes and said, "Sir?" She said it respectfully, as her mom had taught her. "Sir, please don't hurt my friend. She didn't mean anything."

"We don't like smart-mouthed freaks around here," he said. "We got our ways."

"Yes, sir. We understand now. We were just trying to have a little fun. We won't be any trouble, I promise. Please let my friend go." She kept her tone calm, sweet, reasonable—all the things she'd learned to do when Myrnin was running off his rails.

Orange Cap blinked, and she thought he was seeing her for the first time. "You need better friends, little girl," he said. "Shouldn't be running around with a bunch of freaks. If you was my daughter—" But he'd lost his edge, and he let go of Eve's hair and wiped his hand on his greasy jeans as he folded up his knife. "You get on up out of here. Right now. You let Berle go, and we'll let this pass. Nobody gets hurt."

"We're going," Claire said instantly, and grabbed Shane's hand. Michael let go of the angry guy, Berle, who snatched his arm back and rubbed at his wrist as if it hurt. It probably did. Claire could see white marks where Michael had held him. That was restraint for Michael; he probably could have broken the bone without much effort. "Sir?" She spoke again to Orange Cap, treating him like the man in charge, and he nodded and clapped his friends on the shoulders.

They all stepped back.

Claire slipped out of the booth and squeezed by the men, practically dragging Shane with her. Eve and Michael followed. They walked away from the table, into the store, and Claire pushed open the door and led them all outside, into the harsh white light near the gas pumps and the car.

She looked back at the store. The three men, the people working the restaurant, and practically everyone else were looking out the windows at them.

Claire turned on Eve first. "Are you *crazy?*" she demanded. "Just couldn't shut up, could you? And *you!*" She pointed at Michael. "You're not in Morganville anymore, Michael. Back there you were a big dog. Out here, you're what *we* were back *there*. Vulnerable. So you need to stop thinking that people owe you respect just because you're a vampire."

He looked stunned. "That's not what I—"

"It was," she said, interrupting him. "You acted like a vamp, Michael. Like any vamp getting back-talked by a human. You could have gotten us hurt. You could have gotten Eve killed!"

Michael looked at Shane, who lifted his shoulders in a tiny, apologetic shrug. "She's not wrong, bro."

"That's not what it was," Michael insisted. "I was just trying to—look, Eve started it."

"Hey! That thump you heard was me under the bus, there!"

Shane shrugged again. "And now Michael's not wrong. Hey, I like this game. I don't have to be the wrong one for once in my life."

"Shut up, Shane," Eve snapped. "What about you, Miss *Oh, sir, please let my friends go; I'm such a delicate little flower?* What a crock of shit, Claire!"

"Oh, so now you're mad because I got you out of it?" Claire felt her cheeks flaming, and she was literally shaking now with anger and distress. "You started it, Eve! I was just trying to keep you from getting killed! Sorry you didn't like how I pulled that off!"

"You just—can't you stand up for yourself?"

"Hey," Shane said softly, and touched Eve's arm. She whirled toward him, fists clenched, but Shane held up both hands in clear surrender. "She stood up for *you*. Might want to consider that before you go calling Claire a coward. She's never been that."

"Oh, *sure*, you take her side!"

"It's not a side," Shane said. "And if it is, you ought to be on it, too."

Michael had been watching, calming down (or at least shutting down), and now he reached out and put his hands on Eve's shoulders. She tensed, then relaxed, closed her eyes, and blew out an impatient breath. "Right," she said. "You're going to tell me I can't be upset about nearly getting my face cut off."

"No," Michael said. "But don't take it out on Claire. It's not her fault."

"It's mine."

"Well . . ." He sighed. "Kind of mine, too. Share?"

Eve turned to face him. "I like my blame. I keep it close like a warm, furry blanket."

"Let go," he said, and kissed her lightly. "You're taking my side of the blame blanket."

"Fine. You can have half." Eve was calmer now, and relaxed into Michael's embrace. "Damn. That *was* stupid, wasn't it? We nearly got killed over ice cream."

"Another thing I don't want on my tombstone," Shane said.

"You have others?" Claire asked.

He held up one finger. "I thought it wasn't loaded," Shane said. Second finger. "Hand me a match so I can check the gas tank." Third finger. "Killed over ice cream. Basically, any death that requires me to be stupid first."

Michael shook his head. "So what's on your good list?"

"Oh, you know. Hero stuff that gets me rerun on CNN. Like, I died saving a busload of supermodels." Claire smacked his arm. "Ow! *Saving* them! What did you think I meant?"

"So," Claire said, taking the high ground, "what now? I mean, I guess ice cream is kind of off the table, unless you're okay with random violence as a topping."

"Got to be something else in town," Michael said. "Unless you just want to sit here and take up a gas pump until Oliver gets his act together."

"He told us to wait here."

"Yeah, well, I'm with Michael on this one," Shane said. "Not really into doing what Oliver wants, you know? And this is supposed to be our trip, not his. He's just along for the ride. Personally, I like moving the car. Even if we're not leaving him behind."

"You really *do* have a death wish."

"You'll save me." He kissed Claire on the nose. "Mikey, you're driving."

FIVE

Durram, Texas, was a small town. Like, *really* small. Smaller than Morganville. There were about six blocks to it, not really in a square; more like a messy oval. The Dairy Queen was closed and dark; so was the Sonic. There was some kind of bar, but Michael quickly vetoed that suggestion (from Shane, of course); if they'd gotten into trouble asking for ice cream, asking for a beer would be certain doom.

Claire couldn't fault his logic, and besides, none of them was actually bar-legal age, anyway. Though she somehow doubted the folks in Durram really cared so much. They didn't seem like the overly law-abiding types. Cruising the streets seemed like a big, fat waste of time; there weren't any other cars on the streets, really, and not even many lights on in the houses. It seemed like a really boring, shut-up town.

Shades of Morganville, though in Morganville at least you had a good *reason* to avoid being out after dark.

"Hey! There!" Eve bounced in the front seat, pointing, and Claire squinted. There was a tiny, dim sign in a window, a few lights were on, and the sign *might* have said something about ice cream. "I knew no self-respecting small Texas town would shut down ice cream service at night."

"That makes no sense."

"Shut up, Shane. How can you not want ice cream? What is wrong with you?"

"I guess I was born without the ice cream gene. Thank God."

Michael pulled the car to a stop in front of the lonely little ice cream parlor. When he switched off the engine, the oppressive silence closed in; except for street signs creaking in the wind, there was hardly a sound at all in downtown Durram, Texas.

Eve didn't seem to care. She practically flung herself out of the car, heading for the door. Michael followed, leaving Claire and Shane behind in the backseat.

"This isn't going at all how I'd thought," Claire said with a sigh. He laced their fingers together and raised hers to his lips.

"How'd you think it would go?"

"I don't know. Saner?"

"You *have* been paying attention this last year, right? Because saner isn't even in our playbook." He nodded toward the ice cream parlor. "So? You want something?"

"Yes." She made no move to get out of the car.

"Then what—oh." He didn't sound upset about it. He'd been telling the truth, Claire thought. He really didn't have the ice cream gene.

But he *did* have the kissing gene and didn't need that much of a hint to start using it to both their advantages. He leaned forward, and at first it was a light, teasing brush of their lips, then soft, damp pressure, then more. He had such wonderful lips. They made her ignite inside, and it felt like gravity increased, all on its own, dragging her back sideways on the big bench seat, pulling him with her.

Things might have really gone somewhere, except all of a sudden there was a loud metallic knock on the window, and a light shined in, focusing on the back of Shane's head and in Claire's eyes. She yelped and flailed, shoved Shane away, and he scrambled to get himself together, too.

Standing outside of the car was a man in a tan shirt, tan pants, a big Texas hat. . . . It took a second for Claire's panicked brain to catch up as her eyes fastened on the shiny star pinned to his shirt front.

Oh. Oh, *crap*.

Local sheriff.

He tapped on the window again with the end of a big, intimidating flashlight, then blinded them again with the business end. Claire squinted and cranked down the window. She licked her lips nervously, and tasted Shane. Inappropriate!

"Let's see some ID," the man said. He didn't sound like the Welcome Wagon. Claire searched around for her backpack and pulled out her wallet, handing it over with trembling hands. Shane passed over his own driver's license. "You're seventeen?" The sheriff focused the beam on Claire. She nodded. He shifted the light to Shane. "Eighteen?"

"Yes, sir. Something wrong?"

"Don't know, son. You think there's something wrong about taking advantage of a girl who's under eighteen on a public street?"

"He wasn't—"

"Sure looked that way to me, miss. Out of the car, both of you. This your car?"

"No, sir," Shane said. He sounded subdued now. Reality was setting in. Claire realized they'd just made the same mistake that Michael had—they'd acted as if they were home in Morganville, where people knew them. Here, they were a couple of troublemaking teenagers—one underage—making out in the back of a car.

"You got any drugs?"

"No, sir," Shane repeated, and Claire echoed him. Her lips, which had felt so warm and lovely just a minute ago, now felt cold and numb. *This can't be happening. How could we be this stupid?* She remembered Shane's list of ways not to die. Maybe this ought to be number four.

"You mind if I search the car, then?"

"I—" Claire looked at Shane, and he looked back at her, his eyes suddenly very wide. Claire continued. "It's not our car, sir. It's our friend's."

"Well, where's your friend?"

"In there." Claire's throat was tight and dry, and she was holding Shane's hand now in a death grip. *If he searches the car, he'll open the coolers. If he opens the cooler and finds Michael's blood . . .*

She pointed to the ice cream shop door. The sheriff looked at it, then back at her, then at Shane. He nodded, switched off his flashlight, and said, "Don't you go nowhere."

Through all of that, Claire had only a blurry impression of him as a person—not too young, not too old, not too fat or thin or tall or short—just average. But as he walked away, his belt jingling with hand-cuffs and keys and his gun strapped down at his side, she felt cold and short of breath, the way she had when she'd faced down Mr. Bishop, the scariest vampire of all.

They were in trouble—*big* trouble.

"Fast," Shane said, as soon as the door started to close behind the sheriff. He yanked open the door, grabbed Michael's cooler, and looked around wildly for someplace to put it. "Go to the door. Cover me."

Claire nodded and walked up to the door, looking in the grimy glass, blocking any view past her of the street. She made little blinders out of her hands as if it were hard to see in. It wasn't. The sheriff had walked straight up to Michael and Eve, who were still standing at the counter of the ice cream shop. Eve had an ice cream cone in her hand, fluorescent mint green, but from the look on her face, she'd forgotten all about it.

Claire glanced back. Shane was gone. When she looked back into the store, the sheriff was still talking to Michael, Michael was answering, and Eve had a terrified look in her eyes.

Claire nearly screamed when someone touched her shoulder, and she jumped back. It was Shane, of course. "I put it in the alley, behind a trash can. Covered it with a stack of newspaper," he said. "Best I could do."

The sheriff had finished his conversation, and he, Eve, and Michael were heading for the door. Claire and Shane backed up to the car. Claire leaned against him and felt his heartbeat thudding hard. He looked calm. He wasn't.

Eve didn't even *look* calm. She looked, well, distressed. "But we didn't *do* anything!" she was saying, as they came outside. "Sir, please—"

"Got a report of trouble up at the Quik-E-Stop," the sheriff said. "People fitting your description threatening folks. And to be honest, you kind of stand out around here."

"But we didn't—" Eve bit her lip on blurting that out, because in fact they had. Michael had, for sure. "We didn't mean anything. We just wanted to get some ice cream, that's all."

Hers was starting to leak in thin green streams. Eve, startled, looked down and licked the melted stuff off her fingers.

"Better eat that before it's all over you," the cop said, sounding relaxed and almost human this time. "Do I have your permission to search your vehicle, ma'am?"

"I—" Eve's eyes fixed on Shane, behind the sheriff, who was giving a thumbs-up. "I guess so."

He seemed surprised, maybe even a little disappointed. "Sit down over there, on the curb. All of you."

They did. Eve had trouble doing it gracefully in the poofy black skirt she was wearing, but once she was down, she started wolfing down her ice cream. Halfway through, she stopped and pounded her forehead with an open palm. "Ow, ow, ow!"

"Ice cream headache?" Claire asked.

"No, I'm just wondering how the hell we could be so *bad* at this," Eve said. "All we were supposed to do was drive to Dallas. It shouldn't be this hard, right?"

"Oliver made us stop."

"I know, but if we can't stay out of trouble on our own—"

"That *was* an ice cream headache, right? Not an aneurysm?"

"That's where things explode in your brain? Probably that last thing." Eve sighed and bit into the cone part of her dessert. "I'm tired. Are you tired?"

Michael wasn't saying anything. He was staring at the car, and the cop searching it—going through bags, purses, glove box, even under the seats. He finally glanced over at Shane. "What about the weapons?"

Shane's mouth opened, then closed.

"Uh—"

Right at that moment, the cop opened Claire's suitcase and pulled out a sharp silver stake. He held it up. "What's this?"

None of them answered for a few seconds; then Eve said, "It's for the costumes. See, we're going to this convention? And I'm playing the vampire, and they're playing the vampire hunters? It's really cool."

That almost sounded real.

"This thing's sharp."

"The rubber ones looked really fake. There's a prize, you know? For authenticity?"

He gave her a long look, then dropped it back into Claire's bag, rummaged around, then closed it. He left the suitcases and bags outside the car, scattered around, and after checking in the wheel wells and in the spare tire section, he finally shook his head. "All right," he said. "I'm going to let you all go, but you need to go right now."

"What?"

"I need to see your taillights disappearing over the town limits. And I'm going to follow to make sure you get there nice and safe."

Oh *crap*. "What about Oliver?" Claire whispered.

"Well, we can't exactly give him as an excuse," Eve whispered back fiercely. She ate the last bit of ice cream cone and smiled at the cop. "We're ready, sir! Just let us get loaded up."

Michael grabbed Shane, and they had an urgent conversation, bent over Eve's giant suitcase. Eve leaped up, tripped over a random bag, and went down with a yelp that turned into a howl.

The sheriff, proving he wasn't a total jerk, immediately came to bend over her and see if she was okay.

This gave Michael enough vampire-speed time to retrieve the cooler from the alley, put it back in the car, and be innocently reaching for the next bag before the sheriff helped flailing, clumsy Eve up to her feet.

"Sorry," Eve said breathlessly, and gave Michael a trembling little smile and wave. "I'm okay. Just bruised a little."

"That's it," Shane said. "No more ice cream for you."

They finished loading things in the car, and Claire took a last look at the deserted streets, the flickering, distant, dim lights. There was no sign of Oliver; none at all.

"Well?" the sheriff said. "Let's go."

"Yes, sir." Eve slid into the driver's side, closed her eyes for a second, then fumbled for her keys and started the car. Michael took the passenger seat in front, and Claire and Shane climbed in the back.

The sheriff, true to his word, got in his cruiser, parked across the street, and turned on the red and blue flashers; no siren, though.

"Thanks," Michael said, and sent Eve a quick smile. "Good job with the tripping. It gave me time to get the blood."

"Wish I'd meant it, then." She put the car in reverse. "And could we please have another word for blood, outside of Morganville? Something like, oh, I don't know. Chocolate? Red velvet cake?"

"Why is it always sugar with you?" Shane asked.

"Shut up, Collins. This one was all on you, you know."

He shrugged and put his arm around Claire's shoulders. "Yeah, I know. Sorry."

"What are we going to do?" Claire asked. "About Oliver?"

Nobody had an answer.

The sheriff's cruiser let loose a shocking little *whoop* of siren, just to let them know he meant business. Eve swallowed, put the car in reverse, and backed the sedan onto the street. "Guess we'll figure it out as we go," she said. "Anybody got his cell number?"

"I do," Michael and Claire said, simultaneously, and exchanged guilty looks. Michael took out his phone and texted something as Eve drove—staying well under the speed limit, which Claire thought was very smart—and as they passed a sign announcing the town limit, the sheriff's car coasted to a stop. The lights were still flashing.

"Keep going?" Eve asked. She kept looking in the rearview mirror. "Guys? Decision?"

"Keep going," Shane said, leaning forward. "We can't get back as long as he's watching. If we're going back at all. Which I don't vote for, by the way."

"Better idea," Michael said, and pointed up ahead, on the left side of the narrow, very dark road. "There's a motel. We check in, wait for Oliver to join us. We're going to have to sit the day out somewhere, anyway."

"*There?*" Eve sounded appalled, and Claire could see why. It wasn't exactly the Ritz. It wasn't even as good as that motel in the movie *Psycho*.

It was a little, straight line of cinder-block rooms with a neon sign, a sagging porch, and one big security light for the parking lot.

And the parking lot was empty.

"You can't be serious," Eve said. "Guys. People get *eaten* in places like this. At the very least, we get locked in a room and terrible, evil things get done to us and put on the Internet. I've seen the movies."

"Eve," Michael said, "horror movies are not documentaries."

"And yet, I really think a serial killer owns this place. No. Not going to—"

Michael's phone buzzed. He flipped it open and read the text. "Oliver says to stop here. He'll join us in about another hour."

"You are *kidding.*"

"Hey, you're the one who had to have the ice cream. Look what kind of trouble we got ourselves into. At least this way we're safe in a room with a door that locks. And the sign says they have HBO."

"That stands for Horrible Bloody Ohmygod," Eve said. "Which is the way they kill you. When you think you're safe."

"Eve!" Claire was starting to get creeped out, too. Eve put her hands up, briefly, then back down to the wheel.

"Fine," she said. "Don't say I didn't warn you, while we're all screaming and crying. And I'm sleeping in my clothes. With a stake in both hands."

"It's probably not run by vampires."

"First, you wanna bet?" Eve hit the brakes and put the car in park. "Second, sharp pointy things tend to work on everything else, too. Including cannibals running creepy motels."

They sat in silence as the engine ticked and cooled, and finally Shane cleared his throat. "Right. So, we're going in?"

"We could stay in the car."

"Yeah, that's safe."

"At least we can see them coming. And also run."

Claire sighed and got out of the car, walked into the small office, and hit the bell on the counter. It seemed really, really loud. She heard doors slamming behind her—Shane, Michael, and Eve finally bailing out. The office was actually nicer than the outside of the building, with carpet that was kind of new, comfortable chairs, even a flat-screen TV playing on the wall with the sound turned off. The place smelled like . . . warm vanilla.

Out of the back room came an older lady with graying hair tied back in a ponytail. Claire couldn't imagine anyone looking *less* like a serial killer, actually—she looked like a classic grandma, even down to the small, round glasses. She was wiping her hands on a dish towel and was wearing an apron over blue jeans and a checked shirt. "Help you, honey?" she asked, and put the towel down. She looked a little nervous as the others came in behind her. "Y'all need a room?"

"Yes, ma'am," Claire said softly. Michael and Shane were doing their best to look like nice boys, and Eve was, well, Eve. Smiling. "Maybe two, if they're not too expensive?"

"Oh, they're not expensive," the lady said, and shook her head. "Ain't exactly the Hilton, you know. Thirty-five dollars a night, comes with breakfast in the morning. I make biscuits and sausage gravy, and there's coffee. Some cereal. Ain't fancy, but it's good food."

Michael stepped up, signed the book, and counted out cash. She read the register upside down. "Glass? You from around here?"

"No, ma'am," he said. "We're just passing through. Heading for Dallas."

"What the hell possessed you to come all the way out here?" she asked. "Never mind; glad you did. Fresh sheets and towels in the rooms, soaps, some complimentary shampoo. You need anything, you just call. You kids have a good night. Oh, and no hell-raising. We may be outside of town, but I know the sheriff personally. He'll make a special trip."

"Why does everybody think we're so insane?" Eve asked, and rolled her eyes. "Honestly, we're *nice*. Not everybody our age rolls with anarchy."

"You would, if anarchy offered free ice cream," Michael said. He accepted the two keys and smiled. "Thank you, ma'am—"

"Name's Linda," the lady interrupted. "Ma'am was my mother. Though I guess I'm old enough now to be ma'am to you folks, more's the pity. You go on. Let me finish up my baking. You stop back later. I'll have fresh chocolate chip cookies."

Eve's mouth dropped open. Even Michael looked impressed. "Uh—

thanks," he said, and they retreated out to the parking lot, staring at one another. "She's making cookies."

"Yeah," Shane said. "Terrifying. So, how are we doing this thing?"

"Girls get their own room," Eve said, and plucked one of the keys out of Michael's hand. "Oh, come on, don't give me that face. You know that's the right thing to do."

"Yeah, I know," Michael said. "Looks like they're right next door to each other."

They were, rooms one and two, with a connecting door between. Inside, the rooms—like Linda's office—were really pretty nice. Claire checked out the bathroom; it was nicer than the one at home—and cleaner. "Hey, Eve?" she called, sticking her head around the door. "Should I be terrified now, or later?"

"Shut up," Eve said, and flopped on one of the two beds, crossing her feet at the ankles as she reached for the remote on the TV. "Okay, it's not Motel Hell. I admit it. But it could have been. . . . Hey, check it out—there's a *Saw* marathon on HBO!"

Great. Just what they needed. Claire rolled her eyes, went out to the car, and helped the boys unload the stuff they needed—which was, actually, pretty much everything by the time they finished. Eve remained loftily above it all, flipping channels and searching for the most comfortable pillow.

Shane dragged her suitcase into the room and dumped it on the floor beside her bed. "Hey, Dark Princess? Here's your crap. Also, bite me."

"Wait, here's your tip—" She flipped him off, without taking her eyes off the TV. "Nice to know we can still be just the same even outside of Morganville, right?"

He laughed. "Right." He looked at Claire, who leaned her own suitcase against the wall and looked around. "So I guess this is good night?"

"Guess so," she said. "Um, unless you guys want to watch movies?"

"I'll bring the chips."

Two hours later, they were lying on the beds, propped up, groaning and wincing and yelling stuff at the screen. The sound was turned up loud, and what with all the screaming and chain saws and such, it took a few seconds for the sound *outside* the room to filter through to any of them. Michael heard it first, of course, and nearly levitated off the bed to cross the room and pull back the curtains. Eve scrambled to mute the TV. "What? What is it?"

Out in the parking lot, Claire could now hear hoots, drunken laughter, and the crash of metal. She and Shane bounced off the bed, too, and Eve came last.

"Hey!" she screamed, and Claire winced at the rage in her voice. "Hey, you assholes, that's my *car!*"

It was the three jerks from the truck stop, only about a case of beer more stupid, which really didn't seem possible, in theory. But they were going after Eve's car with a great big sledgehammer and two baseball bats. The glass in the front window shattered at a blow from the sledgehammer, which was swung by Angry Dude. Orange Cap swung a baseball bat and added another deep dent to the already horribly damaged hood. The last guy knocked off the side mirror, sending it to left field with one hard blow.

Orange Cap blew Eve a gap-toothed kiss, reached in his back pocket, and pulled out a glass bottle filled with something that looked faintly pink, like lemonade. . . .

"Gas," Michael said. "I have to stop them."

"You'll get your ass killed," Shane said, and flung himself in the way. "No way. This ain't Morganville, and if you end up in a jail cell, you'll *die.* Understand?"

"But my *car!*" Eve moaned. "No, no, no . . ."

Orange Cap poured gas all over the seats inside, then tossed in a match.

Eve's car went up like a school bonfire at homecoming. Eve shrieked again and tried to lunge past Shane, too. He backed up to block the door and dodged a slap from her. "Claire! Little help?" he yelped, as Eve actually connected. Claire grabbed her friend's arms and pulled her backward. It wasn't easy. Eve was bigger, stronger, and more than a little crazy just now.

"Let go!" Eve yelled.

"No! Calm down. It's too late. There's nothing you can do!"

"I can kick their asses!"

Michael had already come to the same conclusion as Shane, and as Eve broke free from Claire, he got in her way and wrapped his arms around her, bringing her to a fast stop. "No," he said, "no, you can't." His eyes were shimmering red with fury, and he blinked and took deep breaths until he was himself again, blue-eyed Michael, under control—barely.

The three men in the parking lot whooped and hollered as Eve's car burned, then scrambled for their big pickup truck as the motel's office door slammed open.

Grandma Linda stood there, looking like the wrath of God in an apron. She had a shotgun, which she pointed at an angle at the sky and fired. The blast was shockingly loud. "Get lost, you morons!" she yelled at the retreating three men. "Next time I see your taillights I'll give you a special buckshot kiss!"

She racked another shell, but she didn't need to reload; the truck was already peeling out, spitting gravel from tire treads as it flew out of the parking lot, did a quick, drunken U-turn, and headed back inside Durram's town limits.

Grandma Linda shouldered the shotgun, frowned at the burning car, and went back into the office. She returned with a fire extinguisher, and put the blaze out with five quick blasts of white foam.

Shane opened the door and got immediately mowed down by Eve, who blew past him, with Michael right behind. Shane and Claire followed last. Claire felt physically sick. The car was utterly *trashed*. Even with the fire put out, the windows were shattered, the bodywork dented and twisted, the headlights broken, tires flat, and the seats were burned down to the springs in several places.

She'd seen better wrecks at the junkyard.

"Those three ain't got the sense God gave a virus," Linda said. "I'll call the sheriff, get him out here to write up a complaint. I'm sorry, honey."

Eve was crying, violent little jerks of sobs that came with shudders as she stared at the wreckage of the car she'd loved. Claire put her arm around her, and Eve turned and buried her face in Claire's shoulder.

"Why?" she cried, full of rage and confusion now. "Why did they follow us? Why'd they do that?"

"We scared them," Michael said. "Scared people do stupid things. Drunk, scared bullies do even stupider things."

Linda nodded. "You got that right, son. It's a damn shame, though. Hate to see something like this happen to nice kids just minding their own business. People like that, they just got to pick on somebody, and everybody around here's had enough of 'em. Guess they figured you for the new toys."

"They figured wrong," Michael said. His eyes glittered briefly red, then faded back to blue. "But we've got problems. What are we going to do for a car?"

"Just be glad we got our stuff out of it," Shane said, and Michael, knowing what he was getting at, looked briefly sick, then nodded. "Eve and I will do some shopping tomorrow. See what we can get in town."

Eve sniffled and wiped at her eyes, which made a mess of her mascara. "I don't have the money for a new car."

"We'll find a way," Shane said, as if it made sense and happened to him on a regular basis. Claire guessed, with his history, it probably had. "Come on, moping around out here isn't fixing anything. Might as well go in for the night. We're not going anywhere."

Linda sighed. "Hate to see this kind of thing happen," she said again. "Damn fools. You wait here a second."

She went back into the office, carrying the fire extinguisher, and came back out with a small ceramic bowl full of . . .

"Cookies," Shane said, and accepted it from her. "Thanks, Linda."

"Least I can do." She kicked a rock, frowning, and shook her head. "Damn fools. I'll sit up the rest of the night, make sure they don't come back here."

Somehow, Claire didn't think they'd take the chance. Linda had looked pretty serious with that shotgun.

The joys of the movie party were over, but the cookies were warm, fresh, and delicious. Eve's tears dried up and left a feverish anger in their place.

She took a long shower to burn it off, and when she came out of the bathroom, wreathed in steam, she looked small and vulnerable, stripped of all her Goth armor.

Claire hugged her and gave her a cookie. Eve munched it and hugged her black silk kimono around herself as she climbed onto the bed. "Boys gone?" she asked.

"Yeah, they're gone," Claire said. "Mind if I—?"

"No, go ahead. I'll just sit here and watch my car smoke." Eve stared moodily at the curtains, which were closed, thankfully.

Claire shook her head, grabbed her stuff, and went in to take her own shower. She did it at light speed, half convinced that Eve would find some way to get herself in trouble while she was gone, but when she emerged pink and damp and glowing from the hot water, Eve was exactly where she'd left her, flipping channels on the TV.

"This is the worst road trip *ever*," Eve said. "And I missed the end of the movie."

"Jigsaw always wins. You know that."

There was a soft sound at the motel room door. Something like a scratching sound; then a thud. Eve came bolt upright in bed. "What the hell was that? Because I'm thinking serial killer!"

"It's Shane, trying to freak you out. Or maybe it's those guys again," Claire said. "Shhh." She went to the curtains and peeked out, carefully. The light was dim in front of the door, but she saw someone slumped against the wall. Alone. "Just one guy—I can't really see him."

"So the serial killer option's still on the table? New rule. The door doesn't open."

They both jumped as a fist thudded once on the door. "Let me in," Oliver's voice commanded. "Now."

"Oh," Eve said. "In that case, new rule. Also, technically, he *is* a serial killer, right?"

Claire didn't really want to think too much about that one, because she was afraid Eve might have a point on that.

She slipped back the locks and opened the door, and Oliver came into the room. He made it two steps before his knees gave out on him, and he fell.

"Don't touch him!" Claire said as Eve slipped off the bed to approach him. She could see cuts and blood on him. "Get Michael. Hurry."

That wasn't a problem; Michael and Shane were already opening their own door, and the four of them were standing together when Oliver rolled over on his side, then to his back, staring upward.

He looked bad—pale, with open wounds on his face and hands. His clothes were cut, too, and there was blood soaked into them. He didn't speak. Michael dashed back into his room and came back with the cooler. He knelt next to Oliver and looked over his shoulder at the three of them. "You guys need to leave. Go next door. Now. Hurry."

Shane grabbed the two girls and steered them out, closing the door behind him and leaving Michael alone with Oliver.

Claire tried to turn around.

"No, you don't," Shane said, and shepherded them into his room. "You know better. If he needs blood, let him get it from the cooler. Not from the tap."

"What happened to him?" Eve asked the logical, scary question, which Claire had been at some level trying not to face. "That's *Oliver*. Badass walking. And somebody did that to him. How? Why?"

"I think that's what we have to ask him," Shane said. "Providing he's not having a serious craving for midnight snacks."

"Damn," Eve said. "Speaking of that, I left the cookies. I could use another cookie right now. How screwed are we, anyway?"

"Given the car and whatever trouble Oliver stirred up? Pretty well screwed. But hey. That's normal, right?"

"Right now, I wish it really, really wasn't."

They sat around playing poker until Michael came back, with Oliver behind him. He was upright and walking, though he looked as if he'd put his clothes through a shredder.

He didn't look happy. Not that Oliver ever really looked happy when he wasn't playing the hippie role, but this seemed unhappy, plus.

"We need to leave," he said. "Quickly."

"Well, that's a problem," Shane said, "seeing how our transpo out there is not exactly lightproof anymore, even if we didn't mind sitting on half-burned seats." Not even the trunk, anymore, thanks to the sledgehammer's work. "Plus, we've got t-minus two hours to sunrise. Not happening, anyway."

Michael said, "Oliver, it's time to tell us why we came here in the first place. And what happened to you."

"It's none of your business," Oliver said.

"Excuse me, but since you dragged us into it with you, I'd say it *is* our business now."

"Did my business destroy your car? No, that was your own idiocy. I say again, you don't need to know, and I don't need to tell you. Leave it." He sounded almost himself, but subdued, and he sat down on the edge of the bed as if standing tired him—not like Oliver.

"Are you okay?" Claire asked. He looked up and met her eyes, and for a second she saw something terrible in him: fear—overwhelming, tired, ancient fear. It shocked her. She hadn't thought Oliver could really be afraid of anything, ever.

"Yes," he said, "I'm all right. Wounds heal. What won't is what will happen if we remain trapped here. We can't wait for rescue from Morganville. We must get on our way before the next nightfall."

"Or?" Claire asked.

"Or worse will happen. To all of us." He looked . . . haunted. And very tired. "I need to rest. Find a car."

"Ah—we're not exactly rolling in cash."

Without a word, Oliver took out a wallet from his pants, grimaced at the scratches and tears in the leather, and opened it to reveal a bunch of crisp green bills.

Hundreds.

He handed over the entire stack. "I have more," he said. "Take that. It should be enough to buy something serviceable. Make sure it's got sufficient trunk space."

After a second's hesitation, Eve's fingers closed around the money. "Oliver? Seriously, are you okay?"

"I will be," he said. "Michael, do you suppose there is another room in this motel I can occupy until we are ready to leave?"

"I'll get one," Michael said. He slipped out the door and was gone in seconds, heading for the office. Oliver closed his eyes and leaned back against the headboard. He looked so utterly miserable that Claire, without thinking, reached out and, just being kind, put her hand on his arm.

"Claire," Oliver said softly, without opening his eyes, "did I give you permission to touch me?"

She removed her hand—quickly.

"Just—leave me alone. I'm not myself at the moment."

Actually, he was pretty much like he always was, as far as Claire could tell, but she let it go.

Eve was fanning out the money, counting it. Her eyes were getting wider the higher she went. "Jeez," she whispered. "I could buy a genuine pimped-out land yacht with this. Wow. I had no idea running a coffee shop was this good a job."

"It's not," Shane said. "He probably has piles of gold sitting under his couch cushions. He's had a long time to get rich, Eve."

"And time enough to lose everything, once or twice," Oliver said. "If you want to be technical. I have been rich. I am currently . . . not as poor as I once was. But not as wealthy, either. The curse of human wars and politics. It's difficult to keep what you have, especially if you are always an outsider."

Claire had never really thought about how vampires got the money they had; she supposed it wouldn't have been easy, really. She remembered all the TV news shows she'd seen, with people running for their lives from war zones, carrying whatever they could.

Oliver would have been one of those people, once upon a time. Amelie, too. And Myrnin. Probably more than once. But they'd come through it.

They were survivors.

"What happened out there?" Claire asked, not really expecting him to answer.

He didn't disappoint her.

SIX

Once Oliver had his own room—room three, of course—at the motel, Claire, Eve, and Shane set out lightproofing the rooms Michael and Oliver would be staying in during the day. That wasn't so hard; the blackout curtains in the windows were pretty good, and a little duct tape around the edges made sure the room stayed dim—that and a DO NOT DISTURB sign on each knob.

"Dead bolt and chain," Shane told Michael as the three of them left the room. Dawn was starting to pink up on the eastern horizon. "I'll call when we're at the door again, on your cell. Don't open for anybody else."

"Did you tell that to Oliver?"

"Do I look stupid? Let him figure out his own crap, man."

Michael shook his head. "Be careful out there. I don't like sending the three of you out by yourselves."

"Linda's riding shotgun with us," Eve said. "Literally. With an actual, you know, *shotgun*."

"Actually," Shane said, "Linda's driving us. We said we'd buy her breakfast and haul some heavy stuff for her at the store. Kind of a good deal, plus I think everybody likes her. Nobody's going to come after us while she's with us."

It might have been wishful thinking, but Michael seemed a little relieved by it, and he knocked fists with Shane as they closed the door. They heard the bolts click home.

"Well," Eve said, "it's the start of a beautiful day in which I have had no sleep, had my car burned, and can't wear makeup, which is just so great."

The no-makeup thing was Shane's idea, and Claire had to admit, it was a good one. Eve was, by far, the most recognizable of their little group, but without the rice powder, thick black eyeliner, and funky-colored lipsticks, she looked like a different person. Claire had lent her a less-than-Gothy shirt, although Eve had insisted on purple. With that and plain blue jeans, Eve looked almost . . . normal. She'd even pulled her hair back in a single ponytail at the back.

Not a skull in sight, although her boots still looked a little intimidating.

"Think of it as operating in disguise," Shane said. "In a hostile war zone."

"Easy for you to say. All you had to do was throw on a camo T-shirt and find a ball cap. If we can find you some chewing tobacco, you're gold."

"I'm not in disguise," Claire said.

Eve snorted. "Honey, you *live* in disguise. Which is lucky for us. Come on, maybe Linda's still got some cookies left."

"For breakfast?"

"I never said I was the Nutrition Nazi."

Linda was up—yawning and tired, but awake—when they opened up the office door. She was sipping black coffee, and when Eve said good morning, Linda waved at the plate of cookies on the counter. Eve looked relieved. "Ah—could I have some coffee, too?"

"Right there on the pot. Pour yourself a big one. It's already a long day." Linda had put on another shirt—still checked, but different colors—but otherwise, she looked pretty much the same. "So, you kids get any sleep at all?"

"Not much," Shane mumbled around a mouthful of cookie as Eve poured a chunky white mugful of coffee. He held out his hand in a silent demand for her to get him some, too. She rolled her eyes, put the pot back on the burner, and walked past him to the cookie tray. "Hence, Miss Attitude."

"The attitude comes from *someone* not even wanting to fetch his own coffee."

Shane shrugged and got his own, as Eve raided the cookie tray and Claire nibbled on part of one, too. She supposed she ought to feel more tired. She probably would, later, but right now, she felt—excited? Maybe nervous was a better term for it. "So," she ventured, "where do you go to buy a car here?"

"In Durram?" Linda shook her head. "Couple of used places, that's all. Any new cars, we go to the city for them. Not that there's many new cars round here these days. Durram used to be an oil town, back in the boom days, pumped a lot of crude out of the ground, but when it folded, it hit the ground hard. People been leaving ever since. It never was huge, but what you see now ain't more than half what it was fifty years ago, and even then a lot of those buildings are closed up."

"Why do you stay?" Shane asked, and sipped his coffee. Linda shrugged.

"Where else I got to go? My husband's buried here; came back dead from the war in Iraq, that first one. My family's here, such as they are, including Ernie, my grandson. Ernie runs one of the car lots, which is why I figure we can find you what you want at a good deal this early in the morning." She grinned. "If an old woman can't make her own grandson get out of bed before dawn to do her a favor, there's no point in living. Just let me finish my coffee and we'll be on our way."

She drank it fast, faster than Shane and Eve could gulp their own, and in about five minutes the four of them were piling into the bench seat of Linda's pickup truck, which had more rust than paint on the outside, and sagging seats on the inside. Claire sat on Shane's lap, which wasn't at all a bad thing from her perspective. From the way he held her in place, she didn't think he objected, either. Linda started up the truck with a wheezing rattle of metal, and the engine roared as she tore out of the gravel parking lot and onto the narrow two-lane road heading toward Durram.

"Huh," she said as they passed the town limits sign, barely readable from shotgun blasts. "Usually there's a deputy out here in the mornings. Guess somebody overslept. Probably Tom. Tom likes those late nights at the bar, sometimes; he's gonna catch hell for blowing it again."

"You mean fired?"

"Fired? Not in Durram. You don't get fired in Durram; you get embarrassed." Linda drove a couple of blocks, past some empty shops and one empty gas station, then took a right turn and then a left. "Here it is."

The sign said HURLEY MOTORS, and it was about a million years old. Somebody had hit it with buckshot, too, once upon a time, but from the rust, it had been a while ago—maybe before Claire was born; maybe before her *mother* was born. There was a small, sad collection of old cars parked in front of a small cinder-block building, which looked like it might have been built by the same guy who'd built Linda's motel.

Come to think of it, it probably had.

The cinder blocks were painted a pale blue with dark red trim on the roof and windows, but the whole thing had faded to a kind of pale gray over time. As Linda stopped the truck with a squeal of brakes, the front door of the shack opened, and a young man stepped out and waved.

"Oooh, cute," Eve whispered to Claire. Claire nodded. He was older, maybe twenty or so, but he had a nice face. And a great smile, like his grandma.

"Oh, he *is* cute!" Shane said in a fake girly voice. "Gee, maybe we can ask him out!"

"Shut *up*, you weasel. Claire, hit him!"

"Pretend I did," Claire said. "Look, he's bleeding."

Shane snorted. "Not. Okay, out of the truck before this gets silly."

Linda, ignoring them, had already gotten out on the driver's side and was walking toward her grandson. As they hugged, Claire scrambled down from Shane's lap to the pavement. He hopped down beside her, and then Eve slithered out as well. "Wow," she said, surveying the cars on the lot. "This is just—"

"Sad."

"I was going more for horrifying, but yeah, that works, too. Okay, can we agree on nothing in a minivan, please?"

"Yep," Shane said. "I'm down with it."

They wandered around the lot. It didn't take long before they'd looked at everything parked in front, and from Eve's expression, Claire could tell there wasn't a single thing she'd be caught dead driving—or, more accurately, caught *with* the dead driving. "This *sucks*," Eve said. "The only thing that has decent trunk space is *pink*." And not just a little pink, either; it looked like a pink factory had thrown up all over it.

Linda's grandson wandered over, trailed by her. He caught the last bit of Eve's complaint, and shook his head. "You don't want that thing, anyway," he said. "Used to belong to Janie Hearst. She drove it fifteen thousand miles without an oil change. She thinks she's the Paris Hilton of Durram. Hi, I'm Ernie Dawson. Heard you're looking for a car. Sorry about what happened to yours. Those fools are a menace—have been since I was a kid. Glad nobody was hurt."

"Yeah, well, we just want to get the heck out of town," Eve said. "It was my car. It was a really nice old classic Caddy, you know? Black, with fins? I was hoping maybe somebody could tow it in, fix it up, and I could pick it up later on, maybe in a couple of weeks?"

Ernie nodded. He had greenish eyes, a color that stood out against his suntanned skin; his hair was brown, and wavy, and got in his face a lot. Claire liked him instinctively, but then she remembered the *last* cute stranger she'd liked. That hadn't turned out so well. In fact, that had turned out very, very badly, with her blood getting drained out of her body.

So she didn't smile back at Ernie—much.

"I think I can set that up," he said. "Earle Weeks down at the repair shop can probably work some magic on it, but you'd have to leave him a pretty good deposit. He'll have to order in parts."

"Hey, if you can make me a good deal on a decent car that isn't *pink*, I'm all good here."

"Well, what you see is pretty much what you get, except—" He gazed at Eve for a few long seconds, then shook his head. "Nah, you won't be interested in that."

"In what?"

"Something that I keep out back. Nobody around here will buy it. I've been trying to make a trade with a company out of Dallas to get it off my hands. But since you said big classic Caddy—"

Eve jumped in place a little. "Sweet! Let's see it!"

"I'm just warning you, you won't like it."

"Is it pink?"

"No. Definitely not pink. But"—Ernie shrugged—"okay, sure. Follow me."

"This ought to be good," Shane said, and reached into his pocket for a cookie he'd hidden there. He broke it in half and offered it to Claire.

"Can't wait," she said, and wolfed it down, because Linda was world-class with the cookies. "I can't believe I'm eating cookies for breakfast."

"I can't believe we're stuck in Durram, Texas, with a burned-out car, two vamps, and the cookies are this *good.*"

And . . . he had a point.

Eve had a look on her face as if she'd just found the Holy Grail, or whatever the Gothic equivalent of that might be. She stared, eyes gone wide and shiny, lips parted, and the glee in her face was oddly contagious. "It's for sale?" she asked. She was trying to play it cool, Claire thought, although she was blowing it by a mile. "How much?"

Ernie wasn't fooled even a little bit. He rubbed his lips with his thumb, staring at Eve, and then at the car. "Well," he said thoughtfully, "I guess I could go to three thousand. 'Cause you're a friend of Grandma's."

Linda said, "Don't you go cheating this gal. I know for a fact you paid Matt down at the funeral parlor seven hundred dollars for the damn thing, and it's been sitting for six months gathering dust. You ought to let her have it for a thousand, tops."

"Gran!"

"Don't *Gran* me. Be nice. Where else in this town are you going to sell a hearse?"

"Well," he said, "I've been working on making it more of a party bus."

It was *gigantic.* It was gleaming black, with silver trim and silver curlicues on the trim, and faded white curtains in the windows at the back. Grandma Linda was right—it was covered in desert dust, but underneath it looked sharp—*really* sharp.

"Party bus?" Eve said.

"Yeah, take a look."

Ernie opened the back door, the part where the casket would have gone . . . and there was a floor in there, with lush black carpet, not metal runners or clamps as there would have usually been for coffins. He'd built in low-riding seats down both sides, two on each side, facing each other.

"I put in the cup holders," he said. "I was going for the fold-down DVD screen, but I ran out of money."

Eve, as though in a trance, reached in her pocket and pulled out the cash. She counted out three thousand dollars and passed it over to Ernie.

"Don't you want to drive it first?" he asked.

"Does it run?"

"Yeah, pretty well."

"Does it have air-conditioning?"

"Of course. Front and back."

"Keys." She held out her hand. Ernie held up one finger, ran back to the shack, and returned with a set dangling from one finger. He handed them to her with a smile.

Eve opened the front door and started up the hearse. It caught with a cough, then settled into a nice, even purr.

Eve stroked the steering wheel, and then she *hugged* it—literally. "Mine," she said. "Mine, mine, mine."

"Okay, this is starting to seriously creep me out," Shane said. "Can we move past the obsessive weird love and into the actually driving it part?"

"You guys go on and take it out for a spin," Ernie said. "I'll get the paperwork ready for you to sign. Be about fifteen minutes."

"Shotgun!" Shane said, one second before Claire. He winked at her. "And you get the Dead Guy Seat."

"Funny."

"Wait until there are actual dead guys sitting back there."

It wasn't safe to say that, not in front of Ernie and Linda; after a second, Claire saw Shane realize that. He blinked and said, "Well, maybe not. But it would be funny."

"Hilarious," Claire agreed, and went around to the back. Getting in was a bit of a challenge, but once she was sitting down, it felt kind of like what she imagined a limo would be. She looked around for a seat belt and found one, then strapped herself in. No sense dying in a car crash in a hearse. That seemed a little too tragically ironic even for Eve. "Hey, there really *are* cup holders."

"Fate," Eve said with a sigh.

"I'm not sure fate had to burn up your car to get the point across," Shane said, buckling his own seat belt.

"No, not that. The hearse. I'm going to name it Fate."

Shane stared at Eve for a long, long few seconds, then slowly shook his head. "Have you considered medication, or—"

She flipped him off.

"Ah. Back to normal. Excellent."

Eve pulled the hearse around carefully, getting used to the size of the thing. "It probably gets crap gas mileage," she said. "But *damn*. It's so *dark*!"

Claire moved aside the white curtains to look out the back window as they drove past the front of the used car lot. Linda and Ernie were standing in front of the shack, waving, so she waved back. "I'm probably the first person to wave from back here," she said. "That's weird."

"No, that is *awesome*. Awesome in the deliciously creepy sense. Okay, here we go, hold on. . . ." Eve hit the gas, and the hearse leaped forward. Shane braced himself against the dash. "Wow. Nice. I thought it might only go, you know, funeral speed or something."

"You're not seriously naming this thing."

"I am. Fate."

"At least call it Intimidator. Something cool."

"My car," Eve said, and smiled. "My rules. You can go buy the pink one if you want."

He shuddered and shut up.

Eve made the block without incident, and pulled the hearse back into the car lot about five minutes later, bumping it carefully up the drive and parking in front of the shack. As she switched the ignition off, she sighed and wiggled in the big leather seat in satisfaction. "This is the *best road trip ever.*"

Shane bailed out. Claire scrambled to slide out the back and found him waiting for her, grabbing her around the waist and helping her out. He didn't let go immediately, either. That was nice, and she felt herself sway toward him, as if the world had tilted his direction. "I guess we'd better go in and make sure she doesn't pay him even more money," Shane said, "because you know she would, for this thing."

"She's a giver," Claire agreed. "Also, maybe Linda's got more of those cookies."

"That's a good point."

Inside, they found Eve already signing the papers. Her driver's license and proof of insurance were already on the table, and as Ernie said hello to the two of them, he gathered up her information and made a copy at the back of the office. It was small, and crowded, and pretty dusty. It looked as though Ernie was the only one who worked here, at least most of the time. Linda was leaning against the wall, staring out at the car lot through the big glass window. She looked pensive.

"Is there something wrong?" Claire asked her. Linda glanced at her, then shook her head.

"Probably nothing," she said. "I just wonder why the sheriff hasn't been around yet. He's usually circling the town pretty regular, and he hasn't been here yet. Deputy wasn't at the sign, either. Strange."

Ernie filled out the title and handed it over, along with the paperwork and Eve's driver's license and insurance. Eve juggled all the paper to shake hands with him, and he gave her a smile that was definitely flirting. "Thanks," he said. "You staying in town long?"

"Oh—ah, no, I'm—we're heading out. To Dallas. With my boyfriend." Eve said it without too much emphasis, which was good; Claire didn't think Ernie was a bad person or anything. And Eve was cute, even when she hadn't made an effort to dress herself up Goth-style.

Ernie winced. "Should've seen that coming," he said. "Well, enjoy the new ride, Eve. And don't be a stranger."

"No stranger than I am already," she promised, straight-faced, and then they went out to admire the big black hearse again.

Linda moved straight past them to her own truck. "Hey," Shane called. "How about breakfast? We were going to buy you—"

"No need," she said, and climbed into the cab. Through the open window she said, "I'm going to go see the sheriff, see if I can find out what the heck's going on today. If I don't see you kids before you go, have a safe trip. And thanks for livening up my week. Hell, my whole month, come to that."

"No, thank *you*," Shane said. "Your motel is great."

She gave him a tight, quiet smile. "Always thought so," she said. "Good-bye, now."

She took off in a spray of gravel, raising plumes of dust as she skidded back onto the road. Ernie, who'd come out with them, sighed. "My grandma, the race car driver," he said. "Have a good trip, now."

They said their thanks, got into the hearse, and headed back to the motel.

They never got there. As they passed the town limits sign, and the road rose up a little in a mini-hill, Claire caught sight of flashing red and blue lights up ahead. "Uh-oh," she said. Eve hit the brakes, and she and Shane exchanged a look. "That's the motel, right? They're at the motel."

"Looks that way," Shane said. "This is not good."

"Ya think?" Eve chewed her lip. "Call Michael."

"Maybe they're—"

"What, hanging out there looking for somebody else? Call him, Shane!"

Shane dialed the number of Michael's cell phone, listened for a second, then closed his phone. "Busy," he said. "We need to get in there."

"And do *what*, exactly?"

"I don't know! You want your boyfriend dragged out to french fry in the sun?"

Eve didn't answer that. She drummed her fingers on the steering wheel, looking agonized, and then said, "I'll apologize later, then."

She hit the gas, and the hearse picked up momentum coming down the hill. It zipped past the motel, doing way past the speed limit.

One of the police cars—there were two in the parking lot—backed out and raced after them. Eve didn't slow down. She hit the gas.

"Eve, what the hell are you doing? We can't outrun them in a *hearse*, in the middle of the desert!"

"I'm not trying to," she shot back. "Claire, look out the back. Tell me if the other car joins in."

It took a few seconds, but then Claire saw another flare of red and blue flashers behind them. "They're both following," she called back. "And how is this good, exactly?"

"Text Michael," Eve told Shane. "Tell him the coast is clear and to get his butt out of there."

"What about Oliver?"

"Michael's too much of a Boy Scout not to tell him, too. Don't worry about that."

Shane texted fast. "It's still kind of sunny out, you know."

"Oliver's older," Claire said. "He can stay out in the sun a lot longer than Michael. Maybe he can lead the police away, or something."

"That's up to them," Eve said. "I just need to keep driving as long as I can before we give up. The more we piss these guys off, the more chance Michael and Oliver have of getting away."

It turned out, as the police cars cranked it up, that Eve's hearse really wasn't made for car-chase speeds. They were overtaken in about another mile, and boxed up in another two.

Eve, surrendering, eased off the gas and hit the brakes to slow down and pull over.

"Okay, here's the deal," Shane said. "Keep your hands up, and play nice. You panicked, that's all. We were telling you to pull over, but you locked up. Got it?"

"It's not going to help."

"It will if you play the ditz. Better sell it, Eve. We're in enough trouble already."

The rest of it went straight out of the reality-TV-show playbook. The police ordered them out of the car, and before she knew it, Claire was being thrown up against the back of the hearse and searched. It felt humiliating, and she heard Eve crying—whether that was acting or not remained to be seen; Eve cried over smaller things. Shane was answering questions in a quiet, calm voice, but then, he'd spent a lot of time getting hassled by the Morganville police. For Claire, it was kind of a new experience, and not at all a good one. She had the deputy, she supposed; he was a tall, skinny guy whose uniform didn't fit very well, and he seemed nervous, especially when he put handcuffs on her.

"Hey," Shane called as his own hands were secured behind his back. "Hey, please don't hurt her. It wasn't her fault!"

"Nobody's hurting anybody," said the sheriff from the night before. "Okay, let's just calm down. Now, let's have some names. You?" He pointed at Claire.

"Claire Danvers," she said. Oh *man*, there went any chance at all of ever getting into MIT. She was going to have a mug shot that got pasted all over Facebook. People were going to mock her. It would be high school all over again, times a million.

"Address?"

She gave him the address in Morganville, on Lot Street. She didn't know what the others would have done; maybe she ought to have lied, made something up. But she didn't dare. Like Shane had said—they were in enough trouble already.

Eve gave her name in a trembling, small voice, and then Shane finished things up. They both gave the Glass House address.

"So, you're all, what, sharing a house?" the sheriff asked. "Where's the blond kid from last night?"

"I—" Eve bit her lip and closed her eyes. "We had a fight. A big one. He—he left."

"Left how? Seeing as the car you came in is still smoking in the parking lot back there, and it ain't going anywhere. There's no bus coming through here, young lady."

"He hitched a ride," Eve said. "With a truck. I don't know which one. I just heard it on the road."

"A truck," the sheriff repeated. "Uh-huh. And he wouldn't be back there in Linda's place with the door all locked up, then."

"No, sir."

That, Claire reflected, might be almost true, because if Eve's gamble had paid off, Michael and Oliver weren't there any longer. Where they *were* was another story.

"Well, we're waiting for Linda to get back; then we'll open up those doors and see what's going on. Sound okay to you?"

"Yes, sir," Eve said. "Why the handcuffs?"

"You three are a bunch of desperate characters, way I see it," the sheriff said. "I find you causing trouble last night, get a report your car's been trashed by the very same boys who say you threatened them, and next thing you know, I've got one man dead and two men missing this morning. The dead one got found in his pickup truck just about a mile up the road from your motel."

"I—" Eve stopped, frozen. "Sorry. What?"

"Murder," the sheriff repeated, slowly and precisely. "And you were the last ones to see them alive."

SEVEN

For a long, long moment, nobody moved, and then Shane said, "You don't think we killed—"

"Let's just stop right there, son. I don't want to be making any mistakes about how we do this." The sheriff cleared his throat and recited something about rights and remaining silent. Claire couldn't make sense out of it. She felt sick and horribly faint.

She was being *arrested.*

She was being arrested *for murder.*

Eve's crying was uncontrollable now, but Claire couldn't help her. She couldn't help herself.

Shane stayed uncharacteristically silent as they loaded him into the back of the squad car, then put Claire and Eve in with him. The sheriff leaned in before he closed the door to look at them. He almost looked kind now. That didn't make Claire feel any less sick.

"I'm going to have the deputy drive your, ah, vehicle back into town," he said. "Can't leave it out here. Might get stolen, and you folks already lost one car in Durram. Don't want it happening again."

He slammed the door on them. Claire felt Eve flinch all over at the boom of solid metal.

"Deep breaths," Shane said softly. "Eve. Sack up. You can't go to pieces like this. Not now."

The sheriff got in the front, on the other side of a wire mesh screen. He put on his seat belt, looked in the rearview mirror, and said, "No talking."

Then they drove back to the motel, where Linda's truck had just pulled in. She looked pale and worried, but she didn't betray much of anything at the sight of her three former guests in the back of a squad car. She listened to the sheriff, nodded, and went into the office to get master keys.

She opened up all three rooms they'd rented. Shane let out a sigh of relief even before the sheriff went in to look around. "They're gone," he said. "They got out. Somehow."

"How can you be sure?"

"Because Michael's smarter than me, and he'd have found a way. Ow, Eve, stop squirming. Not like there's a lot of room in here!"

"Sorry," Eve said. She sniffled uncomfortably. Her eyes were red and puffy, and so was her nose, and in general she looked pretty miserable. Claire bumped shoulders with her gently.

"Hey," she said. "It'll be okay. We didn't do this."

"Yeah, they never put innocent people on death row in Texas," Eve said. "Don't kid yourself. We're in big trouble. *Big* trouble. Like, not-even-Amelie-can-get-us-out-of-it trouble."

Her eyes started to tear up again. Claire repeated the shoulder bump. "Don't. We'll be okay. We'll figure this out."

Sniffle. "You're just Little Miss Optimist, aren't you? Do you come with accessories, like a glass half full and lemons to make into lemonade, too?"

"I'm not an optimist," Claire said. "I just know us."

"Damn straight," Shane said. "Look, they'll separate us at the station. Don't say anything about anything. Just watch and listen, okay? No matter what they say, just stay quiet."

"I've seen cop shows," Eve said, offended. "I'm not stupid, you know."

Shane leaned forward and looked across her at Claire. "Okay, Eve's going to spill her guts the first time they look at her harshly. What about you?"

"Quiet as a mouse," Claire said. Her heart was pounding, and she wasn't sure she could keep that promise, but then again, she'd kept secrets from Mr. Bishop.

This wasn't nearly as bad.

Was it?

The sheriff's station in Durram, Texas, was basically two rooms, if you didn't count the bathroom; there was a small open area with a couple of desks and computers, some corkboards on the walls full of notices and pictures, and behind that, a door with iron bars. But first, before they got to the iron bar part, Claire and Shane were seated on a wooden bench—it was a lot like a church pew, only with big bolts drilled into it on either side—and cuffed to the bench, too far apart for Claire's comfort. She really ached to be held by him right now.

"Hey, sir? Could I use the bathroom?" Shane asked.

"Not until you're processed."

"I'm not kidding. I really need to go. Please? Or would you rather clean it up?"

The deputy stared at him, harassed and doubtful, and Shane did a convincing squirm that Claire wasn't absolutely sure was fake. The deputy finally sighed and unhooked him to escort him to the small bathroom off the main room.

Eve, meanwhile, had been taken straight to the sheriff's desk, where he offered her a big box of tissues and a glass of water.

Claire was wondering what the heck to do, when she saw a flash of a face in the window of the station, behind the sheriff's back. A tall, lean figure in a long black coat, hat, and gloves.

Oliver. Dressed for the sun. Out and moving, getting an assessment of where they were and what had happened. He saw her watching him and gave her a quick nod that told her nothing at all, not even, *Don't worry.* Then he vanished.

Her phone gave out an ultrasonic ringtone. She blinked and looked around, but neither the sheriff nor the deputy had noticed it at all. Eve had, but after that first involuntary glance, she kept her back turned and stared off into space, Kleenex crumpled in both hands.

Claire squirmed and managed to get her phone out of her pocket without attracting attention.

She had a text message, from Michael. It read, *We'll get you guys out of there soon. Meanwhile, stay quiet.*

It was pretty much the same advice Shane had given. She wanted to believe it, but her insides were still shaking. She was *definitely* not meant to be a career criminal.

Right. She should just sit here, then, and—think of something else. Like science. Some people recited baseball scores to distract themselves; Claire liked to go through the entire periodic table of elements, and once she'd finished with that, she started on all of the alchemical symbols and properties Myrnin had taught her. That helped. It made her remember that there was something out there beyond this room, this moment, and that there were people out there who might actually care if she didn't come back.

Shane came back from the toilet and was cuffed in place again. He edged over a little closer to her and leaned forward, elbows on his thighs, head hanging down so his hair covered his face.

"There's a window in the bathroom," he said. "Not very big, but you could get out of it. Doesn't open, though. You'd have to break it out, and that would be noisy."

Claire coughed and covered her mouth. "I'm not breaking out of jail! Are you crazy?"

"Well, it was a thought. I mean, seemed like a good idea at the time." Shane sat back up and looked at her, his forehead crinkling in a frown. "I just don't want you here. It's not—" He shook his head. "It's just not right. Me and Eve, well, yeah, she piled into it head-on, and I'm always in trouble. But you . . ."

"I'm okay." She reached out and put her palm against his cheek, feeling the slightly rough stubble there. It made her steadier. It made her want to be somewhere else, like in the motel room, with the door closed. "I'm not going anywhere without you."

"I am *such* a bad influence on you."

"Trying to get me to stage a jailbreak? Yeah. You really are."

"Well, at least you didn't do it. There's that."

The deputy got up from his desk and came to unlock Shane from the bench. "Let's have a talk, Mr. Collins," he said.

"Oh, let's," Shane said, with totally fake enthusiasm. He winked at Claire, which made her smile for a second, until she remembered there really was something tragic here—one man dead, two missing. Granted, they hadn't been the nicest people, but still . . .

She realized, with a grim, cold, drenched feeling down her spine, that she had no idea what Oliver had been doing when those men were being killed.

No idea at all.

The sheriff kept them talking for hours, then locked them in the cell in the back. Shane went in one cell; Eve and Claire together in the other. All of their stuff was taken away, of course, including cell phones. Claire had erased the text messages, but she figured it was only a matter of time before the sheriff got them, anyway. And then he'd know for sure that Michael was out there, a fugitive from justice.

That sounded romantic, but probably wasn't, especially since he was a vampire caught without shelter in the daytime.

She hoped he and Oliver had remembered to take the cooler of blood with them. They might really need it, especially if they got burned.

And here I am, worrying about a couple of vampires who can take care of themselves, she thought. *I ought to be worrying a lot more about what's going to happen when they call my parents.* They would—and that would make it just about a million times worse.

"Hey," Shane said from the other side of the bars. "Trade you cigarettes for a chocolate bar."

"Funny," Eve said. She was almost back to her old unGothed self again, though there were still red splotches on her cheeks and around her eyes. "How come you're always behind bars, troublemaker?"

"Look who's talking. I didn't try to outrun the cops in a hearse."

"That hearse had horsepower." Eve got that moony look in her eyes again. "I love that hearse."

"Yeah, well, I hope it loves you back, because otherwise, that's just sad. And a little sick." Shane drummed his fingers on the bars. "This isn't so bad. At least I've got better company this time around." And he wasn't scheduled to be turned into a vampire, or burned alive, but that kind of went without saying. "And they even have toilet paper."

"Oh, I *really* didn't need to hear that, Collins." Eve sighed and paced around the cell again, hugging herself tight. "It tells me way too much about your past."

Claire leaned into the bars. Shane leaned in from the other side, and their fingers brushed, then intertwined. "Hey," he said. "So, this is familiar."

"Not for me," she said. "I'm usually *outside* the bars."

"You're doing fine."

Claire smiled at him, then drew in a quick, shaking breath. "I have to tell you something," she said. "It's important."

Shane's fingers tightened on hers, and his index finger stroked gently over the silver claddagh ring, with its bright stone. "I know."

"No, you don't. I saw Oliver," she whispered, quickly and as softly as she could. Clearly, that was not what Shane was expecting to hear, and she watched him go through a whole list of reactions before he finally settled on annoyed.

"Great," he said. "When?"

"Outside the windows while they were talking to you," Claire said.

"Was he barbecued?"

"No, he was wearing a big coat and hat. I don't guess he was any too excited about being out in the daytime, though."

"I guess barbecued was too much to hope for." Shane fell silent as he thought about it, then finally shook his head. "They'll wait for dark," he said. "They'll have to, whatever they plan to do; Michael's just too vulnerable out there in the day. I wish we knew what they were doing."

"I'm pretty sure they're thinking the same thing about us," Claire said.

"Since they probably have no idea what happened. As far as they know, this hassle is all about Eve's bad driving."

"Hey, I heard that!" Eve said.

Shane smiled, but it was brief, and his dark brown eyes never left Claire's. "I don't like this," he said. "I don't like seeing you two in here."

"Yeah, well, welcome to my world," Claire said. "I haven't enjoyed it much seeing you behind bars, either." She laughed sadly. "This was supposed to be a fun little trip, remember? We should be in Dallas by now."

"My dad used to say that life's a journey, but somebody screwed up and lost the map."

Claire wasn't sure she wanted to think about his father right now. Frank Collins wasn't the kind of ghost she wanted drifting around between them, especially since being in jail—again—probably made Shane think a lot about his dad. Not that Frank was a ghost. Unfortunately. He'd been a terrible, abusive father, and now he was a vampire, and she couldn't really imagine that it had improved him all that much.

Even if he had saved her life once.

"As long as we're together," she said. "That's what matters."

"Speaking of that," Shane said, "we could be together and headed anywhere when we get out of this, you know. I'm just putting that on the table."

He was talking about not going back, about leaving Morganville. She'd been contemplating it, and she knew he had, too. "I—I can't, Shane. My parents . . ."

He bent his head closer and dropped his voice to a whisper. "Do you really think they want you to be there? Risking your life, every day? Don't you think they want you out, and safe?"

"I can't, Shane. I just can't. I'm sorry."

Shane was silent a moment, then let out a long breath. "I bet I could convince you if I could get through these bars. . . ."

"You'd get arrested all over again."

"Well, you're just that tempting. Jailbait." He kissed her fingers, which made her shiver all over; his lips lingered warm on her skin, reminding her of what it felt like to be alone with him, in that timeless, special silence. "Not a lot we can do until—" He stopped, then, frowning, looked over at the barred door that led into the sheriff's office. "Did you hear that?"

"What?" Even as she asked it, Claire heard the growl of an engine outside—a big one. It had to be some kind of truck, but not just a pickup—a big delivery van, or an eighteen-wheeler. The brakes sighed, and the roar of the engine cut out. "I guess they're getting some sort of delivery, maybe?"

Maybe, but somehow Claire didn't think so. She had a bad feeling. From the way Shane was staring at the jail door—which wasn't telling them anything—he was feeling the same thing.

And then in the outer office, glass crashed, someone yelled, and Claire heard laughter.

Then more crashing. More yelling.

Shane let go of her. "Claire, Eve—get to the back of the cell." When they hesitated, he snapped, "Just go!"

They did it, not that there was anywhere in particular to go, or to hide. They sat together on one of the two small cots, close together, watching the jail door to see what would come through.

What came through wasn't Oliver. It wasn't even Michael.

It was Morley, the vampire from Morganville, in all his homeless-bum glory. He was dressed in layers of threadbare clothes, and he had a large, floppy black hat on his head over his straggly graying hair.

He looked at the bars on the jail cell door, sneered, and snapped the whole thing off its hinges with a heave. He tossed the iron aside as if it weighed next to nothing.

Morley stepped through the open space, surveyed the three of them, and swept off his hat in a low, mocking bow. He was good at the bowing thing. Claire supposed he'd probably had a lot of practice. He seemed old enough to have lived in a time when bowing well got you somewhere.

"Like lobsters in a tank," he said. "I know we agreed you'd give up your blood to me, but really, this is just too *easy*."

He smiled.

With fangs.

Claire got up and walked toward the bars. She didn't like letting Morley—or any vampire—see she was afraid of him; from working with Myrnin in his crazy days—crazier?—she'd realized that showing fear was an invitation to them. One they found really hard to resist.

"What are you doing here?" she asked. Because for a confusing few seconds, she thought that maybe Oliver had teamed up with Morley to rescue them. But that was flat out impossible. The idea of Oliver and Morley ever being able to have a civilized conversation, much less actually work together, was completely ridiculous. "You're not supposed to leave Morganville!"

"Ah, yes. Amelie's rules." He said that last word with a lot of relish, and there was a muddy red flare in his eyes to match. "Poor, dear Amelie is operating at a disadvantage these days. Rumors said she was unable to keep the boundaries of the town in quite the same condition they had been. I decided to test the theory, and, behold, I am *free.*"

That was really, really not a good thing. Claire didn't know a whole lot about Morley, but she knew he tended more to the bad-old-days model of vampire—take what you want, when you want, and don't care about the consequences. The opposite of how Amelie—and even Oliver—ran things. To Morley, people were just blood bags that could talk—and sometimes outrun him, which only made it more exciting.

"They'll come after you," Claire said. "Amelie's people. You know that."

"And I look forward to seeing how that turns out for her." Morley paced back and forth in front of the bars, humming a song Claire didn't recognize. In the net of his wild hair, his eyes glittered with a kind of silvery light. They expressed not exactly hunger, but something more like amusement. "You look cramped in there, my friends. Shall I get you out?"

"Actually, it's pretty roomy," Shane said. "I'm feeling better about it all the time."

"Perhaps . . ." Morley turned. "Ah, you're playing the gentleman, I see. Of course, by all means. Ladies first."

"No!" Shane lunged at the bars. Morley had his eyes fixed on Eve and Claire now, and Claire thought, with a sinking sensation, that putting on a brave face wasn't going to get her very far—not with him. "Changed my mind. Sure. I'll go first."

Morley shook his finger gently in Shane's direction, but without taking those shining eyes off the girls. "No, you had your chance. And I despise those who think themselves *gentlemen* in any case. You're not making friends that way."

"No!" Shane yelled, and slammed his hand into the bars, which rattled uneasily. "Over here, you ratty fleabag! Come and get it!"

"Fleas suck blood," Morley said mildly. "Quite the cousin of the vampire, those clever little creatures, so why should I find that insulting? You really must find more interesting ways to bait me, boy. Tell me my beard would better stuff a butcher's cushion. Or that I have more hair than wit. Live up to your heritage, I beg you."

Shane had no idea what to say to that. Claire cleared her throat. "Like . . . you're . . . an inhuman wretch, void and empty from any dram of mercy?" She hated Shakespeare. But she'd had to memorize lines back in high school for a production of *The Merchant of Venice*.

And it had finally paid off, from the surprise in Morley's face. He actually took a step back.

"It speaks!" he said. "And in lilting, glorious words. Though I am not so partial to the Bard, myself. He was a pitiful man to drink with, always dashing off to scribble away in the dark. Writers. Such a boring lot."

"What are you *doing* here? Because I know you didn't come to get us," Claire said. She advanced and wrapped her hands around the bars, as though she wasn't at all afraid of him. She hoped he couldn't hear her heartbeat, but she knew he could. "We're not important enough."

"Well, that's certainly true. You're entirely incidental. Actually, we're in search of a town. Something small, remote, easily controllable. This seemed a good possibility, but it's rather too large for our purposes."

We. Morley hadn't just slipped out of Morganville alone. Claire remembered the big, throbbing engine outside. Might be a big truck. Might be a bus. Either way, it would probably hold a lot of vampires—like the ones Morley had applied to be allowed to leave Morganville with in the first place.

Oh, this just got better and better.

"You can't just move in here," Claire said, trying to sound reasonable, as if that would do any good. She let go of the bars and backed away as Morley took a step toward her again. "People live here."

"Indeed, I'm not planning on it. Too much trouble to subdue such a large population. However, we're in need of supplies, and this town's quite well stocked. Couldn't be better." Morley suddenly lunged forward, grabbed the bars of their cell, and *ripped the door off*—just like that, with a shriek of iron and sharp snapping sounds.

Eve, behind Claire, screamed, and then the sound went muffled, as if she'd covered her mouth.

Claire didn't move. There didn't seem to be much point. Shane was yelling something, and for some odd reason the place on her neck hurt, the place where Myrnin had bitten her, where there was still a nasty scar.

Morley stood there for a moment, hands on both sides of the doorway, and then stepped inside. He *glided*, like a tiger. And his eyes turned red, the irises lighting up the glittering color of blood.

"Get down!" somebody yelled from behind him, and Claire hit the floor, not daring to hesitate even for a second. There was a loud roar that it took her a second to identify as gunfire, and Morley staggered and went down to one knee.

The sheriff looked dazed, and there was blood on the side of his head, but he held his gun very steady. "Get down, mister," he said. "Don't make me shoot you again."

Morley slowly toppled forward, face-forward, on the floor. The sheriff breathed a sigh of relief and gestured for Eve and Claire to come out. Claire did, jumping over Morley's outstretched hand and expecting that any second, any second at all, he'd reach up and grab her, just like in the movies.

He didn't. Eve hesitated for a few seconds, then jumped for it, clearing Morley by at least a couple of feet, straight up. The sheriff grabbed them and hustled them off to the side, then unlocked Shane's cell. "Out," he said. "Help me get him inside."

"It won't do any good to lock him up," Shane said. "He already ripped off two of your doors. You want him to go for three?"

The sheriff had clearly been trying not to think about that. "What the hell are these people?" he snarled. "Some kind of damn monsters?"

"Some kind of," Shane said. He'd put his hands on Claire, and now he wrapped his arms around her, and after a second, included Eve in the hug, too. "Thanks. I know you don't believe us, but we're not the bad guys here."

"I'm starting to think you might be right about that."

"What gave you your first clue? The fangs, or the door ripping?" Shane didn't wait for an answer. "He's not dead. He's playing with you."

"What?"

"You can't kill him with that thing," Eve said. "Can't even slow him down, really."

The sheriff whirled to stare at Morley, who was still facedown on the floor. He aimed his gun at the body again and kept it there.

Morley didn't move.

"No, he's down," the sheriff said, and walked over to press fingers to Morley's dirty neck. He yanked his hand away quickly, stumbling back. "He's cold."

Morley laughed, rolled over, and sat up, doing his very best risen-from-the-grave imitation. It helped that he was filthy and looked kind of crazy scary.

The sheriff backed away, far away, all the way to the wall, then aimed his gun at Morley and pulled the trigger, again.

Morley brushed his clothes lightly, dismissing the bullet even before the echoes from the shockingly loud gunshot stopped ringing in Claire's ears. "Please," he said, and practically levitated to his feet. He reached out and took the sheriff's gun from him, then tossed it in the corner of the cell where Eve and Claire had been kept. "I hate loud noises. Unless it's screaming. Screaming's all right. Let me demonstrate."

He reached out and grabbed the sheriff around the neck.

Something pale and very fast flashed through the doorway, and suddenly another vampire was there—Patience Goldman, with her slender hand wrapped around Morley's wrist. She was a dark-haired young woman, pretty, with big dark eyes and skin that would have probably been olive had she still been alive. It added a honey undertone to her pallor.

"No," Patience said. Claire had met her—and the entire Goldman family—more than once. She liked them, actually. For vampires, they had real concern for other people—as demonstrated by Patience's trying to keep Morley from killing the sheriff. "There's no need for this."

Morley looked offended, and shoved her back with his free hand. "Do *not* lay hands on me, woman! This is none of your concern."

"We came to—get supplies," Patience said. She seemed uncomfortable with that, and Claire immediately realized that *supplies* was code for *people*—to eat. "We have what we need. Let's go. The longer we delay, the more attention we attract. It's an unnecessary risk!"

Patience and Jacob, her brother, had been hanging out with Morley for a while, and they'd wanted to break out of Morganville, and their parents' restrictions—Theo Goldman was a good guy, but kind of strict, as far as his family went, or at least that had been Claire's impression. Claire could easily believe that Morley had convinced Patience and Jacob to come along, since he was leaving, anyway, but she also didn't believe they'd go along with killing people.

Not unnecessarily, anyway. Vampires in general were a little shaky on the details of morality in that area—a hazard of being top predator, Claire guessed.

"Hmmm," Morley said, and turned his gaze back to the sheriff. "She does have a point. Fortunately for you." He released the man, who slammed back against the wall, looking sick and shaky. "Stay. If you move, speak, or in any way irritate me, I'll snap your neck."

The sheriff froze in place, clearly taking it all very seriously. Claire didn't really blame him. She remembered her first encounter with vampires, her first realization that the world wasn't the neatly ordered place she'd always been told it was. It could really mess up your head.

In fact, she wasn't entirely sure hers had ever recovered, come to think of it.

She was just starting to relax when Morley reached out and grabbed her and Eve by the arms. When Shane yelled a protest, Morley squeezed, and Claire felt agony shoot in a white bolt up her arm. Yeah, that was *almost* broken.

"Don't cause a fuss, boy, or I'll be forced to shatter bones," Morley said. "The girls come with us. If you want to run, you may. I won't stop you."

Like Shane would. Or even *could*, being Shane. He fixed Morley with a bleak, grim stare and said, "You take them, I'm coming, too."

"How gentlemanly of you," Morley said, smiling. "I believe I already told you how I feel about *gentlemen*. But suit yourself."

He hustled Claire and Eve out into the open room that was the police bull pen. Desks had been shoved around, papers littered the floor, and Deputy Tom was lying half hidden behind one of the chairs. Claire was glad she couldn't really see him. She hoped he was just . . . knocked out.

Somehow, though, she really didn't think so.

Shane followed behind Morley. Patience walked next to him, but she didn't try to touch him—which was probably smart, given the fiery look in Shane's eyes. His muscles were tight, his hands bunched into fists, and the only thing holding him back from punching Morley was the certain knowledge that it would be Claire and Eve who'd get hurt.

Morley shoved open the glass outer door with a booted foot, and glanced up at the blazing sun. "Quickly, if you please," he said, and dragged Eve and Claire across the open ground at a stumbling run to an idling bus.

It was an old passenger bus, with darkened windows, and the next thing she knew, Claire was being shoved up the steep, narrow steps ahead of Morley, with Eve being dragged along behind him. It was dark inside, with only a few overhead reading lights on to show her the interior. There were worn, fraying velvet seats, and in almost every one sat a vampire, at least in the front two-thirds of the bus.

In the back were mostly humans—tied up, gagged, and looking desperate. There were no Morganville residents, at least that Claire could spot offhand, but she saw two immediately familiar faces—Orange Cap and Angry Guy, from the diner, who'd trashed Eve's car. The sheriff had said they'd disappeared; she'd assumed they were dead, like their friend who'd been left with his pickup truck.

Morley had grabbed them. Claire thought that the other one, the one who'd died, had been more of an accident than deliberate murder, although maybe he'd done something to make Morley angry, too. There was no way to tell, really.

The two bullies weren't looking quite so in control now. Their eyes were wide, their noses were running, and they kept wrestling against the ties that held them in place.

"Friends of yours?" Morley asked, seeing her expression. "I'll see if I can seat you in the same section. Aisle or window?" He shoved Eve into a seat next to a window, across from Orange Cap, and then slung Claire into the empty seat beside her, on the aisle. Then he turned to Shane.

Shane sat down silently in the chair in front of Claire. Patience, watching this, bit her lip and shook her head, but when Morley snapped the orders, she broke out some plastic cable ties and fastened Claire and Eve to the seats, then turned to Shane.

"I'm sorry for this," she said softly. "You should have gone. Gotten help. I would have made sure no harm came to them."

"I don't trust their lives to anybody but me," he said. "No offense."

"None taken," Patience said with a sigh. "But Morley will require you to provide blood. He's promised not to drain any of our captives, but I'm sure you understand his temper. Resistance would not be wise."

Shane shuddered and looked away. He didn't like giving blood, even at the Bloodmobile or the blood bank, and that was a lot more removed from having a vampire taking it, no matter whether they used medical equipment or went the old-fashioned way. Claire wasn't too cool with it herself, and she knew Eve well enough to know she'd fight it, hard.

"Let us go," Claire blurted. Morley had wandered away toward the front of the bus now, talking to someone else, and Patience was leaning over her, checking her bonds, which were very tight. "Patience, please. You know this isn't right. Just let us go."

"I can't do that."

"But—"

"I *can't*," Patience said, with soft but unyielding emphasis. "Please don't ask again."

She straightened and walked away without another glance, leaving them in the back, pinned like the other UnHappy Meals. At least she hadn't gagged them. Claire supposed she would, if they started screaming. *Note to self: don't scream.* Good advice.

Shane twisted around in his seat to peer at her over the top of the seat. "Hey," he whispered. "You okay?"

"I'm fine. Eve?"

Eve was fuming, her cheeks bright, her eyes hot with fury. "Fine," she snapped, biting off the word and leaving a sharp, broken silence. After a second, she softened a little. "Pissed off. *Really* pissed off. What kind of stupid trip is this? So far, I've been assaulted, insulted, arrested, and now I'm tied to a seat by a bunch of vampires in case they crave a little O negative at lunch. And my boyfriend is out there somewhere, dodging sunbeams. This *sucks!*"

"Ah—" Claire didn't quite know how to answer that. She looked at Shane, who shrugged. "He'll be okay."

"I know," Eve said with a sigh. "I'm just—I need him right now, you know? Shane was all gallant and came with you. I feel . . . abandoned, that's all."

"You're not abandoned," Shane said. "Dude, don't bag on Michael. It's a whole different problem when you're flammable."

Eve turned her face away, toward the window, and said, "I know. I'm just—gah, seriously, I *hate* being helpless! We have to do something," she said. "We have to get out of this."

But, as Morley dropped into the driver's seat of the bus, slammed the doors closed, and put the beast in gear, Claire wasn't at all sure what options they really had. Morley wasn't interested in bargains, and they had nothing to trade, anyway. No way they could threaten him, not even with Amelie; he'd already given Amelie the finger on his way out of Morganville, and he clearly wasn't worried about her coming after him—or, if so, what would happen when she did. Claire didn't have anything else in her bag of tricks, nothing at all.

"Wait it out," Shane said, as though he knew what she was thinking—and he probably did, actually. He was starting to get really good at that. "Just wait and watch. Something will happen. We just need to be ready to move when it does."

"Fantastic," Eve muttered sourly. "Waiting. My favorite. Next to skinny-dipping in acid and having vampires *suck my blood*."

"Sorry," Shane said to Claire.

"For what?"

"That you're sitting next to Little Miss Sunshine. It's not going to be a fun trip."

He was right about that. It wasn't.

EIGHT

Eve mostly sat in silence, but she was just crackling with anger. Claire could feel it coming off her like static electricity. She wasn't cooling off anytime soon, either; Claire thought she was being angry to keep from being scared, which wasn't a bad choice. Being scared under these circumstances wasn't going to get them anywhere. It certainly hadn't helped Orange Cap and Angry Guy much, or the five other people Claire could spot who were bound and gagged, waiting for a vamp to get hungry.

She saw it happen once, but in the medically approved way; Jacob Goldman—Patience's vampire brother, and under other circumstances kind of an okay guy—had fixed somebody up with a tourniquet and drawn out about ten tubes of blood from one of the men sitting two rows up. He was good at it. Theo, his dad and a doctor, had probably taught him how to do it. She supposed there was one advantage to having a vampire draw your blood—he wasn't likely to miss a vein and have to try again.

Jacob looked unhappy about what he was doing, and at the end, even patted his victim on the shoulder in a gentle, reassuring way. Claire half expected him to hand over a lollipop—although since the man was gagged, that probably wouldn't make much sense.

"Not happening," Eve whispered next to her. "No, not happening. This cannot be *happening*. Where the hell is Oliver? Isn't he supposed to be our chaperone?"

Claire didn't know and couldn't begin to reassure Eve, because there was a creeping sense of doom coming over her, too. Michael wasn't showing up, and neither was Oliver, and that had to be bad. It just had to be, somehow. Oliver, at least, could stand the sun; she'd seen him outside the jail before Morley had made his dramatic entrance. So why wasn't he stepping in?

Because you're not important, Claire's little, traitorous voice whispered. *Because you're just human. Fast food on legs.*

No, that wasn't true. Even Oliver had treated them—well, not exactly *nicely*, but he had developed a kind of basic respect for them. Maybe, in Eve's case, even a little liking.

He wouldn't just stand by and watch things happen.

Unless he thought he couldn't win, the little voice responded, and ugh, the little voice was way too logical for Claire to argue with. Oliver wasn't the self-sacrificing type, except maybe—*maybe*—where it applied to Amelie— and only in little glimpses.

But Michael was, and Michael would have shown up unless something had stopped him.

Or someone.

Claire cleared her throat. "Jacob? Can I ask you something?"

Jacob slipped the blood vials into a pocket of his jacket and came back down the aisle of the bus. He swayed gracefully with the motion of the road, not even bothering to check his balance against the tops of the seats, the way a human probably would have. He crouched down next to Claire, bringing them to eye level.

"I'm so sorry," he said immediately. "This was not what we'd planned. We never intended to do it this way, but we couldn't get to either the blood bank or the Bloodmobile—they were both well guarded. We had to choose—leave without supplies, or . . ."

"Or pick them up at the convenience store?" Claire tried to keep the judgy tone out of her voice, but it was hard. "That's not what I wanted to talk about."

Jacob nodded, waiting.

"Have you seen Michael?"

Jacob's eyes widened. "No," he said, and he was an even worse liar than Claire expected. "No, did he come with you?"

"Jacob, you know he did." Claire said it softly, and hoped that Eve couldn't hear what she was saying. "Did something happen to him?"

Jacob stared at her for a few long, sick seconds, then said, "I don't know."

He stood up and walked away. Claire bit her tongue on an almost-overpowering urge to yell something after him; it probably would have just gotten her gagged, anyway.

Shane was turned in his seat, as much as his bonds would allow, and he was staring at her. He knew, too.

Claire risked a glance over at Eve, but she was staring out the window. Not crying, not anymore. She just looked . . . distant, as if she'd removed herself from everything happening around her.

Shane was right. There was nothing to be done now except wait.

Claire was bad at it, but she spent the time trying to think through the problem. What would Myrnin do? Probably invent some device made out of fingernails and coat threads that would cut through plastic handcuffs. Then again, Myrnin would be cheerfully chugging down the blood, so maybe he was not such a good example to follow. Sam. What would Michael's grandfather have done? Still a vampire, but he'd never have gone along with this stuff. He'd have stood up for people. He had his whole life, both as a human and a vampire.

And he'd have never been handcuffed to a seat, genius, Claire's little voice reminded her. *How about Hannah Moses?* That was a good suggestion, for once. Claire couldn't imagine how Hannah, who'd been a big-time soldier, would have gotten out of this, but it probably would have involved a concealed knife—which, of course, Claire didn't have.

The steady throb of the road was hypnotic, and since the windows were blacked out, there wasn't much to see out there except some passing shadows. The vampires were mostly whispering among themselves, and she could feel their suppressed excitement. It was strange, but the vampires seemed to feel they'd been prisoners in Morganville, too—mostly prisoners of its strict rules of conduct, but Claire knew they hadn't been allowed out of town freely any more than the human residents.

It was odd that the *vampires* would now be feeling that same freedom that she, Eve, Michael, and Shane had felt leaving the town borders. It seemed . . . wrong.

"Eve?" Claire tried bumping Eve's shoulder with her own. She did it often enough to finally pull Eve out of her staring trance and get her attention. "Hey. How you doing?"

"Fantastic," Eve said. "Adventure of a lifetime." She dropped her head back against the seat's built-in pillow and closed her eyes. "Wake me for the massacre, okay? Don't want to miss it."

Claire had no idea what to say to that, so she just settled her own head back, closing her eyes, too. The road hiss became a kind of white noise in her head, and then . . .

She was asleep.

When she woke up, the bus was pulling to a stop. Claire flinched, tried to lift her arms, and immediately was reminded that plastic handcuffs *hurt* as they cut into her skin. She took a deep breath and relaxed, deliberately, looking around. Eve was awake, too, her dark eyes narrow and glittering in the dimness. In the row ahead, Claire could see the back of Shane's head as he tried to make sense of whatever was outside the window.

"Where are we?" Claire asked. Shane's head shook.

"No idea," he said. "Can't really see a whole lot. It looks like maybe some little town, but I can't tell."

"They don't need more, uh, supplies. No empty seats."

"That's what I was thinking," Shane said. There was nothing in his voice, but Claire knew he was feeling just as worried as she was about this development.

Morley brought the bus to a stop with a hiss of air brakes and a lurch, then opened the door and descended the steps. It was still daylight out there; the light spilling in from the opened accordion doors was milky white and intense.

None of the other vampires tried to follow. They just waited. Morley came back, stood at the front of the bus, and grinned. "Brothers and sisters," he said, "I have stopped for gas. Feel free to snack while I attend to the fuel."

"Oh no," Eve whispered. "No, no, *no.*"

Claire tried to get her hands free, again. The plastic handcuffs cut deep, almost drawing blood, and she had to stop; the smell of blood wouldn't be a good thing, just now.

The vampires were turning to look at those in the back of the bus, and their eyes were glowing.

Patience and Jacob Goldman weren't among them. They were closer to the back, and they had their heads bent together, whispering. Patience seemed upset at something Jacob was saying, but he was insistent, and as the first vampire got up to get his snack, Jacob suddenly flashed out of his seat and stood in the way.

The vampire was a woman, nobody Claire had ever met; she looked older, and not very nice. She also didn't like Jacob's getting in her face, and she said something in a language Claire didn't recognize. Jacob must have, because he spouted something right back.

Patience finally got out of her seat and stood nearby, clearly backing him up.

Jacob reached into his pocket and handed over two blood vials. He switched to English to say, "This will hold you for now. There's no need for anyone to be killed, and you know what will happen if we allow feeding in here. Take it and sit down."

"Who do you think you are, *Amelie?*" The woman bared her fangs in a mocking laugh. "I left Morganville to escape these stupid rules. Give me what I want, or I'll take it."

"The rules are not stupid," Patience said. "The rules are sensible. If you want to alert humans to our presence and restart the bad old times, the times when we ran for our lives, owned nothing, *were* nothing—then wait until we have reached our destination. You can go off on your own and do what you will. But while Jacob and I are here, you *will not* feed directly from these people. I will not see them dead because you can't control yourself."

She sounded absolutely sure about what she was doing, and very matter-of-fact, as if only an idiot would argue with her. The other vampire frowned, thought about it, and then made a sound of frustration. She grabbed two vials from Jacob's outstretched hand. "I'll expect more," she snapped. "You'd better start draining them. You have a lot of mouths to feed."

Jacob ignored her. "Who else? I can give out four more. . . ."

Four more vampires got up and accepted the vials. Jacob took out his medical kit and handed it to Patience. "I'll stay here," he said. "Draw the blood."

"Yeah, don't make any of them short!" one of the other vampires called, and there was a ripple of laughter.

"Enough," Jacob said, and there was a hint of relaxed humor in his voice. "You'll all get what you want. Just not now. And not here."

He looked over his shoulder at Patience, who was strapping a tourniquet around the first human she'd found—a woman, this time. There was a little resistance, but not much, and Patience proved herself to be just as good at drawing blood as her brother. She filled ten more vials, which she handed over to Jacob for distribution as she moved on to the next donor.

So it went, even after Morley came back inside after fueling up the bus. He saw what was going on, and shook his head. "You can take the vampire out of Morganville . . . ," he said, and left the rest unsaid as he dropped into the driver's seat. "Right, young ones, bloodbath later. First, we drive."

Claire half hoped that the vamps would be done with lunch before Patience worked her way back to her row, but no such luck. However, she turned left, and started with Angry Guy, whose bug eyes and muffled shrieks seemed to make no impression on her at all. She did the blood draw quickly and easily, pocketed the vials, and moved on to Orange Cap, who'd lost his cap now and was crying wet, messy tears. His nose was dripping, too.

When Patience was finished tapping him, she turned to Claire. She looked at her for a long moment, then said, "I will not take your blood. Nor that of your friends. Not yet."

Next to Claire, Eve let out a little sigh of relief. Shane, who'd been sitting tensely in the row ahead, relaxed as well.

Claire didn't. "Why?"

"Because—we owe you a favor, I think. Let this be payment." She started to move on to the next row.

"Wait," Claire said. Patience's dark, strange eyes returned to her face. "They're going to kill us all. You don't want that, you and Jacob."

"Jacob and I are outnumbered," Patience said softly. "I am sorry, but there is little we can do more than we are doing now. Forgive me."

"There has to be something—" Claire bit her lip. Eve was paying attention now, and Shane, although Claire was trying to keep the whole conversation to a whisper. "Can't you maybe let us loose? We promise, we won't tell Morley."

"Child, you have no idea what you're saying," Patience said, a little sadly. "He'll catch you, and then Morley will find out what he wants to find out. He has no reason not to rip this information from you, and it would be suspicious enough that I haven't drawn blood. He already thinks Jacob and I are too weak. You put us at risk, as well as yourselves."

"So what's our choice?" Eve hissed, leaning over as far as she could. "Getting fanged to death? No, thank you. Pass. If I'd wanted that kind of gruesome, horrible horror-movie ending, I could have stood on a street corner in Morganville and saved myself the trouble!"

Patience looked even more uncomfortable. "I can't help you," she said again. "I'm sorry."

That was her final answer, apparently. Claire watched her continue on with her blood work, apparently satisfied that she'd done her good deed for the day.

"We're screwed," Shane said, in a matter-of-fact voice, and turned back, face forward. "Still want to go back to Morganville? Because every day is pretty much just like this, one way or another."

Eve sighed, slumped against the window, and looked as if she was close, again, to bursting into tears. She didn't. Claire almost wished she would. It wasn't like Eve, all this nervous anger. It made *her* nervous, and the last thing she needed right now was more to raise her pulse rate.

"Michael will find us," Eve said. "They'll come for us."

Claire wished she felt that sure about it.

Patience and Jacob distributed all of the collected blood, two vials per vampire, and gave the rest to Morley, who chugged them back like shots at happy hour. It was disgusting, watching all the vampires having their snack; Claire's stomach turned, and she found it was easier staring down at her feet than actually paying attention.

Some of the blood donors had actually passed out, though whether that was just sleep, low blood pressure, or panic, Claire wasn't sure. It was quieter, at least. Morley kept driving, and it seemed like hours before he slowed the bus again. He didn't stop, just geared down and beckoned to a vampire sitting behind him. The vampire nodded, pointed to three others, and gestured for them to follow.

"What's going on?" Shane asked. "Can you tell?"

"No," Claire said, and then gasped as Morley opened the bus doors. The bus was still rolling along at maybe thirty-five or forty miles an hour. The four vampires up front put on coats, hats, gloves—sunny-day wear—and lined up on the stairs.

One by one, they bailed out.

"What the hell?" Shane twisted around awkwardly to the limit of his ability. "Eve, can you see anything? What's going on?"

"I can't—wait, I think—" Eve squinted, leaned her head against the window, and finally continued. "I think they're going after something behind us. A car, maybe."

Four vampires had just bailed out of a moving bus, in broad daylight, to attack a car that was behind them. Following them?

Claire gasped as an electric shock zipped up her spine. Michael. Oliver. It had to be! They'd figured it out. They were right behind them.

Yeah, her tragic, pessimistic little voice said in her head. *They're right behind us, and four vampires are about to drag them out of the car and leave them to fry.*

"Can you see—" Claire's voice was shaking now. Eve didn't answer. "Eve!"

"I'm trying!" Eve snapped. "It's all just shadows out there, okay? I can barely tell there's a car! Oh no . . ."

"What?" She and Shane blurted it out together, leaning toward Eve as if somehow they could make things out any better.

"The car," Eve said. "I think—I think it crashed. It's not behind us now." She sounded dull again, defeated. "It's gone."

"Dammit," Shane said. "Probably was some farmer driving to market. Didn't have anything to do with all this crap."

"Doesn't matter now," Eve whispered. "They're not coming now."

She began to cry, producing wrenching sobs that made her whole body vibrate, and banged her forehead against the window glass—hard. Claire instinctively tried to reach out for her, and came up against her restraints, again. "Hey," she said, trying hard to sound compassionate and soothing. Her heart just ached for Eve, who sounded so . . . lost. "Eve, please don't. Please don't do that. It's going to be okay; it's all—"

"No, it's not!" Eve screamed, and turned toward Claire in a tearful fury. "It's not okay! Michael! Michael!"

She started thrashing against her restraints. Shane tried to calm her down, too, but Eve wasn't listening anymore—not to anybody.

Patience came and, with a sad but determined look at Claire, leaned over and gave Eve a quick injection in her shoulder. It was so fast Claire couldn't react to try to stop her, and Eve stopped thrashing to say, in blank surprise, "Ow!"

Then her eyes rolled back in her head, and she went completely limp in her chair, her head tilting toward the window, wild strands of hair covering her face.

"What did you do?" Claire demanded, and tried not to scream it. She'd just seen what screaming got you.

"She'll sleep," Patience said. "She's not injured. It's better this way. She could hurt herself, otherwise."

"Yeah, can't have that," Shane said bitterly. "Gotta save that for you guys. What was that, with the vamps getting off the bus?"

Patience put the cap back on the needle she'd used to inject Eve and put it in her pocket. "Someone was following," she said. "They're not now. That's all you need to know." The bus changed its pitch again, air brakes sighing, and slowed to a relative crawl. The doors banged open again, and two vampires got on, wearing hats and gloves and long coats against the sun.

One of them was smoking, even with all the protective gear.

The other one, a little taller and thinner, grabbed Morley by the neck, dragged him out of the driver's seat, and tossed him right out the door.

"Go!" he shouted, and stripped off his hat.

The tall one was Oliver.

Michael—who was the incoming vampire trailing wisps of smoke— raced down the aisle, slammed into Patience and Jacob, and knocked them out of the way. Nobody else had time to stand up, although a few vampires lunged and caught pieces of his coat as he ran toward the back of the bus. Oliver was right behind him, and as they reached the rows where the humans were, Oliver turned and snarled at the other vampires, who were starting to get to their feet. They were hampered by close quarters, but there were a lot of them.

Jacob bounded up, gave Oliver a second's dark look, and then jumped up on top of the headrest of the seat next to him, crouching like a bird of prey. Patience did the same on Oliver's other side.

"No," she said flatly, as the vampires started to move toward them. "Stay where you are."

Michael reached them and snapped Claire's bonds first. It took him a precious few seconds, because the plastic was tougher than he'd thought, and he had to try not to hurt her. As soon as she was free, he leaned over Eve and pushed out the side window with one powerful punch. Metal bent and shrieked, glass shattered, and the whole window assembly fell out onto the road.

Light streamed in, pure and white-hot, and hit him full in the face. Michael jerked back into the shadows with a choked cry. Claire had a blurred impression of burns, but he didn't give her time to worry about him. "Out!" he yelled, and grabbed her by the waist to boost her toward the window. The inch of skin exposed between his coat and gloves sizzled like frying bacon. Claire grabbed hold of the jagged edge of the window and looked down. The bus was still rolling, and it was picking up speed as it started down the hill. "Claire, jump!"

She didn't really have a choice.

Claire jumped, hit the hard pavement with a stunning thump, and rolled. She managed to protect her head and curled up in a ball on the white-hot surface.

The bus kept on rolling. She could hear screaming—and fighting. Another window broke, next to Shane.

"Come on," Claire whispered, and clambered to her feet. She hurt all over, and her ankle felt as if she'd sprained it, but that didn't matter right now.

She watched the bus.

Nobody came out the window.

Claire started to run after the bus—limped after it—and had to stop when her ankle folded under her after a dozen steps. "Shane!" she screamed. "Shane, come on! Get out!"

Her attention was completely fixed on the bus, but she had good survival instincts, thanks to Morganville's harsh training; she sensed a shadow behind her, and dropped just in time.

Morley. He was baking in the blazing day—not sizzling like Michael, but definitely turning toxic-sunburn red. And he was angry. His hand blurred through space where she'd been, and if she'd been in the way, he would have broken her neck. She rolled and stumbled back to her feet, felt the left one give way again, and hopped backward.

Morley gave her a feral, awful grin. "Nobody leaves the tour," he said. "Especially not you, little girl. Amelie wants you back. I'm certain of that. You're my insurance. No fair limping off on your own."

He reached for her, and out of the corner of her eye, Claire saw a black shape hurl itself from the shattered bus window and streak toward them. At first she thought it was Michael, but no—Oliver.

He hit Morley like a brick wall and threw him fifty feet down the road in a rolling, slapping mess. Then, after an irritated look at her hopping on one foot, he scooped Claire up in his arms, then turned back to shout, "Michael, leave it! Get out!"

A car was roaring over the hill behind them—a police car, with half the light gear ripped off and dangling, and holes punched in the doors and windows. It had clawlike scrapes in the hood.

It didn't slow down for Morley, who scrambled to his feet and dived out of the way as the cruiser rocketed past. It screeched to a sliding halt, crossways in the road, and the driver threw the passenger door open, then the back. Oliver tossed Claire into the back of the car, left the door open, and raced back to the bus. He leaped up, clinging to the open window, reached in, and grabbed something—a handful of black coat—and dragged.

Michael toppled out the window and fell heavily on the road. Oliver dropped down, cat-steady, and reached down to pull Michael to his feet. He took off his own hat and jammed it down on Michael's bare blond head, stripped off his own long black coat, and flung it over him as additional protection.

Michael fought to get free, but as Claire flailed and struggled to sit up, Oliver dragged her friend all the way to the police car, shoved him in the back door, and slammed it, hard, penning Michael inside. The handles didn't work, of course. Michael landed half on top of her, heavy and smelling like burning hair, but he quickly rolled up and tried to smash out the window glass—which, Claire realized with a shock, was painted over black—spray painted. Only the driver's side part of the front window was left unaltered.

Oliver got in the front, turned, and drove a fist through the metal grating that separated the back of the squad car from the front. He peeled back the metal, grabbed Michael's arm, and said, "You can't help them by dying. You tried. We'll try again. This isn't over."

"Eve's still in there! I can't leave her there!" Michael yelled, and yanked free.

Oliver, with a weary, impatient sigh, grabbed him by the neck this time, and pinned him back against the stained vinyl seat. "Listen to me," he said, and peeled back more of the grate so their eyes could meet, and hold. "Michael, I swear to you that we will not abandon your friends. But you must stop this nonsense. It's doing nothing to help them, and everything to destroy your usefulness to me and everyone you love. Do you understand?"

Michael was still tense, ready to fight, but Oliver held him there, staring him down, until Michael finally let go of Oliver's arm and held up both hands in surrender. His whole body slumped. Defeated.

Still, Oliver didn't let go. "Drive," he told the man behind the wheel. "Follow the bus. Morley's already back on board. He'll keep driving, but we should hang back out of sight."

"I can't follow it if I can't see it!" the driver protested, and Claire knew that voice, but it didn't sound like the sheriff from Durram, or even his deputy. It sounded . . .

No way.

Claire leaned forward and peered through her half of the grate, which was still in place. "Jason?" Jason Rosser? Eve's brother? "What the hell are you doing here?"

"Oliver needed some support that wouldn't combust," Jason said. "Besides, that's my sister in there, right?"

Eve. Eve was still in the bus—that was why Michael was fighting so hard. Claire felt strangely behind the curve right now; maybe she'd banged her head harder than she'd thought. It ached on the right side. She was starting to feel a whole lot of aches, as the adrenaline started to recede a little.

Shane. Shane was still on the bus, too. Why was he still on the bus?

"Jason. Use this to track them," Oliver said, and pulled something out of the glove compartment of the cruiser. It looked like a GPS navigation device. "It's been keyed to follow the bus."

"You bugged the bus?"

"I bugged your sister. I slipped a cell phone into her pocket during the confusion. Hopefully she'll have an opportunity to use it."

He handed the device over to Jason, who stuck it up on the dashboard, angled so he could see the colored road map display. "Nice," he said. "Hey, if you could unlock the shotgun, that would be good, too."

"No," Oliver said flatly. "The last thing I trust you with is a firearm. Just drive."

Claire was having trouble focusing, she realized. "You gave Eve a phone?"

"I put it in her pocket," Oliver said. "Unless they search her again, I doubt they'll find it. There were plenty of distractions."

"What about Shane? Is he okay?"

"I don't know." Oliver kept staring at Michael. "Was he?"

"I got one of his hands free," Michael said. "I could have gotten them both out. You just had to give me one more—"

"One more second and you'd have been pulled to pieces, which would have done me no good at all," Oliver said. "Patience and Jacob were stepping aside. They know a lost cause when they see one, and you couldn't have gotten Eve and Shane both out in any case. It's better to leave them together, where they can protect each other. Now, are you going to behave yourself? Or do I need to prove to you, again, who is master here?"

Michael didn't answer, but he dropped his hands to his sides.

Oliver let him go. "How do you feel?"

Michael let out a brittle little laugh. "What, you're concerned?" He looked bad, Claire realized, even in the dim light bouncing in from Jason's side of the front window. He was burned red, his face swollen.

"Not really," Oliver said. "I'm concerned you'll be a liability. Which is almost certainly going to be the case, if you continue to act like some lovesick boy instead of a thinking man. Are we understood? If you want to save your fragile little friends, you must be a great deal smarter about when you risk your own safety."

It was hard to tell what the expression on Michael's swollen face was, but there was no mistaking the flash of hate in his eyes. Claire swallowed, hard. Michael took a deep breath and turned toward her. "You're okay?" he asked, and stripped off his gloves. His hands were pale, but just above the line where the gloves had been were vivid black and red burns. He gently touched her face, turning it to one side, then the other. "You're going to have some action-star bruises, tough girl." But she knew what he was looking for, really.

"No fang marks," she said. "Well, none that weren't already there, from before, you know. Look, not even any needle marks."

"Needle marks?"

"Patience and Jacob, they insisted that all blood get drawn with a needle. I think they were trying to sort of ration it out."

"They were trying to keep you alive," Oliver said, turning back to face the front. "That many vampires in an enclosed space, a feeding frenzy would be inevitable. None of you would have survived it, especially not restrained as you were."

As Eve and Shane still were. Claire felt sick. She also felt horribly, horribly guilty. "Why me?" she asked. "Why save me, not Eve? Or Shane?"

"You were the closest," Michael said. "And—you're the youngest. Eve and Shane would both kick my ass if I tried to save them ahead of you." But he looked sickly guilty, too, and she knew he was thinking, just as she was, of Eve. "I heard her screaming for me. That was why we—why we decided to go in."

"It was that or listen to his yowling the rest of the drive," Oliver said. "I've never been in love, and more and more, I'm glad I haven't. It seems to make you foolish, as well as very tiresome."

Jason snorted; it might have been a choked laugh. "Yeah, you got that right."

Oliver smacked Jason in the back of the head. "I don't need your agreement. Drive."

Claire tried to pull her head back together. "Wh-what are we going to do?" she asked. "Just follow them? What if—what if something happens on the bus? Are we just going to sit here?"

"Yes," Oliver said. "Because going back now, we've lost the element of surprise, and Morley will be ready for us. In fact, he may try to engineer a provocation, to force us to do something stupid. We follow them until they stop. Once they're off the bus, we have a much better chance."

Jason said, "What about, you know, ramming the bus? Out here in the sun, they can't really chase us down on foot. Not for long."

"Ramming a bus will simply yield us a car that will no longer drive, and will not ensure the bus is disabled," Oliver said. "It would take something larger. Much larger. In any case, it's not prudent. Too much risk of damage to your delicate little humans on board."

"But—"

"Oh, just shut up and follow," Oliver snapped. "I am tired of debate. There will be no more."

Claire knew a door slamming when she heard it. She twisted around a little and pulled up the pant leg over her left ankle. It was puffy and starting to bruise. Yep. That was sprained. "Do we have any first aid stuff in here?"

Oliver dug out a box and passed it through the torn grate on Michael's side. She found some of that rubberized wrapping bandage stuff, and tried to do it herself, but Michael took it away from her, removed her shoe and sock, and wrapped it for her without saying a word.

"Thanks," she said softly. It felt better, once that was done, although there was still a dull red ache that flared up every time she moved. "Is there anything—"

"I'm healing," Michael said. He put the medical kit down and let his head fall back against the seat. "Man. This has not been the trip I planned."

"Really?" Oliver's voice was dry. "It's exactly what I expected. Sadly."

NINE

They drove for what seemed like a very long time, but according to the clock built into the cruiser's dashboard, it was only a couple of hours. The bus kept taking crazy back-road turns, as if they were searching for something. Finally, though, the dot stopped moving. "What is that?" Jason asked, and tapped the screen. It magnified. "Is that a town?" Claire couldn't see anything through the grate, other than a dot on a map. "It's tiny, if it is. Smaller than that last place where you got yourselves jacked."

"No other roads in," Oliver said, looking at the display. "They'll see us coming in any case. The land is as flat as a griddle. And just as hot."

"Yeah, who ever decided to locate Vampireville in Texas, anyway? Whose good idea was that?" Jason asked.

"Amelie's," Oliver said. "And none of your business why she chose it. It'll do us no good to wait until dark—they will only have sharper senses with which to detect us. Better to strike in the day, if we can. Unfortunately, my army consists of one unreliable criminal, one girl with a disability, and one incredibly foolish young vampire with a tanning issue. I am not confident."

"We don't have a choice," Claire said. "We have to go. Eve and Shane—"

"I am more concerned with what Morley is doing," Oliver interrupted. "He's defying Amelie. Defying *me*. I can't allow that to go unanswered."

It boiled down to the same thing, luckily—they didn't have a choice, and Oliver had to help. He thought about it in silence for a few minutes as the cruiser continued on its path to the dot on the map, then nodded sharply. "All right," he said. "We go in. Now. But when we do, you must be fast, and you must be ruthless. Michael, since you're so hell-bent on saving the girl and your friend, that will be your mission. Claire, Jason, you will stay with me. I may require someone to act as distraction."

"He means bait," Michael said. "You're not using Claire."

"She's a wounded deer," Oliver said. "She's perfect."

"*You're not using Claire*. And that's not optional. I don't care if you think you're the boss; you're not using her." Michael sounded utterly, completely dedicated to that proposition, and Oliver, after a second's frozen silence, nodded.

"Very well. I'll use the criminal. He's serviceable, I suppose."

Jason cleared his throat. "Do I get the shotgun if you're staking me out for bait?"

"No," Oliver said. "Not ever."

Claire was struck by a random thought, which was proof her brain was finally shaking off the effects of bailing out of the bus at low speed. "Hey," she said. "It takes hours to get here from Morganville. How did Jason—"

"Jason says shut up," Eve's brother snapped. "It's none of your business, okay? Let's just say I was in the neighborhood."

Oliver said nothing. That meant that either Jason had tried to get out of Morganville and managed to get himself caught by Oliver—or he'd been on Oliver's business errands. Either way, there was some kind of relationship there that Claire was sure hadn't been in force a month ago. In fact, Oliver had been pretty definitely on the "Let's execute the jerk" team. So why was Jason suddenly part of his crew—and a trusted part, if Jason had gotten some kind of permission to leave Morganville?

Claire figured she would probably never know. Jason was angrily not talking; Oliver was never Mr. Great Communicator even when he was in a good mood, and this wasn't one of those times.

He looked angry, focused, and very, very dangerous.

"Take us in," Oliver said. "You all know what's required. Do it. Get allies from Morley's people if you can, by whatever means you can. Intimidate if you can't persuade. Don't allow yourself to be surrounded. Arm your friends, destroy your enemies, and whatever the cost, *win*. Are we understood? I will take care of Morley."

Michael nodded. His face was healing faster than Claire had expected, but she guessed it wouldn't last, not if they were going out in the daylight again. She wondered how much he could really take, before the pain and damage got too much and just overwhelmed him.

She hoped she wouldn't have to find out.

Jason drove way too fast, gunning the engine to race-car levels, chasing dust devils down the road, and grinning like the maniac he was, from Claire's glimpses of his expression. He looked more than ready for a fight. She'd never exactly seen him like this, and it was more than a little frightening.

Next to her, Michael was closed off, focused on controlling the pain he had to be feeling, and the worry. Oliver probably didn't feel anything. He'd sneer at the idea of being worried.

Claire wanted to throw up, but she was determined to hang on and be as strong as she could. She rooted through the first aid box and found a couple of extra-strength pain relievers, not that they would help much. She also asked Michael, quietly, if he had any kind of weapon he could give her.

He silently dug a silver-coated stake out of his pocket and handed it to her. It had a wicked-sharp tip, enough to slice as well as stab, and it felt cold and solid in her hand as she gripped it hard enough to leave sweat prints on the shiny surface. "Last resort," he told her. "Don't get close enough to need it, okay?"

"Okay," she agreed, and tried for a smile. She thought she actually managed to pull one off. "Does it hurt? Never mind; stupid question. Of course it hurts. I'm sorry."

His pale hand, with its vivid red burns at the wrist, gripped hers tightly for a few seconds. "You're a good person, Claire. You know that, right?"

"So are you."

"Technically not really a person anymore, as Shane likes to remind me."

"Shane can be an idiot."

"But a good friend."

"That, too." She sighed. "We have to get them back, Michael. We have to."

"And we will," he said. "I promise."

He might have said more, but just then the car's acceleration slowed. Jason eased off the gas and said, "Okay, we're here. Looks like about three blocks' worth of town, if that. Maybe thirty buildings total? What's the plan?"

"Find the bus," Oliver said. "They won't have gone far."

"Why not?"

"Because Morley is a lazy sod, and he won't want to put himself out. Look for the biggest building, and you'll likely find the bus parked right in front of it."

Sure enough, as Jason turned the sharp corner into town—if you could call it a town; it was more like a random collection of buildings— the bus was immediately and obviously parked right in front of what looked like a miniature version of the Morganville Courthouse—sort of Gothic, with towers and peaked roofs, and constructed of gray stone blocks. It looked about twenty years out from any kind of maintenance work; the iron fence around the place was leaning, rusted through, and the grass inside was ragged and overgrown.

The sign said BLACKE TOWNSHIP CIVIC HALL AND COURTS. In front of the entrance sat some kind of civic monument—a big, not very good greenish bronze statue of an old man wearing an antique suit, looking very self-satisfied. The plaque at his feet, visible even from the street, said HIRAM WALLACE BLACKE. Hiram hadn't fared too well. There were dents in his bronze form, and the whole thing leaned a little to the left, as though built on unsteady ground. Another few inches, and the whole thing was going to do a face-plant of Hiram into the overgrown grass.

The bus looked deserted. The doors were wide-open. There was no sign of Morley, his people, or anybody else.

"How do you blow this screen up? Oh yeah, I see," Jason said. "Okay, the phone is inside the building. That's where they've got Eve, anyway."

"You know what to do. Michael, when you find your friends, bring them back here if you can. If you can't, find a defensible position and hold it, and wait for me."

"What are you going to do?"

"Find Morley," Oliver said. "And explain to him why it is a terrible idea to make me come after him. This will be over quickly. Morley's not a brave man, and he'll order his people to comply. The only risk is that something could happen before I find him and . . . convince him."

The way he said that last part made Claire shiver. Oliver was capable of a lot of things, and some of them were really not very civilized. She'd seen some of it. It still woke her up at night, with her heart pounding.

But right now, at least he was pointed in the right direction. Kind of like a cannon.

"Go," Oliver said. He didn't yell it, and there wasn't any special emphasis to it, but Claire heard the absolute flat command in the word. He flung open his door, opened Michael's side in the back, and then he was moving toward the door, walking, not running, moving with deliberate speed, as if he had all the time in the world, and couldn't be stopped by anything or anyone. Jason scrambled out and scurried to keep up. He forgot to open Claire's side, but that was okay; Michael zipped around in less than two seconds, opened it, and flung Oliver's extra coat over his head to give himself extra protection from the fierce afternoon sun. "Check the bus!" he ordered.

"Wait, where are you—"

Too late. Michael was gone, racing at an angle across the overgrown grass, heading for the leaning shadow of the building. He got there and slammed his back against the stone, bent over and shaking, and finally stripped off the coat and shattered one of the windows that led into the courthouse.

It was odd, Claire thought, that there wasn't a single person coming out of the buildings to see what was going on—not even out of the Civic Hall and Courts. There wasn't a soul anywhere in sight. Blacke couldn't have very many people in it, but it must have at least a hundred or so.

They couldn't *all* be completely clueless, especially if Morley had been his usual obnoxious self.

Claire lurched for the bus, hobbled up the steps, and found the whole thing deserted. None of the prisoners were still in their seats, and the floor was littered with cut plastic ties in the back.

She left the bus at a limping run, crossed to the broken window—Michael hadn't waited—and groaned when she realized it was almost head-high to her. With no time to complain about it, she jumped, grabbed the sill, and ignored the cuts she got from the broken glass. Michael had swept away most of it; what was left was irritating, that was all. Her arms trembled with the strain, but she managed to lift herself up, get the toes of her right foot into one of the cracks in the stone, and boost up onto the window's broad ledge. From there it was easy enough to swing her legs in, but it was a longer drop to the floor than she'd thought, and she hit too hard. Her left ankle let out a fiery burst of pain, and she paused to brace herself against the cold stone wall, panting and waiting for the agony to subside.

She was in some kind of office, but it hadn't been used in recent years; the desks looked like something left over from the turn of the century, but these weren't antiques; they were junk. The wood was rotten, drawers were cracked and hanging loose, and in some cases the legs had actually broken off.

She surprised a mouse in one of the broken drawers, and nearly screamed as it zipped across the dirty floor in her path. *Deep breaths. Come on, keep it together; they need you. Shane needs you.*

Claire pulled the heavy silver-coated stake out of her pocket and held it in her left hand as she opened the door with her right, ready to attack if she had to . . . but the hallway was empty.

She could hear running footsteps, though. Noise upstairs. That didn't mean there weren't bad guys down here, however. Thanks to a thorough education in Morganville—Survival 101—she *always* assumed there were bad guys around every corner.

There was a lot of chaos going on upstairs—furniture crashing, thumping, running feet. People yelled—Claire tried not to think of it as screaming—and it sounded like that might be where Oliver had chosen to go after Morley.

But where was Michael?

Claire opened another door and found an office, with a desk and a computer and an old cup of molding coffee sitting on top of some papers. Nobody there. She tried the next door—same result, only no coffee.

In the third one, she found a woman slumped in the corner. She was unconscious, not dead, thankfully, as Claire discovered on checking her pulse, which proved to be strong. Claire moved the woman into a more comfortable position, rolled over on her side; recovery position, it was called. Shane had taught it to her—he was good at first aid.

The woman was older, kind of heavy, and she looked tired and pale. *Pale.*

Claire checked her neck on both sides, but found nothing. Then she checked the woman's wrists and found a slowly bleeding wound, and not a neat one, either. Claire shuddered, breathed in a few times to steady herself, and then looked around for something to use to tie up the wound. There was a scarf on the woman's desk; Claire carefully wrapped it around her wrist and tied it tight, and checked the woman again. She was still unconscious, but didn't seem to be in any trouble.

"It'll be okay," Claire promised, and went on. The thing that was worrying her now was that while she certainly wouldn't put it past Morley and his crew to be snacking on random people, this hadn't just happened. The blood streaking the woman's hand had been mostly dried and flaking off, the wound had been half healed, and Morley's party bus had only just arrived in town.

That didn't sound right at all.

Out in the hall, the fight was still going on upstairs, and as Claire carefully edged toward the stairs, trying to get a look, there was a sudden thump-rattle-crash, and a body came flying into view, hit the wall, and tumbled down the big, scarred wooden steps to sprawl at her feet.

It was a vampire.

It was *not* one of Morley's vampires. She'd gotten a look at every one of them on the bus, and they'd all been typical Morganville folks. None of them had looked Shane's age, or been wearing a bloodstained, tattered old football jersey that smelled like dead feet even from twenty yards away.

This was *not* a Morganville vampire.

This was something else.

And it rolled up, bared terrifying lengths of fangs, and came after her with a roar full of fury, hunger, and delight.

TEN

Claire yelped, backed up, and got the stake level just in time to bury it in his chest. His momentum drove him onto the silver-coated wood, and pushed her into the wall behind her with a bruising slam. Her head hit the bricks, and she felt a hot yellow burst of pain, but she was more concerned with his bloody red eyes, crazy with rage, and those sharp, sharp fangs. . . .

Then he slumped against her; she shoved, and he toppled off her and down to the floor with a crash, hands thumping out to either side. Man, he really *stank*, as if he hadn't bathed or washed his clothes in a year. And he smelled like old blood, which was sick.

His eyes were open, staring at the ceiling, but Claire knew he wasn't dead—not yet. The silver in the stake was hurting him, and the stake itself was keeping him immobilized for now. Whether or not the silver would kill him was a question of how old he was, but somehow she didn't think he was one of the ancient ones, like Amelie and Oliver and Morley. He was more like some bully who'd turned vamp a few years back, if that.

The silver was burning him. She saw black around the wound now.

He tried to kill me. She swallowed hard, her hand tentatively touching the stake, then dropping away. *I should let him die.*

Except she really needed that stake. Without it, she was unarmed. And she knew—because Michael had told her—that getting staked was painful. Getting staked with *silver* was agony.

Claire reached for the stake to pull it out. She'd just grabbed hold when a voice behind her said, in a rich, rolling English accent, "You don't want to be doing that."

Morley. He must have come down the stairs while she was otherwise occupied. He was bloody, clothes ripped even worse than they had been before, and he had open scratches across his pale face that were healing even as Claire turned to stare at him.

She tightened her grip on the stake and yanked it free as she rose out of her crouch, turning to fully face him.

Morley sighed. "Do any of you fools actually ever *listen*? I said *don't* do that!"

"He's hurt," Claire said. "He's not getting up any time soon."

"Wrong," Morley said. "He's not getting up at all. But then, he doesn't really have to."

She felt something cold brush her aching ankle, then wrap hard around it. The teen vamp had grabbed her and was pulling himself toward her.

Morley reached out, grabbed the stake from her hand, and stabbed the vampire again, with easily three times the strength Claire had used. She heard the crunch as the stake pushed through bones and into the wooden floor beneath.

The boy, no older than Shane, went limp again. His skin started to smolder from the silver.

"You can't—," she began, and Morley turned on her, his face hard.

"It might have dawned on you by now that I *can*," he snapped. "It might also have occurred to you that this boy is not one of my little flock. Doesn't that make you at all alarmed, Claire?"

"I—"

"It should," he said, "because apart from those vampires gathered in Morganville, there shouldn't *be* more. Amelie, whatever you think of her, is a thorough sort. Those who didn't agree to participate in her social experiment in Morganville were put down. There *are* no vampires still walking that I don't know." He nudged the boy with one worn boot. "But I don't know him, or his pack of jackals who just ate my supplies!"

"*Pack?*" Claire looked up, startled, at another thump and crash from upstairs. Morley ignored her and dashed for the stairs, racing in a blur. There was screaming up there. "Hey, wait! Ate your—*supplies*—you don't mean—"

Morley got to the top of the stairs and disappeared before she could manage another word. "My friends?" she finished lamely, and then blinked, because two seconds after Morley had crossed out of sight, Michael emerged from the shadows up there, with Shane beside him.

Michael was carrying Eve, who still seemed unconscious.

They came down the stairs fast, and Claire didn't like the tense worry she saw on Michael's face—or on Shane's. "We have to go," Michael said. "Now. Right now."

"What about Oliver? And Jason?"

"No time," Michael said. "Move it, Claire."

"My stake—"

"I'll make you a shiny new one," Shane promised. He sounded short of breath, and he grabbed her hand and towed her at a fast limp after Michael, who was heading down the hall for the broken window where they'd entered. "You all right?"

"Sure," she said, and controlled a wince as she came down wrong, again, on her ankle. But in the great scheme of things, yeah, she was all right—more all right than the people upstairs, from what Morley had said. "What is going on up there?"

"Morley's having a very bad day," Michael said. "Tell you later. Right now, we need to get out of here before—"

"Too late," Shane said, in a flat, quiet voice, and the four of them stopped in the middle of the hall as two vampires glided out of the shadows at either end, blocking them in. One was a shuffling, twisted old man with crazy eyes and drifting white hair. The other was a young man, wearing a football jersey—teammate of the vamp Claire had already staked, she guessed. This one was broader than Shane, and taller. Like the old man, he looked . . . weird; crazy, even for a vampire.

"Give," the old man said in a rusty, strange voice. "Give."

"Holy crap, that's creepy," Shane said. "Okay, plans? Anybody?"

"In here." Michael slammed his foot against the door on the opposite side of the hall and blew it back on the hinges with a splintering crash. Shane hustled Claire ahead of him into the room, and Michael jumped in after, slamming the door in the faces of the two vampires and shoving his back against it. "Barricade!"

"On it!" Shane said, and nodded for Claire to grab the other end of a heavy wooden desk, which they slid across the floor to block the door as Michael, with Eve in his arms, jumped effortlessly up onto the desk's top and then lightly down as it slid past. "Think that'll hold?"

"Hell no," Michael said. "Did you *see* that guy?" Eve stirred in his arms, murmuring, and he looked down at her, his face going still with concern. As she restlessly turned her head, Claire saw a matted spot in her hair—blood, almost invisible against the black.

"What happened?" Claire blurted.

Michael shook his head. "I don't know," he said.

"She got on Morley's bad side," Shane said. "He backhanded her into a wall. She hit her head on the corner. I thought—" He went quiet for a second. "Scared the shit out of me. But she's okay, right?"

"I don't know," Michael said.

"Well, use your superpowers or something!"

"I'm a *vampire*, idiot. I don't have X-ray vision."

"Some supernatural monster you are," Shane said. "Remind me to trade you in for a werewolf, bro. Probably be more useful right now."

Claire ignored the two of them and moved to the other side of the room. There was a window, but as she unlocked it and threw up the sash—which didn't want to move, and was caked with dust and old, dead bugs—she discovered that the grime had disguised a thick set of iron bars on the other side. "Michael," she said, "can you break these?"

"Maybe. Here." Michael handed Eve over to Shane, who balanced her with a lot more difficulty. He looked at the bars, which were in full, blazing sunlight. "That—could be a problem."

He was still wearing his leather coat, but his gloves were ripped—it looked as if somebody had shredded them with claws. Pale strips of skin showed through on the backs of his hands.

Shane, who was leaning against the desk that blocked the door, was almost knocked over as the vampires on the other side slammed into the barrier, sliding the desk nearly a foot before Shane dug in his feet and shoved back. The desk slid toward the door, inch by slow inch, until he'd jammed it hard against the old vampire's grabbing hands caught in the doorway. "Decide quick!" he yelled. "We're running out of time!"

Michael took a deep breath, grabbed one of the ancient, dusty drapes on the side of the window, and yanked it down. He wrapped it over both hands, then grabbed the bars. Even then, the sleeves on his coat rode up, and Claire saw the strips of reddened skin, already burned from before, start to smoke and turn black. Michael shook with effort, but the sun was too much for him. He let go of the bars and stumbled backward, panting, eyes gone red and wild. "Dammit!" he yelled, and tried kicking the bars. That worked better; his booted feet and jeans protected him better, and the first kick landed solidly, bending the bars and rattling the bolts.

He didn't have time for another one, because the vampires on the other side of the door hit it again, sliding the desk halfway into the room and sending Shane stumbling into Claire. Michael whirled in time to face the first vamp in, which was the younger one in the ragged football jersey.

Michael was fast, but his multiple exposures to the sun had slowed him down, and the other vamp hit first and hard in a blocking tackle, and Michael was thrown all the way into the back wall. He shook it off and rolled back to his feet just as the bloodsucking jock reached out for Claire.

Michael wrapped a fist in the back of the boy's jersey and yanked him off his feet, throwing him down with a bang flat on his back. He planted a knee on the guy's chest, holding him down, but that wasn't a permanent solution, and as Claire watched, the other vampire, the twisted old man, shuffled into the room, grinning with one side of his mouth. He looked even more dead than most vampires, and there was something familiar about the disorganized way he was moving, something—

She didn't have time to think about it, because the old man jumped at them like some creepy hunting spider, hands outstretched and hooked into claws. Shane dived one way, burdened by Eve; Claire dived the other. That put Shane and Eve closer to the door, and with a tormented look back, Shane ducked out.

"Claire, go!" Michael said. "Run!"

"I can't run," she said, very reasonably. Hobbling wasn't really an option; either one of these vamps could take her down in seconds. One slow, sliding step at a time, she backed away from the approaching old vampire, heading for the window.

He didn't seem to get her plan until he'd followed her into the sunlight and begun to burn. Even then, it seemed to take a few seconds to really sink in that he was in trouble. He kept coming in that awkward crab walk even as his clay white skin turned pink, then red, then began to smoke.

Then, finally, he howled and ducked away into the shadows.

Claire, pressed up against the windowsill and bathed by the hot sun, breathed a sigh of relief. Briefly.

"Smart," Michael said. He stayed where he was, holding Vamp Boy down, and watching the older vampire shuffle around and stalk Claire. "Stay where you are. He may try to grab you and pull you out of the sun. If I let this one go—"

"I know," Claire said. "I've got it." She didn't, really, but what choice did she have? She looked around frantically for something, anything, to use, and blinked. "Can you throw that over here?" she asked, and pointed. Michael looked around and picked up something off the floor, frowning.

"This?"

"Throw it!"

He did, and Claire snatched it out of the air just as the older vampire made his run at her, howling.

Claire buried the pencil in his chest. She got lucky, sliding it between his ribs just as Myrnin had taught her to do in his occasional, completely random self-defense classes, and the older vamp's eyes went wide and he fell at her feet, in the sun. Claire rolled him out of the way, but she left the pencil in his chest.

"You've *got* to be kidding," Michael said, and shook his head. "That is just embarrassing."

"Have you noticed something about them?" Claire asked, shaking now that the surge of adrenaline was passing. The vampire Michael was leaning on swiped at him, but Michael easily avoided the blow.

"These guys? They're not too smart."

"They're sick," she said. "I recognize the way the older one moved. Notice that they're not really talking? They can't. They've been broken down to basic levels. Hunt and kill. Like the worst-off vampires in Morganville when I got there."

Michael clearly hadn't thought of that. His whole body language changed, and for a second Claire thought he was going to get up and move away from the other vampire, but sense won out over fear, and he stayed put. Michael had never gotten sick from the disease the rest of the vampires had carried; as the youngest, he'd never had the chance. But he'd seen what it had done to some of the others in Morganville. He'd seen the creatures they'd become, confined for their own protection in cells in an isolated prison.

"It's okay," she said. "You've had the shot, Michael. I don't think you can get it now."

She hoped that was true, anyway. If this was some new strain of the disease, then that was worse. Lots worse, especially if—as she suspected, from the condition of these two vampires, and the one she'd staked in the hall—they were actually getting sicker a lot faster than the typical Morganville vampire had.

Shane came pelting into the room, almost tripped over the pencil-staked vampire, and looked around, lost. "Uh—what happened?"

"Where's Eve?"

"I left her next door," he said. "She's okay."

"You *left* her?" Michael snapped. "Oh, you'd better tell me you didn't just say that."

"She's fine, Mike. She's awake, kind of. I left her with a letter opener, hiding under a desk. She's safer than any of us right now." Shane looked down at the staked vamp at his feet. "Claire?"

"Yes?"

"You staked a vampire with a number two pencil."

"I didn't actually check the number."

"Have I told you lately how freaking awesome you are?"

She tried to smile, but her heart was fluttering in her chest now, and not in a good way. "Compliments later. We really need to get out of here and get to the car. Any ideas?"

"Find another pencil and I'll pin this one down, too," Michael said.

"You know how weird that sounds, right?" Shane said. "Right, never mind. Number two pencil, coming up. Why do I feel like we're taking a test?"

"Claire." Michael looked past Shane at her. "Go to Eve. Make sure she's okay."

Claire nodded and hobbled out the door, across the hall. The door was shut but not locked, and she pushed it open . . .

Only to have to duck an awkward lunge from Eve, who was standing up, clinging to a chair and holding a glittering silver letter opener in one deathly tight-gripped hand. Eve yelped and opened her fingers to drop the knife when she saw what she'd almost done, and fell into Claire's arms with a sob of relief. "You're okay, you're okay," Eve whispered, and hugged her with feverish, shaking strength. "God, so sorry. I thought you were one of the creeps."

"Not today," Claire said, and winced at the blood trickling down the side of Eve's face. "That must hurt."

"Not so much now." Eve's eyes looked kind of vague and unfocused, but she was staying on her feet. That had to be a good sign. "I thought—I thought I saw Michael. But then Shane was here, and—"

"Michael's here," Claire said. "He was carrying you, but he had to fight. He's coming, Eve. I told you he would."

Eve squeezed her eyes shut for a moment, breathing deep. "Okay," she said then, and her voice sounded stronger. "Okay. We'll be okay."

From the other room, Claire heard the sound of metal bending, and then a loud *clang*. "Yo!" It was Shane's voice, ringing off stone and wood. "Girls, the party's over. We are *leaving*!"

"Come on," Claire said, and put her arm under Eve's shoulders to keep her upright. "Time to go."

"Where's Jason?" Eve almost sounded in focus now, and on just the wrong topic. "We have to find him!"

"He's with Oliver," Claire said. "We'll find him. First, we have to make sure we stay alive, okay? Very important."

The two of them staggered together across the hall into the room where two vampires were lying on the floor, pinned by pencils, and Michael and Shane were standing at the window. The bars were broken out. Michael was sensibly off to the side, away from the sun, and he'd draped one of the thick, dusty curtains over his shoulders. Claire supposed he was going to use it to cover his head.

But neither he nor Shane was moving.

"What?" Claire asked, and as she came to the window and looked out, she realized what the problem was.

The police car was on fire.

And so was the bus, with big, crackling, very public flames.

And nobody, *nobody* had come out to gawk. No police had come running. Not even the volunteer fire department.

Blacke was a dead town—literally.

"We are screwed," Shane said, very matter-of-factly. "Plan B?"

"There isn't one," Michael said.

"You know, I kind of saw that one coming," Eve said. "Even with a concussion."

They stood there for a moment, watching the car and bus burn, and for a few seconds nobody said anything. Then Michael said, "Morley didn't do that. Morley isn't that stupid."

"It damn sure wasn't Oliver," Shane added. "So what the hell is going on around here?"

"You should tell us. You were riding with Morley; we just got here."

"Yeah, funny thing, getting tied up and hustled around by hungry vampires made me not notice the little things. All I know is that we got into the building, Morley was making some speech, and next thing

I knew, one of Morley's crew was yelling that we were being attacked. I grabbed Eve and tried to get her under cover, but she got clocked by Morley when she got between him and some guy he was fighting. She hit her head." Shane paused and glanced at Michael. "What's your excuse?"

"I lost track a while ago," Michael said. "Right about the time Oliver detoured us into Crazytown for no good reason. Unless this is what he was looking for all along."

"What, a town full of sick vampires?" When Claire said it, suddenly it made sense. "He *was*. He knew they were here. Somewhere, anyway. He was looking for them!"

"He thought they were in Durram," Michael agreed. "That's why he went off in the middle of the night searching. But if they ever were there, they moved on, to here. Smaller town. Easier to control, before they got too sick to care."

"But these dudes are not exactly historical," Shane said, and nodded toward the kid in the football jersey. "That's not some vintage outfit he's wearing; he can't have been vamped more than a few months ago, a year at the most. So how did he—"

"Bishop!" Claire interrupted. "Bishop was looking for Amelie. And he was making new vampires all the time, just making them and leaving them." She shuddered. "He must have come through here, or someplace close." Bishop was Amelie's father—both physically, and in a vampire sense, apparently. And in neither sense was he going to win a Father of the Year award. Or get a humanitarian plaque, either. He'd snacked on necks, and this was what he'd left behind him.

Scary, and disgusting.

"If Oliver was looking for them, he must have some kind of plan," Eve said. She was leaning against the wall now, holding one hand to her must-be-aching head, and she still looked kind of vague and unfocused. "Find him. He'll know what to do."

"He might have had a plan, but that was before Morley and his merry bunch of idiots crashed into it," Shane said. "Now we're in the middle of a three-sided vampire war. Which would be an awesome video game, but I'm really not interested in playing for real. I like my reset buttons."

"Then we have to find another car," Michael said. "One that runs."

"No, man, *I* have to find another car," Shane said. "And black out the windows. And get it back here so you don't combust strolling around town shopping for one. So here's an idea: *you* take care of the girls; *I'll* get the wheels."

"Did you just tell me to stay with the girls?" Michael said, and grinned. Shane did, too.

"Yeah," he said. "In your *face*, man. How does it feel?"

They tapped fists. Eve sighed. "You are both *morons* and we're all going to die, and my head hurts like crazy," she said. "Can we please just get out of here? Please?"

Michael went to her and put his arms around her, and Claire heard her let out a little, sad sob as she melted against him. "Shhh," he whispered. "It's okay, baby."

"So not," Eve said, but she'd lost her edge. "And where the hell were you while I was getting dragged along on the party bus, nearly getting fanged?"

"Racing after you," he said. "Jumping onto the bus? Breaking out windows? Almost rescuing you?"

"Oh yeah," Eve said. "But I was unconscious for all that part, so I couldn't really appreciate how brave you were. This is all right, though. Being with you."

Shane exchanged a look with Claire, made a gagging sound, and got her to laugh. Then he took her hand, held it for a second, then lifted it to his lips. His mouth felt so warm, so soft, that she felt every muscle in her body shiver at the touch. His thumb brushed over the claddagh ring, their secret little promise.

"Wait for me," he said. "Any requests on the kind of car?"

"Something with armor?" she said. "Oooh, and headrest DVD. Bonus for surround sound."

"Rocket launchers," Michael said.

"One hot yellow Hummer with optional mass destruction package, coming up." Shane squeezed her fingers lightly, one more time, then ducked out the window. Claire watched him drop to the grass, roll to his feet, and take off at an angle through the afternoon glare.

The glare, she realized, was at a lower level than before.

It was late afternoon, and the sun was heading west, fast.

"Nightfall," she said. Michael stepped up near her, out of range of the sun still flooding the window. "We don't have too long before it gets dark, right?"

"Right," he said. "But if we stay here in this building, I think we're going to have even less time. There are a lot of these . . . other vampires. And they're not exactly shy."

He grabbed the two fallen vampires and dragged them out into the hallway, where he dumped them next to the one still decorated with Claire's silver stake—that one was definitely dead now, burned by the silver. She tried not to look too closely.

Michael barricaded the doors again and sat Eve down in a somewhat secure chair in the corner. "Stay," he told her. "Rest." He ripped down the other half of the dusty, thick curtain and wrapped it around Eve; one of those cute romantic gestures that was a little spoiled by her bout of uncontrollable sneezing as a gray cloud floated up around her face.

Claire stayed by the window, staring out. Not that it would help; even if she saw Shane, even if she saw he needed help, what was she going to do? Nothing, because she was human, slow, and had a torn-up ankle on top of all that.

But somehow, it was important that she stand there and watch for him, as though it were some agreement they'd made, and if she didn't keep it, something bad would happen.

Superstition. *Well, I'm standing in some kind of pseudo-Gothic castle thingy with a bunch of vampires fighting in the halls. Maybe superstition just makes sense.*

"Did you see Jason?" Eve was asking Michael. "Was he okay?"

Michael acted as if he didn't hear her. He came to join Claire at the window, although just to the dark side of the sunlight. "Anything?"

"Nothing yet," she said. "Did you see him? Jason?"

"Not really."

"That's not really an answer, is it?"

Michael shot her a look. Whatever he was about to say was interrupted by a thump from overhead—a hard one, followed by what sounded like scratching. Lots of scratching, like very sharp claws. Maybe knives.

Like something was digging *down* through the floorboards from the second floor.

"Okay, that's not a good sound," Eve said. "Michael?"

He was standing very still, staring upward, his face marble white in the shadows.

Dust filtered down from the ceiling. Pieces of old plaster rained down in flakes, like snow. Claire backed away from the window, away from that *sound*—all the way back to the heavy desk blocking the door leading into the room.

Suddenly the door shoved against her, as someone *outside* the room hit the door with a shocking crash and howled. More scraping, this time at the wooden door. Michael lunged forward and slammed the desk back in place and held it there as the door shook under the force of the battering. "Dammit," he hissed. "Where is he?"

Overhead, something snapped with a dry crack—boards being broken and peeled away, ripped free, and tossed aside.

They were digging through.

Eve stood up, bracing herself on the wall, and kicked loose the leg of a rickety smaller table lying near her chair. It broke loose with a splintered end, not as sharp as a spear, but not as blunt as a club, either. She gripped it in both hands, dividing her attention between the ceiling, which was now snowing plaster like a blizzard, and Michael, who was struggling to hold the desk in place as a barricade at the door.

We're going to die here, Claire thought. It came to her with terrifying clarity, as if she'd already seen the future through an open window in time. Eve would be lying there, her eyes wide and empty, and Michael would die trying to protect her. Her own body would be a small, broken mess near the window, where Shane would find it....

No.

The thought of Shane's finding her, more than just the dying itself, made Claire refuse to accept it. He'd seen enough, suffered enough. Adding this on top of it—no. She wouldn't do it to him.

"We have to live," she said out loud. It sounded half crazy. Michael glanced at her, and Eve outright stared.

"Well, duh," Eve said. "And *I'm* the one who got clocked today."

The ceiling gave way with a low groan of wood and a flood of plaster and debris, and three bodies, covered in blood where they weren't white with plaster dust, dropped through the opening. They looked like monsters, and as the taller one turned to Claire and she caught the glint of fangs, she screamed.

The scream lasted for about a heartbeat, and then recognition flooded in—and relief. "Oliver?" Great. She was relieved to see *Oliver.* The world was officially topsy-turvy, cats were living with dogs, and life as she knew it was probably over.

Oliver looked . . . well, like a monster—like a monster who'd fought his way out of hell, inch by inch, actually, and, weirdly, loved every minute of it. He grinned at Claire, all wickedly pointy fangs, and whirled toward Eve as she lunged at him with the business end of her broken stick. He took it away from her with contemptuous ease and shoved her into Michael, who had checked himself before attacking, but was clearly just as stunned as Claire felt.

"At ease, soldiers," Oliver said, and it was almost a laugh. Next to him, Morley slapped white dust from his clothes, raising a choking cloud that made Claire's eyes water as she coughed. "I think we're still allies. At least for now."

"Like Russia and England during the Second World War," Morley agreed, then looked thoughtful. "Or was that the first? So difficult to remember these things. In any case, enemies with a common worse foe. We can kill each other later."

The third person in the group was Jason, who looked just as bad as the other two, and not nearly as fine with it. He was shaking, visibly shaking, and there were rough bandages wrapped around his left wrist and hand that were soaked through with blood.

Eve finally, belatedly, recognized her brother, and reached out to grab him into a hug. Jason stayed frozen for a moment, then patted her on the back, awkwardly. "I'm okay," he said. That was a lie, Claire thought, but a brave one. "You've got blood on your face."

"Hit my head," Eve said.

"Oh, so, no damage, then," Jason said, which was *such* a brother thing to say that Claire smiled. "Seriously, that looks bad, Eve."

"No broken bones. My head hurts, and I feel dizzy. I'll live. What the hell happened to you?"

"Don't ask," Jason said, and stepped away. "Need some help, man?"

Michael had grabbed hold of the desk and shoved it back against the door again, and he was now struggling to keep it in place. "Sure," he said. Not that Jason's muscle power was going to work any miracles, Claire thought; he was stringy and strong, but not vamp-strong.

"Let them in," Morley said, and finished redistributing dust from his clothes to the rest of them with a final slap. "It's my people. Unless you don't trust us?"

"Now, why wouldn't we?" Eve said sweetly, and turned to Michael. "Don't you dare!"

"You'd rather leave them out there to be torn apart?" Morley asked, without any particular emphasis, as though it didn't really matter to him one way or the other. "I would have thought someone with so much compassion would be less judgmental."

"Excuse me, but *you tied us to seats.* And *put needles in our arms.* And *drank our blood.* So no, I'm not really seeing any reason to get all trusty with you!"

Morley shrugged. "Then let them die. I'm sure you'll have no problem listening to their screams."

Someone was, in fact, shouting on the other side of the door now, not so much battering on it as knocking. "Michael! Michael, it's Jacob Goldman! Open the door! They're coming!"

Michael exchanged a quick look with Claire, then Eve, then Oliver. Oliver nodded briskly.

Michael grabbed the desk and pulled it backward, nearly knocking Jason to the ground in the process. "Hey!" Jason protested. "A little warning next time, man!"

"Shut up." Michael shoved him back as the door pushed open from the outside, and vampires started flooding into the room.

Morley's people. They, like Morley, hadn't come through this unharmed; every one of them, including Jacob and Patience Goldman, looked as if they'd fought for their lives. A few were wounded, and Claire knew from experience that it took a lot to hurt a vampire, even temporarily.

Jacob was cradling his right arm, which was covered in blood. Patience was supporting him from the other side. Even Eve looked a little concerned at the sight of his ice white face and blind-looking eyes. He seemed to be in serious pain.

Patience settled him against the wall and crouched next to him as Morley and Oliver, with Michael's help, engineered some kind of barrier for the door when the last of Morley's people were crammed into the small room.

There weren't nearly so many as before.

"What happened?" Claire asked Patience. The vampire girl looked up at her, and there was a shadow of fear in her face that turned Claire cold inside.

"They wouldn't stop," Patience said. "They came for our prisoners. They wouldn't—we couldn't make them stop. Even when we destroyed one, two came out of the shadows. It was—we couldn't *stop* them." She looked down at Jacob, who had closed his eyes. He looked dead—more dead than most vamps. "Jacob almost had his arm torn off trying to protect them. But we couldn't help."

She sounded shocked, and deeply distressed. Claire put a hand on her shoulder, and Patience shuddered.

"You're okay," Claire said. "We're okay."

"No, we're not," she said. "Not at all. These are not vampires, Claire. They are animals—vicious beasts. And we—we are just as much prey for them as you are."

"Right," Morley said, raising his voice over the rising babble of conversation. "Everybody, shut it! Now, we can't stay here—"

"The bus is burning," someone said from near the window. Morley seemed to pause, obviously not expecting that, but he moved past it at light speed.

"Then we don't use the bus, clot-for-brains. We find another way out of this accursed graveyard of a town."

"In the sunlight?" Jacob asked. His voice was soft and thready with pain. "Not all of us will survive for long, and those who do will suffer. You know that."

"Your choice—go and burn; stay and be torn apart." Morley shrugged. "For my part, burns heal. I'm not sure that my disconnected pieces would, and I'd prefer not to find out."

"Something's coming," a voice called from the window. "A truck. A delivery van!"

Claire shoved through the crowd of vampires, ignoring the cold touch of skin and the hisses of annoyance, and managed to get a clear space right in front of the window, where a solid couple of feet were still bathed in sunlight. Eve had already claimed it, but she let Claire squeeze in beside her.

The van was a big yellow thing, some kind of bread truck, with a boxy, windowless back. As Claire watched, it jumped the curb and bounced up onto the lawn, charged forward, and knocked down the leaning iron fence around the Civic Hall. It missed the statue of what's-his-name, the town's patron saint, but the vibrations caused the whole thing to wobble uncertainly, and as Claire watched, it toppled over that last couple of inches, and gravity took over, slamming the smug statue's face into the grass once and for all.

Thankfully, not in the way of the van.

The van reversed, turned, and then backed up fast toward the window. It stopped a few feet away, and Shane hopped down from the driver's side. He ran to the window and grinned at Eve and Claire.

His grin faded fast as his eyes adjusted to the shadows, and he saw all the vampires in the room. "What—"

"Morley's people," Claire said. "I guess we're all in this together right now."

"I'm . . . not loving that."

"I know. But we all need to get out of here."

Shane shook his head, shaggy hair sticking in damp points to his face, but he turned and opened up the back doors of the van. Inside, there wasn't much space, but there was enough to hold all the vamps—maybe.

"I'll take as many as can fit," he said. "But seriously, once they're out of here, all bets are off."

"Agreed," Morley said, and stepped forward into the sun. If it bothered him, it was only enough to make him narrow his eyes a little. He grabbed the frame of the window and, with one hard pull, ripped it right out of the stone and tossed it out into the overgrown grass. "Right, youngest first. Go, now."

There was hesitation, until Morley gave a low-decibel growl, and then vampires started stepping up, quickly throwing themselves out into the sunlight and moving fast to the sheltering darkness of the van. In only a few seconds it was just Claire, Michael, Jason, Eve, Morley, and Oliver, with Shane standing outside the window.

"I said *youngest first*," Morley said, glowering at Michael. Michael raised pale eyebrows at him. "Idiot."

"I stay with my friends."

"Then it would appear you get to tan with them, as there's no more room in the back."

"No," Oliver said. "Michael goes in the back. You and I ride outside."

Morley let out a black bark of a laugh. *"Outside?"*

"I'm sure you're familiar with the concept." Oliver, without even looking at him, grabbed Michael by the shoulder and almost threw him across the open space to the back of the van. Michael crashed into the small open space left and was pulled inside by Patience Goldman, who looked anxious, almost frightened. Shane slammed the back doors of the truck and ran to the front. "Right. Move it, ladies."

Jason didn't wait for girls first; he jumped out and went. Oliver boosted Eve up to the window, and she ran for the cab of the truck, where Jason was already climbing inside. Claire followed, avoiding any help from Oliver, and as she pulled herself up on the truck's mounting step, she saw Oliver and Morley jump out of the building and flatten themselves on top of the truck, in full sun, arms and legs spread wide for balance. She banged the door shut behind her and squeezed in next to Eve, with Jason on the other side next to Shane.

"We couldn't have done this boy/girl?" Shane complained, and started up the car. "Back off, freak!" That last was for Jason, who was pushing too close for Shane's comfort, evidently. Claire tried wiggling closer to the passenger door, but the cab wasn't made for four, no matter how relatively skinny they might be. And Shane wasn't small.

"Just drive, smart-ass," Jason snapped. Shane looked like he was considering hitting him. "Unless you want the two on top baked golden brown."

"*Crap*," Shane spat, and glared at the steering wheel as if it had personally offended him. He put the truck in gear, ground the gears, and got it roaring through the grass. It bumped hard over the curb, sending Claire into the dashboard, and she flailed to regain her balance as the truck slewed back and forth, got traction, and roared off down the street.

"Where the hell are you going?" Jason yelled.

"Your sister gets to talk. You don't."

"Fine," Eve said. "Where the hell are you going, Shane?"

"The library," he said. "I promised I'd bring the truck back."

Claire blinked, looking over at him, and Eve, wide-eyed, shook her head.

"You know it's desperate," she said. "Shane is going to the *library*."

And in spite of everything, that was actually funny.

ELEVEN

The library was about a block down, on the left. They passed a lot of empty, blank buildings, broken windows, destruction that seemed like the aftermath of a good looting. It didn't seem recent, though.

The library's windows were all intact, and there were people patrolling outside it—the first living people Claire had seen in Blacke, actually. She counted four of them, armed with shotguns and crossbows.

"My kind of library," Shane said. "What with all the weapons and everything. I tried to boost the truck, and they finally let me have it, but I had to bring it back. This looks like the place to be. At least we can find out what the hell is going on, maybe get a bus or something."

The guards outside the library were certainly paying attention. The guys with shotguns tracked the truck as it approached, and they looked really serious about firing, too. Claire cleared her throat. "Uh, Shane—?"

"I see it," he said. He slowed the truck to a crawl. "So, I'm guessing *Hi, we're friendly strangers with a bunch of vampires in your bread truck* probably isn't the way to go here." He put the truck in reverse. "Guess this wasn't as good an idea as it looked at a distance."

"Maybe we should—"

Whatever Eve was about to suggest became useless, because two po-

lice cruisers, carrying *more* armed bubbas, came screaming out of alleys
on either side of the library building and blocked Shane's exit. Shane hit
the brakes. In seconds, Claire's door was yanked open, and a huge man
with a shotgun glared at her, grabbed her, and dragged her out onto the
hot pavement. He pressed fingers to her throat for a second, then yelled,
"Live one!"

"This one, too!" yelled his buddy, who was pulling a fighting, screaming Eve out of the cab. "Watch it, girl!"

"*You* watch it, you pervert! Hands!"

"Hey, leave her alone!" That was Jason, flinging himself out after Eve,
looking every bit the feverish little maniac Claire remembered from the
first time she'd seen him. Maybe a little cleaner. Maybe.

He must have moved too fast for the armed guard's comfort, because
he got hit in the gut with the stock of the shotgun, and collapsed to the
street. Eve screamed his name, and got picked up and bodily carried into
the library, along with Claire. "No!" Claire screamed, and looked back at
the truck. Shane was getting wrestled out of the driver's side, and Jason
was being dragged to his feet.

This was *not* going well. And where the *hell* were Oliver and Morley?
They weren't on top of the van anymore. . . .

Oliver dropped from the overhanging roof of the library and drop-
kicked the bubba holding Claire. He shoved Claire out of the way as the
one holding Eve aimed a crossbow and fired; Oliver snatched the arrow
right out of the air and snapped the thick shaft with a twist of his fingers,
grinning. "Let the girl go," he said. "I've played this game with many better than you. And they all died, friend."

He was looking pink from exposure to the sun, but not burned. Not
yet. Uncomfortable, maybe. The guard's eyes darted around, looking for
support, and found it in the form of two more cowboy-hatted men racing to the rescue.

With shotguns.

Claire threw herself forward, throwing her arms wide. Eve let out a
warning cry, but Claire stepped in front of Oliver as the shotguns came
up. "Wait!" she yelled. "Just wait a second! He's with us!"

The shotguns focused on *her.*

Oh, crap.

"You're running with the bloodsuckers?" one of them said in a soft, dangerous voice. "Little girl like you?"

"He's not like—like those things at the courthouse," she said. She put her hands up in the surrender position and took a step toward them. "We're not supposed to be here. We just want to leave, okay? All of us. We want out of town."

"Well, you ain't leaving town," the guy holding Eve said. "You or any of your fanged little friends. We're not letting this thing spread any farther. Blacke is under quarantine."

The heavy library doors opened, and a small, gray-haired woman stepped out. She didn't look much like a leader—Claire wouldn't have picked her out of a crowd at first glance—but immediately, everybody looked toward her, and Claire felt the gravity of the scene shift in her direction.

"Charley?" the woman asked. "Why are you pointing a shotgun at this pretty little girl? I heard somebody say she was a live one."

"She's with them!"

"There are no collaborators, Charley. You know that. Either she's infected, or she's not. There's no in-between. Now lower your gun, please." The woman's pleasant voice took on a steely undertone. "Lower it. Now."

"That one behind her, *he's* infected," Charley said. "Guaranteed."

"Actually," Oliver said, "in the sense you mean it, I'm not infected. Not in the way you're thinking."

The older woman, without so much as a pause, unslung a strap from her shoulder, loaded a crossbow bolt, and fired it right into Oliver's chest.

He toppled over and hit the ground with a heavy thud. Claire screamed and ran to his side. When she reached for the bolt to pull it out, the woman grabbed her arm and pulled her back, struggling. She shoved Claire at one of her guards, who held her securely. "You know what to do," she said to another one of them, nodding toward Oliver. "Let's get these kids inside. I don't want them to see this."

"No, you don't understand!" Claire shouted. "You can't—"

"I understand that he's a vampire, and for whatever twisted reason, you want to protect him," the woman said. "Now be quiet. You're not in any danger here."

Claire thought about all the vampires locked in the back of the truck. *Michael.*

She couldn't tell them about that. If they were going to kill Oliver, just like that, she couldn't imagine what they might do to a whole confined load of vampires. It'd probably be way too easy. The sun was sliding steadily toward the horizon. Maybe, when it was blocked by the eastern buildings and there was enough shadow, they could get out of the truck and scatter.

The woman looked at her sharply. "You seem to be thinking very hard," she said. "About what?"

"Nothing," Claire said.

"I see. What's your name?" When Claire didn't answer, the woman sighed. "All right. I'm Mrs. Grant. I'm the librarian. I'm what passes for authority in Blacke these days, since all our peace officers and elected officials are dead. Now, let's be friendly. I've told you my name. What's yours?"

"Claire," she said.

"And where are you from, Claire?"

Claire looked her right in the eyes and said, "None of your business."

Mrs. Grant's graying eyebrows hitched up, but under them, her faded green eyes didn't seem surprised. "All right. Let's get you and your friends inside, and you can tell me why you thought that vampire was someone you ought to be caring about."

Claire looked back over her shoulder as she was pushed/pulled along. Oliver was being carried away, limp as a bag of laundry.

And there was nothing she could do about it.

The inside of the library was cool and dark, lit mostly by the natural sunlight trickling in the windows, although there were some camp-style fluorescent and LED lanterns scattered around, and even some old-fashioned oil lamps on the tables. The Blacke library was larger than Claire would have expected, with rows and rows of books, and lots of rooms off to the sides. In the middle was a kind of command center, with a small desk, a laptop computer, and some kind of small pedal-powered generator. Ranked on the shelves nearby were weapons, including a pile of silver chains—jewelry, Claire guessed, ransacked from all over town. There were a lot of first aid supplies, too.

Inside the library there were about twenty or thirty people; it was hard to see, because they were scattered around on cots between the aisles of books. Claire heard a small voice, then someone crying; it sounded like a little kid, maybe four or five. "What is this?" she asked, looking around. Mrs. Grant led her over to a long reading table and pulled out a chair for her.

"This is what's left of our town," she said. "The survivors. We're a tough bunch, I'll tell you that."

"But"—Claire licked her lips and settled into the seat—"what *happened* here?"

Mrs. Grant waited while the others—Eve, Shane, and Jason—were deposited in chairs around the table, with varying degrees of gentleness. Shane was furious, and he looked as if he were seriously thinking of grabbing a fistful of weapons from the racks. Mrs. Grant evidently saw that, because she pointed at two of her burly cowboy guards and had them stand behind Shane, blocking him in at the table.

"Blacke's never been what you might call a crossroads," Mrs. Grant said. "Most folks living here were born here. Their families have been here forever; we don't see new people real often out here." That was, in fact, pretty much like Morganville, minus the attraction of Texas Prairie University. It was pretty much like every other small town in the area, too. Claire nodded. "One night, we got us some visitors. An old man in a suit, and his niece and nephew. Foreign people. French, maybe."

Claire looked at Eve and Shane. Eve mouthed *Bishop.* Confirmation for what they already had guessed—Mr. Bishop had hit Blacke on his way through to Morganville.

And he'd had fun.

"They stayed at the Iron Lily Inn," Mrs. Grant continued. "It's the closest thing we've got to a hotel. Or had, anyway. Mrs. Gonzalez owned it. She made the best apple pie in the world, too." She slowly shook her head. "Next morning, Mrs. Gonzalez was missing; never showed up at the school—she worked in the office up there. Sheriff John went around to the hotel and found her dead. No sign of those . . . people."

That couldn't be the whole story, Claire thought; she knew how vampires were made, and if Mrs. Gonzalez had been drained to death, she wouldn't have come back. So she just waited. Mrs. Grant seemed to want to take her time, and Claire was trying hard not to think about what might be happening outside, with Oliver. Morley had run off, she supposed. And she had no idea what would happen to the vampires still in the back of the truck.

"We thought the murder of Mrs. Gonzalez was the end of it— shocking, first serious trouble this town had seen in close to thirty years, but still the end. And then the next night Miss Hanover just vanished from her store—gas station, right up the street. Best we can tell, those two women were the first victims. We know the three strangers left town that night; somebody saw them driving that big, black car of theirs like a bat out of hell. Didn't matter. They left *this* behind."

Mrs. Grant looked down at her hands, which were spread out on the table in front of her. Strong and scarred, they suggested she hadn't always been a librarian. "It started slow. People started disappearing, maybe one every few weeks. Disappearing, or dying. Then it got bad, fast, just—in days, it all of a sudden seemed like half the town was gone. Sheriff John didn't call for help soon enough. Next thing we knew, we saw *them* for the first time, in force. Terrible things, Claire. Terrible things happened. And we had to do terrible things to survive."

"Why didn't you just—," Eve began to ask, but was interrupted as Mrs. Grant's head came up sharply.

"Leave?" she snapped. "Don't you think we tried? Phones were out, landlines and cells. Internet went down with the power the first day; they ripped the power station apart while they were still thinking. We sent everybody we could out of town on the school buses. They never made it. Some kind of trap on the road, blew out all the tires. Some made it back here. Most didn't."

It was like some horror movie come to life. Claire had thought Morganville was bad, but *this*—this was beyond bad.

"I'm sorry," she whispered. "But why stay here? Why don't you just—try again?"

"You know how many people used to be in Blacke?" Mrs. Grant asked. "One hundred seventy-two. What you see here in this building is what's left. What's left still breathing, anyway. You think we can just walk away? These were our friends, our families. And if we leave, what happens? How far does this spread?" Mrs. Grant's eyes hardened until they were like cold green ice. "It stops here. It has to stop here. Now, you explain to me how you're traveling around with one of *them*."

"What's more important is that Oliver wasn't—like those people you're talking about. They're sick. He's not."

Mrs. Grant let out a sharp laugh. "He's *dead*. That's as sick as it gets, Claire from nowhere."

"Look," Shane said, leaning forward and putting his elbows on the table, "I'm not saying the vampires aren't the essence of freaky; they are. But they're not *like* this. Not—normally. They can be—"

"And how do the four of you know anything at all about vampires?" Mrs. Grant asked. None of them answered, and her eyes narrowed. "There are more out there. More of them. Even if we finish here, there are more."

"Not like these!" Claire said again, desperately. "You have to believe me; they're not all—"

"Not all bad," said Morley, who stepped out of the shadows of one of the racks of books, looking terrifying and bloody and as unreassuring as possible. "No, we're not. Although some of us are no doubt better than others."

And *Oliver* appeared on top of the bookcase, looking down. In his long black coat, he looked very tall, very strong, and even more intimidating than Morley. More came out of the shadows, too. Claire spotted Patience and Jacob near the edges of the group.

And Michael, golden Michael, who smiled at Eve as though it would all be all right, somehow.

Mrs. Grant came out of her chair and lunged for the weapons.

Shane slammed his chair backward, throwing the two guards behind him off balance. That was all the time Oliver needed to jump from the bookcase to the table, then to the floor, and take the guns out of their hands.

He didn't hurt them. He didn't have to.

Morley did that way-too-fast vampire thing and was suddenly at the weapons rack ahead of Mrs. Grant, baring his fangs and grinning. He made a little finger-wagging gesture, and she skidded to a stop and backed off, breathing fast. Scared to death, of course, and Claire didn't blame her.

Michael, meanwhile, was already at Eve's side. She threw her arms around his neck. "How did you get out?" she asked, her voice muffled against his shirt. He rubbed her back gently and rested his chin against her hair.

"The building across the way casts a pretty big shadow," he said. "We bailed as soon as we could. From there it wasn't hard. They thought they had everybody they needed to worry about."

"You didn't—"

"No," Michael said. "We didn't hurt anybody. Patience made sure of that."

The townspeople of Blacke—all twenty or thirty of them—were gathering together in a tight block now, with their kids safely in the center. They looked about to make their last stand. Not one of them, Claire realized, thought they were going to live through this.

"Hey," she said to Mrs. Grant. "Please. Don't be afraid. We're not going to hurt you."

Morley laughed. "We're not?"

"No, we're not," Oliver said, and piled the weapons on the table. "Shane, get the silver."

"Can I keep some?"

Oliver smiled grimly. "If it makes you happy."

"You have no idea."

"Distribute the chains to everyone else. Make sure they're wearing silver at their necks and wrists. It'll help protect them, should some of us,

Morley, suffer a lapse of character." He checked each shotgun for shells, and tossed them to specific individual vampires, who snatched them out of the air with lazy accuracy. "Right. I'm afraid Mrs. Grant is quite right; we can't allow this infection—and it *is* an infection—to spread any farther than it has already. We must hunt down and dose everyone who's contracted the disease, or destroy them. That's as much for our kind as yours, you see."

"*Dose* them?" Mrs. Grant blurted. "What are you—"

Patience Goldman opened up a small black satchel—her father's doctor bag, Claire realized—and inside were dozens of vials of liquid, as well as some bottles of red crystals. Claire herself had helped develop those; the liquid contained a cure for the blood-borne disease that Bishop had spread here, or at least she hoped it did. The crystals would help restore people's sanity, temporarily. It worked best doing the crystals, then giving the shot. It had worked for the far-gone vampires in Morganville.

"They can be saved," Oliver said. "Your family and friends can be restored to sanity, we believe. But they can't be restored to human. You understand? What's done is done on that score. But you can have them back, if you can adjust to that small difference."

"This is insane," one of the guards said, a little wildly. His crossbow was now in the hands of one of Morley's vampires, a little guy with a lined, twisted face and a limp. "We have to fight! Lillian—"

"We're not here to fight you," Oliver said. "And we're not here to save you. *I* am here to stop the spread of this infection by any means necessary, which, as I see it, aligns with your goals. My other friends," he said, putting some irony into that last word, "are just passing through your fine town. None of us have any reason to want to harm you."

"You're *vampires*," Mrs. Grant said blankly.

"Well, obviously. Yes." Oliver snapped another fully loaded shotgun closed and tossed it through the air.

To Mrs. Grant.

"Any questions?" he asked.

She opened her mouth, closed it, and looked around. There were a lot of vampires—just about as many as there were humans. And none of them were making threatening moves. Shane walked around, handing out silver chairs to people, smiling his best I'm-a-nice-guy smile. Even Jason seemed to be doing his best to be nonthreatening, which wasn't exactly easy for him.

"Then let's sit down," Oliver said, and pulled out a chair at the table. "I, for one, have had a very hard day."

TWELVE

Night fell as tensions gradually eased; the people of Blacke never quite got comfortable, but they loosened up enough to put on some stew in the library's small kitchen, which had a miniature stove that ran on gas. Apparently, the gas was still flowing, even though the electricity was out. As the light faded outside the windows, Mrs. Grant and three of her burly cowboy-hatted guards—Claire guessed the cowboy hats were a kind of uniform—made the rounds to barricade the doors and windows.

Morley joined them, and after a long, uncomfortable moment, Mrs. Grant decided to ignore his presence. The guards didn't. Their knuckles were white on their weapons.

"May I assist?" he asked, and put his hands behind his back. "I promise not to eat anyone."

"Very funny," Mrs. Grant said. Morley gave her a grave look.

"I wasn't joking, dear lady," he said. "I do promise. And I never make a promise I don't intend to keep. You should feel quite secure."

"Well, I'm sorry, I don't," she said. "You're just—"

"Too overwhelmingly dashing and attractive?" Morley grinned. "A common problem women face with me. It'll pass. You seem like the no-nonsense sort. I like that."

Claire smiled at the look on Mrs. Grant's face, reflected in the white LED light of the lantern she was holding. "You are really—odd," the older woman said, as if she couldn't quite believe she was even having the conversation.

Morley put his hand over his heart and bowed from the waist, a gesture that somehow reminded Claire of Myrnin. It reminded her she missed him, too, which was just *wrong*. She should not be missing Morganville, or anyone in it. Especially not the crazy boss vampire who'd put fang marks in her neck that would never, ever go away. She was doomed to high-necked shirts because of him.

But she *did* miss him. She even missed Amelie's dry, cool sense of power and stability. She wondered if this was a kind of vacation for Amelie, too, not worrying about Oliver, or Claire, or Eve, or any of them.

Probably. She couldn't imagine Amelie was losing any sleep over them—presuming she slept, which Claire really wasn't sure was the case, anyway.

"Hey." Shane's hip nudged her chair, and he bent over, putting his mouth very close to her ear. "What are you doing?"

"Thinking."

"Stop."

"Stop thinking?"

"You're doing way too much of it. It'll make you go blind."

She laughed and turned her face toward his. "I think you're thinking of something else."

"I'm *definitely* thinking of something else," he said, and bent over to kiss her. It was a long, sweet, slow kiss, full of gentle strokes of his tongue over her lips, which parted for him even though she was *sure* she hadn't exactly told them to do that. Warmth swept over her, making her oddly shivery, and she grabbed the neck of his shirt when he tried to pull away and kissed him some more.

When she let go, neither of them moved far. Shane sat down in the chair next to her, but scooted it over and leaned in so they were as close together as possible. There weren't many lights here in the corner, where Claire had retreated to eat her cup of stew and think, and it felt wildly romantic sitting together by candlelight. Shane's skin looked golden in the glow, his eyes dark, with only a hint of shimmering amber when the light hit them just right. His chin was a little dark and rough, and she felt it with her palm, then smiled.

"You need a shave," she said.

"I thought you liked me scruffy."

"Scruffy is for good dogs and bad rockers."

"Oh yeah? And which am I, again?" He was *so close* to her, and in this little bubble of candlelight it felt as if everything happening around them, all the craziness, all the bad things, was taking place a world away. There was something about Shane that just made it all okay, for as long as she was with him, for as long as he was looking at her with that wonderful, fascinated glow in his eyes.

He moved a little strand of hair back from her face. "Some road trip, eh?"

"I've had worse," Claire said. His expression was priceless. "No, really. I have. I went on a trip with my parents all the way to Canada once. A week in the car, with my folks, having educational experiences. I thought I'd go nuts."

"I thought you liked educational experiences."

"Bet *you* could teach me a few things."

He kissed her again, hungrily, and there was such focus in him that it took her breath away. She wanted—yeah, she knew what she wanted. She knew what *he* wanted, too. And she knew it wasn't going to happen, not here, not tonight—too bad, because if she got killed before getting some privacy with Shane again, she was going to be *really* upset with Oliver.

Somebody coughed out in the shadows, at the edges of their candlelight, and Shane sat back. Claire licked her damp lips, tasting him all over again, and struggled to focus on something else, such as whoever was interrupting them. "What?" That came out a little harsh.

"Sorry." That was Jason, and he didn't sound sorry at all. He sounded kind of amused. "If you want to go on with the porn show, please, I'll wait."

"Shut up," Shane growled.

"You know, we could get into this make-me-no-you-make-me kind of thing, but I think we have better things to do," Jason said. "I'm not talking to you, anyway. I need Claire."

She needed a lot of things, all from Shane, and she couldn't think of a blessed thing right now that she needed from Jason Rosser. It made her voice go even colder. "Why?"

He rolled his eyes, just like his sister, which was creepy. She didn't even like to think they came from the same gene pool, much less shared things she thought were cute and funny in Eve. "Because Oliver wants you, and what Oliver wants, Oliver gets, right? So get your sweet little butt up already."

"Hey," Shane said, and stood up. "I'm not telling you again, Jase. Stop."

"What, because I said she had a sweet little butt? You don't think she does? Hard to believe, since you spend so much time staring at it."

Shane's hands closed into fists, and Claire remembered Jason on the street in the dark outside Common Grounds, coming after them—after her and Eve, specifically; at least that was what he'd said to Shane.

Shane hadn't forgotten.

"You and me, man, one of these days, we're going to finish this," he said softly. "Until that day, you stay the hell away from my girl. You understand?"

"Big tough guy," Jason said, and laughed. "Yeah, I understand. Personally, she's too skinny for me, anyway."

He walked off, and Claire saw a tremor go through Shane, something she figured was an impulse to slam into Jason and knock him flat, and then pound him.

But Shane didn't move. He let out a slow breath and turned back to face her. "That guy," he said, "is not normal; I don't care what Eve says. And I don't like him around you."

"I can take care of myself."

"Yeah, I know." He forced a smile. "It's just that—" This time, he shrugged and let it go. "Oliver, huh?"

"I guess." Claire picked up the candle and headed through the stacks for the unofficial—or official?—command desk, where Oliver was now sitting, talking to a couple of vampires whose faces glowed blue-white in the light of the fluorescent lamp.

"About time," Oliver said. "I need you to see if you can get a message out on this thing." He nodded to the computer, which sat there dead and unresponsive.

"There's no electricity."

"They've been trying to use this," he said, and pointed toward the pedal generator. "They tell me it should work, but there's some problem with the computer. Fix it."

"Just like that."

"Yes," Oliver said. "Just like that. Whine about it quietly, to yourself."

She seethed, but Shane just shrugged and looked at the pedal generator, which was sort of like an exercise bike. "This thing could be a real workout," he said. "Tell you what: I'll pedal; you do the magic. Sound fair?"

She liked that he was willing to help. Their fingers intertwined, and he kissed her again, lightly.

"Sounds fair," she agreed.

She turned the laptop over and took a look at it. Nothing obviously wrong jumped out—nothing cracked or broken, anyway. Shane climbed on the seat and started turning the pedals—which must have been harder than it seemed, because even *he* seemed to be working at it. The resistance built up energy, which translated into electricity, which went into a power strip with some kind of backup battery built into it. Immediately, the battery began beeping and flickering a red light. "Right, that's working," Claire said. "It'll probably take a while to recharge the backup, though."

"How much time are we talking?" Shane asked.

She grinned. "Slacker."

"Well, yeah, obviously."

In a few moments, the computer's power light finally came on, and she booted up and started looking into the computer problem. It took her thirty minutes of diagnostics before she located the problem and got the operating system booted up.

Shane, the poor thing, kept pedaling. He stopped wasting his breath with quips after a while. When the power strip's battery finally clicked over to green, he stopped, gasping for breath, slumped over the handlebars. "Okay," he panted, "let's not screw it up, shall we? Because I do not want to do that again. Next time, get a vamp. They don't need to breathe."

Claire looked over at Oliver, who was ignoring them and jotting down notes on a map of Blacke.

But he was smiling a little.

"It's booting up," she said, watching the lines scroll by. "Here goes...."

The Windows tones sounded, and it felt like everybody in the library jumped. Mrs. Grant and Morley abandoned their security sweep and came back to stand by Claire's elbow as the operating system load finished, and the desktop finally appeared. She let it finish, then double-clicked the Internet icon.

"Four oh four." She sighed.

"What?" Morley peered over her shoulder. "What does that mean?"

"Page not found," she said. "It's a four oh four error. Let me try something else." She tried for Google. Then Wikipedia. Then Twitter. Nothing. "The ISP must be down. There's no Internet service."

"What about e-mail? It is e-mail, yes?" Morley asked, leaning even closer. "E-mail is a kind of electronic letter. It travels through the air." He seemed very smug that he knew that.

"Well, not exactly, and would you please either *back off* or go find a shower? Thanks. And to send e-mail you have to have Internet service. So that doesn't work."

"I pedaled for nothing," Shane said mournfully. "That deeply bites."

"Does anyone else think it's too quiet?" Oliver asked, and looked up from the map.

There was a moment of silence, and then Mrs. Grant said, "Sometimes they don't come at us for a few hours. But they always come. Every night. We're all there is for them."

Oliver nodded, stood up, and gestured to Morley. The two vampires stalked off into the dark, talking in tones too quiet for human ears to catch at all.

Mrs. Grant stared after them, eyes narrowed. "They'll turn on us," she said. "Sooner or later, your vampires will turn on us. Count on it."

"We're still alive," Claire said, and pointed to herself, Shane, Jason, and Eve. Eve was sitting a few feet away, curled in Michael's arms. "And we've been at this a whole lot longer than you."

"Then you're deluded," Mrs. Grant said. "How can you possibly trust these—*people?*" She acted as if that wasn't the word she wanted to use.

"Because they gave you back your guns," Claire said. "And because they could have killed you in the first couple of minutes if they'd really wanted to. I know it's hard. It's hard for all of us, sometimes. But right now, you need to believe what they're telling you."

Mrs. Grant frowned at her. "And when exactly do I *stop* believing them?"

Claire smiled. "We'll let you know."

There weren't a lot of kids in the library, but there were a few—seven total, according to Claire's count, ranging from babies who were still being bottle-fed to a couple of trying-to-be-adult kids of maybe twelve. Nobody was too close to Claire's own age, though. She was kind of glad; it would have been just too creepy to see the kind of blank fear in their faces that she saw in the younger kids. Too much like seeing herself, in the beginning of her Morganville experience.

She wound up thinking about the kids because Eve had brought over a lantern, gotten them in a circle, and started reading to them. It was something familiar, from the few words Claire could hear; it finally clicked in. Eve was reading *Where the Wild Things Are.* All the kids, even the ones who would probably have said they were too old for it, were sitting quietly, listening, with the fear easing away from their expressions.

"She's got the touch, doesn't she?" That was Michael, standing behind Claire. He was watching Eve read, too. "With kids." There was something quietly sad in his voice.

"Yeah, I guess." Claire glanced over at him, then away. "Everything okay?"

"Why wouldn't it be? Just another day for us Morganville brats." Now the *smile* was quietly sad, too. "I wish I could take her away from all this. Make it all—different."

"But you can't."

"No. I can't. Because I am who I am, and she is who she is. And that's it." He lifted his shoulders in a shrug so small it almost didn't even qualify. "She keeps asking me where we're going."

"Yeah," another voice said. It was Shane, pulling up a chair beside Claire. "Girls do that. They've always got to be taking the relationship somewhere."

"That's not true!"

"It is," he said. "I get it; somebody's got to be looking ahead. But it makes guys think they're—"

"Closed in," Michael said.

"Trapped," Shane added.

"Idiots," Claire finished. "Okay, I didn't really mean that. But jeez, guys. It's just a question."

"Yeah?" Michael's blue eyes were steady on Eve, watching her read, watching her smile, watching how she was with the kids clustered around her. "Is it?"

Claire didn't answer. Suddenly, *she* was the one who felt closed in. Trapped. And she understood why Michael was feeling so . . . strange.

He was watching Eve with kids, and he was never going to have kids with Eve. At least, she didn't *think* vampires could. . . . She'd never really asked. But she was pretty sure she was right about that one. He looked like someone seeing the future, and not liking his place in it one bit.

"Hey," Shane said, and nudged Claire's shoulder. "You noticed what's going on?"

She blinked as she realized that Shane wasn't figuring out Michael— that he hadn't even really noticed all the personal stuff at all. He was, instead, looking out into the shadows, where there had been vampires patrolling at the edges.

"What?" she asked. She couldn't see anyone.

"They're gone."

"*What?*"

"The vampires. As in, no longer in the building. Unless there's a big line for the bathroom, all of a sudden. Even Jason's gone."

"No way." Claire slid off her chair and went to the desk. There was no sign of Oliver, or Morley. The map of Blacke was still spread out on the table, anchored with weights on the corners, marked in colored pencils with things she didn't understand. She grabbed the lantern and went to the library doors, where Jacob Goldman had been standing.

He wasn't there.

"See?" Shane said. "They've bailed. All of them."

"That's impossible. Why would they just leave us?"

"You have to ask?" Shane shook his head. "Claire, sometimes I think your head's not really in the survival game. Think: why would they leave us? Because they can. Because as much as you want to believe the best about everybody, they're not the good guys."

"No," she blurted. "No, they wouldn't. *Oliver* wouldn't."

"The hell he wouldn't. Oliver is a rock-solid bastard, and you know it. If he added up the numbers and it looked like it might benefit him by adding even a second or two to his life, he'd be out of here, making up some sad story. It's how he survives, Claire." Shane hesitated for a second, then plunged on. "And maybe this is a good thing. Maybe if he's taken off, we should, too. Just—run. Get as far away, as fast as we can."

"What are you saying?"

"I'm saying . . . ," he began with a sigh. "I'm saying we're out of Morganville. And Oliver is all that's stopping us from heading anywhere in the world, other than there."

She really didn't want to believe that Oliver was gone. She wanted to believe that Oliver was, like Amelie, someone who took his word seriously, who, once having granted his protection, wouldn't just walk away because the going got tough.

But she really, really couldn't be sure. She never was, with Oliver. She had absolutely no doubts about Morley; he was all vampire, all the time. He'd smile at you one minute and rip out your throat the next, and wouldn't see any contradiction in that at all.

Shane was right, though. Oliver *was* all that stood between them and a life out in the world; a life free of Morganville.

Except for the people they'd leave behind.

She glanced back at Eve, surrounded by the kids in a circle of light, and at Michael, watching her from the shadows with so much longing and pain in his face.

And it hit her.

"Michael," she blurted. "Whatever Oliver might do to us, he can't leave Michael behind to die. He *can't*. Amelie would kill him."

No doubt about that. Amelie had deeply loved Sam, Michael's grandfather, and when she'd turned Michael into a vampire, she'd considered him family—*her* family. If Oliver planned to throw them to the infected wolves, he was going to have to figure out how to do it *and* somehow save Michael, without letting Michael know what had happened to the rest of them.

Michael must have heard her say his name, because he looked over at her. Shane crooked a finger at him. Michael nodded and walked over.

He was much more observant than Claire was, because before he ever reached them, Michael looked around and said, "Where are they?"

"Thought maybe you knew," Shane said. "They being your fellow fanged ones. Isn't there some kind of flock instinct?"

"Bite me, blood bank. No, they didn't tell me anything." Michael frowned. "Stay here. I'm going to check the rest of the building. Be right back."

He was gone in a whisper of air, hardly making any sound at all, and Claire shivered and leaned against Shane's solid, very human warmth. His arms went around her, and he touched his lips lightly to the back of her neck. "How can you smell this good after the kind of crappy day we've had?"

"I sweat perfume. Like all girls."

He laughed and squeezed her. He smelled good, too—more *male*, somehow, a little grungy and edgy and sweaty, and although she loved soap and water and shampoo, sometimes this was better—wilder.

Michael was back in—true to his word—just a few minutes, and he didn't look at all happy. "I found Patience," he said. "She and Jacob are guarding the doors from the outside. Oliver went out to do a patrol."

"And everybody else?" Claire asked.

"Morley took everybody else to go after the enemy. He said he wasn't going to wait for them to come to us. At least, that's what he said he was doing. For all Patience knows, Morley may be trying to find another truck or bus and get his people out of town."

"Did Oliver know about this?"

Michael shook his head. "He's got no idea, although he might now, if he spotted them outside. Don't know how he'd stop them on his own, though."

Claire didn't, either, but it was *Oliver*. He'd figure out something, and it probably wouldn't be pretty.

"How long until dawn?"

"A couple of hours," Michael said. He looked over at Eve, who had finished up the story and was hugging kids who were on their way to their beds. "Mrs. Grant said they always come during the night. That means they'll be coming soon, if Morley's people didn't screw up their whole day. And we'd better be ready."

When there had been a bunch of vampires running around on *their* side, Claire hadn't felt too worried, but now she was. And looking at Michael and at Shane, she knew they were, too.

"So let's hat up, guys," Shane said. "Nobody gets fanged tonight. New rule."

He and Michael did a fast high-low five, and went for the weapons.

Claire got Eve and updated her; then they joined the boys to get their vampire-repelling act together. Mrs. Grant had been dozing in an armchair, shotgun across her lap, but she woke up as soon as the four of them started raiding the weapons pile on the table. Claire was impressed; for an old lady, she woke up fast, and the first thing she did was look for trouble. When she didn't find any immediately, she looked at the four of them and said, "Are they coming?"

"Probably," Michael said, and picked up a couple of wooden stakes, leaving the silver-coated ones for the humans to handle. He also grabbed up a crossbow and some extra bolts. "We're going to help with patrols. Looks like we're a little light on guards."

"But Morley—" Mrs. Grant's mouth slammed shut, into a grim line. She didn't need to be clued in, obviously. "Of course. I never doubted he'd stab us in the back."

"I'm not saying he has," Michael said. "I'm just saying he's not here. So we need to be sure that if things go wrong . . ."

Mrs. Grant rose from her chair, winced, and rubbed at a sore spot on her back. She looked tired, but very focused. "I'll get my men up," she said. "Should have known we couldn't do a whole night without some kind of alert. I just hoped for a miracle."

"How long have you been doing this?" Claire asked. "Fighting them off?"

"It wasn't all at once," the older woman said. "At first we thought the people we couldn't find were just sick—regular human sick. And they were clever at first, good at hiding out, picking off people who weren't paying attention. Like wolves, going after strays. By the time we knew, they came in force and took out most everybody who could have gotten things organized against them. All told, I guess we've been living out of this library for almost three weeks now." She almost smiled, but it was just a bitter twist of her lips, really. "It seems longer. I can hardly remember what it was like before. Blacke used to be a real quiet town; nothing ever happened. Now . . ."

"Maybe we can get it back to that quiet town it used to be," Claire said.

Mrs. Grant gave her a long look. "Just you and your friends?"

"Hey," Shane said, snapping a shotgun closed with a flick of his wrist. "We're just trying to help."

"And stay alive," Eve added. "But trust me, this is not the worst situation we've ever been in." She sounded confident about that. Claire raised her eyebrows, and Eve considered it for a few more seconds. "Okay, maybe *tied* for worst. But definitely not the Guinness record for awfulness."

Mrs. Grant looked at each of them in turn, and then just walked away to rouse her own men.

"Seriously," Shane said, "this kind of *is* the worst situation we've ever been in, right?"

"Speak for yourself," Michael said. "I got myself killed last year. Twice."

"Oh yeah. You're right—last year really sucked for you."

"Boys," Eve interrupted, when Michael started to make some smart-ass comeback. "Focus. Dangerous vampire attack imminent. What's the plan?"

Michael kissed her lightly on the lips, and his eyes turned vampire-bright. "Don't lose."

"It's simple, yet effective. I like it." Shane extended his fist, and Michael bumped it.

"I am *never* taking a trip with either of you ever again." Eve said. "Ever."

"Excellent," Shane said. "Then next trip, we hit the strip bar."

"I have a gun, Shane." Eve sighed.

"What, you think I actually loaded yours?"

Eve flipped him off, and Claire laughed.

Even now, things just stayed normal, somehow.

An hour passed, and nothing happened. Eve got anxious about Jason's absence, but Claire was starting to feel a little confident that nothing *would* happen tonight at the library, as the minutes clicked by and the night around the library remain quiet, with nothing but the wind stirring outside in the streets.

And then the walkie-talkie Mrs. Grant had given her squawked for attention, making her jump. Claire figured it would be Shane; he'd stationed himself on the other side of the building, apparently because she was so distracting (which really didn't disappoint her, when she thought about it).

But it wasn't Shane.

It was Eve. "I'm coming out," she said. She sounded breathless and worried. "You need to see this."

"I'm here," Claire said. "Be careful."

In under a minute, Eve was beside her, holding out an open cell phone. Not hers—this one, for instance, didn't have all the usual glow-in-the-dark skulls on it. Eve wouldn't have a boring cell like this one.

Oh yeah. It was the one Oliver had slipped into her pocket on the bus. The only one they had now, since the rest were probably still dumped in a drawer back in the Durram police station.

There was a text message on the phone. *Wounded*, it said. *Bring help. Garage.*

It was from Oliver.

And that was it. Just the four words. Claire had gotten the occasional phone call from Oliver, but *never* a text.

"Oliver texted me," Eve said. "I mean really. Oliver *texted.* That's weird, right? Who knew he could?"

"Mrs. Grant said the cell phones didn't work here."

"No, she said they went out. This one's working. Kinda, anyway."

"Michael!" Claire called, and he jumped down from the top of a bookshelf next to the window to land next to her, barely seeming to notice the impact. She didn't see him coming, either, which made her fumble the phone and almost drop it. "Hey! Scary-monster move! Don't like it!"

"I'll try to whistle next time," he said. "What?"

She showed him. He *did* whistle, softly, and thought for a few seconds.

"What if it's not him?" Claire said. "What if it's, I don't know, *them?* They got him, and they're using his phone to lure us in?"

"They didn't strike me as particularly clever with the planning, but you've got a good point. It could be a trap." He frowned. "But if Oliver is calling for help, it's about as bad as it gets."

"I know." Claire felt short of breath. "What do we do? He probably thinks Morley's here!"

"Well, Morley's not." Michael looked around at the library, at the cluster of kids sleeping on cots in the middle of the room. "I don't like leaving them, but we can't just ignore it. Not if there's a chance he's really in trouble. It's close to dawn, at least. That's good for them, bad for Oliver."

They found Mrs. Grant, who listened to them, read the text message, and shrugged.

Shrugged.

"You want to go, go," she said. "We held out before any of you got here. We'll hang on long after you're gone, too. This is our town, and we're going to be the last ones standing around here. Count on it."

"Yes, ma'am," Claire said softly. "But—the kids—"

Mrs. Grant smiled bleakly. "What do you think we fight so hard for? The architecture? We'll fight to our last for our kids, every one of us. Don't you worry about that. You think your friend needs you, go on. Take the weapons—we've got plenty. This used to be a big hunting town." Mrs. Grant paused, eyeing Claire. "In fact, hold on. Got something for you."

She rummaged in a closet and came up with something that was huge, bulky, and looked very complicated—but once Claire had it thrust into her hands, she realized it wasn't complicated at all.

It was a bow. One of those with the wheels and pulleys—a compound bow?

Mrs. Grant found a bag stuffed full of arrows, too.

"I don't know how to shoot it," Claire protested.

"Learn."

"But—"

"If you don't want it, give it back."

"No," Claire said, and felt ashamed of herself. "I'm sorry. I'll figure it out."

Mrs. Grant suddenly grinned and ruffled Claire's hair as one would a little kid's. "I know you will," she said. "You got spark, you know that? Spark and grit. I like that."

Claire nodded, not quite sure *what* to say to that. She clutched the bow in one hand, the bag of arrows in the other, and looked at Michael. "So I guess we're—"

"Saving Oliver," Michael said, straight-faced. "Maybe you'd better try shooting that thing first."

While Michael, Shane, and Eve straightened out whatever it was they were going to do to get to Oliver—who was, according to the map and Mrs. Grant, at an old adobe building near the Civic Hall called Halley's Garage—Claire set up a couple of hand-drawn paper targets on pillow-padded chairs, pulled one of the arrows out, and tried to figure out how to put it on the bowstring quickly. That didn't work so well, so she tried again, taking her time, then pulling back the arrow and sighting down the long, straight line.

It was surprisingly tough to pull the string back, *and* hold the arrow in place, *and* not waver all over the place. She didn't even hit the chair, much less the target, and she winced as the arrow hit the wall at least four feet away. But at least she'd fired it. That was something, right?

She picked out another arrow and tried again.

Twenty arrows later, she'd managed to hit the pillow—not the target, but the pillow—and she was starting to understand how this whole thing worked. It was easier when she thought of it in terms of physics, of potential and kinetic energy, energy and momentum.

As she was working out the calculations in her head, she forgot to really worry about all the physical things that were getting in the way—the balancing of the bow, the aiming, the fear she wasn't going to get it right—and suddenly it all just *clicked*. She felt it come into sudden, sharp focus, like a spotlight had suddenly focused on her, and she let go of the arrow.

That instant, she *knew* it would hit the target. She let the bow rock gracefully forward on the balance point, watching the arrow, and it smacked into the exact center of her crudely drawn paper circle.

Physics.

She *loved* physics.

Shane arrived just as she put the arrow into the center, and slowed down, staring from the target to Claire, standing straight and tall, bow still held loosely in one hand and ready to shoot again. "You look so hot right now," he said. "I'm just saying."

She grinned at him and went to pick up all the arrows. One or two had suffered a little too much from contact with the wall, but the rest were good to reuse, and she carefully put them back into the bag, fletching end up. "You just like me because I might actually be able to be useful for a change."

"You are *always* useful," Shane said. "And hot. I mentioned that, right?"

"You're mental. I need a shower, clean clothes, and about a year of sleep."

"Okay, how about a hot mess?"

"Let me be Eve for a minute," she said, and flipped him off. He laughed and kissed her.

"Not even close," he said. "Come on, we've got some cranky old vampire to rescue."

THIRTEEN

It was still dark outside, but it felt ... different, as if the world was still dreaming, but dreaming about waking up. The air felt cool and light, and the darkness was just a tiny bit lighter than before.

"Not long until dawn," Michael said. "Which is good news and bad news."

"Good news for us," Shane said. "Present company excepted."

"You're such a bro."

"You start smoking, I'll roll you into the shade," Shane said. "Can't ask for more than my being willing to save your bloodsucking ass." They stood outside of the doors of the library for a few seconds, getting their bearings. Mrs. Grant had equipped them with sturdy LED lanterns, but it didn't feel like the light fell very far. There could be anything lurking ten feet away, Claire thought. And there probably was.

Michael shut off his lantern and just ... disappeared. It was startling, but they knew he was going to do it, at least; the plan was that he'd get out ahead of the light and look for trouble. Kind of a cross between a scout and bait. Claire's walkie-talkie clicked a moment later—no voice message, just the quiet electronic signal. "Go," she said. "We're okay."

The three of them went at a jog, watching their steps as best they could in the confusing jumble of shadows and harsh, flickering light.

Blacke looked like a nightmare, or Hollywood's idea of a disaster movie—cars abandoned, buildings closed and dark, windows shattered. The big, Gothic Civic Hall loomed over everything, but there weren't any lights showing inside. The statue of Hiram what's-his-face remained facedown in the thigh-high weeds, which Claire thought really might have been the best place for it. At least it wasn't leaning over and threatening to fall on people. Especially on her, because that would have been the worst Darwin Award–qualifying death ever.

They made it to the sidewalk beside the Civic Hall. Shane pointed. "That way," he said. "Should be on that corner, facing the hall."

Michael suddenly zipped into view at the edge of the light. "They're coming," he said. "Behind us and to the left. Back of the Civic Hall."

"Run!" Shane said, and they took off, lanterns throwing crazy, bouncing light off broken glass and metal, turning shadows into ink-filled blots. The iron fence around the Civic Hall was leaning outward, into the sidewalk, and Shane had to flinch and duck to avoid a sharp, rusty arrow-point bent low enough to scrape his face. Claire almost tripped over one of the metal bars that had fallen loose from the fence. She kicked it out of the way, then paused and grabbed it, juggling the lantern.

"Don't stop!" Eve hissed, and pulled her on. The iron bar, with its sharp arrowhead top, was heavy, but straight, like a spear. Claire managed to hang on to it as they ran, but at the next curb she missed her footing and had to scramble. Her lantern broke free of her fingers and smashed on the ground. It flickered, brightened, then faded and died.

Out of nowhere, Michael was next to her, handing her his own switched-off lantern and grabbing the iron bar from her. "Keep going!" he said, and turned with the iron bar to guard their backs. Eve looked back, her face pale in the white LED lights, and her dark eyes looked huge and terrified.

"Michael?"

"Don't stop!"

He fell behind in the dark after only three or four steps and was lost to them. Claire heard something like a snarl behind them, and what sounded like a body hitting the ground.

Then came a scream, high and wild.

Up ahead, she saw a flash of what looked like faded pink. There was a leaning metal sign flapping and creaking in the predawn wind, and Claire wasn't sure, but she thought the rusty letters might have said GARAGE.

It was a square adobe building with some old-fashioned gas pumps off to the side that looked as if they hadn't worked since Claire's mom was a kid. The windows were broken and dark, but they were blocked up with something, so there was no way to see inside.

Shane arrived at the door of the building—a big wooden thing, scarred and faded, with massive iron hinges—and banged on it. "Oliver!" he yelled. "Cavalry!"

Funny, Claire didn't feel much like the cavalry at the moment. They rode in with guns blazing to save the day, right? She felt more like a hunted rabbit. Her heart was pounding, and even in the cool air she was sweating and shaking. *If this is a trap . . .*

The door opened into darkness, and a hand reached out and grabbed Shane by the shirt front, and yanked him inside.

"No!" Claire charged forward, lantern blazing now and held high, and saw Shane being dragged, off balance, out of the way. Not having time or room for the bow, she dropped it, grabbed an arrow out of the bag, and lunged for the vampire who was taking Shane away.

Oliver turned, snarling, and knocked the arrow out of her grip so hard her entire hand went numb. She gasped and drew back, shocked, because Oliver looked . . . not like Oliver, much. He was dirty, ragged, and he had blood all down his arm and the front of his shirt.

There was a raw wound in his throat that was slowly trying to heal.

That was his own blood on his clothes, she realized. Something— someone—had bitten him, nearly killing him, it looked like.

"Inside," he ordered hoarsely, as Eve hovered in the doorway, peering in. "Michael?"

Michael appeared out of the darkness, racing fast. He stopped to grab up Claire's fallen bow, and then practically shoved Eve inside the building as he slammed the door and turned to lock it. There were big old-fashioned iron bolts, which he slid shut. There was also a thick old board that Oliver pointed toward; Michael tossed Claire her bow and slotted the bar in place, into the racks on either side of the door.

As he did, something hit the door hard enough to bend the metal bolts and even the thick wooden bar. But the door held.

Outside, something screamed in frustration, and Claire heard claws scratching on the wood.

Michael wasn't hurt, at least not that Claire could see; he hugged Eve and kept one arm around her as they came toward Claire, who was still in a standoff with Oliver.

And Oliver was still holding Shane with a white, clenched fist twisted in the fabric of his shirt.

"Hey," Shane said. "Off! Let go!"

Oliver seemed to have forgotten he was even holding him, but as he turned to look at Shane, Claire saw his eyes turn muddy red, then glow hotter when Shane tried to pull away.

"Don't," she said softly. "He's lost a lot of blood; he's not himself. Stay still, Shane."

Shane took a deep breath and managed to hold himself steady, but Claire could tell it really cost him. Everything in him must have been screaming to fight, rip free, run away from that glowing red hunger in Oliver's eyes.

He didn't. And Oliver, after a few eternal seconds, let go of him and stepped back, then suddenly turned and stalked away.

Shane looked over at Claire, and she saw the real fear in his eyes, just for a second. Then he pushed it away, and smiled, and held up his thumb and index finger, pushed about an inch apart. "Close," he said.

"Maybe you're not his type," Michael said.

"Oh, now you're just being insulting." Shane reached out for Claire's hand, and squeezed it, hard. He didn't mind letting her feel the nerves that still trembled in him, but he wasn't going to let Michael see it, obviously. "So what the hell is going on in here?"

A vague shape loomed up behind him out of the shadows. Then another one. Then another. Shane and Claire quickly moved to stand back-to-back. So did Eve and Michael. Among the four of them, they were covering every angle.

"Lurking isn't answering," Shane said. "Oliver? Little help?"

Instead, one of the shapes stepped forward into the light. Morley. Claire felt relieved, and annoyed. Of *course* it was Morley. Why had she ever doubted it? He was the champion lurker of all time.

"What did you bring?" Morley rasped.

"Besides charm and beauty?" Eve said. "Why? What did you need? What are you doing here?"

"They've been helping us," whispered someone out of the dark. Eve turned up the power on her lantern to max, and the dim, cold light finally penetrated the shadows enough to show the people lying crumpled on the dirty floor of the garage. Well, *people* might have been a little bit misleading, because Claire realized they were all vampires; their eyes caught the light and reflected it back.

She didn't recognize them. And then it finally occurred to her why she wouldn't.

These were the vampires of Blacke. The sick ones. And there must have been at least ten of them, in addition to another ten or fifteen of Morley's crew, crammed into the small adobe building.

"We went after them one by one," Morley said. "We've been at it for hours now. Some of them were a damn nuisance to bring here, let alone dose. But your witch potion does seem to work, little Claire. If we can get some of the crystals in them, they become rational enough to accept the cure."

Claire was stunned. Somehow, having seen how far gone things were, she'd never really expected them to be able to *save* people—but here they were, lying exhausted on the floor, shaking and confused. Unlike the vampires Claire had dealt with in Morganville, these were newbies, like Michael; people who'd been turned against their will in the first place, and made sick at the same time. For some reason, they'd been more suscep-tible to getting on the crazy train than Michael; maybe that was because he was originally from Morganville, and had some kind of better resistance. But they'd certainly gotten sick a lot faster, and a lot worse, than any vampires she'd ever seen.

Consequently, they were healing a whole lot more slowly. It hadn't taken Myrnin and Amelie and Oliver long to recover after taking their doses when Bishop was safely out of the way, but then, they were far older, and had already coped with being vampires.

Claire focused on a boy about her own age. He looked scared, devastated, and alone. He looked *guilty*, as if he couldn't forget how he'd been surviving these past few weeks or what he'd done.

"They're coming around," Morley continued. "But the more we get of them, the more vulnerable we are; they can't get up and fight yet, even if we'd trust them to do so. And the others over there, they've tracked us here. Oliver did a gallant job, but they're no doubt on their way here now."

"Uh, I think we might have pretty much led them straight over," Eve said. "Sorry. Nobody specified stealthy in the message."

"I was hoping one would take it as implied," Oliver snapped. "I should have known better."

"And where the *hell* is my brother, you jerk?"

"He has orders," Oliver said. "That's all you need to know."

"Children, children, this anger gets us nowhere," Morley said, in a mocking, motherly tone. "There are about fifteen of them left we haven't been able to catch and give the cure, and sadly, we have very little left at this point. The ones we can't cure, we must confine, until we can get the drugs from Morganville."

Funny, Claire had never really thought of him as being a humanitarian—vampiritarian? Anyway, someone who put the best interests of others first. But getting out of Morganville—and away from Amelie—seemed to have done something good for Morley. He seemed to almost *care*.

Almost.

"Confine, not kill," Oliver said, and turned to come back toward them. His eyes had gone safely dark again, although Claire could see how tired and hungry he was in the sharp moves he made, and the tense set of his muscles. "And how precisely do you think we should do that, Morley?

It's been difficult enough to trap these creatures singly and pacify them. Morning isn't far away, and in case you have failed to notice, you're down quite a few followers on your side."

Morley shrugged. "Some stayed near the library. Some simply wanted to go, so I let them. The whole purpose of this exercise was to earn our freedom, Oliver. Even if you don't understand the concept of freedom in the slightest—"

"Freedom?" Oliver barked out a laugh. "Anarchy is what you want, Morley. It's what you always wanted. Don't dare to—"

"Hey!" Claire said, and stepped away from Shane, facing both vampires. "Politics later! Focus! What are we going to do, if they're coming? Can we hold them off?"

"This is the most defensible position in town, other than the library," Morley said, suddenly all business. "We can hold it with the men we have, even against the local talent."

"I'm sensing a *but* coming up soon," Shane said.

"*But*," Morley said, "we failed to bring much in the way of supplies. In fact, most of ours ended up stuck between the teeth of our friends across the way. And those who are recovering will need to feed, quickly."

There was a short, deadly silence. Oliver said nothing, but he looked drawn and weary.

"Wait," Eve said slowly. "What are you saying?"

More silence. Claire felt cold trickle down her spine. "You're saying we just volunteered to be blood donors."

"You are *not* serious," Shane said. "You are *not* snacking on us."

"Not all of you, obviously," Morley said. "The girl's exempt; she's Amelie's toy, and I wouldn't harm her for the world. Michael, of course, isn't the appropriate meat for our table. But you and our lovely living dead girl—"

"No," Claire said. "Never going to happen. Back off."

"My dear, do you think I'm actually offering you a choice? It's an *explanation.* An apology, of sorts. Oliver didn't send you the message. I held him down, took his telephonic device, and used it myself. Why do you think he's so badly mussed?"

It was weird, Claire thought, to feel so clear at this moment. So calm. "You're telling me you're going to take Eve and Shane and drain them."

"I could make them vampires when we're done, if you just can't face losing them. I'm terribly progressive that way. Then you would be the *only* breather in your little pack, Claire. How long do you imagine you'd last, especially if your boyfriend there declared his *undying* love?" Morley fluttered his eyelashes like a cartoon character and put both hands over his heart. "If I were you, I'd volunteer to join them. Being human is not precisely a clever plan."

"Yeah? How's this?" Claire, in one smooth, fast motion, pulled an arrow from the bag on her shoulder, slotted it home on the string, and pulled the compound bow back to full extension. She was aiming the arrow straight at Morley's crossed hands, over his heart.

He laughed. "You aren't serious——"

She fired.

The arrow went through both of Morley's hands, pinning them to his chest with the fletching at the end. He stared down in shock at the wood piercing his chest, stumbled, and went down to his knees.

Then just down, face forward. The arrow stuck up out of his back, like an exclamation point.

"I will," Claire said softly, and let the bow rock forward as she reached one-handed for another arrow and nocked it home. "I'm not a really good shot, but this is a really small room, so let me make this very clear: the first vampire who tries to lay a hand on either of my friends gets a new piercing, just like Morley. Now, if you need food, I will figure it out. But you don't get to use my friends like vending machines. Are we clear?"

Around the room, vampires nodded, casting disbelieving looks at Morley. Even Oliver was staring at her as if he'd never really seen her before. She didn't know why; he'd known she could do it—hadn't he?

Or was she different, somehow?

"Shane?" Claire asked. He stepped up to her side. "Use Eve's phone. Call Mrs. Grant at the library. We need to organize something."

"What?"

"A blood drive," she said.

"Hang on—"

"Shane." Claire tilted her head up to look at him, and didn't smile. "They'll do it. These are their friends and family. They'll do it to save them. I'd do it to save *you*."

He touched her cheek gently. "I think you would," he said. "Crazy girl."

"Ask Morley how crazy I am," she said. "Oh, wait. You'll have to take the arrow out, first."

"Maybe later. Facedown is a good look for him." Shane gave her a quick, beautiful smile, and turned away to make the call.

Michael was shaking his head. Claire, without loosening her draw on the bow, gave him a quick, nervous look. "What?"

He laughed. "You," he said. "Jeez, Claire. If I didn't love you, you'd scare me."

"I don't love her," Oliver said acidly. "And if you *ever* point that arrow anywhere near me, Amelie's pet or no, I will take it away from you and introduce you to the sharp end, with great pleasure. Are we clear, girl?"

"Yeah," she said, and kept the arrow pointed away from him. "You got your butt kicked by Morley, and you're threatening me because I actually solved your problem for you. I think we're very clear. But don't worry. I won't hurt you, Oliver."

For a brief, deadly second, there was utter silence.

Then Oliver laughed.

It wasn't the bitter, angry, terrible laugh she expected. Oliver actually sounded almost *human*. He sagged back against the wall, still laughing, and sank down to a crouch, hands loosely braced on his knees. It sounded as if he hadn't laughed that much, or that deeply, for a very long time. It was weirdly infectious; Eve giggled in little hiccups, trying not to; Michael started laughing at her struggle not to laugh. Before too long, even Claire was fighting to keep her aim steady with the arrow.

"Ease up," Michael said, and touched her arm, which was trembling with effort. "You made your point. Nobody's coming after us. Not in here."

She sighed, finally, and loosened the draw on the bow. Her shoulders were aching, and her arms felt like raw meat. She hadn't even felt the strain until it was gone.

"Claire," Oliver said. She looked over at him, suddenly alarmed and wondering if she had the strength to try to draw the bow again, but he was smiling. It gave his sharp face a relaxed look she wasn't really used to seeing, and his eyes held what looked like genuine warmth. "It's too bad you're not a vampire."

"I guess that was a compliment, so thanks, but no thanks."

He shrugged and left it at that. Still, Claire had a second's flash of temptation. *All those years. All those things to learn, to feel, to know . . .* Myrnin lived for the excitement of knowledge; she knew that. The only difference between the two of them, really, was that he could go on forever learning.

But despite all of that, despite all the shiny immortality and the fact that there were a few vamps she didn't actually hate—even Oliver now— Claire knew she was meant to be human. Just plain Claire.

And that was really okay.

As if to prove it, Shane slid his arm around her waist and kissed her cheek. "You rock, you know that?"

"I'm a rock star," she said, straight-faced. "I'm probably the saddest little rock star ever, though. What did Mrs. Grant say?"

"She says they'll set up a donation center there and bring it over in bottles. She's not risking her people to bring it over. Somebody has to go pick up and deliver."

"Does she believe us?"

"She wants to," Shane said. "Her husband's in here, somewhere. So's her son."

And that, Claire thought, was why Morley had been right about this, even if he was a complete *vampire* about it.

You had to save what you could.

Amelie had understood that all along, Claire realized. That was why Morganville existed. Because you had to try.

Oliver ended up doing the blood pickup himself, maybe as a kind of off-hand apology for putting Eve and Shane at risk in the first place, though that of course went unsaid. As the stuff was being passed around—one small plastic cup per vampire, to start—Claire knelt beside Morley's still body, rolled him on his side, and snapped the arrow off just below the point. Then she pulled it out of his chest and hands with one sharp tug, dropping it to the concrete.

Morley took in a huge gasp of air and let it out in a frustrated shout. He held up his hands and stared at the holes punched through them until the flesh and bone started to knit themselves again.

He rolled over on his back, staring up at nothing, and said, "I was going to say you aren't a killer. And I still stand by that statement, because evidently I'm not dead. Only *very* upset."

"Here." Claire handed him a cup of blood. "You're right. I'm not a killer. I hope you're not, either."

Morley sat up and sipped, eyes narrowed and fixed on her. "Of course I'm a killer, girl," he said. "Don't be stupid. It's my nature. We're predators, no matter what Amelie likes to pretend in her little artificial hothouse of Morganville. We kill to survive."

"But you don't have to," Claire pointed out. "Right now, you're drinking blood someone gave you. So it doesn't have to be kill-or-be-killed. It can be different. All you have to do is decide to be something else."

He smiled, but not with fangs this time. "You think it's so simple?"

"No." She got up, dusting her knees. "But I know you're not as simple as you like people to think you are."

Morley's eyebrows went up. "You know nothing of me."

"I know you're smart, people follow you, and you can make something good happen for the people who trust you. People like Patience and Jacob, who've got good instincts. Don't betray them."

"I wouldn't—" He stopped, and looked away. "It doesn't matter. I promised to get them all out. They're out. What they do now is up to them."

"No, it's not," Oliver said. He was standing near them, leaning on a stack of old tires as he sipped from his own plastic cup. "You made yourself responsible for them when you left Morganville, Morley. Like it or not, you're now the patriarch of the Blacke vampires. The question is, what are you going to do with them?"

"Do?" Morley looked almost panicked. "Nothing!"

"Not an answer. I suggest you devote some thought to it." Oliver smiled, eyes unfocused as he drank with evident pleasure. "Blacke could be an ideal location, you know. Remote, isolated, little traffic in or out. The humans remaining have a vested interest in keeping your secrets, since their own have been turned. It could be the start of something quite . . . interesting."

Morley laughed. "You're trying to make me *Amelie*."

"Goodness, no. You'd look terrible in a skirt."

Claire shook her head and left them arguing. Dawn was rolling over the town's sky in waves of gold, pink, and soft oranges; it was beautiful, and it felt . . . new, somehow. The destruction was still there; Hiram's statue was still facedown in the weeds; there were still a dozen feral vampires hiding out somewhere in the shadows.

But it felt as if the town had just come alive again. Maybe that was because across the square, the Blacke library doors were wide-open, and people were coming outside into the cool morning air.

Coming across the square to see those they'd thought they'd lost forever.

Shane was sitting on the curb next to the old, cracked gas pumps, eating a candy bar. Claire plopped down next to him. "Half?" she asked.

"And now I *know* you're my girlfriend, since you're not afraid to demand community property," he said, and pulled off the uneaten half to hand it over. "Look. We're alive."

"And we have chocolate."

"It's not just a miracle; it's a miracle with chocolate. Best kind."

Eve emerged from the garage doorway and settled down next to Claire, leaning her chin on her fists. "I am so tired, I could throw up," she said. "What's for breakfast? Please don't say blood."

Claire separated her half of the candy bar into two pieces and gave Eve one. "Snickers," she said. "Breakfast of—"

"Champions?" Eve mumbled around a mouthful of sticky goodness.

"Not unless it's competitive eating," Shane said. "So, Morley's staying? He's becoming King of Blacke?"

"I think it's more like Undead Mayor, but yeah. Probably."

"So can we ditch Oliver now?"

"Don't think so," Claire said. "He says we leave soon."

"How are we planning to do that, exactly?"

"No idea—"

She heard the engine first as a faint buzz, like a stray but persistent mosquito; then it built into a roar.

A big, black hearse slewed around the corner from the highway and skidded to a stop in front of the garage.

The window rolled down, and Jason Rosser looked out. He grinned. "Anybody need a ride? I figured I'd head back to Durram and grab yours, sis. Since it's officially legal and all. Oh, and I got your cell phones, too."

"Bro, you *rock*." Eve lunged up to her feet and ran possessive hands over the paint job. "Okay, creep, out of my driver's seat. Now."

Jason held the door open for her. As she started to get in, she threw her arms around his neck and hugged him, hard, even with the door between them. He looked surprised.

And so relieved, it hurt Claire a little to see it.

"Come on," Eve said. "We have to lightproof the back."

"Give me a sec," Jason said. "I need a bathroom."

"There's one in the library," Shane said. "Hey, how'd you get out of town?"

"I stole a tractor," Jason said.

"What?"

"A tractor. It took me all night to get to Durram. Wasn't sure if I'd ever make it, either. I ran out of gas two miles from where they'd towed the car."

"Huh." Claire could tell Shane was grudgingly impressed. "So you walked?"

"No, I flew on angel wings."

"Ass."

"How'd you get it out of impound?"

"Trade secret," Jason said. "But it involves not actually asking. Same with the phones. Speaking of which..." He dug in the pocket of his hoodie and came up with them, which he handed over to Shane. They didn't tap fists or high-five or anything, but Shane nodded, and Jason nodded back.

"No signal," Claire said, checking hers. "Man, the Morganville provider network sucks."

"It works when Amelie wants it to work," Shane said. "Apparently, she doesn't want it working right now."

"Michael needs to call the guy in Dallas. You know, let him know we're on the way."

"Let him know we got trapped in a vampire town and fought off a vampire zombie army, you mean?"

"I was thinking maybe car problems."

"Boring, but effective," Shane said. "I'll go see if we can make it work. Maybe cell phone wastage doesn't apply to vampires."

As they were talking, Jason walked across to the library, head down, looking like a thin stick in blue jeans. Claire wondered if maybe, just maybe, there was a chance for Eve's brother.

Not much of one, but... maybe.

EPILOGUE

"It's you," Eve said, and gave the wig a final tug on Claire's head, setting it just right. All of a sudden, it *looked* right—not just some random collection of plastic threads stuck on top of her scalp, but... hair. Pretend hair, sure, but, it looked...

Claire couldn't decide how it looked. She cocked her head first one way, then the other. Tried a pose.

"Is it cool? I think it's cool. Maybe?" The girl looking back at her wasn't just a mousy, skinny girl anymore. The new, improved Claire Danvers was taller, a little more filled out, and she was wearing a new hot pink shirt layered over black, a pair of low-rise jeans with skulls on the pockets, and pink and white hair. She was *rocking* the streaked wig. It flowed down over her shoulders in careless waves, and made her look mysterious and fragile and smoky, and Claire just knew she had never been smoky or mysterious in her entire life.

"That is absolutely so you," Eve said with a happy sigh, and jumped around in hoppy circles in her new patent leather black shoes with red skull imprints. "You have *got* to get it. And wear it. Trust me, Shane will go nuts. You look so *dangerous!*"

"Shane's already nuts." Claire laughed. "Did you *see* him in the T-shirt aisle? I thought he was going to cry. So many sarcastic sayings; so few days of the week to wear them. And I'm not sure I really feel comfortable looking, y'know, *dangerous.*"

Eve gave her a long, serious look. "You are, you know. Dangerous."

"Am not."

"It's not the hair. You just—you're something else, Claire. It's like when all the rest of us don't know where to go, you . . . just go. You're not afraid."

"That is so not true," Claire said with a sigh. "I'm scared all the time. Down to my bones. I'm lucky I don't run away like a screaming little girl."

Eve smiled. "That's my job. You're the heroic one."

"Not!"

"Oh, just shut up and get the wig already," Eve said.

"No."

"Get it, get it, get it!"

"Okay! Jeez, you're scaring the other freaks!"

They both broke into manic giggles, because it was true; a couple of very Gothy Goths were edging away, casting them both odd, apprehensive little looks. Being from Morganville gave you an attitude, Claire guessed. And that wasn't a bad thing, especially when you were in a scary-big city like Dallas, where everything seemed to move ten times faster than she was used to, including the traffic. She didn't know how Eve had managed to get them to the hotel, or get Michael to his studio appointment after dark, but she had, and it was *fabulous.*

The hotel rooms had free soaps and shampoos and *robes.* It was amazing. And they were all modern, with flat-screen, high-definition TVs, and beds so soft that sleeping on them was like sleeping on angel wings.

It was so not like the life she was used to living, which was, she supposed, what made it extra special cool.

"I am a rock star," Claire said to her reflection. Her reflection seemed to agree, although it still made her laugh inside to think it. She remembered Morley's surprise when she'd actually shot him, and Oliver's laughter, his genuine approval.

Maybe she was, a little *tiny* bit.

She flipped the hair over her shoulders and thought about makeup. "What do you think about heavy eyeliner?" Claire asked, which was totally redundant, because Eve never went anywhere without heavy eyeliner. It was her number one fashion tool.

Instantly, Eve whipped out her Mac tools and began doing Claire's eyes for her. When she checked again, Claire looked . . . *really* mysterious. Her face had taken on depth, shadows, secrets.

Wow. It was amazing what a little change could do.

And a little sleep, Claire thought. She felt better than she had in *months,* knowing there was nobody lurking around the corner to kidnap her, munch her neck, or otherwise present a serious danger.

"You look absolutely fantastic," Eve said. "Drop-dead gorgeous."

"Not literally, hopefully."

"The idea is to knock *other* people dead, sweetie. I didn't think I really had to explain that part."

Shane rounded the corner of the aisle with a double armload of T-shirts, every one of them bound to offend *someone* in Morganville, and skidded to a stop at the sight of the two of them. His mouth opened and closed. Eve stepped away, but Shane didn't notice; his eyes were fixed on Claire, and he looked as if he'd been hit in the forehead with a two-by-four.

"How do I look?" she asked, which was a completely ridiculous question, given how he was staring at her.

He dropped the T-shirts and kissed her, long and sweet and hard, and she felt a fierce kind of joy blow into a storm inside, wild and crazy and *free.*

The Gothy McGoth twins, in their leather and spikes and dyed hair, sniffed and walked off, clearly offended by the sight of so much happiness in one place.

When Shane let her up for air, Claire said, "Maybe we should actually buy the stuff before we celebrate?"

"Why wait?"

And he kissed her again.

Dallas was *amazing.* All the lights, the dizzying buildings, the crazy amounts of traffic, the noise, the people. After a long morning of shopping, Claire was dog-tired, too tired and dazed to even properly admire how awesome their hotel was, with all the glass and marble and fancy furniture. Michael wasn't due to be in the studio until eight p.m., so she fell into bed and slept in her clothes, for a long time. When she woke up, Eve was just finishing her makeup—back to Goth Girl Gone Wild— and checking her lace skull-patterned minidress in the mirror. Her legs looked taller than Claire's entire body.

"Wow," Claire mumbled, and sat up. The mirror showed her just how horrible her bed head could be. "Ack."

"The shower is amazing," Eve said, and turned to the side, smoothing down her dress. "Is it too much?"

"For Morganville? Yeah. For Dallas? No idea. But you look fantastic."

Eve smiled, that secret little smile, and her eyes glittered brightly.

She was thinking about Michael, obviously.

Claire yawned, slipped off the bed, and went to try the shower. Thirty minutes later, her hair fluffed into relative cuteness, she was clean, dry, and dressed in jeans and her best cute blue top, the one Shane said he liked. She even stopped for a little makeup, although she knew it was a lost cause, considering Eve's outfit.

Shane rapped on their door ten minutes later, and when she answered, he looked sleepy but relaxed. He was freshly showered, which was always a look she loved on him; his hair was even more insane than usual, as if he'd toweled it dry and then forgotten about it. She smoothed it down. He kissed her and called, "Yo, Eve? Crazy train's leaving the station!"

"I'm coming!" Eve yelled breathlessly, and came out of the bathroom, again, smoothing down her dress.

Shane blinked, but he didn't say anything. "Michael's waiting. He's freaking out that he's going to be late."

"Well, he won't be," Eve said. "Do I look okay? Like a rock star's girlfriend?"

"No," Shane said, and when she looked hurt, he laughed. "You look much better than that, scary girl."

She blew him a kiss and set off down the hall. Michael was pacing next to the elevators, crackling with nervous energy; his gear was piled next to the wall, and he had a strange, closed expression on his face that disappeared the second he saw Eve.

Claire sighed in sympathetic happiness as Michael kissed his girl-friend and leaned over to whisper something in her ear—something that made Eve laugh and cuddle even closer.

Shane rolled his eyes. "I thought you were in a hurry, man."

"Never in *that* much of a hurry," Michael said, and picked up one of the guitars.

Shane picked up the other and offered him a fist to bump. "Let's go rock it, Mikey." Michael just looked at him for a second. Shane held steady, and said, "Michael. You can do it. Trust me."

Michael took a deep breath, returned the fist bump, and nodded as he pushed the elevator call button.

There was a car downstairs—a big black town car, like a limousine only not as fancy—with a driver in a black jacket. He gave Eve a hand in, then Claire; Michael and Shane took the facing bench seat. The guitars, Claire assumed, went in the trunk.

Michael was looking pale, but then, when didn't he? He reached across the open space and took Eve's hand as the car began to roll. "Love the dress," he said.

"Love you," she said, very simply. His eyebrows rose a little, and he smiled.

"I was getting to that part."

"I know." Eve patted his hand. "I know you were. But you're a boy. I thought I'd just cut to the chase. You're going to be great, you know."

They didn't say anything the rest of the short drive; the roof overhead was clear, and it gave them an amazing view of the tall buildings and the colored lights. Claire felt her heart pounding. *This was really happening.* She couldn't imagine what was going on in Michael's head—or heart. It seemed like a dream. *Morganville* seemed like a dream, one that had happened to someone else, and the idea that they'd leave this reality and go back to that one . . .

Shane didn't have to, Claire thought again. Of the four of them, he was the one who could walk away, and there was nothing in Morganville to hold him.

Nothing but her, anyway.

At the studio, which was in a plain-looking industrial building at the edge of downtown, the driver unloaded the guitars and saw them inside, where two people waiting immediately focused on Michael. Claire, Eve, and Shane suddenly became his entourage, which was funny and kind of awesome, and trailed along as the two recording people explained the process to Michael.

Shane carried both the guitars. He did it with a smile, too, that said clearly how proud he was of his friend. Michael looked fierce—he was concentrating on every word, and Claire could see him already putting himself into performance mode, that place that made him so different when he was onstage.

At the studio door, one of the two studio guys turned and held out a hand to Eve, Claire, and Shane. "You guys need to wait in the box," he said. "Through that door." He pointed to a thick metal door with a window inset, and took the guitars from Shane. Then he flashed them a quick grin. "He'll be great. Trust me, he wouldn't be here if he wasn't."

"Damn right," Shane said, and led the two girls into the box—which, it turned out, was the recording studio's control room. A big man with frizzy hair was sitting at the mixing board, which looked more complicated than the inside of the space shuttle. He said hello and gestured for them to take a seat on the big, plush couch at the back of the room.

It was an amazing place, the studio, full of people who were all just really, really great at their jobs. The engineer behind the giant, complicated mixing board was relaxed, calm, and very easygoing, and the two on the other side of the glass helped Michael get set up, did some sound checks, and then left him alone and joined the rest of them in the control room.

"Right," the engineer said, and nodded to his two assistants—if that was what they were; Claire wasn't sure. "Let's see what he's got." He flipped a switch. "Michael? Go ahead, whenever you're ready."

Michael started out playing a slow song, with his head down, and Claire felt the mood in the room change from professional to really interested as he settled into the music. It flowed out of him, silky smooth, beautiful, as natural as sunshine. It was an acoustic guitar thing, and it put tears into Claire's eyes; there was something so soft and sad and aching about it. When he finished, Michael held the chord for a long moment, then sighed and sat back on his stool, looking through the glass toward them.

The engineer's mouth was open. He closed it, cleared his throat, and said, "What's that called, kid?"

"'Sam's Song,'" Michael said. "It's for my grandfather."

The engineer closed the microphone, looked at the other two, and said, "We've got a live one."

How darkly hilarious, Claire thought. *If only he knew.*

"He's great," Shane said softly, as if he'd never actually realized it before. "Seriously. He's *great.* I'm not crazy, right?"

"You're not crazy," the engineer said. "Your buddy has insane skills. They're going to love him out there."

Out there. In the world.

In the real world.

Where Michael couldn't really go for long.

The booth door opened, and Oliver walked in. He was in normal human mode, looking fatherly and inoffensive. The aging hippie, complete with tie-dyed T-shirt and faded jeans and sandals. Claire bet that if she'd told the engineer Oliver was a vampire, he'd have laughed and told her to lay off the crack.

Oliver perched on the arm of the sofa, listening. They all scooted over, because even Claire didn't really want to lean against him, no matter how nice he was apparently being. He said nothing at all. After a while, they all relaxed a little, as Michael continued to pour out the amazing rivers of music on the other side of the studio glass. Fast, slow, hard rocking—he could do it all.

When the last song was over, two hours later, the engineer hit the microphone into the studio and said, "Perfect. That was perfect; that's a keeper. Okay, I think we're done. Congratulations. You are officially on your way, my man."

Michael stood up, smiling, holding his guitar in one hand, and caught sight of Oliver watching him.

His smile almost faded, but then he moved his gaze over to Eve, who was on her feet, blowing him kisses. That made him laugh.

"Rock star!" Eve yelled, and clapped. Claire and Shane stood up and clapped, too.

Oliver sat quietly, no expression at all on his face, as they celebrated Michael's success.

It was their last night in Dallas.

Oliver had allowed them to have a nice dinner out, at a fantastically expensive restaurant where all the waiters were better dressed than Claire ever had been. He didn't go, of course, but somehow Claire could feel his presence, feel him watching.

It was still an amazing meal. She tried everything on her plate, on Shane's, even on Michael's and Eve's. They laughed and flirted, and after the dinner—which went on Oliver's credit card—they went to a dance club across the street, full of beautiful people and spinning lights. No liquor allowed for them, thanks to the glowing wristbands they didn't get, but they danced. Even Shane, although he mainly held on to Claire as *she* danced—which was fantastic. Hot, sweaty, exhausted, happy, the four of them piled into a cab and headed back to the hotel.

It was on the elevator ride up that Shane asked, "Are we really going back?"

It was a long ride; their rooms were on the very top floor of a very tall building. Nobody spoke, not even Michael. He rested his chin on top of Eve's head and held her close, and she put her arms around him.

Shane looked at Claire, the question plain in his eyes. She felt the heavy weight of it, the absolute vital *importance* of it.

The claddagh ring on her right hand felt cold, suddenly.

"Seriously," Shane said. "Can you leave all this? Just go back to *that*? Michael, you've got a future out here. You really do."

"Do I?" Michael asked. He sounded tired and defeated. "How long do you think I could last before something went wrong, man? Morganville's safety. This is—beautiful, but it's temporary. It has to be temporary."

"It doesn't," Shane insisted. "We can figure it out. We *can*."

Before Michael could answer, the floor dinged arrival, and they had to get out.

Oliver was standing in the hallway, wearing his leather coat and serious expression. No more Mr. Nice Hippie, obviously. He was standing as if he'd been waiting for them for a while.

Creepy.

All four of them came to a sudden halt, staring at him; Claire felt Shane's arm tighten around her waist, as if he was considering moving in front of her. To protect her from what?

There was something odd about the way Oliver was looking at them—because he *wasn't* looking at them, exactly. It was not his normal direct stare at all.

Instead, he silently dialed a number on the cell phone in his hand and put it on speaker, right there, standing in the middle of the hotel hallway. All the plush carpet and lights and normal life seemed to fade away as Claire heard a calm voice on the other end of the phone say, "Do you have them all?" Amelie. Cool, precise, perfectly in control.

"All except Jason," Oliver said. "He's on an errand. He's not involved in this in any case."

Silence for a few seconds, and then Amelie said, "I want you to know I take no pleasure in this. I have made it clear to you, Claire, that I value your service to me and to Morganville, that you are important to us. Do you understand?"

"Yes." Her throat felt dry and tight, and her skin cold.

"Michael," Amelie continued, "I have spoken with you in private, but I will make this public: you must return to Morganville. This goes equally for Claire. You *must* return. There is no argument, no mitigation. Oliver understands this very well, and he is standing as my enforcer in this matter. No doubt the lights are very bright in Dallas, and Morganville seems far away. I assure you it is not. I don't doubt you have spoken of running away, of securing your freedom, but you must understand: my reach is long, and my patience is not infinite. I would much rather your parents continue in blissful ignorance of their danger, Claire. And yours, Eve.

And even yours, Michael—even though they have left Morganville, they remain under my control, and always will."

"You bitch," Shane muttered.

"Mr. Collins, I will tolerate much from the four of you, including your occasional rudeness. I will allow you a great deal of freedom and latitude. But make no mistake: I will not let you go free. Make your peace with it as you can. Hate me if you must. But you *will* come back to Morganville, or suffer the consequences. You of all people know that I am quite serious about that."

Shane went pale, and Claire felt every muscle in his body draw tighter. "Yeah, I know," he said hoarsely. "Found my mom floating in a bathtub full of her own blood. I know how serious you can get."

Amelie was silent again, and then she said, "Morganville may not be paradise, and it may not be the future you believe you deserve. But in Morganville, you and your families will remain safe and alive while it is within my power to ensure it. I give you my word, as Founder, that this will be so. Is this understood?"

"You're holding our families hostage," Claire said. "We already knew that."

"And I wanted you to hear it from my lips, so there would be no mistakes," Amelie replied. "And now you have. I will expect you back tomorrow. Good night."

Oliver shut the phone off and put it away. He said nothing to them, just moved out of the way. For a few seconds the four of them just stood there, and then Shane said, "So that's it."

"Yes," Oliver said. "Tomorrow, we return. I suggest you make the most of the time you have tonight." He turned to leave, and then looked back over his shoulder—just one, fast glance. "And I am sorry."

Shane, without another word, took Claire's hand and led her to his room.

In the morning, with the sunlight falling over the two of them as dawn rose on their last day of freedom, Shane rolled over to look at her, propped himself up on an elbow, and said, "You know I love you, right?"

"I know."

"Because I suck at saying it," he said. "It's a work in progress, all this relationship stuff."

She hadn't really slept all night. She'd been too busy thinking, worrying, wondering. Imagining all kinds of futures. Imagining this moment. And she felt as if she were falling from a very tall building as she asked, "Shane? Are you—are you going to come back? To Morganville?"

Apart from Frank, his now-vampire dad, there was nobody Amelie could hold over his head . . . nobody but Claire and Eve and Michael, and, anyway, Amelie had never really needed Shane. *Claire* needed him, though. With every heartbeat she needed him more.

He looked at her, holding the stare for so long it felt as if the fall would go on and on, falling forever. . . .

And then he said, very quietly, "How can I not go back? How can I let you go, Claire? We all stay, or we all go back. I'm not letting you go on your own." He touched a fingertip to her nose, startling a laugh out of her. "Somebody's got to be your bodyguard."

She kissed him, and their skins warmed together in the sunlight; silently, Shane raised her right hand to his lips, and kissed her fingers and kissed the claddagh ring glittering there, that promise of the future that had so much meaning for him in the past.

And then, one more time, while they were still completely free, he told her how much he loved her.

Afterward, going back to Morganville didn't seem so dark.

TRACK LIST

As always, music drives the creative bus for me, so here are some songs that rocked this little road trip. Feed the artists, please. They deserve your support.

"Good 2 U"	Dave Mason
"Fire"	Daniel Lanois
"Guilty as Charged"	Gym Class Heroes
"Call in the Cavalry"	The Shys
"Troubled Land"	John Mellencamp
"Luisa's Bones"	Crooked Fingers
"Looking Pretty, Pretty"	TAB the Band
"Post Blue (Dave Bascombe Mix)"	Placebo
"Running up that Hill"	Placebo
"Sister Rosetta (Capture the Spirit)"	Noisettes
"Circle the Fringes"	The Gutter Twins
"Nighttiming"	Coconut Records
"I Can't Do It Alone"	3OH!3
"Wish We Were Older"	Metro Station
"That Dress Looks Nice on You"	Sufjan Stevens
"Kill Kill"	Lizzy Grant
"I Love You Good-bye"	Thomas Dolby

"Prime Mover"	Steve Stevens
"I Don't Live in a Dream"	Jackie Greene
"Down Boy"	Yeah Yeah Yeahs
"People C'mon"	Delta Spirit
"The Future's Nothing New"	The Alternate Routes
"Snakes and Lions"	Melpo Mene
"Gift"	Curve
"World Can't Have Her"	Cobra Verde
"Go My Way (The iPod Song)"	Bacon Brothers
"Don't Let the Devil Take Your Mind"	Jackie Greene
"Keeper"	Butterfly Boucher
"Lonely Ghosts"	O+S
"Mama Told Me (Not to Come)"	Three Dog Night
"2080"	Yeasayer
"Wild Life"	Bacon Brothers
"Architeuthis"	Bacon Brothers
"On Fire"	JJ Grey & Mofro
"I'm Good, I'm Gone"	Lykke Li
"Disappearing"	Simon Collins

More playlists at www.rachelcaine.com

Read on for an exciting excerpt from
the next Morganville Vampires novel,

BITE CLUB

by Rachel Caine
Available from
New American Library.

L ooking back on it later, Claire thought she should have known trouble was coming, but really, in Morganville, *anything* could be trouble. Your college professor doesn't show for class? Probably got fanged by vampires. Takeout forgets to put onions on your hamburger? The regular onion delivery guy disappeared—again, probably due to vampires. And so on. For a college town, Morganville had a remarkable lot of vampires.

Claire was an authority on all those subjects: Texas Prairie University and, of course, the vampires. And mysterious disappearances. She'd almost been one of those, more often than she wanted to admit.

But this problem wasn't a disappearance at all. It was an appearance . . . something new, something different, and something cool, at least in her boyfriend Shane's opinion, because as Claire was sorting the mail for their weird little fraternity of four into the "junk" and "keep" piles, Shane grabbed the flyer she'd put in "junk" and read it with the most elated expression she'd ever seen on his face. Scary. Shane didn't get excited about much; he was guarded about his feelings, mostly, except with her.

Now he looked as delighted as a little kid at Christmas.

"Mike!" he bellowed, and Claire winced and put her hands over her ears. When Shane yelled, he really belted it out. "Yo, Dead Man, get your ass down here!"

Michael, their third housemate here at the Glass House, must have assumed that there was an emergency under way . . . not an unreasonable assumption, because hey, Morganville. So he arrived at a run, slamming the door back, looking paler than usual, and more dangerous than normal, too. When he was acting like a regular guy, he seemed quiet and sweet, maybe a little *too* practical sometimes, but Vampire Michael was a whole different, spicy deal.

Yeah, she was living in a house with a vampire. And strangely, that was not the weirdest part of her life.

Michael blinked the tinges of red away from his blue eyes, ran both hands through his wavy blond hair, and frowned at Shane. "What the hell is your problem?" He didn't wait to hear, though; he walked over to the counter and got down one of their mismatched battered coffee mugs. This one was black with purple Gothic lettering that spelled out POISON. It was their fourth housemate Eve's cup, but she still hadn't made an appearance this morning.

When you slept later than a vampire, Claire thought, that was probably taking it a little too far.

As he filled the mug with coffee, Michael waited for Shane to make some sense. Which Shane finally did, holding up the cheaply printed white flyer. It curled around the edges from where it had been rolled up to fit in the mailbox. "What have I always wanted in this town?" he asked.

"A strip club that would let in fifteen-year-olds?" Michael said.

"When I was *fifteen*. No, seriously, what?"

"Guns R Us?"

Shane made a harsh buzzer sound. "Okay, to be fair, yeah, that's a good alternate answer. But no. I always wanted a place to seriously train to fight, right? Someplace that didn't think aerobics was a martial art? And look!"

Claire took the paper from Shane's hand and smoothed it out on the table. She'd only glanced at it when sorting mail; she'd thought it was some kind of gym. Which it was, in a way, but it wasn't teaching spin and yoga and all that stuff.

This one was a gym and martial arts studio, and it was teaching self-defense. Or at least that was what Claire took from the graphic of some guy in a white jacket and pants kicking the crap out of the air, and the words DEFEND YOURSELF in big, bold letters at the bottom.

Michael leaned over her shoulder, slurping coffee. "Huh," he said. "Weird."

"Nothing weird about people wanting to learn a few life-preserving skills, man. Especially around here. Not like we're all looking forward to a peaceful old age," Shane said.

"I mean it's weird who's teaching," Michael said. "Being that this guy"—he tapped the name at the bottom of the page—"is a vampire."

Vassily was the name, which Claire made out only when she squinted at it. Small type. "A vampire's teaching self-defense," she said. "To us. Humans."

Shane was thrown for just about a minute, and then he said, "Well, who better? Amelie put out a decree that humans were free to learn this stuff, right? Sooner or later, some vamp was bound to make some cash off of it."

"You mean, off of us," Claire said. But she could see his point. A vampire martial arts instructor? That would have to be all kinds of scary, or awesome, or both. She wouldn't have gone for it, personally; she doubted she had half as much muscle or body mass as it was going to require. But Shane . . . Well, it was a natural for Shane, really. He was competitive, and he didn't mind taking some punishment as long as he enjoyed the fight. He'd been complaining about the lack of a real gym for a while now.

Claire handed the flyer back to him, and Shane carefully folded it up and put it in his back pocket. "Watch yourself," she said. "Get out of there if anything's weird." Although in Morganville, Texas, home of everything weird, that was a pretty high bar to pass. After all, there was a vampire teaching self-defense. That, in itself, was the strangest thing she'd seen in a while.

"Yes, Mom," Shane said, but he whispered it, intimately close to her ear, and then kissed that spot on the neck that always made her blush and shiver, every time. "Eat your breakfast."

She turned and kissed him full-on, just a sweet, swift brush of lips, because he was already moving . . . and then he did a double take, and came back to kiss her again, slower, hotter, *better*.

Michael, sliding into a seat at the kitchen table with his coffee cup, flipped open the thin four-page Morganville newspaper, and said, "One of you is supposed to be somewhere right about now. I'm just saying that, not in a Dad kind of way."

He was right, and Claire broke off the kiss with a frustrated growl, low in her throat. Shane grinned. "You're so cute when you do that," he said. "You sound like a really fierce kitten."

"Bite me, Collins."

"Whoops, wrong housemate. I think you meant that for the one who drinks plasma."

Michael gave him a one-fingered salute without looking up from his study of the latest Morganville high school sports disaster. Claire doubted he was actually interested in that, but Michael had to have reading material around; she didn't think he slept much these days, and reading was how he passed the time. And he probably got something out of it, even if it was just something to impress Eve with on his knowledge of local football.

Claire grabbed her breakfast—a Pop-Tart just ringing up out of the toaster—and wrapped it in a napkin so she could take it with her. Book bag acquired, she blew Shane (and Michael) an air kiss as she hit the back door, heading out into a cold Morganville fall morning.

Fall, in other parts of the world, was a beautiful season, filled with leaves in brown, orange, yellow. . . . Here, the leaves had been brown for a day, and then dropped off the trees to rattle around the streets and yards like bones. Another depressing season, to add to all the others that were depressing in this town. But at least it was cooler than the blazing summer; that was something. Claire had actually dug out a long-sleeved tee and layered another shirt over it, because the wind gusts carried the sharp whip of approaching winter now. Pretty soon, she'd need a coat, and gloves, and a hat, and maybe boots if the snow fell hard enough.

Morganville in summer was dull green at best, but now all the grass was burned dry, and most of the bushes had lost their leaves, leaving black skeletons to shiver in the cold. Not a pretty place, not at all, although a few house-proud people had tried some landscaping, and Mrs. Hennessey on the corner liked those weird concrete animals. This year, she had a gray deer fake-sipping from an empty stone fountain, and a couple of concrete squirrels that looked more menacing than cute.

Claire checked her watch, took a bite of her Pop-Tart, and almost choked as she realized how little time she had. She broke into a jog, which was tough considering the weight of the bag on her shoulder, and then kicked it to a full run as she passed the big iron gates of Texas Prairie University. Fall semester was a busy time; lots of new, stupid freshmen with maps wandering around confused, or still unpacking boxes from their cars. She had two or three near-collisions, but reached the steps of the Science Building without much incident, and with two whole minutes to spare. Good, she needed them to get her breath back.

As she munched the rest of her breakfast, wishing she had a bottle of water, others she knew by sight filtered past her . . . Bruce from Computational Physics, who was almost as out of place here as she felt; Ilaara from one of the math classes she was in, but Claire couldn't really sort out which one. She didn't make close friends at TPU, which was a shame, but it wasn't that sort of a school—especially if you were in the know about the inner workings of Morganville. Most of the just-passing-through students spent the year or two they were here with the usual on-campus partying; except for specific college-friendly stores that were located within a couple of blocks, they hardly ever bothered to leave the gates of the university. And that was probably for the best.

It was dangerous out there, after all.

Claire found her classroom—a small one, nothing at her level of study had big groups—and took her usual seat in the middle of the room, next to a smelly grad student named Doug, who apparently hated personal hygiene. She thought about moving, but the fact was there weren't many other places, and Doug's aura was tangible at ten feet away anyway. Better to get an intense dose close-up so your nose could adjust quickly.

Doug smiled at her. He seemed to like her, which was scary, but at least he wasn't a big chatterbox or one of those guys who came on with the cheesy innuendos—at least, not usually. She'd certainly sat next to worse. Well, maybe not in terms of body odor, though. "Hey," he said, bending closer. Claire resisted the urge to bend the other way. "I hear he's springing a new lab experiment on us today. Something mind-blowing."

Given that she worked for the smartest guy in Morganville, maybe the entire world, and given that he was at least a few hundred years old and drank blood, Claire suspected her scale of mind-blowing might be a little bigger than Doug's. It wasn't unusual to go to Myrnin's secret lair/ underground lab (yes, he actually had one) and find he'd invented edible hats or an iPod that ran on sweat. And considering that her boss built blood-drinking computers that controlled dimensional portals, Claire didn't really anticipate any problems understanding a mere university professor's assignments. Half of what Myrnin gave her to read wasn't even in a living language, anyway. It was amazing what she'd learned—whether she wanted to or not.

"Good luck," she said to Stinky Doug, trying not to breathe too deeply. She glanced over at him, the way you do, and was startled to see that he was sporting two spectacular black eyes—healing up, she realized after the first shock, but he'd gotten smacked pretty hard. "Wow. Nice bruises. What happened?"

Doug shrugged. "Got in a fight. No big deal."

Someone, Claire thought, had disliked his body odor a whole lot more than usual. "Did you win?"

He smiled, but it was a private, almost cynical kind of smile—a joke she couldn't share. "Oh, I will," he said. "Big-time."

The door banged open at the far end of the room, and the prof stalked in. He was a short, round little man, with mean close-set eyes, and he liked Hawaiian shirts in obnoxiously loud colors—in fact, she was relatively sure that he and Myrnin might have shopped at the same store. The Obnoxious Store.

"Settle down!" he said, even though they weren't exactly the rowdiest class at TPU. In fact, they were perfectly quiet. But Professor Larkin always said that. Claire suspected he was actually deaf, so he just said it to be on the safe side. "Right. I hope you've all done your reading, because today you get to do some applications of principles you should already know. Everybody, stand up, shake it off, and follow me. Bring your stuff."

Claire hadn't bothered to unpack anything yet, so she just swung her backpack to her shoulder and headed out in Professor Larkin's wake, happy to be temporarily out of the Doug Fug. Not that Larkin was any treat, either. . . . He smelled like old sweat and bacon, but at least he'd bathed in recent memory.

She glanced down at his wrist. On it was a braided leather band with a metal plate incised with a symbol—not the Founder symbol that Claire wore as a pin on the collar of her jacket, but another vampire's symbol. Oliver's, apparently. That was a little unusual; Oliver didn't personally oversee a lot of humans. He was above all that. He was the Don in the local Morganville Mafia.

Larkin saw her looking, and sent her a stern frown. "Something to say, Miss Danvers?"

"Nice bracelet," she said. "I've only seen one other like it." The one she'd seen had been around the wrist of her own personal nemesis, Monica Morrell, crown princess (she wished!) of Morganville. Once the daughter of the mayor, now the sister of the *new* mayor, she thought she could do whatever she wanted . . . and with Oliver's Protection, she probably could still, even if her brother Richard wasn't quite as indulgent as Daddy had been.

Larkin just . . . didn't seem the type Oliver would bother with, unless he wasn't what he seemed.

Larkin clasped his hands behind his back as they walked down the almost-empty wide hallway, the rest of the class trailing behind. "I ought to give you a pass from today's experiment," he said. "Confidentially, I'm pretty sure it's child's play for you, given your . . . part-time occupation."

He knew about Myrnin, or at least he'd been told *something*. There weren't many people who actually knew Myrnin, and fewer still who'd been to the lab and had any understanding of what went on in there. She'd never seen Larkin, or heard his name mentioned by anybody with clout.

So she was careful with her reply.

"I don't mind. I like experiments," she said, "provided they're not the kind that try to eat me or blow me up." Both of which, unfortunately, she'd come across at her job at the lab.

"Oh, nothing that dramatic," Larkin said. "But I think you might enjoy it."

That scared her, a bit.

When they arrived at the generic lab room, though, there didn't seem to be anything worth breaking a sweat over: some full-spectrum incandescent lights, like you'd use for indoor reptiles; some small ranked vials on each table of what looked like . . .

Blood.

Oh, crap, that was never a good sign in Morganville (or, Claire thought, anywhere else, either). She came to a sudden stop, and sent Larkin a wide-eyed look. The rest of the class was piling in behind her, talking in low tones; she knew Doug had arrived because of the blanket of body-smog that settled in around her. Of course, Doug took the lab stool beside her. Dammit. That blew, as Shane would have said; Claire covered it by sending him a small, not very enthusiastic smile as she dropped her backpack to the ground, careful of the laptop inside. She hated sitting on lab stools; they only emphasized how short she was. She felt like she was back in second grade again and unable to touch the floor in her chair.

Larkin assumed his position in the center of the lab tables, and grabbed a small stack of paper from his black bag. He passed out the instructions, and Claire read them, frowning. They were simple enough—place a sample of the "fluid" on a slide, turn on the full-spectrum lighting, observe and record results. Once a reaction was observed, mix the identified reactive blood with control blood until a nonreaction was achieved. Then work out the equations explaining the initial reaction, and the nonreaction, to chart the energy release.

No doubt at all what this was about, Claire thought. The vamps were using students to do their research for them. Free worker bees. But why?

Larkin had a smooth patter, she had to admit; he joked around, said that with the popularity of vampires in entertainment it might be fun to apply some physics to the problem. Part of the blood had been "altered" to allow for a reaction; part had not. He made it all seem very scientific and logical, for the benefit of the eight out of ten non–Morganville residents in the room.

Claire caught the eye of Malinda, the other one in the room who was wearing a vampire symbol, and Malinda's pretty face was set in a worried, haunted expression. She opened her eyes wide and held up her hands in a silent *What do we do?*

It'll be okay, Claire mouthed. She hoped she wasn't lying.

"Cool," said Stinky Doug, leaning over to look at the paper. Claire's eyes watered a little, and she felt an urge to sneeze. "Vampires. *I vant to drink your bloot!*" He made a mock bite at her neck, which creeped her out so much, she nearly fell off the stool.

"Don't *ever* do that again," she said. Doug looked a little surprised at her reaction. "And by the way, showers. Look into them, Doug!"

That was a little too much snark for Claire's usual style, but he'd scared her, and it just came out. Doug looked wounded, and Claire immediately felt bad. "I'm sorry," she said, very sincerely. "It's just— You don't smell so great."

It was his turn now to look ashamed. "Yeah," he said, looking down at the paper. "I know. Sorry." He got that look again, that secret, smug look. "Guess I need to get rich enough nobody cares what I smell like."

"That or, you know, showering. That works better."

"Fine. Next time I'll smell just like a birthday bouquet."

"No fair just throwing on deodorant and aftershave or something. Real washing. It's a must."

"You're a tough sell." He flashed her a movie-star grin that looked truly strange with the discoloration around his mouth and nose. "Speaking of that, once I take that shower, you interested in going out for dinner?"

"I'm spoken for," she said. "And we have work to do."

She prepped the slide, and Doug fired up the lamp. The instant the full-spectrum lighting hit it, there was a noticeable reaction—bubbling under the glass, as if the blood had been carbonated. It took about thirty seconds for the reaction to run its course; once it had, all that was left was a black residue of ash.

"So freaking cool," Doug said. "Seriously. Where do you think they get this stuff? Squeeze real vampires?" There was something odd about the way he said it—as if he actually knew something. Which he shouldn't, Claire knew. Definitely, he shouldn't.

"It's probably just a light-sensitive chemical additive," Claire said. "Not sure how it works, though." That was true. As much as she'd studied it, she really didn't understand the nature of the vampire transformation. It wasn't a virus—exactly. And it wasn't a contaminant, either, although it had elements of that. There were things about it she suspected that all of their scientific approaches couldn't capture, try as they might. Maybe they were just measuring the wrong things.

Doug dropped the uncomfortable speculation. He wasn't so bad as a lab partner, if you forgot the stinky part; he was a good observer, and not half bad with calculations. She let him do most of the work, because she'd already done most of this with Myrnin; interesting that Doug came up with a slightly different formula, in the end, than she had on her own, because she thought his was a little more elegant. They were the first to come up with a stable mixture of the blood, and the second to come up with calculations—but Doug's, Claire was confident, were better than the other team's. You didn't have to finish first to win, not in science. You just had to be more right than the other guys.

All was going okay until she caught Doug trying to pocket a sample of the blood. "Hey," she said, and caught his wrist, "don't do that."

"Why not? It would be awesome at parties."

Again, there was that unsettling tone, a little too smug, a little too *knowing*. Whatever it was he intended to do with it, she doubted he was going to show off at parties with it.

"Just don't." Claire met his eyes. "I mean it. Leave it alone. It might be—toxic." Fatal, she meant, because if the vamps found out Doug was sneaking out samples . . . Well, accidents happened, even on the TPU campus. Stupidity wasn't covered by the general Protection agreement, and Doug seemed to have caught a little bit too much of a clue.

Doug grudgingly dropped it back to the table. Professor Larkin came around, checked out the sample bottles, and recorded them against a master sheet. As he walked away, and she and Doug packed their bags, Claire said, "See? I told you they'd be auditing."

"Yeah," Doug whispered back. "But he already checked us out."

And before she could stop him, he grabbed a couple of the vials, stuck them in his bag, and took off.

Claire swallowed the impulse to yell, and a second one to kick the table in frustration. She didn't dare tell Larkin; he was Protected, and Doug had no idea what he was getting into. She had to get him to give the vial back. Dumb-ass wouldn't have any idea what to do with it, anyway.

She hoped.

Photo by Sharon Sams-Adams

Rachel Caine is the *New York Times* bestselling author of more than thirty novels, including the Weather Warden series, the Outcast Season series, and the Morganville Vampires series. She was born at White Sands Missile Range, which people who know her say explains a lot. She has been an accountant, a professional musician, an insurance investigator, and, until recently, still carried on a secret identity in the corporate world. She and her husband, fantasy artist R. Cat Conrad, live in Texas with their iguanas, Popeye and Darwin. Visit her Web site at www.rachelcaine.com, and look for her on Twitter, LiveJournal, Myspace, and Facebook.